EMPIRE OF SHADOWS

BOOK 1 *of the* RAIDERS OF THE ARCANA

Crimson Fox
PUBLISHING

EMPIRE OF SHADOWS

BOOK I
RAIDERS OF THE ARCANA

JACQUELYN BENSON

Elements of this story were included in *The Smoke Hunter* by Jacquelyn Benson, first released by Grand Central Publishing in 2016 and re-released by Vaughan Woods Publishing in 2020.

First edition: April 2024

Library of Congress Catalog Number: 2023919942
ISBN: 978-1-958051-33-7

Published by Crimson Fox Publishing
www.crimsonfoxpublishing.com

Stay up-to-date on new book releases by subscribing to Jacquelyn's newsletter at JacquelynBenson.com.

Content warnings for Empire of Shadows:
Contains instances of kidnapping and restraint, animal death, animal attack, minor field surgery, alcohol consumption, and ritual (not psychological) self-mutilation.

Contains references to past sexual harassment and micro-aggressions, a smallpox epidemic, forced religious conversion, and human sacrifice.

For the revolutionaries.

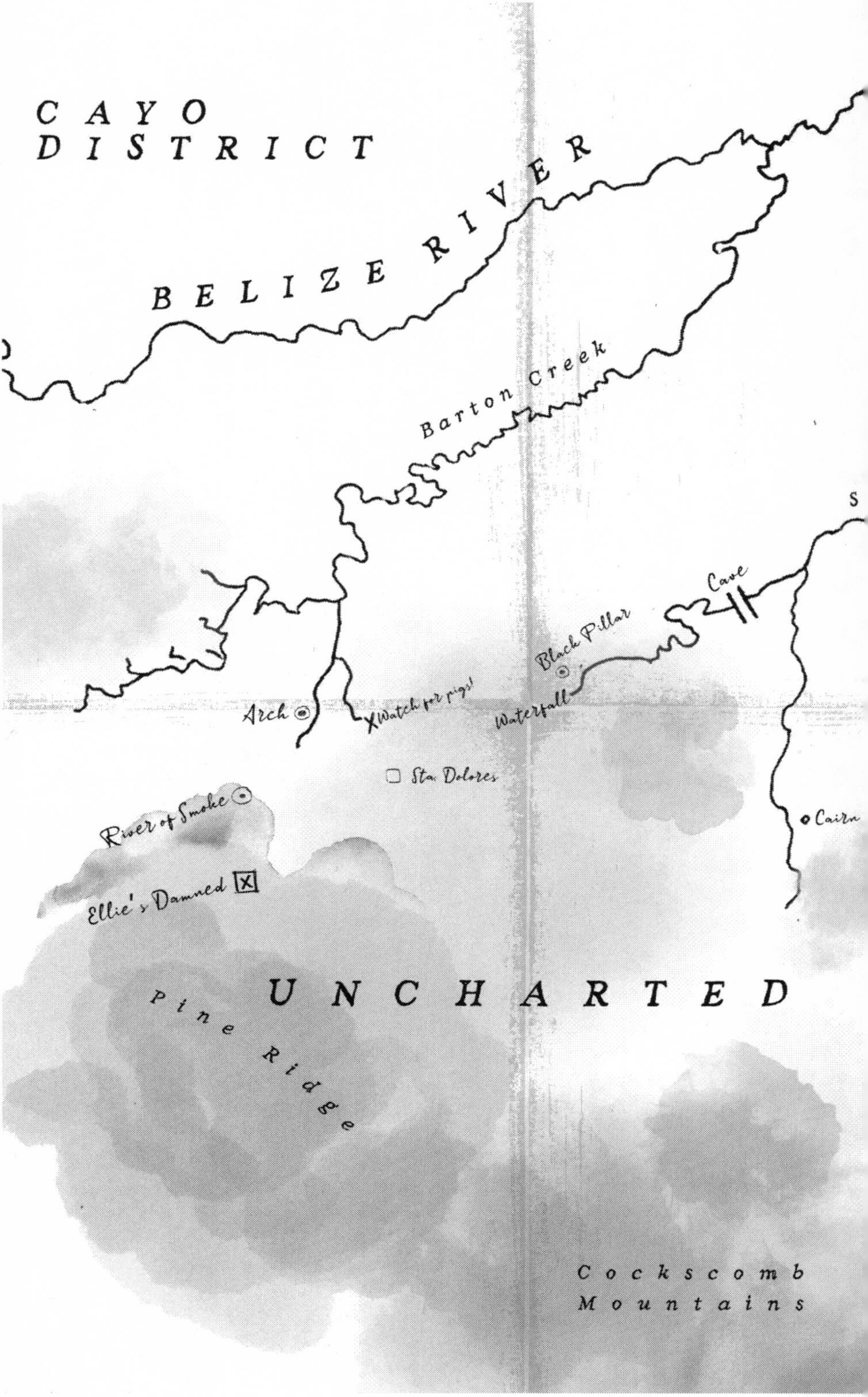

CAYO DISTRICT
BELIZE RIVER
Barton Creek
Cave
Black Pillar
Arch
Watch for pigs!
Waterfall
Sta. Dolores
River of Smoke
Cairn
Ellie's Damned
UNCHARTED
Pine Ridge
Cockscomb Mountains

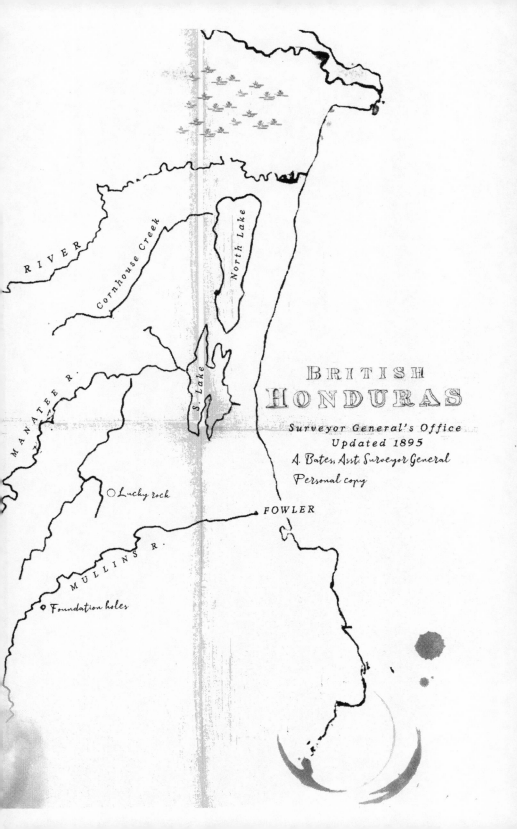

RIVER

Cornhouse Creek

North Lake

MANATEE R.

S. Lake

BRITISH
HONDURAS

Surveyor General's Office
Updated 1895
A. Bates, Asst. Surveyor General
Personal copy

○ Lucky rock

FOWLER

MULLINS R.

◇ Foundation holes

BEFORE WE BEGIN

$\mathcal{I}$ HAVE A CONFESSION to make.

The story you hold in your hands is not wholly original. It is possible that some privileged few of you will recognize certain characters and plot points in this tale from my debut novel, *The Smoke Hunter,* which was released in 2016 by Grand Central Publishing.

I had always intended for *The Smoke Hunter* to be the first of several adventures for Ellie and Adam, but for various reasons I had to put that dream aside for several years.

When I finished writing my *London Charismatics* series, I knew that I wanted to come back to these characters and their world—but the story needed a brush-up. (Ten years more writing experience shows.)

The brush up turned into a complete reinvention. New scenes were added, while others were taken away. Characters were more elegantly defined or changed up entirely. Plot threads were transformed and tightened. A great deal more history found its way into the story.

The result is the book that I always wanted to write, but simply didn't have the know-how to create a decade ago. Readers of *The Smoke Hunter* will recognize elements of the story they enjoyed, but they will also find much that is new, and I believe they will enjoy even more fun and adventure than they did before.

And yes, my loves—there will be more to come for Ellie and Adam.

Happy reading.

And so the Forefathers held counsel again. "What shall we do with them now? Let their sight reach only to that which is near; let them see only a little of the face of the earth! ... Are they not by nature simple creatures of our making? Must they also be gods?"

THE POPOL VUH
ENGLISH TRANSLATION BY DELIA GOETZ AND SYVANUS G. MORLEY

PROLOGUE

Cayo District, New Spain, 1632

𝒻RIAR VINCENTE SALAVERT had never imagined that he would await holy martyrdom while covered in hives.

For weeks now, he had been imprisoned in a hole in the ground. It was a relatively comfortable hole, as holes went. His captors had lowered down woven blankets and a rough mattress stuffed with dried palm fronds, dropping them through the ragged gap thirty feet overhead. There was even a convenient crack in the stone floor through which Salavert could take care of the more humiliating necessities.

The mosquitoes still managed to find him.

It was all rather in keeping with the theme of the last six years of Salavert's life—a saga of dreams, itching, and abysmal disappointment.

Six years ago, Salavert crossed the sea to the New World alight with visions of sainthood. What other fate could possibly await a man who had committed his body and soul to the salvation of a continent yet ignorant of Christ's grace?

The reality of his situation became clear to him shortly after he arrived in the festering, fly-infested mission of San Pedro Flores.

Some of the local people had received the blessing of being relocated from their wretched villages to the mission's settlement, a move that brought them from ignorance into the light of the Holy Roman Church. Yet as soon as they were done mouthing the proper responses to the Latin liturgy, they returned to their cabins to set out flowers and fruit for strangely-named saints whom Salavert knew no pope would ever recognize.

The villagers who didn't trudge along to services simply ran away, or engaged in outright revolt—or they died as smallpox ravaged through the community, forcing the mission's hired mercenaries to go out and round up a new batch of converts.

None of this boded well for Salavert's heavenly prospects. He had dreamed of doing great things in the name of God—the sort of things that might eventually see him rewarded with a nice, cushy cathedral post or maybe even a move to the Vatican. But one did not get to the Vatican by way of mass graves and followers who ran away from you.

Then Salavert heard the whispers of a great city hidden in the unexplored vastness of the mountains to the west—rumors of a gleaming metropolis where even the poor laborers drank from jeweled goblets and the kings slept in rooms paved with gold.

No man Salavert spoke with had seen this legendary place for themselves. The stories came in tantalizing hints and fragments... but it was enough to resurrect a tiny seed of hope from the rot of Salavert's dying ambitions.

If he could gain the ear of a true king, Salavert had no doubt that he could bring the great man into the grace of the church. And where a king went, surely his subjects would be compelled to follow. Salavert could be single handedly responsible for converting an entire nation.

Surely this was the great destiny that he had known awaited him since he was first called to the service of his faith.

Salavert pleaded with his abbot until at last he was granted permission to investigate the rumors of the hidden city. Accompanied by one of his brothers in Christ, he headed into the wilderness alongside two dozen of their new local converts, who had been assigned to carry the essential food and supplies.

Half of the converts escaped as soon as they left the mission.

Salavert trekked northwest with the others through crocodile-infested swamps and snake-riddled wasteland. Halfway through the second week, the food ran out. The converts harvested strange plants and killed animals that Salavert felt certain were forbidden in Leviticus. He stoutly refused to sully himself by eating them... at least, until he got a bit hungrier.

At last they reached a range of high, dark mountains where no Christian foot had ever stepped. What lay within those unknown peaks was a mystery even the wildest men could not illuminate.

Salavert plunged into that wilderness, trusting God to lead him to his destiny.

God was determined to test him. Salavert and his brothers remained lost for weeks in a verdant hell, subsisting on fruits that made his skin break out in a rash, and insects—which were surprisingly palatable.

Eventually, he knew he must find civilization or die… and at last, his prayers were answered. Like a dream glimpsed through a haze of desperation, the clouds before him parted, and the light of heaven gilded the secret Salavert had been seeking.

The city was even more magnificent than the rumors had promised. Truly, there was no place on earth so near to paradise… or to hell.

The people of the gilded kingdom took Brother Francesco first, restraining his arms and holding a bowl of smoldering herbs under his nose. His eyes rolled up in his head as he went limp in their arms. A band of painted acolytes dragged him up the massive steps of their gleaming pyramid and disappeared inside the idolatrous temple at its summit.

Francesco did not emerge again.

Three days later, Salavert was forced, stumbling, toward a neat row of rectangular pyres on the outskirts of the city. He feared he would be compelled onto one of them to meet his death in flames—and then realized that the pyres were already full. The pitch-soaked stacks of kindling held the bodies of several of his converts. The bodies bore no sign of violence, but Salavert knew without doubt that their deaths had not been natural. They had been murdered by some foul means for their failure to recant, or as a sacrifice to the demon gods of this place.

The people of the city gathered around the pyres, watching with a solemn stillness Salavert might almost have mistaken for grief.

As one of their demon priests set his torch to the wood, Salavert realized with a start that several of the corpses were marked with raw, red lesions.

He knew the significance of those signs all too well. The oozing pustules were a clear indication of the smallpox pestilence.

Flames whirled up to consume the bodies—but it was too late. The disease had already been unleashed. It would sweep across this place like a wind. Salavert had seen how it ravaged the villages near the mission of San Pedro de Flores, leaving them empty of everything but ghosts and flies.

He realized that he had indeed been called to this unholy place by God— but the instrument of redemption that he had been chosen to deliver was not prayer.

It was death.

Weeks passed, and the regular deliveries of food and water Salavert had enjoyed in his prison became more sporadic. He took to shouting through the ragged opening overhead about the deplorable conditions in which he was being held.

No one answered.

At last, he resigned himself to the truth. It was not the red robes of a cardinal or a choice post at the Vatican that God had chosen for him. Salavert had been destined for martyrdom.

He strove to await his glorious death with grace and equanimity—at least when he wasn't frantically scratching himself and cursing at the ever-present bugs.

Finally, a rope unfurled from above, slapping down to the stones beside him. Salavert woke from his doze with a jerk of surprise, and was hauled back to the surface.

The men who fetched him were weak with fever and covered with sores. As they marched him to the center of the city, Salavert found that the paradise he had seen on his arrival had been transformed into a nightmare.

Black clouds rose from burning fields. Bodies were piled in fly-haunted masses. More of them lay where they had fallen along the verges of the great plaza. The air was dense with smoke and the stench of rot.

His captors dragged him to the tiered pyramid that loomed like a pale ghost through the haze. Salavert staggered up each massive step, half-carried by the guards until they reached the pinnacle.

Someone waited for him there—a slight figure made larger by the elaborate feather headdress and jade breastplate of a priest.

But this was no priest. It was a woman of perhaps thirty with umber-hued skin and fiery golden eyes. The beauty of her face was marred by an unseemly old scar on her cheek, a jagged lightning bolt of puckered skin that any self-respecting lady back in Spain would have kept hidden under a veil.

Around her neck hung a medallion of dark stone. Salavert had last seen the ornament on the chest of the most prominent man who had watched over the slaughter of his converts. It was a symbol of rank he was sure this mere woman would never have attained if not for the plague.

With horror, Salavert wondered whether martyrdom at the hand of a *female* would even count in the eyes of God.

The priestess made an authoritative gesture, and the two guards pulled a dark hood over Salavert's head. The cloth stank of another man's fear as it enclosed him in darkness.

He stumbled blindly along an obscure, tortuous path of rough stones and low, tight turns. The air around him grew cool.

At long last, the bag was pulled from his head. To his profound surprise, Salavert found himself inside a massive cave filled with soaring pillars and graceful veils of stone. It looked like a cathedral formed by the hand of God from the very earth itself. The vast space whispered with the soft hush of the glittering water that ran across the floor to a deep pool at the far end of the cavern.

At the center of the vast space lay a flat, black disk, smooth and clear enough to reflect phantom glimmers of the nearby torches.

It was a mirror—a great mirror made of stone. The dark perfection of its surface in the still, haunted atmosphere of the cavern transfixed him.

As the guards pushed Salavert closer, he was haunted by the unexpected sense that something murmured to him through the soft crackle of the flames and the gentle susurration of the water.

It sang of dreams—and of glory.

The priestess took a black obsidian dagger from the sheath at her belt.

The spell over Salavert broke in a fresh, desperate pulse of fear. His scream echoed off the delicate frills of stone, but the guards held him fast, dragging him to the edge of the glass as the priestess began her incantation.

The melodic tones of her profane liturgy melded with the fading echo of his terror, and the uncannily resonant walls of the cave transformed her worship and his fear into a symphony.

Salavert began to recite the last contrition, grasping frantically for some semblance of control. He would not achieve sainthood while shrieking like a maniac. As a row of insect bites on his back took up itching again, he determined that he would meet his end with dignity.

The priestess drew the blade across the skin of her palm. She whispered a few phrases laced with grief and desperation, then knelt at the edge of the mirror and pressed her bleeding hand to the surface.

Smoke welled up from between her fingers. The priestess leaned into it, breathing deeply. Her eyes glazed over.

The air around Salavert grew colder as he realized that something was at work in that unholy cathedral—something old and powerful.

Something that had nothing at all to do with God.

With her eyes still unfocused, the woman extended her free hand, uttering a single word of command. Salavert bit back another yelp as the guards forced him to his knees. He closed his eyes, preparing for the inevitable blow.

Instead, the woman grasped the neck of his robe. With shocking strength, she pulled his face into the column of smoke that rose from the place where her blood met the mirror's surface.

With a gasp, Salavert inhaled… and the cave around him vanished.

Vincente Salavert stood in the soaring nave of the cathedral at the heart of his native Valencia—a rich and glorious monument to the might of God.

He wore the robes of a bishop. They looked very fetching on him, as he'd always known they would.

The pews were deserted. Candles flickered along the aisle, but all the reverent activity that Salavert should be nobly overseeing—the murmured prayers and quiet footsteps—was gone.

Only silence remained... silence, and a woman.

The barbarian priestess with the unsightly scar on her face stood at the altar, holding the cathedral's prize—the Santo Cáliz, a chalice of finely wrought gold and blood-red agate believed by many to be the Holy Grail itself. It fit her small brown hands as though it had been made for them.

Her heathen trappings had been replaced by white robes. She looked as sad and solemn as the Holy Virgin.

"What is this witchcraft?" Salavert cried, mustering an admirable tone of holy outrage as he pointed a finger at where she stood.

The fiendish woman ignored him as she held the chalice to her breast.

"I do not know what I will see," the woman said.

Her words had the aura of a confession. They met Salavert's ears in the warm tones of his native Valencian, yet other languages with which Salavert was far less comfortable seemed to weave within and between.

"I am torn by too many desires. I want... conquest." Her gold-flecked eyes flashed to Salavert. The cold, fierce rage in them made his bowels go over a bit shaky. "I want to raise the dead," she continued, and her expression shifted to one of fresh and terrible grief.

"Those are unholy desires," Salavert pronounced, mustering a little spurt of holy authority.

"They are," the woman softly agreed.

She looked down at the holy chalice in her hands.

"We have been like gods," she said. "But we bought our power with blood... and death."

The cathedral around Salavert shivered—and then changed. The space grew immense. Pews stretched into a dim and terrible distance.

All of them were full. The seats were packed with row upon row of seated corpses, their skin blackened with death. Unnatural red mouths opened over hearts and across throats.

The horror of it rooted Salavert where he stood—and then the woman was there, her eyes blazing as she glared up at him from a breath away.

"You would give it more," she declared fiercely. "You and those who rule you. You who already tear the world apart for what you *want*."

The priestess hissed the word like a curse. Salavert felt the sting of it like a whip against his skin and flinched back from her.

"I have seen you," she said coldly. "I saw you long before you came here. I know exactly what you are."

She closed her eyes and stepped back. The cathedral returned to a familiar space of candlelit shrines and a soaring nave that would have framed Salavert's sermons very nicely.

"We bought it all with blood," the woman repeated softly.

She raised her eyes to him with a look of desperation. The look shifted, hardening into determination, and Salavert was overcome by a sense of terrible anticipation.

"W-What are you going to do?" he stammered.

The priestess turned to face the altar where the chalice of Christ glimmered in red glory.

"I will choose," she declared.

The words echoed through the emptiness of the cathedral like the tolling of a bell.

She dropped to her knees, pressing her small hands to the stones of the floor. Salavert felt the tremor of it through his shoes. Gold flaked from his vestments, shivering to the ground.

"*I want to end this,*" the woman vowed.

Her voice broke against the force of her words.

An answer rasped through the hollow space around them. It smelled of dry earth and bones—of incense and the green of growing things. A strange wind stirred the folds of Salavert's robes, chasing uncanny chills up his skin.

The wind passed, and the cathedral was deserted once more.

The woman let out a short, hard laugh like the croak of a carrion bird.

"So that is to be the way of it," she said.

It seemed to Salavert that he could see flames burning behind her eyes.

"Wake up," she ordered.

He came to himself choking as he lay at the edge of the devilish mirror. Beside him, the priestess pushed herself upright with shaking arms as the two guards watched from a distance in stoic silence.

She climbed painfully to her feet and gave a sharp command in her idolatrous language. The two men responded with a shocked exclamation, clearly doubting the evidence of their own ears—but the priestess's look left no room for debate.

The guards grabbed Salavert by his tattered cassock and yanked him away from the mirror.

Clearly they were moving him somewhere. Perhaps they would bring him to a more prestigious place for his martyrdom.

He *hoped* that was the case. If his death took place in this devil-haunted underworld, Salavert found himself terribly afraid that God might fail to notice it.

Salavert's captors shoved him forward. He staggered to keep upright. The men marched him up a close, winding staircase to a dim chamber carved with images of pagan idolatry. Glancing through its narrow windows, Salavert realized that he stood inside the temple at the top of the city's massive pyramid.

The priestess was the last to emerge. As she straightened, she turned to where Salavert waited between the two guards.

She drew her black knife.

Salavert swallowed another undignified shriek at his impending demise— but once again, the woman's blade moved to her own body rather than his. She severed a leather thong at her throat and caught the weight of the black medallion in her hand.

Grabbing his wrist, the priestess forced the cursed thing into his palm.

Salavert gaped down at it. A demon grinned back at him from the medallion's carved black surface. The stone felt cool against his palm—uncannily so, given that it had just been worn against a woman's skin.

He knew that he should toss it aside. He was a man of God. He should not suffer such a wicked object to contaminate his holy person.

But Salavert did *not* toss it aside. Instead, his fingers curled over the stone as though of their own accord.

They *wanted* to hold it. They wanted to keep it close.

The priestess watched his fingers clench around the medallion. As she did, the great effort that had been bearing her up suddenly gave way. She looked younger and more vulnerable than she had before. Sorrow and exhaustion darkened her eyes.

She spoke a single word. Though he did not know the tongue, Salavert found himself entirely certain of its meaning.

Go.

He offered no resistance as the guards hauled him toward the doorway that would lead them out of the temple. Only as he was about to pass from that heathenish space did he look back.

Stones rasped together as the entrance to the passage slid shut and sealed with a thud. Kneeling on the ground where the opening had been, the priest-ess pushed a small, square block back into place against the wall.

As Salavert watched, she lifted the knife over her head—then plunged it deep into her own chest. She slumped back against the wall, her blood seeping out across the stones.

With nothing but smoke and silence at his back, Friar Vincente Salavert hitched up his tattered robes and ran.

ONE

Morning
April 7, 1898
Whitehall, London

$\mathcal{I}$T WAS JUST ONE little riot.

Eleanora Mallory certainly hadn't meant for it to be a riot. She had gone to the gates of the Palace of Westminster, home of the two houses of Parliament, for a peaceful demonstration in support of women's suffrage. The great Gothic facade of the building rose up behind her in an imposing confection of skinny windows and unnecessary spires.

Inside those walls, the fate of the nation was decided—a fate that Ellie and every other woman in England was entirely, unjustly excluded from.

Ellie had painted a sign on some nailed together slats of wood that she had liberated from an empty crate at her place of employment. It read: *United Against Tyranny!*

She had mulled over the exclamation point for a bit, but had decided that it was quite justified given a thousand centuries or so of systematic oppression.

The organizers of the demonstration had instructed her to hold up her sign and project deep, abiding scorn at the black-suited Members of Parliament who made their way through the gates. Ellie's dignified bearing would shower shame upon the men walking past her—men who refused to grant her the basic human right of self-determination in matters of politics.

Not that shame had been getting the suffrage movement very far. The men in the suits seemed to lack that particular piece of the emotional spectrum.

Most of the members strolled past the protesters as though the women weren't even there. Others busied themselves by rattling off self-important instructions to scurrying underlings.

As Ellie watched the parade of gentlemen walk into their looming building without sparing her and her fellow protesters so much as a glance, her frustration grew until she was gritting her teeth against it.

A pair of MPs with overly tight waistcoats chortled at the demonstration, nudging each other in the ribs. The woman beside Ellie lowered her sign a bit. Her shoulders pulled in as though she were slightly wilted.

Another man nearly walked into the lady beside Ellie, as his nose was pressed to the pages of his newspaper. He looked alarmed when he realized that the suffragists were there, and then sighed as though the whole thing were a bit of bother.

One of the demonstrators behind Ellie whispered softly. The muffled words were heavy with demoralization. A colleague shushed her gently.

Ellie held her back straighter. She hefted her sign higher and tried to look even more shame-provokingly dignified.

She was managing it very nicely until a pair of aristocratic bucks in flash waistcoats stopped in front of the suffragists.

"Which one of 'em would you like to bring you your slippers tonight, Atkins?" the first asked.

"Don't know that I'd let any of them near my slippers," Atkins replied. "The look of them might put me off my port."

He followed this with a theatrical shudder.

One of the ladies beside Ellie flinched as though struck. Another looked close to tears, but she held up her head in spite of it.

The simmering feeling in Ellie's chest grew hotter... and tighter.

"Make sure you're all home in time to put the tea on!" Atkins' companion called out.

The two men broke into a chorus of raucous laughter as they turned to stroll away.

Ellie snapped.

Somehow, the sign flew from her hand. It soared across the pavement and struck Atkins firmly in his black-suited back. He stumbled forward, irritably adjusting his hat.

"I say, now!" he protested.

Whatever it was Atkins planned to say was cut off as Ellie roared out, raising a fist to the sky.

"To the gates, sisters!" she shouted. *"We shall not let them pass!"*

The words sparked through the demonstration's careful facade of dignity, breaking open the roiling emotions that hid beneath. The women around Ellie ignited.

A group of the demonstrators surged forward, charging the enormous wrought iron gates that separated the public pavement from the palace yard. The press of women shoved the heavy doors forward, bringing them to a resounding close.

Now that the MPs were entirely blocked from getting inside, they actually began to pay attention to what was going on.

There were surprised exclamations of *Good Lord!* and *Rather unexpected, wot?* A few of the men managed to reach around the white clad bodies of the suffragists to grasp the gates and give the bars a shake. The iron grid behind Ellie's back rattled alarmingly even as she twined her arms through either side of it.

"We can't hold it closed!" one of her fellow demonstrators cried out.

The gate behind Ellie lurched, knocking off her hat.

"This might help!" someone in the crowd shouted.

A familiar figure pressed forward through the melee, holding up a set of thick gray chains that ended in sturdy manacles.

Earlier, Ellie had seen Miss Reynolds holding the chains in her upraised hands as a prop. At the time, Ellie had thought them quite effective as a piece of symbolic theater. Based on the solid thunk they made as Miss Reynolds approached, the metal links were more than purely decorative in function.

"I can use these to secure one of us to the opening," Miss Reynolds called out breathlessly as the iron clanked in her hands. "But fair warning, I have no idea where the key has gone off to. I wasn't exactly expecting to—"

"Bugger off, you daft witches!" a voice called angrily from the cluster of politicians.

In the face of the flood of verbal bile as the bars jerked with frenzied force behind her back, Ellie felt a remarkable sense of calm wash over her.

"Good morning, Florabelle," she said firmly through the outraged male faces pressing toward her. "You may affix the manacles to me."

The following afternoon, Ellie watched the relentless gray rain wash down the high, narrow windows of the Public Record Office as she waited to be fired.

The PRO was charged with cataloging and archiving official government documents for the entirety of the United Kingdom. Ellie had been told many times that she ought to be grateful for the opportunity to work there… despite the fact that she had scored nearly perfectly on her civil service exams and was eminently qualified for the position. After all, she was the only woman thus far in the PRO's history to be offered the position of archivist instead of being relegated to the typing pool.

Of course, even though Ellie had been working in the great, gray monolith of a building for the last three years, she was still regularly stopped in the halls and directed to the typing pool rather than the archivists' room. There was one gentleman, Mr. Ruddingford, who had very courteously directed her to the typing pool no less than twenty-six times. There was no deliberate malice in it. During each and every encounter, he simply neglected to bother remembering who she was.

On this particular rainy afternoon, Ellie was not in the archivists' room. She sat in an uncomfortable chair in the office of Mr. Charles Henbury, Assistant Keeper of the Rolls—Ellie's supervisor, who at any moment would enter the office and gleefully issue her notice of dismissal.

All for the teensy bother of having been arrested.

Her reflection stared waveringly back at her from the rain-streaked glass, sporting brown hair of a standard hue and hazel eyes, which were currently a bit more gray than green. The neat spray of freckles across her nose was accented by a colorful bruise on her cheekbone. Ellie had acquired said bruise when a flailing, portly baron tripped over the leg of a policeman and fell into her where she hung at the gates.

A framed certificate with a gilded seal and a tricolor ribbon hung on the thick, gray stones behind Mr. Henbury's desk. It was signed by the Master of the Rolls, a silver-haired gentleman who was both the ceremonial head of the PRO and the second-most-senior judge in the kingdom. The certificate honored Mr. Henbury for exceptional work compiling a complete descriptive catalog of the ancient deeds among the PRO's holdings.

Mr. Henbury had not had much to do with it. Ellie had compiled the catalog, and had done quite a bit of work stabilizing the moldering and irreplaceable documents while she was at it. For his part, Mr. Henbury had ignored her requests for necessary supplies and occasionally interrupted her to demand that she fetch him biscuits.

(Mr. Henbury did not ask the male archivists to fetch him biscuits.)

Mr. Henbury had also ignored Ellie's concerns about the level of humidity in Room B14, where the deeds were stored. Several of the fourteenth-century parchments were already damaged by mildew. Finally, Ellie had asked her colleague, Mr. Barker, to bring the issue to Mr. Henbury's desk. Though Mr. Barker was unfortunate enough to be a socialist, he was still a man, and at last the order for a new ventilation shaft was put in.

The dreary halls of the PRO were not what Ellie had dreamed of when she had fought her way into University College, achieving the highest possible marks on her entrance exams. She had elected to focus on the study of Ancient History, picking up additional classes in Greek and Latin. She had taught herself to read Egyptian hieroglyphs in her spare time.

Ellie had done all of it in order to prepare herself for a career as an archaeologist. Her stepbrother Neil—now Dr. Fairfax, she reminded herself—had been more or less handed that life on a silver platter when he had graduated from Cambridge. As Ellie sat in Mr. Henbury's office and watched the rain streak down the glass, Neil was at the ancient and fascinating necropolis of Saqqara in Egypt, excavating a very promising eighteenth-dynasty tomb cluster.

She closed her eyes and imagined the feel of hot sun on her skin as she brushed the debris of centuries away from ancient stones.

Uncovering knowledge lost for millennia was all that Ellie had ever wanted. It had been a ten-year-old Ellie, not Neil, who had come up with the idea of excavating the sedimentation layers under the roses at their semi-detached house in Canonbury. Ellie could still remember her stepmother's screech of dismay. Florence had not been appeased by Ellie's insistence that she would put the plants back once she had determined that there were no indications of a Roman camp or Medieval settlement beneath them.

At that tender age, it had never occurred to Ellie that the life she wanted was an impossibility—that no amount of intelligence and determination would ever overcome the handicap of her gender.

Now aged a ripe twenty-four, Ellie knew the limits the world imposed upon women all too well. Working as an archivist had at least allowed her to get her hands on history, if not quite in the way that she had dreamed.

Now, it seemed even that would be taken away from her. She wasn't entirely certain what would be left once it was gone.

Ellie knew what her stepmother would say… because Florence *had* said it, more or less once a month for the last three years.

It is far past time you got yourself a husband.

Ellie didn't want a husband. Marriage would mean the end of any occupation for her besides *managing the household*—a fate even less desirable than being eaten alive by a boa constrictor.

But what was the alternative? Only teaching, the last resort of most women unfortunate enough to be educated. The thought was more depressing than the weather.

Ellie glanced up at the clock. Mr. Henbury was running late. That was hardly surprising. The man couldn't even be bothered to arrive on time to lay her off—a moment she was certain he had been eagerly anticipating for years.

Ellie eyed the pile of documents on Mr. Henbury's desk. The polished surface was almost invisible under a mountain of teetering files and bundles of loose papers. Mr. Henbury's shelves weren't much better. Books and files were stuffed onto them in a shocking state of disorganization.

Mr. Henbury was ostensibly responsible for sorting out the fate of any items the archivists weren't sure how to categorize. As he was terrible at it, the other archivists usually came to Ellie first with their questions about catalog numbers or difficulties translating Old French.

Ellie had prevented quite a few tough nut cases from landing on Mr. Henbury's messy desk. She allowed herself a small burst of satisfaction at the thought of how much more work he'd be stuck with once she was gone.

Mr. Henbury wasn't particularly keen on working.

Rising from her chair, Ellie risked a quick glance into the hall. It was empty. Satisfied that she had a moment or two before Mr. Henbury entered wielding the ax of dismissal, she slipped over to the desk and plopped herself down in his chair with a happy little sigh of rebellion.

It should have been her chair, really. She certainly never would've let the assistant keeper's desk become such a muddle.

Ellie glanced idly through the papers, searching for anything her colleagues might have sent along for Mr. Henbury to examine. Such odds and ends occasionally made for interesting reading.

She plucked up a set of agricultural reports and frowned at them. They clearly should have been filed within Section DD 168 over in Room 207.

Shelf A, she thought distantly as she reached for a piece of notepaper. *Box 281C.*

Ellie caught herself, stifling a huff of frustration. Mr. Henbury was happy enough for her to do his work for him, but he would raise a holy furor should he discover she'd had the temerity to sit at his desk.

Though it pained her, she refrained from noting the proper catalog reference for the reports. Instead, she turned her attention to a promising-looking ledger sandwiched in the middle of one of Mr. Henbury's stacks. It refused to come loose from the paper mountain until Ellie gave it a more forceful tug—and sent a tower of files sliding to the floor.

"Drat!" she muttered, hurrying around the desk to tidy up the mess.

It would be just her luck for Mr. Henbury to find her rifling through his papers on the floor.

She quickly gathered up an assortment of eighteenth-century shipping logs—*CC 467*, she noted absently—and then paused as she realized that something lay beneath them. Clutching the thick bundle of documents to her chest, Ellie reached out with her free hand and retrieved it.

It was a black book, moderate in dimensions but fairly stout, tied closed with a faded black ribbon. Ellie recognized it as a psalter—an early printed book of psalms. *Calf binding,* Ellie thought as she turned it over in her hands. *Mid-seventeenth century.*

A psalter was most certainly not a government record, and therefore had no business being on the assistant keeper's desk—or in the PRO at all, really. How it had come to be there at all was a mystery.

Most of the mysteries Ellie encountered in the records office weren't particularly alluring. She was far more likely to stumble across the mystery of why some long-dead clerk had decided to add extraneous vowels to all of his adverbs or why another had chosen to file a count of the royal herds alongside a translation of Geoffrey of Monmouth.

Ellie hefted the volume thoughtfully in her hand. It felt oddly heavy.

Footsteps sounded as Mr. Henbury's voice echoed from down the hall.

"Tell Edwards that there will be no extension. The calendar will be done by next Friday or I will find someone else to enjoy his position!"

Ellie hurriedly shoved the tumbled files onto Mr. Henbury's desk, then gave them a quick and uncertain adjustment. Had she set them back at the right angle?

Oh—why was she worrying? Mr. Henbury wasn't going to notice.

She paused at the psalter. It itched under her fingers, begging to be explored. Before Ellie could think further about it, the stout little book had slipped into the pocket of her skirt. She dashed to her seat and quickly arranged herself as the footsteps neared and Mr. Henbury entered the room.

He was a shorter man, and decidedly balding—however much he tried to hide it by combing the remaining hair across his forehead. It was secured there with a generous quantity of pomade that gave off a special glimmer when Mr. Henbury stood beneath an electric light, as he did now.

"Miss Mallory," he announced. "I suppose you must be wondering why you have been summoned here today."

Mr. Henbury had taken on an air of stuffy self-importance. It was one of his favorite airs. Ellie schooled her face into a placid blandness that concealed her frustration.

"I am sure I could not possibly guess, Mr. Henbury," she replied tiredly.

Henbury straightened his back, puffing his chest out a bit. He believed it made him look authoritative.

"It has come to our attention that you were arrested yesterday afternoon," he said. "I am sure you must see that such behavior is quite inappropriate for an employee of Her Majesty's Public Record Office."

"Is it?" Ellie returned dryly. "I had no idea."

Mr. Henbury didn't respond. He wasn't really listening to her anyway.

"I am afraid I must therefore inform you that your employment here at the PRO is to be terminated, effective immediately," he continued. "You will collect any personal items from your desk over the next hour and remove yourself from the premises."

"No letter of reference, then?" Ellie asked in a bland tone.

Mr. Henbury blinked at her, startled.

"A reference letter?" he echoed. "You were arrested!"

"Just one little arrest," Ellie offered cheerfully, "which they aren't even pressing charges for. It's not as though I was denying half the population of the United Kingdom one of their most basic and essential civil rights, consigning them to a life of virtual slavery thinly disguised as 'domestic bliss' and forbidding them from any meaningful or profitable employment."

"You don't require employment," Mr. Henbury spluttered. "That's what you get a husband for!"

Ellie's fury snapped to life.

"I don't want a *husband*," she seethed, cold and dangerous.

Mr. Henbury opened his mouth to respond—then closed it again, blinking at her. It seemed he hadn't the foggiest notion of what to say to that.

"In any event," he went on a bit more loudly, "here is your notice." He took a neat white envelope from his pocket and held it out to her. "Best of luck to you."

Ellie wanted to throttle him. She wanted to scream with pure outrage—not just at her dismissal, which she had fully and grimly anticipated since the moment she had been dragged from the gates of Parliament by a pair of uniformed constables, but at *all of it*. The open disdain of her PRO colleagues. The snide comments in the halls of the university. The insidious, affectionate, unrelenting pressure from even those who loved her.

The dream that she had ached for since childhood—the one the world relished telling her, over and over again, could never be hers.

Ellie calmly extended her hand, taking the white envelope from Mr. Henbury's grasp and slipping it into her pocket.

"Mr. Henbury," she acknowledged evenly.

"Yes, yes," Mr. Henbury replied, waving her away as he turned back to his desk. "Oh, and do ask one of the ladies in the typing pool to run me up a couple of biscuits on your way out."

TWO

$\mathcal{E}$LLIE WOULD NOT be asking anyone to bring Mr. Henbury his biscuits.

She kept her back straight as she walked down the long, gloomy hallway to the archivists' room. As she stepped inside, she was greeted by a rush of schoolboy whispers from a trio of her colleagues who were lingering by the tea service. One of them distinctly chortled under his breath.

Ellie staunchly ignored the sound as she crossed to her desk and sat down in her chair.

Of the six desks in the archivists' room, Ellie's was by far the most tidy. Her drawers were neatly labeled: *To Be Reviewed, In Process, Inquiry Required, Ready to File.* The surface of the desk itself was clear of everything save her desk pad, blotting paper, ink, pen, and letterbox. She slid open the top drawer. It held a box of sharp pen nibs, a stack of perfectly-sized notepaper, and her copy of *The Short History of the Yuan Dynasty*, which she had been enjoying on her lunch breaks.

She took out the pen nibs and the book, slipping them into the leather briefcase on the floor by her chair. Her umbrella was already tucked through the bag's straps. Ellie checked to make sure they were tightened.

There was nothing else to do. Her only other personal item was a small potted fern on the windowsill behind her station. Given that it wouldn't fit in her briefcase, she would have to carry it.

Her works in progress were all painstakingly organized. Anyone would be able to pick up from exactly where she had left off without any trouble, so long as they had a modicum of intelligence. Ellie winced at the notion of which of her colleagues might be assigned that responsibility. She hoped it was Mr. Barker. Mr. Lloyd would make an absolute mess of it. Only yesterday, Ellie had barely managed to save a set of maps of Kwangtung Province from being sent by Mr. Lloyd to the Sussex Ordnance Survey file (*OS2 665*) instead of to Hong Kong (*CO 700, Box 3A*).

She forced herself to take a breath. There was nothing she could do about it anymore.

It was time to go.

Mr. Henbury's envelope crinkled in her pocket. She stuffed her hand inside to take it out and pop it into her briefcase—and stopped as her fingers brushed against the calf bound psalter Ellie had knocked off Mr. Henbury's desk.

She had very nearly walked out with it. How silly of her *that* would have been.

Ellie took the book from her pocket and set it on the desk. She supposed she really ought to bring it back to Mr. Henbury... but the notion of receiving the inevitable self-righteous lecture about misplacing records from a man whose desk looked like the aftermath of a rummage sale made her feel ill.

No—she would simply leave the book here. It would undoubtedly find its way back to Mr. Henbury again, where he'd proceed to lose it once more beneath his paper towers. There was no reason for her to humiliate herself any further.

Mr. Barker glanced over at her, looking uncomfortable and slightly guilty. As a socialist, he likely thought he should speak up about her dismissal but lacked the courage to do it.

The other archivists had forgotten her. They were still dawdling over their tea, talking about cricket.

Leaving the archivists' room so quickly after entering it felt terribly like running away—like *losing*. Ellie mustered a spark of rebellion. She would not let them chase her out. She would take a few extra moments to examine the psalter. That way, she could leave it on her desk with a note as to the proper place where it might be either filed or forwarded.

She untied the black ribbon that held the book closed and lifted the cover to examine the title page. It was written in Latin. *Versio Gallicana*, she thought reflexively, *from Jerome's second translation of the Septuagint*. The Gallicana was a version that had been commonly used in the Roman church during the seventeenth century. That made the psalter unlikely to be English, as the printing of Catholic texts had languished there after the Reformation.

Ellie quickly scanned the rest of the page. A word caught her eye—*Salmanticae*. The book had been printed in Salamanca, Spain.

It made the book's presence in the mess of PRO documents on Mr. Henbury's desk even more intriguing. How had a Spanish psalter, of all things, landed in the British records office?

Idly, Ellie flipped through a few more pages… and stared down at a mutilation.

Past Psalm Four—*Give ear unto me when I call*—the interior of the book had been raggedly cut out, the pages gutted to create a secret hollow.

Ellie had to stifle a muted squeak of horror at the sight. The Versio Gallicana was common enough, but when dealing with a book of such venerable age, every volume had to be considered historically valuable. It felt like sacrilege that someone would carve out a square from the middle of the pages.

The hollow in the book had not been left empty. There was a folded piece of parchment inside, yellowed with age. Gingerly, Ellie lifted it out.

The document was oddly heavy for its size. A few lines of faded brown script—iron gall ink, Ellie distractedly noted—were visible on the outside surface of the neatly bundled package of it. Those had also been written in Latin. Ellie struggled a tad with the quirks of the ecclesiastical spelling as she translated it.

Map indicating the location of the Inhabited Kingdom discovered by Fr. Salavert, which May Be Supposed to lie behind the legends of The White City.

Ellie blinked down at the lines and forced herself to check her translation again.

Words leapt out at her. *Inhabited Kingdom. White City.*

The White City was indeed a legend—a myth that had woven its way through the Spanish conquest of South and Central America. The rumors of a flourishing Indigenous settlement of untold riches were often seen as a variation on the more well-known story of El Dorado.

The allure of the White City's wealth was a golden fever-dream that had led countless explorers and adventurers to their deaths.

It was nonsense, of course. The Mayan civilization had flourished in Mexico and Central America for over a thousand years, only to mysteriously collapse sometime between 800 and 1000 AD, centuries before the arrival of the Spanish. The great ruined cities that had been discovered in the Yucatan and further south had been just that—ruins—by the time the first Europeans had reached the region. The Mayan people who remained had lived in smaller villages and settlements that were quickly ravaged by disease, forced relocation, slavery, and murder during the conquest.

The Aztec cities to the north still stood at the start of the colonial period—but those had been well-known to the conquistadors. They would hardly have warranted being described as *legends*.

Ellie gingerly unfolded the parchment. Something slipped loose from it and fell heavily into her lap. Surprised, she picked it up.

The object was a thin disk of stone perhaps three inches in diameter. The glossy black surface caught and reflected glints of the gray light from the window behind her.

The carved image of a single figure dominated the center, surrounded by rows of neat, square hieroglyphs. With their dots, bars, and stylized animal heads, the characters reminded Ellie of the illustrations she had seen in the books on Mayan and Aztec archaeology that she had pored over at the university library. There had not been very many such volumes, of course. The Mesoamerican region was not a part of the world that received nearly as much academic interest as Egypt, Rome, or Ancient Greece.

The figure engraved in the center of the stone obviously represented a deity. Aspects of the iconography were familiar to Ellie from her reading, though the carving combined elements of a few different Mesoamerican gods. Its face was marred by slashing horizontal lines. One of its legs had been replaced by a writhing snake. Angular, batlike wings protruded from its shoulders, with a round disk—a pectoral decoration, perhaps?—dominating its chest.

She turned the medallion over. The back of the object was blank save for a single hieroglyph made up of a circle of swirling lines.

Ellie puzzled over what they might represent. Wind, perhaps? Or smoke? *Smoke*, she thought distantly. *Smoke feels right.*

She shook off the fog of shock as her fingers tightened reflexively on the stone.

Logically, she knew it was possible—perhaps even likely—that the disc was a hoax or a forgery... but if it wasn't, then Ellie could be holding a fragment of an ancient world.

The notion filled her with a sense of awe.

With some effort, Ellie forced herself to set the artifact aside and focus on the parchment. As promised, it was indeed a map, hand drawn in spidery strokes of aged ink. The undulating line of a coast dominated the right hand side of the page. She identified other lines as hills and mountains. Much of the map's expanse was blank, but that was unsurprising. Early seventeenth-century knowledge of Central America would have been largely limited to the areas bordering the sea.

A handful of landmarks had been carefully marked across the interior, written in the same Ecclesiastical Latin. Ellie delicately traced them with her finger—the curving course of a river leading to a *Black Pillar that Draws the Compass*, then a meandering line to an *Arch Hollowed by the Hand of God.*

Beyond that lay the *River of Smoke*—and finally, a stepped pyramid marked with a thin, faded *X*.

Oh, for goodness' sake, Ellie thought as she looked down at the symbol, her mind whirling.

She forced herself to assess the parchment as she would any other historical document. It was impossible to be certain of its age. The degree to which the material became yellow or brittle over time could vary based on a range of environmental factors, and Ellie had no idea where the psalter had been stored prior to finding its way to Mr. Henbury's desk. Certainly, the faded color of the ink indicated that the page was at least a couple of centuries old, and the style of the script was appropriate to the seventeenth century. The use of Ecclesiastical Latin supported the theory that the piece had originated in one of the Catholic missions that peppered the American coast during that period.

Now that Ellie thought about it, there was something vaguely familiar about the shape of the sketched coastline.

CO 700, her brain suggested automatically. *Box 8. Room 306.*

Ellie neatly folded the map back up into its original form, plucking both it and the medallion up from the desk. She hurried out of the room, barely hearing the new rush of whispers that followed her.

She rounded the corner and climbed the familiar flight of stairs to the third floor of the building, steering unerringly to the room she sought.

Like all the other records rooms in the PRO, Room 306 was packed with metal shelves that lined the walls and divided the floor into narrow aisles. Ellie hurried along the rows containing the records of the Commonwealth Office.

She plucked Box 8 from its shelf.

There were no tables in Room 306. The documents were meant to be carried down to one of the reading rooms where those querying the records waited patiently for their papers to be delivered.

Ellie plopped herself down on the floor instead, her tweed skirt pooling around her as she lifted the cardboard lid from the box.

She shuffled carefully through the documents stuffed inside until she found a hand drawn map of New Spain, dated 1688.

The provenance documents for the map were thankfully complete and up-to-date. The piece had been seized along with other papers from a Spanish privateer who had ended up on the losing side of a conflict with the Royal Navy. Ellie had always liked this particular record because the parchment featured marginal annotations in three different hands—likely from a succession of captains who had made use of it.

Ellie swept the dust from the floor with the sleeve of her white blouse, leaving a gray smudge along her arm, and then laid the parchment from the psalter and the confiscated map side by side on the ground before her.

The maps covered slightly different areas, but Ellie could make out the distinctive shape of the Yucatan's Bay of Chetumal on both, and used it to orient herself. The coastlines did not precisely match, nor were they to scale—but that was to be expected, given the limits of seventeenth-century survey methods.

The note on the parchment had spoken of an *inhabited city*. The geography in front of her was nowhere near any of the regions known to have had thriving urban areas at the time of the Spanish conquest. The map depicted the region where the Mayan ruins had been found—the Mayan ruins that had been abandoned for centuries by the time her secret map had purportedly been drawn.

Then again, her map did not claim to show the location of a Mayan ruin. It spoke of a legend.

A rising excitement began to itch at the back of Ellie's mind. She worked to wrangle it into a suitably scholarly submission.

Just fairy tales and hokum, she thought forcefully to herself as she continued her careful, rational examination.

Key river mouths were marked on the map from Box 8, though their routes extended only a few miles from the shoreline. Pirates, after all, had little need to navigate far inland.

On the map from the psalter, one river traced its way much further into the interior, where the other landmarks—like the *Black Pillar* and the *Arch Hollowed by the Hand of God*—peppered the page. The undulating line looked as though it had been drawn based upon the report of someone who had traveled far beyond the boundaries of the colonial settlements into unexplored territory.

Only one coastal community was named on the parchment—a site labeled with a carefully inscribed cross and the initials *S. P. F.*

Ellie turned her attention to the pirates' map, where over a dozen villages had been drawn along the meandering line of the shore—*Port des Chevaux... San Cristóbal... Coban...*

At the southern end of what was now the colony of British Honduras lay another dot—and the neatly written name of *San Pedro de Flores*

Ellie's pulse kicked up. She yanked Box 8 closer and quickly shuffled through the other papers inside. She plucked out a block cut, printed map from the mid-eighteenth century—approximately seventy years later—and studied it furiously.

The place where the mission of San Pedro de Flores should have been was blank. The mission, then, had not survived long into the eighteenth century.

If the map from the psalter was a forgery, whoever had created it must have had access to an extraordinary archive of historical maps, as well as possessing the skills to do a very fine job artificially aging both the material and the ink.

Or else the document really had been drawn two hundred and seventy-odd years ago.

Ellie leaned back against the shelf of records, her eyes wide.

It could still be a hoax—a very old and very convincing hoax.

But as a woman of logic and science, Ellie had to consider the alternative possibility that her discovery was exactly what it appeared to be… a map to an unknown civilization.

After properly refiling the documents in Room 306, Ellie wandered downstairs in a daze. She was surprised to realize that her feet had taken her to Mr. Henbury's door—but then, Mr. Henbury's door was the responsible place for her to go. For all his numerous faults, Mr. Henbury was still the Assistant Keeper of the Rolls. Stumbling across the potential key to an immense archaeological discovery hiding amongst the records was surely the sort of thing Ellie was supposed to bring to his attention.

Her heart sank at the prospect, bringing her to a halt in the hall. She had absolutely no doubt that the moment she gave the map and medallion to Mr. Henbury, she would be cut out of whatever happened next. That would have been true even if she hadn't just been handed her dismissal papers for a bit of high-principled rioting.

A terrible little thought slipped into her mind. Mr. Henbury was clearly unaware of the existence of the artifacts in her pocket. If he had opened the psalter, he hardly would've left it lying around in his stacks of papers. Even someone as dim and self-absorbed as Mr. Henbury would have recognized their significance. If Mr. Henbury had seen them, he would have forwarded them to either the British Museum or the Royal Geographical Society, the two organizations best qualified to further assess the provenance of the map and potentially mount an expedition to the region.

An expedition…

Ellie imagined pushing her way through the virgin rainforest, following the winding path of a game trail as the orchids bloomed around her and tropical birds chattered overhead. She would be carrying basic survey equipment with her, of course. Even a preliminary investigation of a potential archaeological site should entail a thorough documentation of the visible structures.

She might even lay a small grid in a promising location and dig a few test pits. A cluster of chipped stone could turn out to be a remnant of flint knapping activity while a layer of crushed shells might indicate a midden or the site of a past feast.

Trash heaps, she thought with a dreamy sigh. What she wouldn't give to sink her hands into a lovely, ancient trash heap and pull out all those wonderful details about the real lives of people from a thousand years ago.

Of course, that was pure fantasy. No self-respecting British institution was going to fund sending someone like *her* to the other side of the world.

The daydream crashed to the ground, and Ellie realized that there were people speaking on the far side of Mr. Henbury's office door.

One of them, unsurprisingly, was Mr. Henbury. He sounded oddly nervous.

"I'm telling you, it was right here this morning," he said. "I haven't moved it anywhere. I hardly ever move any of these things!"

"Spread this all out."

The other voice in the room was deep and authoritative, for all that it betrayed just a hint of a less-than-respectable accent—a subtle note of the East End, Ellie deduced absently. Ellie certainly hadn't heard it in the records office before, which meant that it didn't belong to someone who worked here.

Even slightly muffled by the interruption of Mr. Henbury's door, the voice reminded Ellie vaguely of the cold wind before a storm.

"I'm sorry, Mr. Jacobs," Mr. Henbury said. "As you can see, there isn't really a great deal of room—"

His words were cut off by the crash of a few hundred papers flying to the floor.

Mr. Henbury emitted an alarmed squeak, and Ellie took a fascinated step closer.

"That simply isn't..." Mr. Henbury started before stammering to a halt. "You—You can't possibly..."

His words were partially drowned out by the further rush of papers being kicked aside. Ellie jumped back a step as a pair of folders slid partially through the crack at the bottom of the door.

Wills and marriages, she thought automatically, glancing down at them. *Gloucestershire. ER 3. Box 12.*

The man behind the door—Jacobs—was violently searching for something... something that had until recently been buried in the pile of neglected work on Mr. Henbury's desk.

The map crinkled against the fabric of Ellie's skirt as the ferocious rustling from within the office settled to a halt.

A crunch of paper sounded from beyond the door. *He is walking on top of them*, Ellie thought with distant alarm. *That intimidating man is walking on top of the records.*

The notion snapped her out of the fog of surprise. She straightened as a burst of outrage cleared her thoughts.

She absolutely could not stand by and eavesdrop when someone was *walking on the records.*

"Not here," the resonant, chilling voice concluded.

Ellie strode forward, raising her hand to give the door a firm knock. Before she could strike, the slab of wood shuddered with the impact of something roughly the size and weight of Mr. Henbury.

Ellie froze. What sort of person resorted to tossing people around in the otherwise civilized confines of the Public Records Office?

Certainly not a fellow archivist. Such intimidation was the sort of thing one might expect from a criminal—but how would a criminal have come to know about the artifacts in the psalter?

The answer to that question was obvious. There was only one way the well-spoken, calmly violent Jacobs would know that there was anything worth looking for in Mr. Henbury's office.

Mr. Henbury had told him.

None of the other records in Mr. Henbury's pile had any real financial value... not like the sort of value one might find in a map that potentially led to a previously unknown city full of precious artifacts.

Ellie's hand instinctively moved to her pocket as a theory whirled into shape in her mind.

The psalter must have come from an uncategorized box of records. Lord knew, there were plenty of them about, as the British government continued to work to consolidate all its old papers under the umbrella of the PRO. One of her colleagues must have come across the psalter and dumped the item on Mr. Henbury's desk.

By some arcane chance, Mr. Henbury had actually bothered to open the book—and when he saw what it contained, instead of properly logging and assessing it, he had determined to try to hawk it for a quick bit of dosh.

As a hypothesis, it was all too terribly plausible. If the man inside the office did not do away with Mr. Henbury, Ellie would be sorely tempted to murder him herself.

"Who has been inside of your office since we spoke?" Jacobs asked.

The question was unsettlingly composed. One might almost think that tossing high-ranking public officials against their office doors was the sort of thing Jacobs did all the time.

"Nobody!" Mr. Henbury spluttered.

Jacobs' reply was cool, controlled, and entirely confident.

"That isn't entirely true. Is it, Mr. Henbury?"

"What?" Mr. Henbury sounded genuinely confused. "I haven't the foggiest idea what you're—"

There was another shudder of impact against the door.

"Wait—wait!" Mr. Henbury hurried to reply. His tone hiked up to a brighter note of panic. "There was that woman! She was here! She was here all by herself for ages! She must have taken it."

Ellie's outrage heated into the sort of inferno which had last seen her chaining herself to the gates of Parliament.

That weaselly little man was *not* about to toss her to a violent ruffian who walked on historical records. Surely, not even Mr. Henbury could sink that low.

"What woman?" Jacobs calmly pressed.

Ellie took a quiet, instinctive step back from the door as a quick blade of fear mingled with the fury roiling under her skin.

"Miss Mallory," Mr. Henbury replied to the obviously dangerous man currently assaulting him. "It was Miss Eleanora Mallory."

THREE

$\mathcal{E}$LLIE HAD CALCULATED that taking off her boots would allow her to slip away from Mr. Henbury's office both quickly and quietly, gaining herself a brief head start over any pursuit. Her woolen stockings slipped across the floor as she sprinted around the corner into the archivists' room.

Most of her fellow employees ignored her, still absorbed in their discussion of the latest cricket scores as they lumped over their tea.

Only Mr. Barker glanced up from his desk. He blinked owlishly at the walking boots that Ellie held in her hand.

The tea service cohort paid slightly more attention when Ellie plopped down in her chair and set her foot on the desk. She yanked her boots back on with breathless urgency, exposing a scandalous amount of ankle in the process.

"Good God!" one of the tea drinkers mumbled.

Ellie thumped her feet to the ground, snatching up her briefcase and neatly plucking the fern from the windowsill.

Mr. Barker rose from his desk, furrowing his brow with nervous concern. "Miss Mallory," he began, "is everything quite—"

"Just jolly!" Ellie called back as she dashed from the room.

She thundered down the stairs to the ground floor, then burst through a cluster of fellows from the publishing department. Scholars scattered like a flock of alarmed pigeons as she pushed out the door to Chancery Lane.

The gray London drizzle assaulted her, instantly dampening her hair and clothing. Ellie shuffled the fern into the crook of her arm in order to free a hand and yank her umbrella from the straps of the briefcase. She unfurled it with a practiced snap of her wrist.

No villainous clamor rose behind her as she moved quickly into the rain-drenched flow of pedestrians. Slowly, her pulse began to settle. Mr. Henbury had never paid a very great deal of attention to Ellie, and had most likely directed Jacobs to the archivists' room—which she had escaped—or the biscuit tray in the canteen.

Jacobs would not find Ellie at the biscuit tray.

But where was she to go now?

She needed to sort out what she ought to do with the very important historical objects still squirreled away in her skirt pocket. After all, it wasn't as though she had any job to return to—even if there wasn't a violent criminal hunting about the place for her, thanks to her wretched supervisor.

The bells of the nearby Temple Church rang out the hour. The time was exactly three o'clock—and suddenly, Ellie knew exactly where she wanted to be.

If she hurried, she would make it to her destination just in time.

Ellie splashed heedlessly through the growing puddles in the street on her way to Charing Cross Road, and stopped outside a nondescript blue door sandwiched between a chip shop and a cobbler. She juggled the fern and her briefcase until she managed to get her umbrella closed, then pushed her way inside.

The blue door opened onto a dim, narrow stairwell. As Ellie climbed, familiar noises drifted down to her from above—the forceful *huh* of a dozen bodies exhaling together in sequence and the squeak of bare feet on the floorboards.

On the upper landing, she gratefully deposited her things on one of the shelves placed there for that purpose. She slipped into the room, forcing herself to stop at the threshold despite the urgency surging through her veins.

The space was broad, high-ceilinged, and entirely empty of furniture. Twelve women in comfortable attire were arrayed before an elegant young Japanese man with a dashing mustache who held a solidly built schoolteacher in his arms.

"Elbow," he said in careful, strongly accented English as he took a firm grip on the schoolteacher's arm. "Pull close. Tuck the hip." He twisted at the waist to slip his rear against the woman's pelvis. "Hold and bend."

He turned neatly, folding the woman over his hip and flipping her onto her back on the floormats.

"No arms! Pull from the belly." He indicated the sides of his abdomen. "Yes?"

"Hai, Sensei!" the women replied in quick harmony.

Many of the twelve students in the dojo had been present at the suffrage demonstration the day before. Two of them sported visible bruises, like Ellie did. The police had not been particularly gentle when removing them from the gates.

"Next Thursday, two o'clock. Good day!" Sensei Tani finished cheerfully after helping the teacher up. He gave his students a nod, which the women answered with a lower dip of their heads.

The class broke up, whereupon the synchronized attention quickly dissolved into a rapid clamor of chatter as the women filed over to the door. Ellie stepped aside to let the crowd pass as a few acquaintances waved her a greeting.

One of the students—a diminutive whirlwind whose thick, glossy black hair and sun-warmed complexion hinted at her Anglo-Indian heritage—caught Ellie in her arms, pulling her aside with a strength that belied her petite size.

"Ellie!" she exclaimed. "Oh, I am so glad you've come!"

Constance Tyrrell was one of Ellie's oldest friends. The pair had met at primary school and quickly became inseparable. Though they had grown a bit more distant when Ellie went to university and Constance was shipped off to a posh ladies' finishing academy, they had never entirely lost touch.

Three years earlier, Ellie had happily rekindled her friendship with Constance by introducing her to the suffrage movement—which Constance found 'dreadfully thrilling.' Ellie still wasn't certain how much of Constance's interest in the struggle for women's rights was inspired by her passion for the cause... and how much lay in the possible illegality and potential for danger.

Constance had a rather terrifying taste for adventure.

Ellie's friend had been particularly chuffed at the opportunity to join a handful of the other suffragists at Sensei Tani's jiu jitsu classes.

The sensei had to offer the sessions surreptitiously. His passage to London had been paid for by Mr. Barton-Wright, who had his own martial arts studio for gentlemen on Shaftesbury Avenue. Sensei Tani was meant to teach there and almost certainly *only* there—but the sensei had become enamored with a certain Miss McKinnon who had joined the suffrage club a year before. Across the barrier of his limited (though rapidly improving) English and her thick Cork accent, Miss McKinnon had convinced the sensei of the suffragists' urgent need for an effective means of self-defense. He had expressed his willingness to lend aid, and the club had secured lease of this space above the chip shop for the purpose.

Ellie had yet to take advantage of the sensei's classes as her schedule at the PRO conflicted with the time he had available for the lessons, but Constance had found them quite enlightening.

"I'm glad I caught you," Ellie said. "I need to speak to you about something urgent."

Constance flopped onto the bench on the landing. She snapped out her leg and tugged on one of her kid boots. The motion exposed a length of her muscular calf.

"I also have urgent business with you—namely peppering you with a thousand or so questions about what it was like to actually be *arrested*," Constance added.

The second kid boot popped into place. Constance leapt back to her feet, then plucked her coat and hat from the rack.

"Let's nip over to Geraldine's," she declared and dashed down the stairs.

Ellie grabbed her fern and hurried after Constance. She snapped open her umbrella, and the two women huddled under it. They hurried across the street in the increasing downpour to duck into the entrance of a cozy little tea shop.

Geraldine's was decorated with an explosion of potted plants, bold wallpaper, and mismatched chairs. The windows were steamed up against the lingering spring chill. Constance took Ellie by the arm before she'd quite managed to shake off her umbrella, tugging her over to a little nook pressed up against the window.

They settled in—coats, briefcases, umbrellas, and ferns piling up around them. Geraldine herself—a tall, broad-shouldered woman in her forties—strode over a moment later.

"Right, then," Geraldine rumbled as she dropped a pair of cups onto the small, round table. "Earl Gray, hot, and an Assam with too much cream and sugar. Anything else today?"

"No, Geraldine. That'll be lovely," Constance said, tugging the milky Assam over to herself. "Wait—are those eclairs in the pastry case? I'll take two." Constance turned her wide brown eyes over to Ellie. "Do you want anything for yourself?"

"I think not. Thank you." Ellie offered Geraldine a polite nod.

The proprietress answered with a dissatisfied huff, which was as near as Geraldine ever came to general courtesy.

"So!" Constance leaned in closer. "I heard about the demonstration—it's all anyone has been talking about since yesterday evening. I am devastated to have missed it. How was I to know it would be an honest-to-goodness melee instead of another of those desperately boring standing-about sorts of affairs? You must tell me everything. Did they really have to use bolt cutters to remove you from the gates? What was jail like? Were there rats? Did anybody torture you? Were you interrogated by a dashing police inspector? Threatened with deportation?"

"No!" Ellie exclaimed, a bit alarmed by the idea. "None of those things. It was all rather pedestrian."

"How dreadfully disappointing," Constance replied with a sigh. "Perhaps one must be arrested in a less civilized locale in order to have a more interesting experience."

Ellie halted in the process of stirring her Earl Gray.

"Please tell me you will not try to get yourself arrested when you go to Egypt," she ordered flatly.

Constance leaned back in her chair, a devilish gleam brightening her pretty features. "I am sure Egyptian jails have rats. Maybe a little torture, too."

"I am quite certain the Egyptians don't go in for torture," Ellie countered. "Nor do I imagine it would be nearly as fun as you think if they did. That is the whole point."

"You have no imagination," Constance retorted.

Geraldine dropped a pair of eclairs on the table and stalked away without any further niceties.

"I have plenty of imagination!" Ellie protested. "I am desperately imaginative. I simply use my prodigious imagination for more practical purposes."

"I really wish you could come with me." Constance said before taking down half of an eclair in a single dainty bite. Not a smudge of chocolate was left on her lips.

Constance would be leaving for Egypt in just under two weeks. Her father, Sir Robert Tyrrell, had recently been appointed to the post of Comptroller General of Egypt. That made him essentially the lead auditor of the country's government, which was administered by the British Consul General, Lord Cromer.

She gave Constance the same answer she had been repeating since the question of accompanying the Tyrrells to Egypt had first been raised.

"It just isn't feasible," Ellie muttered automatically before taking another sip of her tea.

It *hadn't* been feasible. She couldn't have left her job at the PRO for so long without losing it, and she might never have found another opportunity for something so suited to her skills.

Of course, that wasn't the entire truth. Ellie had also found herself viewing the prospect of joining Constance in Egypt with a terrible sense of sadness. Walking the same sands as the pharaohs while denied the chance to use her extensive education to uncover the secrets of the past would have been a sort of torture.

"I shall have to look up your brother while I am there," Constance mused. "Saqqara is near enough to Cairo, and I haven't seen Neil since we were schoolgirls." She paused to thoughtfully devour the second half of her eclair. "I wonder if he'll even recognize me, or whether he's become any more interesting. He was a bit of a bore back then."

Neil's presence would only have added to the torment of accompanying Constance to Egypt. Even now, Neil was working on a very promising excavation in the Unas South Cemetery of the Saqqara necropolis. He had privately shared with Ellie that he hoped the eighteenth-dynasty ruin he was uncovering would turn out to be the lost, unfinished tomb of the general-turned-pharaoh Horemheb. If Neil's theory turned out to be correct, the tomb could provide invaluable insight into the decline of the Amarna period.

Ellie was extremely interested in the Amarna period.

She was very fond of her stepbrother—despite his annoying habit of constantly trying to tell her what was best for her and his irritating insistence on referring to her as 'Peanut.' Still, the notion of watching him blithely live the life Ellie had always dreamed of was the sort of thing that kept her up in the small hours of the night.

Not that Ellie had told any of that to Constance. She couldn't bear to taint her friend's excitement about her upcoming adventure with her own inconvenient emotions.

"I doubt he's changed much," Ellie returned flatly.

Constance reached for her second eclair.

"But here I am nattering on when you are the one who said you had urgent news." Constance paused with the eclair momentarily forgotten halfway to her lips. Her eyes glittered with excitement. "Is it about a man? Do tell me that it's a man."

Ellie stiffened with alarm.

"Gracious, no!" she exclaimed. "What on earth would I want to do with one of those? No. It's... well, this."

Ellie pulled the map and medallion from her pocket and set them down on the table next to the Earl Gray.

Constance frowned down at the black disk of stone. "Did you find this in one of the shops? It is wonderfully gruesome." She reached out for the objects.

"From the *shops*?" Ellie echoed indignantly. "Hold on—have you any chocolate on your fingers?"

Constance eyed the digits in question and popped three of them in her mouth.

"I'll unfold it for you," Ellie cut in quickly. She pushed aside the eclair plate and the teacups, then carefully opened the parchment.

Constance studied the time-aged lines on the page, blithely reaching out for her eclair.

Ellie cleared her throat pointedly, and Constance retracted the offending hand.

"I know you can't read Latin," Ellie continued, feeling oddly nervous. "But I can assure you that the spelling and syntax are appropriate for this document having been authored by a seventeenth-century Spaniard with a Catholic ecclesiastical education—"

"Ellie," Constance cut in, her eyes bright as she studied the page with her hands obediently tucked into her lap. "You found a treasure map."

"I most certainly did not!" Ellie retorted.

"It has an X on it," Constance countered, pointing a finger at the symbol in question.

"That could be a ten," Ellie pushed back uncertainly. "A measure of distance. A temporary stand-in for an unknown place name."

"It. Is. An. X." Constance's firm tone dared Ellie to disagree. "And what exactly is it that this *X* is meant to indicate?"

"The White City," Ellie replied weakly, sinking down a bit in her chair.

"And what is the White City, Eleanora?" Constance pressed relentlessly.

Ellie felt as though Constance was glaring down at her, though Ellie topped her by a few solid inches even when sitting down.

"A-mythical-kingdom-of-untold-riches-and-splendor," Ellie blurted quickly before clamping her mouth shut again.

"I see," Constance returned archly. "And are you going to tell me where you came by this not-a-treasure-map to a mythical kingdom of untold riches and splendor?"

Two cups of tea and three eclairs later, Constance leaned across the table with conspiratorial glee.

"Are you telling me that you were outside the door while an *actual criminal* used physical violence to intimidate your incompetent supervisor?" she demanded.

Ellie's friend spoke of eavesdropping on an assault as though it were more exciting than stumbling across a parade.

"I'm afraid so," Ellie replied. She popped the last half of a pastry into her mouth and dusted off her fingers.

Constance let out a squeak of outrage. "The nerve of that man! Selling the possible find of the century for his own pecuniary gain! And I would bet my right foot that he didn't even get a proper price for it. From everything you have told me about Mr. Henbury, he would be utterly ignorant of the true potential value of this document." Constance tapped the parchment with a purposeful finger.

Ellie reached across the table and slowly snatched the map back. She slipped it into her pocket as she prayed that Constance's finger had been entirely free of chocolate. The seventeenth-century relic's proximity to so many eclair crumbs was making her distinctly nervous.

"Yes, well… It's all moot now," Ellie said. "Henbury couldn't deliver the objects from the psalter because I'd already—er, borrowed them without asking… and now he has gone and given my name to the criminal in question in order to try and save his own skin."

"The sheer cheek of it, really," Constance noted disapprovingly.

"Quite," Ellie agreed. "And so here I am. I'm afraid I might have panicked and bolted right out of the building. I just knew I needed to talk to someone so I could get my head straight about what to do."

"And have you?" Constance asked.

Ellie's shoulders sank a bit. "I have. It's silly it took me so long to admit it to myself. I must bring the map to the Royal Geographical Society and… and leave it with them," she finished stoutly.

Inside, part of her felt as though it were wilting.

Constance's only answer was an eloquently raised eyebrow.

"Don't do that," Ellie protested. "Don't give me that look."

"What look?" Constance pushed back.

"*That* one," Ellie replied. "The one that says you disapprove of the entirely sensible thing I am planning on doing."

"Now why would I do that?" Constance returned blandly, taking another sip of her tea.

"Because you know the RGS is going to shut me out of it!" The words came out a bit louder than Ellie had intended. She took in a few alarmed looks from the other patrons and lowered her voice to a fervent hiss. "You know that they will take the map and the medallion, wave me off, and be done with me. In the worst case scenario, the objects will end up in some box gathering dust in their archives, and in the best case, they'll dispatch one of their members to British Honduras to track down the site marked on the map and determine whether anything is there."

"And if something is there?" Constance prompted.

"If we are lucky, the fellow assigned to lead the expedition will actually do a reasonable job instead of mucking up the sediment layers and using inconsistent forms of documentation," Ellie replied. "If that is the case, then really, it will all have turned out perfectly fine."

"Will it?" Constance gently pressed.

Something gave a little wrench inside of Ellie's chest. She clutched her cup of Earl Gray a little more firmly as though it was a rope that might keep her from falling.

"It is only that I might have liked to..." Ellie paused, taking an uneven breath. "It would perhaps have meant a great deal to me to simply..."

Her throat tightened. Getting words out of it became difficult.

"I just want to see it, Connie," Ellie finally managed.

The corners of her eyes had begun to feel ever-so-slightly damp.

Constance rose. She circled their little table, hopped neatly over Ellie's briefcase, and dodged the precarious fern.

"Move over," she ordered—then plopped herself on the edge of Ellie's chair and pulled Ellie into her arms.

The gesture was not really the sort of thing one did in a tea shop. It spoke alarmingly of having *feelings*—feelings that were rather too wild and terrible to politely contain.

Ellie didn't protest. She let her friend hold her, dropping her head onto Constance's shoulder.

"Sometimes I am just so very tired of it," she admitted quietly.

"I know, darling," Constance replied, smoothing a hand over her hair. "It is dreadfully unfair."

Ellie didn't answer. Instead, she let herself soak up the warm comfort of Constance's embrace until her soul felt a little steadier again.

"But look," Constance said, pulling back to face her. "I have just had an absolutely marvelous idea!"

"Oh no," Ellie said as her sense of alarm rose.

"*You* should go find the X!" Constance asserted happily.

"What?!" Ellie jolted with surprise and nearly fell off the chair.

"Whyever not?" Constance demanded. "You have the exact same education as those stuffed shirts in the Royal Geographical Society. You are just as well-qualified to pursue the matter as they are."

"You are only forgetting the little matter of how I would manage to get through the uncharted wilderness to the location marked on the map," Ellie pushed back nervously.

"That is what guides are for!" Constance retorted. "Do you think those posh punters at the RGS go jaunting off into the back country on their own? They hire locals to take them, and other locals to carry all of their tents and guns and canoes for them. You won't need half of that—you won't be combining your archaeological survey with a bit of big game hunting on the side and a glass of sherry in the evenings."

"Hardly." Ellie frowned at the very idea.

"So there you are!" Constance exclaimed and gave her a nudge. "What possible reason do you have for turning your map over to those men rather than going after this lost city yourself?"

Ellie fought against a tingling rise of excitement.

"You are forgetting the little matter of the criminal who is after this parchment," she pointed out.

"Yes, that is something," Constance mused thoughtfully. "If your Mr. Henbury were so quick to cough up your identity to that villain, I'm sure he would hardly balk at granting him access to the personnel records."

Ellie straightened in her chair.

"Fiddlesticks!" she cursed. "You're absolutely right! That Mr. Jacobs could very well have my address. He might be heading there as we speak! How are my father and Florence going to handle a violent thug turning up on their doorstep?"

"I expect your father would ignore the fellow and keep reading his newspaper, as he always does," Constance offered. "And your stepmother will serve him tea and pepper him with questions about whether he is eligible to be married."

Ellie rose from her chair, nearly dislodging Constance in the process. She set about quickly gathering her things.

"I must hurry," she declared. "If I am there, then at least I might be able to find some means of putting him off."

Constance plucked up her own hat and coat.

"Excellent plan," she agreed. "We should proceed there immediately."

"Connie, I can't possibly expect you to put yourself at risk for this," Ellie said.

Constance's expression turned stormy.

"Don't you dare try to leave me out of it," she warned. "This is the most exciting thing that has happened to me in ages."

"Oh, dash it!" Ellie burst out, grabbing her fern. "Come along, then!"

FOUR

$\mathcal{T}$HE RAIN HAD LET up by the time Ellie and Constance disembarked from the crowded omnibus. Ellie juggled her briefcase and fern as they hurried up the street.

Her home stood on a tidy little enclave in Canonbury lined with three-story semi-detached houses that were set comfortably back from the road. Most of Ellie's neighbors were reasonably well-to-do clerks of some sort or another. Her father, David Mallory, was an insurance actuary. He earned a high enough salary for the family to employ both a housemaid and a cook, which gave Ellie's stepmother, Florence, less things to be loudly overwhelmed about.

Everything looked quite ordinary as Ellie and Constance approached the house. Florence hadn't yet drawn the curtains for the evening. The train Ellie's father took home every day wouldn't arrive for another twenty minutes.

Ellie slowed as she approached the front steps, regarding the door warily. With its tidy front hedge and white trim, the house did not look at all like a dangerous villain was already wreaking havoc inside of it.

"Well?" Constance prompted. "Are we going in or not?"

"I suppose we had better," Ellie agreed.

Her front hallway was just as unremarkable as the steps. The brass hat stand and potted philodendron gave no indication that any criminals were lurking about.

"Is that you, Eleanora?" her stepmother called from the parlor.

"Yes, Florence," Ellie called back as she divested herself of her hat and umbrella.

Florence popped into the doorway. She was a pretty woman with a generously curved figure, her brown hair accented by streaks of silver. Florence loudly bewailed the presence of those streaks, but Ellie thought they looked nice. They might even have appeared distinguished, if Florence wasn't… well, Florence. It was hard for a person to appear distinguished when they were endlessly complaining about their nerves.

Not that Ellie had any real fears for her stepmother's nerves. Despite all the hand-waving she did, Florence possessed an exceptionally robust constitution.

"I am glad to see you are back at a reasonable hour *today*," Florence said loudly. "How that office of yours can think it appropriate to keep a young lady of good breeding working past eight on a Tuesday evening is utterly beyond my comprehension…"

Constance raised an eloquent eyebrow at Ellie. They both knew perfectly well that it was not the PRO but the Metropolitan Police that had made Ellie late for supper the night before.

Thankfully, she kept quiet about it. Constance was nothing if not a reliable co-conspirator.

Florence was still talking.

"…never mind exposing you to all manner of hazards, like that dreadful bookshelf that fell on you…"

"Yes, well," Ellie hedged, resisting the urge to put her fingers to the bruise that still marked her cheek. "I don't imagine we'll have to worry about rogue bookshelves for the foreseeable future."

"Hello, Constance, darling," Florence said, shifting her attention to Ellie's companion. "I don't suppose *you* would tell her that she can hardly expect to find herself a husband if she spends all her hours poring over musty old papers."

"Florence!" Ellie protested.

"It's only because I care so very much, darling," Florence replied, looking a little emotional.

Beside Ellie, Constance cleared her throat meaningfully.

"Ah—did anyone happen to call by this afternoon?" Ellie asked, taking the hint.

"Why?" Florence demanded cannily. Her eyes sharpened like a hawk sighting marriageable prey. "Are you expecting a caller?"

A clatter and a cry of alarm rose from the kitchen.

"Oh bother," Florence cursed. "Major is after the bacon again."

Florence hiked up her skirts and made an energetic dash toward the kitchen, where Major, her beloved and thoroughly spoiled Jack Russell, was raising havoc.

Ellie tugged Constance up the stairs. They slipped into Ellie's bedroom, which faced the front of the house, and pulled shut the door.

"He hasn't come," Constance concluded.

"It would appear not," Ellie agreed, beginning to pace. "Perhaps we were unfair to Mr. Henbury. Maybe after giving that criminal my name, he resisted any further betrayal of my circumstances."

"I rather doubt that," Constance retorted dryly.

"Then why isn't Jacobs here?" Ellie demanded.

She was answered by a burst of hysterical barking from below—the sound of a manic terrier demanding the opportunity to maul and destroy whatever lay on the far side of the front door.

Someone knocked.

By silent consensus, Ellie and Constance shot to the window and peered down at the front step.

A man stood there. He looked to be in his early thirties and was dressed in a well-made but unremarkable black suit. Ellie couldn't see the details of his face from this angle—only a flash of pale skin and dark hair from under the brim of his bowler hat.

"Is that him?" Constance demanded in a whisper. "Your Mr. Jacobs?"

"I think we must assume that it is," Ellie returned grimly.

Constance craned her head, trying to get a better look around the hat.

"He's a bit dashing," she commented.

"How on earth can you tell that from the top of his head?" Ellie shot back.

Footsteps sounded in the hall. Major's frantic barks were silenced as Florence presumably snatched the dog up in her arms. A moment later, Ellie heard the distinct creak of the front door opening.

She and Constance exchanged an alarmed look.

Ellie quickly weighed her options. She knew Jacobs was not averse to using violence to achieve his ends. Ellie refused to put her friend or her stepmother at risk.

There was an obvious solution to that problem. She might simply give Jacobs what he wanted.

The very thought of it was anathema. Hand the key to a potentially revolutionary archaeological discovery over to someone who walked on historical documents and threw people into doors?

She grasped for an alternative.

A train whistle drifted through the window, emanating from the nearby East London line. The sound was as familiar to her as the clatter of carriage wheels.

Ellie's gaze shot to the books packed neatly onto her shelves.

She hurried over and unerringly plucked *Osgood's English Rail and Steamer*

Timetables from among its brethren. It took Ellie only a moment to find what she sought—the list of steamer departures for the Caribbean, Mexico, and Central America.

Her finger stopped on a single tidy row of type, and her heart began to beat a little faster.

Could she possibly...?

She could, she realized, feeling a jolt of excitement and alarm. She very possibly could.

Ellie flipped to the local rail timetables at the rear of the book—and stopped, staring down at the lines.

She raised her eyes to the clock beside her bed. One of the hands clicked forward.

The time was precisely twenty-two minutes past five.

Her plan fell neatly into place.

It was mad. It would be by far the most rash and irresponsible thing that Ellie had ever done—and that included chaining herself to the gates of Parliament.

It could also work... so long as she could refrain from being assaulted for exactly eight minutes.

What was the alternative? Leaving her map to a well-spoken criminal?

Ellie slammed shut the book and yanked a battered valise from the bottom of her wardrobe, dropping it onto her bed. She began tossing things into it as she spoke.

"I need you to take this to Canonbury Station and buy a ticket for the West India Docks," Ellie ordered.

"The docks!" Constance exclaimed as two practical changes of clothes and a bundle of flannels landed in the suitcase. "Does that mean what I think it does?"

Ellie added a hairbrush and four pairs of spare stockings to the pile.

"I have analyzed the alternatives and—"

Constance cut her off, leaping into action.

"This is marvelous!" she declared. She grabbed a bottle of face cream and a silk scarf from Ellie's dressing table and threw them in as well. "But I don't see why you're running. I can confront the fellow with my jiu jitsu."

"Absolutely not," Ellie shot back as she packed a pair of nail scissors and a still-wrapped bar of soap. "The man is a villain. Your jiu jitsu is most useful when evading capture or restraint, but you cannot expect it to allow you to overcome a person twice your weight."

"But Sensei Tani taught me an excellent maneuver that I have been dying to try out," Constance cut in as she tossed an entirely impractical blue silk dressing gown onto the growing stack of items.

"That will not be necessary," Ellie asserted, snatching up a blank notebook and pen from her writing desk. "This fiend cannot know Canonbury nearly as well as I do. I will lead him on a chase and then double back to meet you."

Not for the first time, Ellie wished that ladies could don a pair of trousers without the garment being seen as an invitation to ridicule or harassment. Thankfully, she at least made a habit of dressing practically. Her boots were sturdy, and her plain tweed skirt wouldn't hamper her movements too badly once she had hiked it up over her shins.

Exquisitely conscious of her limited time, Ellie fought to get the suitcase closed. Constance added her muscle to the effort and finally hopped up to sit on the lid, which allowed Ellie to fix the latch.

Ellie pushed the suitcase at her friend.

"Be ready," she warned. "If I do not succeed in losing him first, I will be cutting this rather fine."

"You may count on me, of course," Constance returned stoutly.

Ellie shoved open the window facing the side of the house and swung a leg over the sill.

"Thank you. You are a true friend, Connie," she said meaningfully.

She grasped hold of the wisteria trellis, setting her boot to one of the sturdy rungs. Casting one final glance back into her bedroom, she took note of the time on the clock as its most slender hand ticked neatly forward.

Five minutes and forty seconds, Ellie calculated.

She swung out onto the wisteria. It took her only a moment to descend the vine, landing solidly between her house and the semi-detached next door. She hurried up the narrow path and emerged into the street.

Constance hadn't been entirely wrong about the man on her doorstep. An idle passer-by might have found him reasonably good-looking. His pale skin and dark hair complemented his lean build and regular features—but his gaze was cool and flat in a manner that reminded Ellie of the unhurried danger in the tones she had overheard from Mr. Henbury's office.

Florence was oblivious to the threat. Based on her pose in the doorway, Ellie's stepmother was mildly flirting as she assessed whether the fellow was a reasonable candidate for a new son-in-law.

A neighbor at the next house was out front watering his garden. A few scattered people strolled down the road. Ellie felt certain that only their presence had prevented the stranger on her threshold from shoving past Florence to get inside.

Thankfully, the neighbors were not an impediment to Ellie's plan.

Five minutes and ten.

"You, there!" Ellie shouted as she yanked the map from her pocket and waved it over her head. "Is this what you're looking for?"

The man's reaction told her everything she needed to know. As he turned toward her, his eyes sharpening like a hound after a fox, Ellie knew that he must indeed be the mysterious Mr. Jacobs—and that she had succeeded in capturing his attention.

"Come and get it, then," she challenged—and bolted.

Her boots pounded down the pavement in a most unladylike manner. A glance back showed that Jacobs was sprinting very capably after her.

Behind him, Constance slipped past Florence, who was gaping after Ellie from the doorway.

Constance whipped off a cheerful salute as she dashed the opposite way up the road, carrying Ellie's valise in her hand.

Ellie hauled up her skirts, exposing her wool stockings as she put on more speed.

Jacobs was fast—but she didn't need to outrun him. She had spent her entire childhood marauding around Canonbury. She knew these streets like she knew her own skin.

She pivoted, skidding to the left and slamming through Mr. Pettigrew's garden gate, the lock of which had been broken for years. Mr. Pettigrew glanced up at her, blinking, from where he stood watering his hydrangeas.

"Sorry, Mr. Pettigrew!" Ellie called as she hopped onto the back of an overturned wheelbarrow and scrambled up onto the wall.

She half-fell into the adjoining garden, landing beside a three-year-old playing in a sandbox.

"Hi Ewwie!" he said cheerfully.

"Keep digging, Clarence!" Ellie replied.

Clarence's mother, Mrs. Lovett, stepped out into the garden with a tea tray. She stared wide-eyed as Ellie dashed around the corner of the house.

Mrs. Lovett's alarmed scream and the crash of breaking porcelain a moment later told Ellie that Jacobs had managed to follow.

Ellie blasted out into another street, swinging left and sprinting past two perambulating widows in elaborate black gowns as she continued to keep her mental count.

Four minutes thirty.

"Well, I never!" the first widow, Mrs. Fairweather, exclaimed.

Only Mrs. Fairweather's grip on her companion's arm kept the sour-faced woman from stumbling over with surprise as she gaped disapprovingly at Ellie's exposed shins.

The tailor, Mr. Granger, tipped his hat politely as Ellie skidded past him. She hopped from the pavement into the road, dodged the plumber's lorry, and ducked to the right to avoid startling Mr. Twyford's temperamental cart horse. The poshly irate driver of a gleaming Vauxhall motorcar shouted after her as he fumbled for his horn.

Ellie ignored him as a more alarmed outburst from the two widows alerted her to Jacobs' proximity.

She raced into a fine little early Georgian chapel. She flew up the nave past the rows of pews, wheeled around the altar, and slammed out the back door into the churchyard. The leaning monument of *G. Edgar Wittlesmith* nearly tripped her, but Ellie managed to right herself by rolling across the surface of a raised tomb, scattering a cluster of terrified squirrels.

Two minutes and twenty seconds.

A door slammed open behind her, and Ellie acknowledged that she was unlikely to succeed in shaking her pursuer.

That was all right. She had recognized the possibility and planned for it.

Ellie was very good at making plans.

She raced up a narrow alley, vaulted over a toppled rubbish bin, and skidded around a corner. Back out on the main road once more, she dashed past the news shop, the post office, and the chandlers. A Pomeranian on the end of a lead barked at her excitedly. A pair of children pointed, staring with wide-eyed wonder as she sprinted past them.

Another train whistle sounded, carrying musically to her on the wind from the east.

One minute twelve.

Ellie swerved onto Grosvenor Avenue. She jumped down into the road again, narrowly avoiding the clustered buckets of blooms that Mr. Cresswell, the florist, always set out on the pavement under his awning.

A loud clatter sounded behind her as Jacobs collided with the display. After a brief delay, he freed himself from the tulips, and his footsteps pounded after her again.

Ellie's legs and lungs burned as she sprinted toward the now-visible sign for Canonbury Station.

Forty six seconds, she thought furiously.

It was too much time.

Ellie raced toward the two sets of stairs that led down to the inbound and outbound platforms on opposite sides of the tracks.

She thought of the whistle that she had heard a moment before, and knew that it must be the five twenty-nine outbound service to Highbury sounding a warning as it approached the station. The five twenty-nine was a train she knew well, as it was the one that her father took home from work every evening.

Yes, she thought. *Yes, that could do nicely.*

Ellie dashed past the inbound stairs, hitting the outbound set instead. She hopped onto the railing and slid down the length of it, buying herself an extra six seconds.

As Ellie reached the bottom, Constance's petite figure waved to her furiously from the inbound platform on the far side of the rail lines. Beside her, the gleaming black engine of the five-thirty express to West Croydon let off a burst of steam and a warning whistle before its departure.

"Inbound express to Shadwell, Rotherhithe, and Forest Hill!" the conductor shouted.

Twenty eight... twenty seven... twenty six...

Brakes screeched from the tracks to the east as the five twenty-nine outbound service slowed for its stop at Canonbury.

Jacobs' footfalls rattled on the grate of the stairs behind her.

Constance shouted over, bouncing nervously up and down where she waited by the inbound train.

"Ellie, you're on the wrong—"

Ellie jumped off the platform.

Her boots landed solidly in the gravel of the track bed. She kicked off against the stones, scrambling across the tracks as the five twenty-nine let off an alarmed whistle.

She felt the rush of the cars behind her as the outbound service crossed the place where she had been standing a moment before.

Ellie hurried in front of the waiting inbound engine and climbed up onto the platform. A small but sturdy hand grasped her arm to help haul her up.

"That was magnificent!" Constance exclaimed with a happy flush in her cheeks.

"Last call for Rotherhithe and Forest Hill!" the conductor shouted.

Constance shoved Ellie toward the first class car. Ellie half stumbled inside as Constance hopped up behind her.

The car jerked as the engine chugged into motion. Constance pushed Ellie into an empty compartment.

Ellie went straight to the window, tugged it down, and stuck her head out through it.

The cars of the inbound train flashed past, and the outbound platform was revealed.

She spotted the trim, mustachioed figure of her father moving toward the stairs, his nose pressed to the pages of the latest edition of the *Financial Times*.

Behind him, Jacobs stood like a dark, still pillar in the midst of a moving mass of evening commuters. His thoughtful, assessing gaze locked onto hers across the growing distance that separated them until he slipped from view.

Ellie collapsed into her seat, releasing her breath in a whoosh.

"That was by far the most exciting thing I have ever done," Constance announced, plopping down across from her.

"Hold on," Ellie said, straightening. "You aren't even supposed to be here!"

"I am seeing you off," Constance retorted breezily. "You never know if you might need someone to engage in physical combat with another dastardly fellow at the docks."

Ellie pressed her fingers to her temples, fighting off a rising headache as reality settled in. "This is madness," she declared.

"Why on earth would you say that?" Constance protested.

"I am throwing myself onto a steamer to British Honduras on less than ten minutes' notice," Ellie shot back, her tone rising. "I just raced a villain through the streets of Canonbury. I haven't the foggiest notion where I'm going or what must be involved in getting there."

She buried her face in her hands. It was becoming a bit harder to breathe.

"I should be doing so much *research...*" she protested helplessly.

Constance grabbed Ellie's hands.

"Eleanora, what is the hieroglyph for truth?" she demanded.

"A feather, or the image of the goddess Maat," Ellie replied automatically.

"Who was the first emperor of China?"

"Qin Shi Huang."

"List the ancient civilizations of Central America in chronological order."

Ellie frowned. "If one includes southern portions of Mexico, we can establish a reliable timeline for the Aztecs, who were preceded by the Mayans to the south. Prior to that, there are still questions as to whether the Toltec or Olmec peoples were genuine or mythological. Of course, the dating methods are notoriously subjective, which makes establishing a clear chronology unreliable at—"

"I have made my point," Constance said firmly. She leaned back, crossing her arms neatly over her chest.

"But there are still so many books I haven't read!" Ellie fought back a flare of panic. "The research is terribly new. Why, just the other day, there was an article in *The Century* on the excavation of a Post-Classical site in Honduras that I have barely had an opportunity to browse, never mind properly annotate…"

Constance was unmoved.

"You are getting on that boat," she declared flatly. "You are going to the Caribbean. You will purchase your equipment with the pile of earnings from your dull job that you have never bothered to properly spend. You will hire a guide, find your city, and become the most famous archaeologist in the world."

Ellie crossed her arms mulishly.

"I am not interested in becoming *famous*," she said tartly. "I would simply like to be permitted to use my skills and education to further our understanding of the ancient world."

"So go do that, then." Constance waved an airy hand. "I don't even know why we're arguing about it. It seems to me that your whole plan to keep your parents from being accosted by that thug relies upon your immediate escape to the colonies and prompt removal into the back country before he can track you down."

"Yes," Ellie agreed, feeling a bit dizzy. "Yes, it rather does. Oh, bother…" She lowered her head to her knees.

"Shoreditch High Street!" the conductor called from outside their compartment. "Next stop, Whitechapel. Change at Shadwell for the London & Blackwell Line."

"That's you," Constance announced. "How long before we arrive at the docks and put you on that boat?"

"Approximately eighteen minutes," Ellie replied unthinkingly.

"Well, then," Constance returned cheerfully. "That should be plenty of time for you to get used to the idea."

The West India Docks were loud and crowded. The narrow waterways were packed with ships. Steam stacks mingled with the tall skeletons of graceful sailboats. Passengers bumped against dockworkers as everyone hurried to load the boats scheduled to leave with the turning of the evening tide. Cranes hefted pallets of tea, oranges, and tobacco onto the wharfs as street vendors hawked whelks, mussels, peppered pies, and apple fritters.

Ellie sniffed at a baked potato cart as a line of dock workers trudged past carrying sides of frozen beef, wrapped in muslin, on their shoulders.

Her stomach grumbled, reminding her that it was nearly time for supper. Constance slipped out the door of the shipping company office and hurried over to join her.

"You're on," she announced, slapping a piece of paper into Ellie's hand. "Though it was a near thing. They're sailing momentarily, and they were loath to deal with the paperwork for another passenger. I had to resort to an outright bribe in order to get you on board."

"A bribe!" Ellie protested. "Connie!"

"It's the sort of thing one does when one is on an adventure," Constance neatly replied as she hooked a hand under Ellie's elbow and dragged her away from the potato cart. "You shall be traveling as Mrs. Nitherscott-Watby, widow."

"Nitherscott-Watby?" Ellie echoed in disbelief. "Did you make that up off the top of your head?"

"Of course I did," Constance returned. "What a silly question."

"Why must I be a widow when I am already a perfectly good spinster?" Ellie demanded.

Constance raised a wry eyebrow at her. "You are hardly some dried up old prune. You are an attractive woman of four-and-twenty. You have only passed as a spinster because you haven't really tried to do anything scandalous yet beyond suffraging."

"Suffrage is not a verb," Ellie retorted.

"What else should I call it?" Constance continued without waiting for a reply. "As a widow, you will be subject to far less scrutiny than an unmarried woman. You will see the sense of it soon enough."

"Should I invent a few imaginary siblings while I'm at it?" Ellie demanded crossly.

"A wealthy uncle might be handy," Constance mused as she hauled Ellie toward the looming ships. "You can think about it on the boat. They've already sent your valise along."

Ellie felt a bolt of panic. "What about my parents? I can't just disappear to the other side of the world without so much as a note."

"I'll tell them you've gone off to Bournemouth on a holiday," Constance breezily assured her. "Heaven only knows you were in desperate need of one."

"Bournemouth?" Ellie's headache threatened to return.

"Bournemouth is lovely, as you would know if you ever went anywhere besides the library. One more to board!" Constance hollered up at the men on the deck, who were in the process of drawing the chain across the gate for departure.

"Perhaps it's too late," Ellie suggested hopefully.

Constance caught Ellie's shoulders, gripping them with a strength that belied her diminutive size.

"You are standing at the foot of the most important thing you have ever done in your life," she declared. "Do you really want to turn around and walk away from that?"

Ellie blinked down at her friend. The answer spilled from her lips, as undeniable as it was terrifying.

"*No.*"

Constance narrowed her eyes with fiery determination. "Then get on the boat, Eleanora."

Ellie yanked Constance into her arms, pressing a kiss to her cheek.

"Thank you," she whispered, and then hurried up the gangplank.

She extended her pass to the porter when she reached the top.

"One more to board," she announced.

"You're cutting it fine," the man retorted irritably before undoing the chain and waving Ellie impatiently onto the deck.

The crew raced to haul in lines as the ship gave off a warning whistle. Behind her, the gangplank clattered as a pair of men pulled it up and tucked it away.

Ellie grasped the rail tightly as she looked out over the docks. Constance had hopped up onto a barrel of salted fish and was waving at her enthusiastically. Behind her, a lean figure with night-dark hair broke the sea of busy, moving people on the pier.

It was Jacobs, gazing up at Ellie from beside the open door of a hackney carriage.

He looked curious, and perhaps a little challenging—but not defeated, Ellie thought with a little chill.

No—he did not look at all like a man whose hopes had just been dashed.

He tipped his hat like a fencer acknowledging a fine parry. Then he was gone, the dark point of him vanishing like a ghost as the ship glided free of the dock and London receded behind her.

FIVE

Noon
April 22, 1898
Approaching Belize Town

*A*T THE END OF Ellie's second week on board the steamer *Salerno,* the green shoreline of British Honduras finally came into view.

The ship had been decidedly short on books, save for a Bible and a catalog of steamer routes. Ellie had gone through the timetables assiduously to calculate how quickly Jacobs might manage to follow her.

Jacobs had seen the boat Ellie had boarded back in London, so it would be little trouble for him to determine where she had gone. Thankfully, direct sailings from England to British Honduras took place only once a month. If Jacobs didn't want to wait that long, he would have to take a ship to New York, then train overland to New Orleans in order to pick up the weekly mail boat to the colony. That journey would take him roughly six days longer than Ellie's more direct route.

All of which meant that Ellie had at least six days to find a guide and abscond to the interior before Jacobs could possibly catch up to her.

On the two-week journey across the Atlantic, Ellie had plenty of time to consider what would need to be done if the map really did lead to a set of undiscovered ruins. Thorough documentation of any potential historical significance was the key to protecting such a find from ne'er-do-wells like Jacobs.

Ellie would submit her findings to both the colonial authorities and the academic journals. In doing so, she would clearly establish the importance of the site and the need for its ongoing investigation and protection.

She was still mulling over which of the journals she would approach first.

The most respectable ones were also the ones most likely to balk at accepting a submission from a woman.

Ellie was also aware that her efforts, if successful, might very well force the world to finally accept her as an archaeologist and scholar—and why not? She had all the training and education required for the job. That she was excluded from the field purely on the basis of her gender was the rankest injustice.

If she were able to crack open the resistant nut of the British scientific establishment, perhaps it would become easier for other women to follow her. The thought added wind to her sails.

Of course, all of that depended upon whether or not anything worth finding actually lay at the end of her map.

British Honduras's capital, Belize Town, lacked a proper harbor. The *Salerno* was forced to anchor two miles from the long, verdant shoreline. The passengers and freight were then shuttled to land by a flotilla of little rowboats and fishing craft, which wove through the dotted coral reefs and cays with obvious expertise. The little islets were lined with stretches of golden sand that bordered thick green forests dotted with colorful flowers and towering palms.

Beneath the ferry, the water was so clear that Ellie could see straight through it to the bits of shell and coral lying on the mud and sand of the sea floor.

The air was warm as a caress, and the sunlight like liquid gold. Ellie soaked up the pure pleasure of both as the sailboat ferrying her and the other passengers approached the colorful buildings that lined Belize Town's waterfront.

As they approached the town, Ellie's hand moved instinctively to the front of her blouse. She could just feel the subtle curve of the medallion beneath the fabric. She had strung the artifact from the psalter along a piece of ribbon trimmed out of an otherwise frivolous nightdress, which Constance had thrown into her valise. The weight of the disk was cool against her skin despite the warmth of the day. Wearing the stone rather than simply concealing it among the rest of her things felt *right*.

The map was tucked into an opening Ellie had picked in the lining of her practical, comfortable corset. When she moved, she could feel the added stiffness of the parchment against her skin.

The river mouth that served as Belize Town's harbor was busy with brightly painted barges and fishing boats. Ellie disembarked and filed onto the customs wharf with the other passengers, where the agent on duty submitted each of them to a cursory examination.

Ellie stepped up to the man's desk as her turn in the queue arrived.

"Where will you be staying?" the agent asked. His English was inflected with a warm, musical rhythm.

"I hadn't quite worked that out yet," Ellie admitted.

"There are two hotels in Belize Town. The Imperial caters to most of our overseas visitors. You will be most comfortable there," the agent assured her.

His description sparked a burst of alarm. Ellie had little desire to be shut up with a bunch of colonial administrators. They were all likely to be Englishmen, and Englishmen were prone to thinking that they knew best what a woman ought to be doing with herself. They were usually quite happy to impose those opinions on any female unfortunate enough to be in their vicinity.

"You said there were two hotels," Ellie quickly cut in. "What about the other one?"

"The Rio Nuevo?" the agent asked. "You will find it on North Front Street by the river. It is quite respectable, but they serve the local sort of food. There is afternoon tea with very nice cream buns at The Imperial."

"I don't require cream buns," Ellie replied shortly. "The Rio Nuevo will do very nicely, thank you."

The agent shrugged and jotted her name into his logbook... her false name, of course.

Mrs. Nitherscott-Watby

Ellie would make Constance pay for that later.

The Hotel Rio Nuevo lay a short distance down the road from the wharf on a lovely avenue of big detached houses with abundant gardens. The hotel was actually one of those same houses, painted white with tidy black shutters, with the addition of a long, two-story wing that extended out from one side of it. Each of the two floors of the wing sported a wide, covered veranda, which looked wonderfully cool and shady.

Ellie paused before climbing the steps, surprised to realize that the building had no foundation. Instead, it had been built on a nest of thick, sturdy pilings driven into the soft ground. She lingered for a moment, distracted by the cleverness of the engineering, before forcing herself to hurry along.

The lobby took up most of the ground floor of the original house. The interior was spacious, with wood-paneled walls and a plethora of potted flowers and tropical ferns. The scattered furniture had seen some years, but all of it was clean and carefully maintained.

Ellie heard the click of billiards balls and a little burst of laughter. She skipped a few steps to the side to peer past the front desk, where a broad doorway led into a well-appointed lounge. A scattering of men of various ethnicities were settled inside. They looked quite comfortable with themselves and seemed more or less respectable.

A pair of posh English accents clanged through the warmer Kriol and Latin inflections, setting Ellie's nerves jangling. She identified the speakers— two pale men in linen traveling suits. Thankfully, they were too engrossed in their game of cards to pay her much mind.

As Ellie approached the hotel's front desk, a gentleman with a glowing amber complexion and a fine black mustache stepped out to meet her. The delicate lines at the corners of his eyes added to his admittedly dashing appeal.

"Good afternoon, madam." His accent revealed a hint of Spanish influence. "I am Mr. Linares Rivas, proprietor. Will you be joining us here at the Hotel Rio Nuevo?"

"I should be very glad to," Ellie replied stoutly.

"And how long will you be with us?" he asked with his pen poised over his book.

"No more than six days, I should think," Ellie replied, thinking uncomfortably of steamer timetables and potentially villainous arrivals.

"Do forgive the question, but are you traveling alone, Mrs...?" He paused, waiting for her answer.

"Nitherscott-Watby," Ellie filled in.

She tried not to wince at Constance's terrible name, and then scrambled to think of the right answer to the proprietor's question.

There had been no one but men in the Rio Nuevo's lounge—or on the *Salerno*, for that matter, though the boat had carried only a handful of passengers as most of its space was given over to freight. The careful concern Ellie had observed in the customs agent earlier also signaled that European women traveling alone did not often visit this remote colony.

Ellie had no desire to draw more attention to herself than was strictly necessary. She needed a story—quickly.

"I will be joined in a few days by my... uncle," she offered awkwardly. "My Uncle Oliver. He's in... investments. Mining. Mining investments."

Mr. Linares blinked at her, though his expression remained otherwise unimpeachably polite.

"Will Mr. Oliver need a room?" he asked.

"What?" Ellie returned, startled.

"Your uncle," he repeated patiently as his warm brown eyes flashed with just a hint of humor. "Will he need a room?"

"Oh! No. No, I am sure that he won't," Ellie quickly replied. "He will—ah... That is, we will be traveling on together as soon as he arrives."

She flashed the hotelier a reassuring smile that hopefully offset her admittedly scrambled explanation.

Blast it. She was going to need to get much better at lying.

Mr. Linares flipped through his register, then turned and plucked a key from the rack on the wall behind him.

"I will put you in Room 201," he announced. "That way, you will be nearest to my wife and myself in case you require any assistance while you are here. We are just down the hall."

Ellie blinked at him, startled by this unexpected thoughtfulness.

"That's very kind of you," she said.

He flashed her a genuine and decidedly charming smile. Ellie felt compelled to smile back.

"The rate is six shillings a day. Unless you are paying in dollars?" he prompted.

Ellie shook her head.

"Dinner is served at seven," he continued easily. "Breakfast at eight and a fine lunch at half past twelve. All are included with your fare. Should you wish to undertake any excursions—a boat ride to the cays or a bit of shell collecting—simply inquire and we will be happy to arrange it. And if you will forgive me for the informality, I do like to mention to our guests that the hotel is in possession of a full bath. I find that our arrivals fresh from the sea are quite appreciative of it. If you would like, I can reserve it for you and have hot water sent over for an additional shilling," he added with graceful delicacy.

Ellie had been making do with ablutions at a basin in her small cabin on the *Salerno* for the last two weeks. The notion of a proper soak in an actual tub sounded like the very picture of luxury.

"That would be delightful," she replied.

"Óscar!" Mr. Linares called out, directing his voice into the back office. "Llene la tina para esta señora. Téngala lista en un cuarto de hora—¿Entendido?"

A lanky teenager poked his head through the doorway.

"Aarite, Papá!" the boy replied with just a hint of adolescent irritation.

Mr. Linares handed Ellie the key.

"You are at the top of the stairs on the right. You will find the bath on the ground floor directly beneath your room—and please let us know if there is anything else we can do to make your stay comfortable. Welcome to Belize Town, Mrs. Nitherscott-Watby," he said, his eyes twinkling.

"I am very glad to be here," Ellie replied—and she found that she meant every word.

SIX

Fifteen minutes later
Hotel Rio Nuevo, Belize Town

ADAM BATES WAS exhausted, mosquito bitten, and covered in mud. At least, he hoped it was just mud.

He had acquired the filth earlier that morning when he had spent the better part of an hour hauling a mule out of a swamp. He had been on his way back from surveying a new land grant upriver when an iguana the size of a small pig wandered onto the trail and spooked the beast carrying Adam's gear.

Adam had been sorely tempted to leave the mule out there for the vultures, but Aurelio would never rent any animals to him again if Adam lost yet another piece of his inventory.

Adam looked like hell. Given that he felt like hell, he supposed that was only fair. When he entered the Hotel Rio Nuevo, which had served as his home base for the last six years, he saw Diego Linares Rivas' face fall into familiar lines of dismay and felt a slight twinge of regret.

In all honesty, Adam might've hopped into the river on his way back to wash off the worst of the muck instead of flaking little pieces of it across the lobby floor, but he had been too damned tired to bother. All he wanted was to crawl into his room and stop moving for a while.

"Dios te salve, María," Diego muttered, his eyes rising dramatically to the ceiling as Adam approached.

"It's not that bad, Diego," Adam countered.

The hotelier answered him with a skeptically arched brow.

Diego's wife, the lovely Ximena Castillo Ramirez de Linares, stepped into the lobby from the back office. Her dark brown hair was lightly streaked with silver and her white blouse contrasted with her brightly colored skirt.

She let out a sharp, high shriek, dropping the basket of laundry she was carrying.

"What are you—a swamp monster?" Ximena exclaimed.

"Kinda what it feels like at the moment," Adam agreed, scratching at his hair. A chunk of mud came loose and dropped onto the floor.

"No!" Ximena protested, raising her hands. "Don't touch it. Don't touch *anything*."

"We could take him out into the garden and throw buckets at him until he's manageable," Diego suggested.

The fact that the hotelier did so in English rather than Spanish made it clear that he intended the remark to be overheard.

"He will scare the other guests," Ximena countered firmly, glaring at Adam. "He should go to his room, strip off all of those clothes, and give them to me to be burned."

"This is a perfectly good shirt," Adam protested.

He tugged the soaked garment away from his chest and frowned at it, trying to remember what color it had been when he had put it on last week.

Ximena drew in a breath, clearly striving for patience.

"Then I will wash it—but I am only touching it with a stick," she declared. "Put it out on the veranda. *All* of it," she emphasized sternly, her green-tinted brown eyes flashing with menace.

"Yes, ma'am," Adam agreed. "Though I was kind of hoping to make use of that bath of yours."

"You want to go into my washroom looking like *that*?" Ximena squeaked.

Adam shrugged. A few more flakes of mud shifted to the ground.

"It's a bath, not an embassy dinner," he noted.

Ximena stepped over the laundry basket and stalked up to him. Her head came roughly to his chin. She jabbed a finger at his chest, stopping just short of actual contact.

"My washroom is *clean*," she seethed. "It is going to stay clean. You are not going to go anywhere near it until you have removed the swamp you are carrying around. ¿Entiendes?"

"Claro, Señora," Adam replied, forcing a straight face.

"Bien." She pulled back her finger, treating him to a haughty look. "Now take off your shoes."

Adam glanced down. His rugged leather boots were completely caked with filth. The mess looked even wetter and less appealing than the stuff on his shirt.

"Yeah, fair enough," he acknowledged with a sigh.

Satisfied, Ximena pivoted back to collect her laundry basket. She set it on her hip and stalked down the hall.

"Just be glad she didn't see that knife," Diego said with a nod toward the sheath at Adam's belt.

Adam's hand moved automatically to his machete. The blade was eighteen inches long and sharp enough to split a palm frond down the middle.

"You know what she said she would do if she caught you wearing it in the hotel again," Diego continued.

"It's useful," Adam countered, giving the top of the hilt a possessive little pat.

"Anyway, someone is already using the bath. You would be out of luck even if Ximena hadn't forbidden you. I'll have Óscar bring you water." Diego eyed Adam tiredly. "Lots of it."

Adam crouched down to tug at the laces of his boots. He gingerly removed them. After a critical look at his socks, he took those off as well.

His toes looked all right.

Diego plucked a key from the rack behind the desk and handed it over. After the fifth time Adam had lost his key while out on a job, the hotelier had declared that it must be turned in for safekeeping anytime he left town.

Adam tossed the comfortable weight of it in his palm as he swung his boots over his shoulder, holding them by the laces. "Has anyone…?"

"Dios, no," Diego asserted, looking mildly aghast. "Nobody goes in your room. Not after the crocodile fell out of the closet."

"Stuffed crocodile," Adam corrected him automatically as he dropped the key into his pocket.

"¡Espera! Your mail." Diego plucked a small pile of envelopes from a slot under the desk and handed them over.

Adam took a quick glance at them. They were return-addressed to San Francisco, which meant they were from his mother—more missives berating him for wasting his time in the colony when he should be preparing to take over the family business.

He mentally pictured himself walking into the boardroom of Robinson, Bates, and MacKenzie in his current state. It would almost be worth the trip just to see the look on the stockholders' faces.

Diego's eyes were already back on his registry book.

"Dinner is at seven," he called without looking up.

"Aye aye, captain," Adam replied.

He trudged down the hall, leaving a trail of flaking mud behind him— which he did feel a *little* bad about. Ximena de Linares ran a tight ship at the

Rio Nuevo.

Adam spent so much time with termites and parrots for company out in the bush that he had a hard time remembering how ordinary people did things.

The rooms that lined the ground floor hall were quiet. At this hour, most of the Rio Nuevo's guests were either out working or had lain down for a siesta—which was probably for the best. There would be fewer people to complain about a swamp monster roaming the hotel.

Adam paused outside the door to the washroom, allowing himself a sigh at the thought of what lay on the other side of it. The tub was large enough for even Adam to sink down into it, and he was a solid two inches over six feet. Without the Rio Nuevo's steam-powered hot water generator, it would have required an hour just to boil enough to fill the thing.

The sign on the door had been flipped over. It read: *Occupied / Ocupado.*

"Woulda been nice," Adam muttered.

He turned to go… just as a quick, feminine scream sounded from beyond the wooden barrier.

There was really only one reasonable way to respond to that. Adam dropped his boots, whipped the machete neatly from his belt, and kicked through the door.

SEVEN

*A*LL ELLIE WANTED was a soak.

The washroom at the Hotel Rio Nuevo had been a delightful surprise. The floor was tiled in cool, clean white. Frosted glass on the windows let in the light without risking any immodest peeks from the outside world. The shelf on the wall was packed with soft, freshly laundered towels. A polished brass rack for them stood beside the tub so that Ellie could wrap herself up as soon as she emerged from her soak. The massive clawfoot bath was currently filled with steaming hot water.

Someone had added a sprinkle of rose-scented soap flakes. They had dissolved into a perfect froth of bubbles that covered the top of the water.

Ellie had peeled off her travel-worn clothes and slipped into the light summer dressing gown that Constance had thrown into the valise back in Canonbury. At the time, Ellie had thought the garment an unnecessary extravagance. Now, she was grateful for the light, airy length of blue silk.

The blissful quiet of the room was everything she hadn't known she wanted since leaving the ship earlier that morning. It should have been the perfect start to her stay in British Honduras.

And it was... right up until Ellie gave the temperature of the water a check with her hand, and a sleek, narrow black head lifted through the bubbles, fixing yellow eyes upon her.

The scream that escaped from Ellie's throat at the sight was not particularly violent. It was really more of a yelp—just an involuntary spasm of the lungs.

The door to the bathroom crashed open, splinters flying from around the shattered lock.

A filth-covered stranger stalked inside. His feet were bare. He lacked a coat, and his muddy shirt sleeves had been rolled up to expose his forearms.

He was holding the biggest knife Ellie had ever seen.

"Where is it?" he demanded.

For possibly the first time in Ellie's life, words flatly deserted her. All she could do was stare at the intruder, mouth agape, as a distant part of her brain wondered if she had caught some tropical ailment and started to hallucinate.

"Hey!" He snapped his fingers. "No fainting. Where's the thing?"

Something in the intruder's words finally began to cut through the fog of shock enveloping Ellie's brain.

"Did you just accuse me of being faint?" she said, ire edging her words.

The ire sparked against a host of other feelings—most of them various forms of horrified outrage—and Ellie's shock was replaced by a sharp, dangerous focus.

"Get out of this room," Ellie demanded, her tone deceptively calm.

"Listen, lady—I'm trying to help here."

The stranger had a flat Yankee drawl. His eyes were a startling blue. The color stood out starkly against the mud that streaked across his sun-darkened features.

"Remove. Yourself. *Now*."

Ellie's last syllable was a threat. Fury rose under her skin. It felt like the rage that had recently gotten her arrested.

The maniac with the knife looked ready to make a retort—which would most certainly *not* have gone well for him—but the creature in the tub chose that moment to whip across the surface of the foamy water.

The stranger lunged across the floor and shoved Ellie against the wall. He pinned her there with his broad, solid back as he held his ridiculous blade ready in front of him.

There was, of course, an entirely reasonable way for a normal, sane person to respond to the presence of an unknown reptile in the tub. It involved dressing, fetching the hotel proprietor, and safely removing the animal so that she might possibly continue with her bath.

It did not include being squished into a corner by a beastly American in his shirtsleeves.

"Get off me!" Ellie barked as she shoved at him.

It was like trying to move a boulder.

"Stop wiggling," he retorted, his eyes glued to the surface of the tub.

Ellie had never wished quite so much that she had made the time for Sensei Tani's jiu jitsu classes. Still, though she lacked martial arts skills, she was quite familiar with the basic principles of physics—like the center of gravity.

She gritted her teeth, making a concerted effort to keep her tone reasonable.

"If you do not remove yourself from my person, I will be forced to use more extreme measures," she informed him.

His eyes narrowed with irritation as he glanced back at her.

"If you'd shut up and think for five seconds, you'd see that I'm trying to—"

Ellie didn't give him a chance to complete the sentence, as it was obvious he had no intention of ending it by getting out of her washroom.

She shoved her right leg between his thighs, feeling him jolt with surprise at the unexpected contact. Hooking her calf around his shin to hold it in place, she twisted her body, forcing more space between his hips and the wall—and then shoved.

The muddy brute flew forward with an ear-burning curse... and promptly tripped into the tub.

Time slowed to a crawl.

His knife clattered against the tiles. The better part of the bathwater washed across the floor in a gentle tide, punctuated by little patches of bubbles.

The foam-covered surface of the bath roiled as the stranger slid to a stop, mud rinsing from his face in long streaks. He went perfectly still as his eyes locked on the surface of the bath framed by the twin peaks of his soaked knees... and Ellie wondered whether she had just inadvertently murdered him.

Her pulse thudded, low and regular, in sync with the drip of the water on the tile. She distantly observed that the man had an objectively nice face. It was strong, with well-cut angles.

A flicker of motion cut through the still-soapy water.

The stranger's arm flashed out with a quick, cat-like movement. He grasped hold of an oily black form—and chucked it across the room.

The snake slid to a stop against the wall. It coiled, hissing with outrage, but the mud-streaked maniac was already surging out of the tub, taking most of the remaining water with him. He snatched up the brass towel rack as his bare feet slapped down against the tiles. He whirled the brass in his hand like a javelin and thrust it at the black, sinuous form of the reptile, pinning the creature's neck.

The snake hissed again, exposing pale, needle-like fangs that made Ellie's stomach clench.

The man took a step closer and peered down. Ellie stared worryingly at his exposed toes. They seemed terribly vulnerable. Her breath stuck in her chest as she wondered what he could possibly do next. Would he try to crush the creature with the towel rack? Order her to run for help?

He did neither of those things. Instead, he smiled and dropped his voice to an indulgent coo.

"Well, *you* gave us quite the scare, didn't you?" he said before tossing the towel rack aside and plucking the snake from the tiles with his bare hands.

He gently forced the reptile's long, angrily whipping body straight and turned back to display it to Ellie.

"No yellow, see?" he said. "She's a snail sucker, not a coral snake. Harmless—aren't you, lil' darling?" He turned the animal's face toward his own and gave it an affectionate little wiggle.

The man was *entirely* insane.

Ellie edged one step toward the door, then stumbled back as he turned in the same direction, carrying the snake out into the hall.

She was torn between the urge to slam the busted door shut behind him or to follow after him and make sure he didn't pose a threat to any innocent passers-by.

Her horrified curiosity about what he intended to do with the snake tipped the scales.

Ellie made a quick adjustment to her dressing gown, which had become hopelessly soaked in the tidal wave from his plunge into her bath, and then hurried out.

The ground floor hallway was empty save for the boy from the lobby, Óscar. The teenager took one look at the snake-carrying lunatic and pivoted, hurrying in the opposite direction. Ellie could hear him call out as he went— something about a *topógrafo loco* and *otra vez*.

Ellie's Spanish was admittedly rudimentary, but she was fairly certain that last part meant *again*.

Her bath invader stopped where the wing ended and kicked neatly through another door. This one gave readily under his foot, opening onto the veranda that faced the extensive rear garden of the hotel—a shady paradise of sprawling calabash trees and flowering oleander.

The stranger strolled outside and extended his arm over the railing.

"Here you go, beautiful," he said and released his grip on the snake.

It slithered free of his arm and dropped into a thick stand of hibiscus. An older couple who had been strolling on the adjacent path stopped and stared, the woman's grip paling on her companion's arm.

The madman wiped his hands on his trousers and came back inside.

"They like the heat," he announced.

The better part of the filth covering him had washed away in the tub. He was soaking wet, his shirt and trousers plastered to his body. He had the sort of male form Ellie had only previously seen in statues at the British Museum. It was admittedly distracting.

"What?" she said numbly.

She was having a difficult time removing her eyes from his pectorals.

"Snail suckers," he repeated, looking at her as though she were a bit thick. "They like the warm water. You should've checked around the tub before you filled it."

"I didn't fill it," Ellie replied absently as she forced her eyes from his chest back to his face. "Óscar did."

"And skip the bubbles," he added pointedly.

Ellie narrowed her eyes. "Óscar added those as well."

"It's rare to find the dangerous ones here in the city," he went on as though she hadn't spoken. "But it isn't unheard of, and you do *not* want to cross paths with a coral snake. It's lucky I was here."

His words sparked her fury back to vivid, blazing life.

"Lucky?" Ellie echoed dangerously. "Exactly who the devil do you think you are?"

"I *think* I'm the guy who just saved you from a snakebite," he replied, sounding a bit put off.

"*Saved* me?" Ellie seethed. "You believe that breaking down the door, waving a knife around, and shoving me into a corner is *saving* me?"

"You screamed," he countered.

"That is not an invitation," Ellie snapped.

"Were you gonna deal with that on your own?" He crossed his arms over his obnoxiously well-formed chest. "Forgive me for saying so, but you don't look like someone who's had a lot of experience with snake wrangling."

"Had I needed help, I would have acquired it. What I did *not* need was some mud-drenched lunatic barging into the washroom with a sword."

"Sorry I wasn't up to your standards of hygiene when I came to your rescue," he shot back.

"This has nothing to do with hygiene!" Ellie exclaimed.

"Listen, Princess." He took a step toward her. The move forced Ellie to crane her neck back a bit—the lunatic was decidedly on the taller side. "In case you hadn't noticed, you're not in jolly old England anymore. Most of the local animal life in the colony is harmless, but there's plenty of stuff that'll kill or maim you before you get a chance to think about it. Around here, if you hear somebody scream, you err on the side of caution—whether or not it's in the damned bathroom."

"*Princess?*" Ellie hissed.

He shrugged. "If the slipper fits…"

Ellie drove an admonishing finger into his sternum. It was like poking a piece of granite.

"I may not be capable of recognizing the different species of local fauna—*yet*—but I am not such a fool as to climb into the bath with one," she retorted. "I was entirely capable of handling the situation on my own without being manhandled by some knife-wielding thug."

"Knife," he repeated.

His hand went instinctively to the empty sheath on his belt. He pushed past Ellie into the bathroom and plucked the huge blade from the muddy puddle where it lay beside the tub. He wiped it off on his soaked sleeve and slipped it back into place at his side.

"Are you quite finished now?" she demanded.

He cocked his head thoughtfully to the side as his eyes dropped to the top of her robe.

"What's that around your neck?" he asked.

Ellie's hand flew to her throat. She pulled up the wet folds of her dressing gown, clenching them over the place where the medallion still rested against her skin.

Fear lent an urgent burst of fuel to her fury. Ellie snatched the fallen towel rack from the ground.

"Out," she ordered as she raised the weighty brass staff menacingly. "Now."

"Are you really threatening to beat me with a towel rack?" the lunatic asked skeptically.

Ellie swung.

"Ow!" He jumped back, rubbing his arm. "All right, I'm going!" he promised, holding his arms up placatingly.

He took a quick step through the door. Ellie slammed it shut, then slumped her back against it. She slid down to the wet floor, clutching both the towel rack and the cold black stone under the soaked silk of her robe.

Her hand shook—but not from the encounter with the snail sucker. Her fear rose from just how close the stranger had come to seeing the secret she wore over her heart.

EIGHT

$\mathcal{E}$LLIE'S PULSE DIDN'T settle back to normal until she had dressed.

The room she had been assigned was spacious, with whitewashed walls and a comfortable bed covered with a worn quilt. A mosquito net hung over the canopy frame, ready to be drawn around in the night, as the windows were obviously meant to stay open for ventilation. There was no insulation, nor any fireplace or parlor stove—but then, such things wouldn't be needed here on the shore of the Caribbean.

Ellie put another pin in her still-damp hair. She further calmed herself by running through the mental list she had built of everything she needed to acquire for her expedition: scissors, mason line, stakes, mosquito netting, hammock, canteen...

And a guide, of course. She was still desperately in need of one of those.

A pair of simple French doors opened onto the veranda. Ellie stepped through them, drawn outside by the warm air and the smell of living things from the garden below.

Her room was on the upper floor of the hotel's wing. The high walkway on which she stood granted her a lovely view over the abundant sprawl of the yard, which was framed by a high wooden fence. Beyond that barrier, she could see the rooftops of more houses. They grew lower and more humble the further they were from the waterfront.

Against the horizon, Ellie could just make out the misty gray haze of the mountains. The soft, distant line of them hadn't been visible earlier in the day when the light had been higher. They looked very far away, lying as they did across miles of flat, tangled swamp—but they were *here*. They were real, and somewhere within them lay the destination marked on her map.

The thought was both thrilling and desperately intimidating.

Ellie's hand rose to the medallion. The artifact could still be part of an elaborate hoax—but if it wasn't, then somewhere out among those distant peaks, an extraordinary secret awaited discovery.

Her reverie was interrupted by the chirp of bright, feminine voices carrying across the air from below. They were speaking Spanish.

She moved to where the veranda ended at the frame of the original house and peered down. The voices were coming from a small area separated from the rest of the garden by a high wooden privacy fence. The space backed onto the hotel's kitchen.

Ellie thought of the rose-scented soap in her bath that afternoon. Adding it to the tub certainly hadn't been the notion of a sixteen-year-old boy—nor did she imagine that Mr. Linares would have thought of it.

The bubbles spoke of a woman's touch.

A spark of inspiration made Ellie's pulse jump. She wasn't a fool. She knew that a lady traveling alone could be vulnerable to rascals. She considered herself to be a person of reasonably good judgment... but no one would know the worth of the various men in the colony as well as a local woman.

Quietly, Ellie slipped down the stairs that led from the veranda to the ground floor. Stepping into the garden, she followed a slender dirt path toward the privacy fence.

A gap in the barrier opened at the end nearest to the house, half-hidden by a stand of young thatch palms. Ellie squeezed herself past the stiff fronds and risked a peek around the corner.

The little yard was obviously a space meant for work rather than for show. Most of the ground was packed earth, except at the fringes where green things came stubbornly springing up.

A fragrant flowering vine meandered cheerfully along the inside of the fence. A few heavy pots of herbs flourished by the steps that led into the kitchen.

A big vat of steaming water squatted in the center of the space. A girl of perhaps sixteen stood by it with her skirts tucked up to expose her shins. Her dark hair was pulled into a messy bun, and her elegant eyebrows were angled crossly. She jammed a polished wooden pole into the vat with a mulish expression on her face.

An older woman sat in the first of a pair of wooden chairs positioned nearby. Her feet were plopped comfortably on a stool as she sipped a glass of something that looked refreshing. Her brightly colored skirt had also been pulled up to expose the lower portion of her legs, but this appeared to have been done for ventilation rather than for work. Her hair was streaked with threads of silver above a markedly lovely face. There was an obvious similarity between her sun-warmed features and those of the girl standing next to the vat.

"Con más fuerza," the older woman ordered, waving a hand at her daughter.

The teenager flashed her a murderous look before whacking at the contents of the vat with her stick more forcefully.

The woman with her feet up had to be the wife that Mr. Linares, the hotel proprietor, had mentioned when Ellie checked in. Ellie felt a flash of guilt at disturbing the lady in a place where she was obviously not expecting any guests. She attempted to creep back to the path, but the heel of her boot slipped, spinning out a little tumble of pebbles.

Mrs. Linares sat up in her chair, suddenly alert.

"Hoo deh?" she called out in Kriol.

Steeling herself against the now-unavoidable embarrassment, Ellie poked her head back around the fence.

"I, er… My apologies. I was just… ah, looking for the…" She cleared her throat, giving up. "I was snooping."

Mrs. Linares's face cracked into a smile. Her eyes twinkled.

"Were you? There is nothing like a good snoop, but I am afraid all you have turned up is two ladies doing laundry."

"Más bien a una," the teenager at the vat muttered under her breath.

Mrs. Linares took another sip of her drink, giving it a little slurp. "Pound it, Rosalita. You are washing, not making soup." She winked at Ellie. "This is the part you guests are not supposed to see."

"I'm terribly sorry for interrupting you," Ellie replied.

"It's no trouble. Was there anything you needed?" Mrs. Linares asked.

There most certainly was, and Ellie's first impressions of this comfortable, confident woman made her feel certain that Mrs. Linares could provide it—but she had no idea how to broach the subject without it seeming abrupt.

Her eyes lit on the glass in Mrs. Linares's hand.

"Is that lemonade?" she asked.

"Limeade," Mrs. Linares replied. "Would you like me to have some sent up to your room?"

Ellie's hopes crumpled a bit.

"Yes. I… suppose that would be appropriate," she conceded.

Mrs. Linares looked amused.

"Or you are welcome to join me here, if you would prefer to watch Rosalita do the laundry while you drink it," she offered with a gracious wave to the other weatherbeaten wooden chair.

"Would you mind that terribly?" Ellie replied, perking up.

"Tito!" Mrs. Linares shouted with impressive volume.

A young boy with messy hair appeared in the door to the kitchen.

"¿Qué, Mamá?" he demanded. He startled a bit at the sight of Ellie. "¿Qué hace esta bakra aquí?"

"The bakra is having limeade with me. Bring her a glass. Con más azúcar!" she shouted after him as he darted away.

"What is a bakra?" Ellie asked as she took the seat beside her.

"It's a Belize word for fancy white people. A little rude, if I am honest," Mrs. Linares said conspiratorially. "Tito will hear about that later."

The boy in question came hopping down the stairs with a limeade in his hand. He handed the glass to Ellie with a neat little bow.

"Your drink, ma'am," he said with perfect courtesy after a slightly nervous look at his mother.

Mrs. Linares dismissed him with a regal wave of her hand. He pounded inelegantly up the steps.

Ellie took a sip of the limeade. It was tart and delicious. She settled back in the chair as the teenager continued to poke halfheartedly at the laundry.

"You must forgive me if I am being too forward... but then, you did invade my yard," Mrs. Linares said playfully. "But I think perhaps you are Mrs. Nitherscott-Watby who joined us earlier this morning, yes?"

"I am," Ellie replied. She hoped that her response to her outrageous alias didn't sound as awkward as it felt.

"It was not such a hard guess," Mrs. Linares admitted. "You are the only woman staying here at the moment other than the sister of some missionary—but she is always in her room, and her face looks like someone just fed her a lemon."

Mrs. Linares shaped her lips into an illustratively disapproving pucker. Rosalita snorted by the tub.

"We get all sorts, as your people would say," Mrs. Linares concluded.

"Yes," Ellie agreed tentatively. "I believe I ran into another—er, guest?— earlier this afternoon. I must say, he was alarmingly pushy."

Mrs. Linares's eyes narrowed dangerously.

"Did one of my guests behave in a way not fitting for a gentleman?" she demanded.

"Oh—not like that," Ellie quickly corrected. "It was all the knife-waving and kicking down doors."

"Kicking down *doors*?" Mrs. Linares echoed. Her voice rose with alarm.

"Well, admittedly, it had something to do with the snake..." Ellie hedged carefully.

Mrs. Linares let out an exasperated sigh as she slumped back against her chair and put her fingers to the bridge of her nose.

"Let me guess. The knife was like this?" She held up her hands roughly two feet apart.

"That's right," Ellie carefully agreed.

"Tall fellow? Beautiful eyes? No shoes?"

"Yes!" Ellie confirmed.

"That is Adam Bates," Mrs. Linares said flatly. "Those are his pants."

She nodded toward the end of Rosalita's pole, which the girl had lifted out from the tub. A pair of khaki trousers were suspended from the end of it.

They looked familiar.

"He is a barbarian, but he is harmless," Mrs. Linares continued. "They would not have made him assistant surveyor general for the colony if he were actually crazy."

Ellie nearly choked on a sip of limeade. "I'm sorry... did you say *assistant surveyor general?*"

"Hard to believe, I know," Mrs. Linares confirmed wryly. "But he is actually very good at it. Before he came—oh, five or six years ago?—everything was a disaster. The surveyor general, he has no interest in going out into the bush, so he just sits in his office and hires whoever comes through the door to do the work for him. But they were all a bunch of grifters. Then Mr. Bates arrived and sorted it all out. He does most of the work himself—and now the others must get proper training and be certified. And he has fixed up all the maps so people actually know where they are going."

Ellie was familiar with the job description. An assistant surveyor general would be responsible for plotting property lines and roads, charting land grants... and expanding the maps of the colony's territories into its as-yet-un-explored regions.

With a silent, dawning horror, Ellie absorbed that the knife-wielding maniac was likely the single person in British Honduras with the most knowledge of the very places she needed to go.

No, Ellie thought furiously. Absolutely not. There had to be a better option.

But she wouldn't find it if she didn't ask. Ellie quickly mulled over her impression of Mrs. Linares. The woman seemed friendly, honest, and straightforward.

"That reminds me of something I was hoping to ask you about," Ellie said carefully.

"Oh?" Mrs. Linares turned a sharp and curious gaze on her.

"I am actually trying to find a reliable guide to the interior. To the mountains, specifically," Ellie explained.

"What do you want to go there for?" Rosalita blurted from her place by the tub.

Mrs. Linares arched a fine black eyebrow thoughtfully.

"Rosalita is being a bit abrupt," the older woman chided with a pointed glare at her daughter.

Rosalita dropped the trousers back into the laundry vat with a wet thwap and began pounding at them again with the stick.

"But she is not wrong," Mrs. Linares continued. "Even those who live here in the colony don't go into the bush unless they are scouting for one of the logging companies or looking for a land grant—and nobody wants a land grant in the mountains. There's nothing out there but monkeys and bugs."

"I know it sounds a bit daft, but it's really quite important," Ellie pressed. "I need to find a guide who knows the land and who won't try to take advantage of a woman traveling alone."

Mrs. Linares exchanged a troubled look with her daughter.

"I am not sure that is such a simple thing to find," she said. "I can think of two I might trust not to rob you or leave you out there, but neither of them would agree to do it for a woman—especially a bakra woman."

"What about Mr. Bates?" Rosalita suggested, resting on her pole.

Ellie froze in her chair.

"He knows the territory better than anyone, and he is honest," Mrs. Linares conceded, oblivious to Ellie's reaction. "He thinks better of women than most... but I think even he would stop at bringing one into the back country. And anyway, he has his own duties to attend to."

Ellie let her head fall against the chair, absorbing this with quiet frustration.

She didn't doubt Mrs. Linares' assessment. As proprietors of the hotel, she and her husband would be deeply connected with the community here. She likely knew as well as anyone what the options available to Ellie were, and it sounded as though none of them were good.

Of course, Ellie's task couldn't be as simple as Constance had made it sound back in London. Nothing was ever that easy for a woman trying to blaze her own path in the world.

Perhaps Ellie should just return to England and give the map to the men of the Royal Geographical Society. Surely, that was better than letting it languish uninvestigated... or fall into the hands of the thug who was almost certainly on her trail.

Ellie clenched her hands on the arms of the chair. She could not give up that easily—not after she had already come so far.

"The two men you said were trustworthy. Could you make arrangements for me to meet with them?" she asked.

"I can," Mrs. Linares replied carefully. "Though I would hate to see you waste your time."

Ellie took a grim sip of her limeade. Perhaps it wouldn't be a waste of time. After all, she had more than just money to offer. She was carrying the key to a possible legend in her corset. Whoever joined her on this expedition would have the chance to be part of making history. Surely there was value in that—perhaps enough value, even, to outweigh the *handicap* of her gender.

"Thank you," Ellie said as she set down her glass and rose. "You've been most kind. Please enjoy the rest of your evening. I am sorry to have disturbed you."

"It is no trouble at all. Good evening to you as well," Mrs. Linares said, eyeing Ellie thoughtfully.

Ellie gave Rosalita a nod as well and slipped back out through the gap in the fence.

Evening was settling over the garden, painting it in deeper layers of shadow. Birds chirped and fluttered through the branches of the calabash trees.

Ellie picked her way back up the path to the guest wing, slapping at a mosquito that buzzed by her ear. Her boots thudded gently on the wooden steps as she climbed back onto the lower level veranda—and spotted at a familiar figure reclined in a rocking chair with his still-bare feet propped up on the railing.

It was the maniac from the washroom—Assistant Surveyor General Adam Bates. He had, at least, donned a clean shirt and trousers.

He was smoking a cigar. The stink of it wafted over to where she was standing. Ellie brushed at the air to chase it away.

"That's a terrible habit, you know," she pointed out.

Bates glanced over at her and raised a skeptical eyebrow. He placed the cigar to his lips and puffed serenely on it before blowing out a long stream of smoke.

"It's a very relaxing terrible habit," he countered. "Goes very nicely with this terribly habitual whiskey."

Ellie shifted her gaze to his feet.

"Still in need of shoes, I see," she commented.

He pointed with the cigar, and she saw a pair of abominably muddy boots tumbled beside his chair.

"Waiting for those to dry out," he replied. "Easier to knock the sludge off."

"You might try stockings in the meantime," Ellie retorted.

He wiggled his toes gratuitously.

"It's good to air them out after a trek," he said. "Keeps the stink down."

"Right. Well, then. Have a delightful evening." Ellie pivoted on her heel, stalking away.

"Sweet dreams, Princess," he called back in reply.

At the sound of that abominable word—*Princess*—she momentarily halted, a violent urge shuddering through her. Ellie controlled it, instead lifting her skirt and walking neatly up the stairs.

No, she thought firmly as she crossed the upper veranda to her room—that was one option she would not be pursuing. She would rather face down a live crocodile than ask Adam Bates to guide her into the interior.

Surely her circumstances could never become *that* desperate.

NINE

The next morning

𝒯HE SUN WAS HIGH and bright as Adam Bates reclined in a wooden chair in the Rio Nuevo's front garden, plowing through a bowl of mamey sapote fruits. The brownish orbs had something of the look of fuzzy avocados, but the rich orange flesh inside tasted of yam and apricot with a hint of spice.

He pried the seeds out neatly with his machete, flicking them into the shrubs. Ximena de Linares hated it when he did that, but Adam always made it a point to yank out any rogue sapote trees that tried to sprout up amongst her parrot flowers.

He had only been back in town for a day, but he was already feeling restless—which wasn't particularly surprising.

Six years ago, he had chosen to come to British Honduras, and he had no regrets about the move. He was glad he lived someplace where nobody knew he was a Bates of the Bates insurance empire. In British Honduras, Adam never had to worry that the people he met would start immediately calculating what they might be able to get out of him.

Sure, the colony was hot. The mosquitoes were obnoxious. The town was a literal swamp, and getting a decent pair of boots took some finagling—but Adam would still take it over San Francisco, where everybody was always trying to measure how relatively important you were.

There were still people who did that here, of course, but they all stayed at the Imperial. Adam didn't have to worry about running into them at the Rio Nuevo—which was why he kept a room there.

That, and the food was great.

For a long time after he'd arrived here, Adam had simply been happy to have escaped his old life—solidly thwarting all of his father's hopes and ambitions for him in the process. Lately, though, some of the shine had been wearing off.

Adam loved his time in the wilderness—living by his knife and his wits, constantly learning about what might kill him and what might make for decent eating. Still, he was less excited than usual about the prospect of heading out on another mapping expedition even as he itched at being confined to the insular world of the capital.

There were reasons for that lack of excitement... reasons he was pretty sure he wasn't going to be able to ignore for much longer.

Every once in a while as Adam listened to the howler monkeys raising a racket outside the glow of his campfire, those same reasons had him wondering whether he was meant to be doing something else with himself.

Or maybe no matter what he did, there was always going to be a down side.

Adam sliced another sliver of orange flesh from his mamey, popping it into his mouth—then paused in his chewing as a trim, feminine figure hurried down the steps from the lobby.

The lady from the bath looked different with all of her clothes on... not that she'd looked at all bad in that soaking wet dressing gown.

Adam was fairly certain she wouldn't appreciate him noticing that—but last time he'd checked, he still had a pulse.

As he swallowed his mouthful of fruit, Adam admitted that maybe kicking down her door with a machete in his hand hadn't been the best move. Would he really have done the same thing if it'd been Diego or one of those annoying English guys from the lounge who'd done the shouting? Maybe he would at least have knocked first before busting the lock.

It simply hadn't occurred to him that a woman would be capable of handling whatever was going on in there. To be fair, if there *had* been a coral snake in that tub, she might not have gotten the chance for a second scream.

Adam wondered what could've brought her to the colony. Foreign women hardly ever came here, and those who did were almost exclusively the wives of some higher-ranking government official—or nuns.

He was fairly certain the lady from the bath wasn't a nun. So what the hell was she here for?

She turned the corner, heading toward the bridge over the river. Her chestnut hair was pinned up into a mercilessly respectable bun under her flat-brimmed hat. He could picture the freckles he knew she had scattered across the back of her neck.

Before he quite knew what he was doing, Adam had tossed his half-eaten mamey into the parrot flowers and followed her.

She moved in the opposite direction of Fort George, which was where most of the colony's white residents and travelers stayed. The neighborhood she headed for instead was still perfectly respectable, but it wasn't the sort of place he would've expected an unaccompanied Englishwoman to trek into.

She finally stopped... at a door Adam recognized.

The tidy clapboard house was set on stilts, like most of the other construction in Belize Town. The paint on the boards was still bright, and the front garden was abundant with a mix of flowers and fruiting shrubs.

Adam tucked himself into a gap between the houses across the street and waited.

The woman was inside for about ten minutes. When she came out again, a deep, cross furrow shadowed her pretty eyebrows.

Whatever she'd heard in there, it clearly wasn't what she'd been hoping for.

Adam fully expected her to head straight back to the hotel, but she continued further down the street instead, stopping at one point to politely ask another woman for directions. As she turned a familiar corner, Adam had the uncomfortable suspicion that he knew exactly where she was going.

Sure enough, the woman stopped at the house of Cedric Barrow—the second-most-reliable and trustworthy guide in town.

The first-most-reliable, Winston Decker, had been the owner of the other house she'd gone to.

Her stop in Cedric's house took a bit longer. That didn't shock Adam. Cedric's wife, Maxime, didn't let a visitor escape until she'd plied them with more snacks than they could eat without bursting.

Finally, the lady emerged, this time with Cedric beside her. The two of them shook hands politely, but Adam could still read the disappointment on her face as she left.

He waited until she was a couple of blocks up the road before jogging across the street to where Cedric lingered on his shaded porch.

"I was wondering why the assistant surveyor general was lurking under Señora Herrara's bougainvilleas," Cedric commented dryly, his tones touched with his Kriol accent.

Cedric was a bit on the shorter side, with tightly curled hair and a neatly trimmed beard. The hair was tinged with gray. Adam knew that Cedric had been making noises about scaling back his work after some trouble with his knees.

"Maybe I was just admiring the flowers," Adam replied innocently.

Cedric scoffed. "You got an interest in this bakra woman, then?" he pressed easily.

Adam rubbed at the bridge of his nose. There wasn't much point in denying it after he'd been spotted skulking about.

"Just curious. What was she after?" he asked casually.

"She wants a guide to take her into the Cayo," Cedric said.

"The *Cayo*?" Adam echoed, blurting out the word with shock.

The Cayo District was the westernmost portion of the colony and by far its most unexplored, underpopulated area. The region was more or less a big, fat blank on Adam's maps, mostly because the rivers ceased to be navigable once they reached the mountains—rugged peaks that topped 3,000 feet, covered in thick forests.

Nobody went to the Cayo. Even the loggers didn't bother with it. Why should they when they'd have to haul any mahogany or dyewoods they harvested out the hard way, instead of just tossing them into a river?

The land wasn't farmable. It took days of slogging through the virgin bush to get there. The Cayo was, in short, a virtually impenetrable wilderness.

"What does she want to go there for?" Adam demanded.

"Du ah luk de fool?" Cedric retorted in crisp Kriol. "A bakra woman like that always got a father or brother or husband somewhere in the background. Doesn't matter how many gray hairs I have in my beard—job like that gonna be nothing but trouble. I didn't let her get to the reasons. Just let her down easy while Maxime filled her up with powderbuns." He nodded up the road. "Better catch up if you want to keep following her."

"Hell," Adam said and darted down the steps.

Cedric's chuckle sounded from behind him.

The woman's figure slipped around a corner. Adam made a quick calculation, then dashed into an alley instead. He dodged a cluster of stray chickens, which squawked at him with alarm.

"Wach dehn fowl, bwai!" an older woman snapped sharply.

"Morning, Miss Ivy," Adam called back.

She waved him on with a huff of disapproval.

Adam spilled out of the alley into the street that led to the bridge, making it just in time to see the Englishwoman walking his way. He adjusted his pace to match her quick steps as he slipped alongside her.

"Nice day for a walk," he commented casually.

She glared at him. Her eyes were hazel, with little sparks of green and silver that flashed at him across the splash of freckles on her nose. They were nice eyes—even when they were shooting daggers at him.

"*You*," she hissed.

"I heard you were looking to make a little jaunt to the interior," Adam said.

She stopped walking, and her glare deepened.

"Were you *spying* on me?" she demanded.

"It's a terrible idea," Adam continued, ignoring the accusation. "The rainy season here is due to start any day now. Once it does, any paths or game trails will turn into muck. The water level rises in all the rivers, and the current turns three or four times as strong. Even with a reliable steam engine to drive you upstream, that's tough going—not to mention the flash floods, the mudslides, and all the fun of trying to set up camp in a mosquito ridden downpour."

"I don't recall asking for your opinion," she shot back.

"Nah," Adam returned easily. "You just asked two of the best guides in the colony—besides myself, obviously. And they both turned you down. I'd like to think you're smart enough to realize that there's not much point going on to the *less* reliable guides... because any of them who tell you yes are either going to rob you or get you killed. What are you after in the Cayo, anyway?"

Her fury was a sight to behold. It slid over her body like another skin, tensing every muscle and turning her eyes to a flashing silver fire. Adam vaguely recalled the way she'd whacked him with the towel rack in the bathroom. If she had that towel rack now, he was pretty sure she'd be using it to try to knock him into the river.

She refrained from assault this time, limiting her response to an outraged growl.

"I have about as much interest in your opinion on the matter as I do in engaging myself to a pig," she seethed. "So unless you are about to direct me to someone who can actually assist me—"

"I mean, I could," Adam mused, cutting in.

That shut her up for a minute.

"Sorry?" she said.

"Apology accepted," Adam replied innocently.

The fury flashed in her eyes again. Adam went on before she took it in mind to express her feelings in the form of a kick to his balls.

"I *could* take you where you want to go," he offered. "As it happens, I know the Cayo better than even Cedric Barrow does."

Adam clamped his mouth shut before it could do anything even more stupid. Had he actually just offered to take this woman into the mountains? She'd get them both eaten by a jaguar in five minutes. She had that jaguar bait air about her.

Nor had Cedric been wrong. She was far too well-dressed and well-spoken not to be respectable—and respectable women usually had a small army of overprotective relatives lurking at their backs. Just because Adam hadn't seen any of them here in Belize Town didn't mean they didn't exist. Adam was better positioned to weather that kind of trouble than a guy like Cedric, but it was still a hell of a lot more hassle than he ought to be asking for.

"Why would you offer that?" she demanded.

"Not entirely sure," Adam admitted. "Now that I think of it, it's probably a terrible idea."

She glared at him with a white hot focus, and then stalked across the bridge toward the hotel.

Adam let her go… but not without a shout at her departing back.

"You know what—just forget about it!" he called out.

She whirled around, flashing him a rude gesture with vehemence.

Someone chuckled beside him. Adam turned to see a grizzled South Asian gentleman carrying a crate with a live rooster on his back.

"What are you laughing at, Mr. Nohri?" Adam demanded.

"About time you found yourself a woman, surveyor," the older man replied with another wheezing laugh before continuing on his way.

TEN

$\mathcal{E}$LLIE STALKED BACK to the Hotel Rio Nuevo. Outrage fired through her blood so hot and fast that she was surprised it didn't come out of her ears in the form of steam.

How *dare* that man follow her? How dare he have the gall to offer to take her to the mountains—as if she would ever agree to travel with some mule-headed surveyor who thought he knew better than everybody else—only to take it back a breath later!

She hoped he stepped on a nettle. Were there nettles in British Honduras?

Something spiky and itchy, at any rate. Ellie hoped he walked through a whole patch of it. She pictured his arrogant face with its unjustly strong cheekbones breaking out in hives, and felt a little burst of satisfaction.

Her conversations with the two guides whom Mrs. Linares had recommended had been frankly disheartening. Both men had seemed honest and well-informed, and both had actively tried to dissuade her from undertaking the journey.

Ellie refused to give up so easily on the promise the map offered. She would find another way to get where she needed to go. She had five days before she risked Jacobs turning up. That was plenty of time to figure something out.

It didn't help that she was also bone-tired. Her sleep the night before had been broken by strange dreams, none of which she could remember clearly.

She had been dreaming more often than usual ever since leaving London. She hoped it wouldn't prove a pattern. If she was going to succeed in securing a guide and navigating her way to the interior, she would certainly need to get her rest.

"Good afternoon, Mrs. Nitherscott-Watby," Mr. Linares said from his place behind the front desk. "Will you be joining us for dinner this evening, or would you like another tray sent up?"

Ellie heard Bates enter the lobby behind her.

She *would* prefer to take a tray in her room—but she wasn't about to let that infuriating man think that she was crawling away in defeat.

"I will, thank you," she replied, making sure that her words were clear enough to be overheard.

"I shall put you at the Reverend Greene's table," Mr. Linares replied. "His sister, who is traveling with him, is the other lady in residence at the hotel. She may help you feel more comfortable."

"That's very kind," Ellie replied. "If you'll excuse me."

She turned from the desk, refusing to spare Bates so much as a glare as she stalked through the door into the guest wing.

———

Dinner was an ordeal.

As promised, Ellie had been seated with a Methodist reverend. His sister had spent the entirety of the meal glaring at Ellie as though expecting her to sprout horns. Clearly, the fact that Ellie was here in the colony without a man made her suspect, despite her widowish cover story.

The reverend himself was a gloomy and apocalyptic sort. Ellie's other dinner companions were hardly better. Two of them were the pair of over-sized English schoolboys she had glimpsed in the billiards room when she arrived the day before. Their names were Galle and Tibbord, and they clearly considered staying at the Rio Nuevo rather than the hotel across town to be 'roughing it.' The two men were on a tour of the region, and they had the sunburns to prove it. Mr. Tibbord—taller, plumper, and less confident—was apparently writing a book about their experiences. Mr. Galle—short, trim, and sporting a carefully waxed mustache—declared that he had provided all of the anecdotes worth mentioning. Based on the blatant hints he dropped, those mostly consisted of excessive alcohol consumption and trips to brothels.

Finally, their company was rounded out by Col. Jeremiah Tuttle, formerly of the Confederate Army, who spent the entirety of the meal arguing that the war between the states had been motivated by "federal overreach" rather than by the shameful economics of slavery. Apparently, British Honduras was afflicted with an entire cohort of Tuttle's fellow rebels, who had fled here after the war to re-establish their plantations. Though slavery was illegal in the colony, as it was in all British holdings, Tuttle bragged about the benefits of cheap South Asian indentured labor in a way that made Ellie wonder whether there was really much difference.

Meanwhile, across the dining room, Adam Bates sat at a table by the veranda, which kept bursting out into raucous laughter. Everyone over *there* was clearly having a grand time. Based on the froth at the top of his glass, he was drinking a beer. Ellie had never been very interested in beer, but she fought back a twinge of jealousy all the same as she wondered whether it might taste better than the wine she had been automatically served—which was unpleasantly sweet.

Ellie still consumed more of the stuff than she normally would have (which was more or less none at all). The grating tones of Bates's laugh and the hive-less state of his cheekbones kept driving the glass to her lips.

The alcohol made her thoughts a bit fuzzy at the edges as she climbed the stairs to her room on the hotel's upper floor. She would probably have a headache tomorrow. She decided to blame Bates for that as well.

Ellie fumbled with her key as she inserted it into the lock. It turned oddly, and she cursed, twisting it again before she pushed the door open and stalked inside.

She froze as she realized that her room was not empty.

A stranger stood in the dim light of the oil lamp on her dressing table—a white man of perhaps fifty with ginger hair and a beard that tended toward gray. Ellie's valise lay open beside him, its contents scattered.

The intruder was middling in height, soft in the middle, and a bit slumped in the shoulders like someone who spent most of his time at a desk. Ellie might almost have assumed that she had stumbled into the wrong room by mistake... if he had not been in the process of shaking out one of her skirts.

"Ah," he said, looking up as she came in. "You must be Miss Mallory."

Something slammed into her from the side.

The tackle thudded her into the wall, jolting the wooden boards under her shoulders. She twisted, opening her mouth to scream—only to have a wad of fabric shoved into it.

Ellie gagged on the cloth as someone wrenched up her arms and pinned her to the wall.

She found herself face to face with Jacobs.

How could he be here? It should have been impossible. Ellie had studied the steamer routes. Certainly, he might have taken a more immediate boat to Cuba or Jamaica from London, but there were no direct connections to Belize Town from any of those ports.

He must have hired a charter. It would have been expensive, and there would be regulatory hurdles and permits to acquire... unless Jacobs had outright smuggled himself into the colony.

Ellie forced her wildly spinning thoughts to a stop. None of that mattered. He was here now, and he had caught her.

"Give me your tie," he ordered.

It took Ellie a moment to realize that he was speaking to the ginger-haired man, who was looking distinctly uncomfortable with the situation.

"Is that really necessary?" the stranger asked.

"Tie, Dawson," Jacobs ordered.

The ginger man—Dawson—jumped, obviously intimidated by his partner. He rapidly removed the garment in question.

Jacobs switched his grip, pinning Ellie with a single hand and grabbing the length of paisley silk with the other. Ellie strained against him with rising desperation as he wrapped the tie around her wrists, then knotted it.

He shoved her onto the bed.

Ellie fought a wilder wave of panic, but it was immediately clear that Jacobs only cared about eliminating the threat posed by her legs. He secured her shins to the mattress with a knee and used a spare stocking from the scattered pile of her clothes to bind her ankles. He wrapped another one around her head to tie the gag in place, then rose, neatly straightening his coat.

"It isn't in the valise," Dawson announced as he watched the proceedings with a distinctly awkward air. "Perhaps you might ask her where she hid it."

His accent was Scottish and a bit posh.

Yes, Ellie thought frantically. They should ask her... because if they took the gag from her mouth for her to answer, she was going to scream bloody murder for help.

Jacobs sat down beside her on the bed, looking entirely unflustered.

"Still have the map?" he asked.

Ellie blinked at him, then made a sound through the gag, signaling her inability to answer.

"Shake of the head will do," Jacobs returned easily.

She narrowed her eyes to a glare.

He leaned closer.

"This could get quite a bit more uncomfortable, if you like," he noted casually.

Ellie glanced over at his companion. Dawson didn't look at all happy about the situation, but he said nothing. She wouldn't be getting any assistance from that quarter.

She forced herself to take a breath. She had to stay calm. She could get through this.

Ellie shook her head.

"She has it," Jacobs announced.

Her eyes widened. She shook her head more pointedly. That had very clearly been a *no*.

Jacobs watched her with an uncomfortable level of focus.

"Is it here in the room with us?" he asked mildly.

Ellie had to get the pair of villains out of here. If she could send them away, then perhaps she could find a way out of her restraints, or make enough of a racket for someone to come looking.

She shook her head again—another sharp *no*.

"Are we going to play guessing games over this all night? She might have squirreled it away anywhere in the colony," Dawson complained.

"It's here," Jacobs replied calmly, still watching her with dark eyes that reminded her of the way an owl looked at a mouse.

Desperately, Ellie nodded her head toward the door. *Out*, she signaled.

"No," Jacobs silkily countered. "That's not quite right. Is it, Miss Mallory?"

A darker, more uncomfortable fear itched along Ellie's spine. Jacobs seemed to have an uncanny ability to see right through her answers—but how was that possible? How could the man tell she was lying when the only clue she gave him was a shake of her head?

"I suppose she might have it on her person," Dawson suggested uncomfortably.

"How very logical of you," Jacobs replied.

Ellie wondered whether Dawson had noticed the slight edge of sarcasm in Jacobs' response.

Jacobs' hands moved neatly and impersonally to the pockets of her skirt, checking their contents. His examination slipped to her waist and then up her torso.

Dawson looked away, reddening a bit.

"Ah," Jacobs said as his fingers patted against the stiffer portion of Ellie's corset through the fabric of her blouse. With neat professionalism, he opened the top three buttons of her shirt and plucked the folded packet of the map from the pocket she had cut into the lining of her undergarment.

He extended the parchment back toward the ginger-haired man without looking at him.

"Professor?" Jacobs prompted when Dawson did not immediately move.

"Right. Yes." Dawson snapped to attention and took the map. He opened it and scanned the page.

"Ecclesiastical Latin," he muttered, bringing the document closer to the lamp. "Sixteenth or seventeenth century, though I should have to examine the fibers in order to be absolutely certain…"

He began walking absentmindedly toward the door with his eyes still glued to the parchment.

"You're forgetting something," Jacobs announced flatly

Without taking his eyes from Ellie's face, he grasped the ribbon around her neck and gave it a quick, sharp tug.

The string snapped loose. He drew the black amulet out from under her blouse and tossed it to the professor.

Dawson fumbled to catch the disk, nearly dropping the map in the process. His eyes widened as he turned the stone in his hands.

"Marvelous," he exclaimed quietly, blinking with surprise.

He jumped a bit as he remembered that Ellie was still there and looked toward her guiltily.

"What about the woman?" he pressed tentatively.

Jacobs stood. The mattress shifted with his movement.

"Check the hallway," he ordered.

Dawson held the map and medallion to his chest, stiffening.

"This really isn't the sort of thing I do…" he began.

"The hall," Jacobs repeated flatly.

Dawson grimaced but hurriedly dodged out of the room. He reappeared a moment later.

"It's clear," he reported.

Jacobs hauled Ellie off the bed and tossed her over his shoulder like a fainting damsel. Though he wasn't a particularly large man, his body felt like iron under her gut.

He stalked from the room into the deserted hallway, carrying Ellie along it until he neatly kicked his way through another door.

This suite was larger than Ellie's, consisting of two adjoining spaces. The room they entered was a small parlor with a table and chair, lit by a single lamp. Beyond it was a bedchamber, swathed in gloom from the falling twilight.

"Why have you brought her to *my* room?" Dawson protested.

"You have work to do on the map," Jacobs replied as he slid Ellie off his shoulder and dropped her onto the floor.

"But what are you going to do with her?" Dawson pressed.

"I'll dispose of her later when there are fewer people about," Jacobs replied.

The remark was not particularly bragging or vicious. Jacobs made Ellie's demise sound as ordinary as taking out the rubbish.

A sharp, cold bolt of terror shot through her.

"Surely you aren't going to—you know—right now," Dawson complained. "You can't expect me to work in here with a... a deceased person."

Jacobs' only answer was a raised, weary eyebrow.

"Well?" Dawson prompted stubbornly as he crossed his arms.

Apparently doing his job with a murdered woman on the floor was a hard line for the professor.

"Fine," Jacobs gracelessly conceded.

He grabbed Ellie by one of her bound arms and dragged her across the floor into the bedroom. The bed inside was built with a squared canopy frame that was meant to be draped with mosquito netting at night.

Jacobs considered her as she glared up at him from the floor.

"A little extra precaution, I think," he concluded.

He hauled her upright by her bound wrists, then knotted the loose ends of Dawson's paisley necktie neatly around the canopy beam. Ellie found herself anchored there, her hands raised above her head.

Jacobs considered the arrangement for a moment—and then walked away, apparently satisfied with it.

Dawson's wide gray eyes watched Ellie from the adjoining room, then disappeared from view as Jacobs pulled the bedroom door shut behind him, leaving her to the gloom.

He didn't bother to lock it.

Ellie's frustrated scream was little more than a choked groan through the fabric of the gag.

Ellie cursed herself roundly. How could she have been so careless?

She had thought she was being terribly clever. It had simply never occurred to her that someone like Jacobs would have the resources to overcome the timetables and forge his own path to the colony.

Now, she might pay for that mistake with her life.

No—Ellie refused to allow that. She would find a way out of this.

The canopy frame was a box fixed to posts at each corner of the bed. Though Ellie could slide herself along the beam to which she had been tied, there was no gap through which she could wriggle her bindings in order to free herself.

Ellie yanked herself closer to one of the posts, trying to study it in the dim light. The bed was perhaps four and a half feet wide. Both post and beam were made of sturdy hardwood, but Ellie couldn't feel any nails. The structure must have been fitted together with wooden dowels and glue.

Dowels were less sturdy than nails. An idea began to take shape in her mind.

Ellie could hear the murmur of low voices through the door to the next room, along with the scrape and shuffle of furniture. She would need to be quiet.

She climbed up to kneel on the mattress, then tugged herself along the beam until her back was pressed up against one of the posts.

Letting her bound wrists take her weight, Ellie swung her feet up and thrust them out toward the opposite post... and missed.

Her shoulders wrenched as she half-fell off the bed. Holding her breath, she froze, listening to the noises from the next room.

No outcry broke the rustling quiet—only the click of a closing door.

She climbed back into place and tried again. This time, her boots connected with the post. Ellie braced herself there, suspended awkwardly over the end of the mattress.

She pushed.

The effort took every muscle in her body—shoulders, abdomen, thighs—all focused precariously on forcing her body into a straight line.

The frame of the bed creaked in protest... and then gave way as the joint between the post and the beam separated with an audible crack.

Ellie slid down the length of the wood and collapsed onto the floor, her heart pounding madly in her chest.

Scrambling to her knees, she tugged her bound wrists free of the beam, then brought up her legs, shoving aside the awkward folds of her skirt to work at the stocking that bound her ankles. She loosened it and kicked her way free of the makeshift rope.

She tried to pull on the gag, but Jacobs had tied it too tightly. With her hands bound, she couldn't reach the knot at the back of her head.

That didn't matter. She didn't need to scream... not if she could run.

Ellie crept to the door, conscious of every subtle creak of the old floorboards. There was no sound from the other side save for the short scrape of a chair adjusting position and the rustling of a few papers.

Silently, she twisted the knob, opened the door the tiniest crack, and peeked through it.

Dawson sat at the table in the parlor. He was bent over some object of study—the map, presumably—scratching away in a notebook with an expression of intense concentration.

Ellie widened the crack in the door and risked a better look. The professor was alone.

The room was stuffed with trunks and cases. Jacobs and his companion had clearly planned on an extended stay in the colony. In fact, some of the equipment she could see strewn about indicated that they had packed for an expedition.

And why wouldn't they, when only a woman stood between them and what they wanted?

The thought sparked a bolt of indignant fury. Ellie supposed *they* wouldn't have any trouble at all finding a guide.

Most of the gear looked brand new. Ellie could also see an entire crate full of books. Books! She couldn't imagine how expensive the freight tariffs on a crate of books must have been.

Whoever Dawson and Jacobs were, they had far more resources at their disposal than Ellie would have suspected for a pair of rogue thieves. The thought was an unsettling one.

A window near the bed behind her opened onto the veranda. Ellie could easily climb through it and dash—but then where would she go? The local constabulary? They would only have Ellie's word that Dawson and Jacobs were criminals. How would she explain where she herself had come by the map and medallion if the pair tried to turn the tables on her?

She couldn't. She'd stolen it herself, more or less—rather more, she admitted ruefully, even if she'd been boxed into it. Who were the colonial authorities here in Belize Town most likely to believe? A lone woman or two well-dressed gentlemen, one of whom apparently boasted the title of *professor* and could afford to carry a crate of books across the sea with him?

The answer to that was obvious.

Dawson's chair scraped again as he rose, muttering to himself. He crossed to the books and started shuffling through them, putting his back to the table.

Ellie's pulse jumped as she realized that she was looking at an opportunity to do something more than simply escape before Jacobs returned to murder her.

She slipped through the door and moved silently behind the professor's back to the makeshift desk.

The map and the medallion lay on top of it, just as she had known they would.

Ellie snatched up the two relics just as Dawson turned, his eyes widening with shock.

"What the devil!" he exclaimed—then jumped nervously at the sound of a key turning in the lock of the door that led into the hall.

Ellie shoved the map and medallion into her skirt pocket and whirled for the French doors at her back. They had been left open to ventilate the room, leaving her way onto the veranda blocked only by a length of mosquito netting.

She easily burst through it.

Voices rose behind her as she darted outside, her footsteps knocking hollowly against the boards of the elevated walkway.

Ellie didn't think much of her chances of outrunning Jacobs. Back in Canonbury, her intimate knowledge of the terrain had given her an advantage. Here, it would all come down to speed—and Jacobs wasn't running with his hands tied.

What she needed to do was disappear.

Thinking quickly, she hurried to the railing of the veranda. Grasping it with her bound hands, she swung an awkward leg over the side. Her skirts hampered the movement. Ellie tugged against them, biting out a curse through the gag.

The fabric loosened, and she nearly toppled. Catching herself, she shifted her grip from the banister to the rails.

Ellie crouched down as low as she could against the outside of the railing, then let her legs drop.

Her shoulders jolted with the impact, an ache shooting through her arms. Her boots dangled over darkness, her feet swinging as she searched for purchase. As her eyes continued to adjust to the deeper gloom, she glanced down to see the railing for the ground floor veranda just a few inches below the soles of her boots.

Footsteps pounded out onto the boards above her.

Ellie let go.

She landed neatly on the railing... and promptly toppled forward. Ellie had a brief moment to ready herself for a crash to the floor—which would undoubtedly reveal her position to Jacobs.

Instead, she slammed into something warm, solid, and decidedly un-floor-like.

An iron arm circled her waist. Her breath left her in a whoosh as her diaphragm hit a rock-hard shoulder. Ellie slid down the front of an intimidatingly large body until her feet met the ground once more.

She looked up into the shocked, twilight-shadowed face of Adam Bates.

"What in the actual black hell—" he began.

Ellie shoved her hands against his mouth and shook her head frantically.

Bates carefully grasped her bound wrists and pulled them back for a better look. His gaze went dark, and his eyes flashed up to the gag that still bound her mouth.

Above them, the footsteps stilled—then started up again with a quick, intentional pace.

Jacobs was heading for the stairs.

With a grim set to his mouth, Bates tossed the remains of a stubby cigar into a tin can by the chair in which he had been sitting. He plucked up a half-empty glass of some brown spirit in one hand, and with the other, he hauled Ellie unceremoniously through the French doors to the room that lay beyond.

He shoved her into the corner.

"Stay," he ordered. His voice was a dangerous murmur, and his blue eyes sparked with threat.

Without so much as a brush of sound, he plucked a chair from the nearby table, whirled it about, and planted it by the opening to the veranda. He slid into it with his drink in his hand.

Ellie stayed where he had put her, pressed back against the wall. The position left her invisible to anyone who happened to pass the French doors, but she would be instantly exposed if someone actually stepped inside the room.

She tried once more to wrench loose the bindings on her hands, but they refused to give.

Even, relentless footsteps approached, stopping as they reached the threshold of the room. Jacobs' voice carried to her from a mere three feet away.

"Good evening," he said. "I was wondering if you had seen anyone come by just now."

There was nothing untoward in his tone. He sounded as though he really were merely out for an evening stroll and not hunting for the woman he intended to murder.

Ellie waited, her heart pounding—and recalled the moment of tension when she had stood outside another door and listened to her supervisor eagerly sell her out.

Was Adam Bates about to do the same thing?

Ellie could see *him* perfectly well. He looked entirely at ease in his chair. He was stripped to his shirt, of course, with his white sleeves rolled up to expose his tanned forearms. The suspenders for his trousers hung at his sides. Bates had obviously shrugged out of them as soon as he had escaped the jacket he had condescended to don for dinner. At least he had shaved since Ellie had seen him that afternoon, but she could already discern the shadow of his beard reemerging along the sharp line of his jaw.

She didn't know him. As far as she knew, he didn't even like her very much. Ellie held her breath as the gag pulled against the corners of her mouth.

"Only the mosquitoes," Bates replied. "And some woman who dropped out of the sky."

She froze. The surveyor didn't so much as glance at her. His eyes were on the man in the doorway.

The bastard. The rotten, irredeemable bastard...

With a liquid grace, Bates rose from the chair. He stalked over to the doorway. The move put him close enough that Ellie could've reached out and touched him if she'd chosen.

He still held the drink. His voice, when he spoke, sounded richly, terribly dangerous.

"Looked to me like somebody put a gag in her mouth," he said. "Tied up her hands."

"Did it," Jacobs countered flatly.

"A man has to wonder," Bates went on with apparent calm as the spirits in his glass twisted into a little tornado. "What sort of fellow would be out looking for a woman trussed up like a goose?"

"Perhaps one concerned for her welfare," Jacobs replied coolly.

"And why would a lady be running from a guy like that?" Bates returned.

A notion burst into Ellie's head—one that was quite frankly bizarre. She willed it toward Bates regardless as though mere urgency could dart it into his brain.

Don't lie, she thought furiously. *Whatever you do, don't lie to him.*

Silence stretched, rich and thick as the night air. Tension swirled around her like the electric potential of the moment before a lightning strike.

"Seems to me," Bates continued softly. "If I had seen a woman like that, you might be the last goddamned person I would tell where she'd run off to." He carefully set his glass down on the nearby table, then raised his gaze to the unseen man across the threshold. "And now I might suggest that you get yourself the hell off my doorstep before I take it in mind to make a more direct intervention in this situation."

There was a pause the length of a breath as Jacobs considered his options.

"Sorry to disturb you," he said at last—and a moment later, his footsteps moved away.

ELEVEN

*E*LLIE BARELY DARED to breathe as she listened to Jacobs depart. Finally, Bates stepped back into the room and closed the French doors behind him.

She exhaled in relief—a feeling that rapidly dispersed as she took in the expression on the face of the man who had just saved her.

It looked terribly like fury.

"Now, I'm going to take off this gag," Bates said evenly. "And then you're going to tell me exactly what sort of trouble you've gotten yourself into. Clear enough, Princess?"

Before she answered, Ellie tore her eyes from his face and took a moment to actually look at the place where she'd inadvertently landed.

The room was a disaster. A single glance revealed that it hadn't been cleaned in months. Every available surface was covered in debris—empty glasses, stacks of papers, teetering piles of books, the cold tail-end of a cigar. The walls were barely visible, buried under pinned-up maps, sketches, and scribbled notes between hooks holding picks, shovels, coils of rope, and wooden tripods. A rifle leaned against the wall in the corner next to a piece of driftwood that looked oddly like a flamingo.

A pair of theodolites, used for accurately measuring distance, sat on a shelf between the skull of an iguana and a jar holding the biggest spider Ellie had ever seen. She was reasonably confident it was dead.

She could feel the crisp pressure of the map in her skirt pocket beside the cold weight of the medallion. An idea began to take shape in her mind.

It was a decidedly terrible idea.

"Well?" Bates prompted, looming over her with all the implied threat of a prowling tiger.

Solemnly, Ellie gave him a nod.

He moved closer. He was a large man, towering over her by a solid six inches. He was near enough for her to feel the warmth that radiated off his very big, very solid body as he reached around her head and gently untied the knot that held her gag in place.

As soon as she felt the tension in the binding give, Ellie ripped it away, coughing at the dryness in her throat. Bates tossed back the rest of his drink, crossed to the washstand, and filled the glass with water from the pitcher there. When he offered it to her, Ellie accepted without protest and gulped down the liquid inside. It burned against her throat before providing a desperate relief.

"I'll get you another," Bates said. He plucked the glass from her hands and carried it over for a refill.

Ellie felt shaky. She looked around the room for a place to sit. The only surface that offered itself was the unmade bed. She dropped down onto it and let her face fall into her bound hands.

Chair legs scraped against the floor. A large hand gently tugged at her wrists.

"Hey," Bates said. "Let me take care of this."

Ellie allowed him to draw down her arms. He set to work on the knots. The bindings fell away to expose raw, red bands of skin where the cloth had chafed against her wrists.

Something about the man in front of her coiled up dangerously at the sight.

"Was he dragging you around?" he demanded as he raised those shockingly blue eyes to meet her own, his voice rich with threat.

"No," Ellie said as she drew her arms back away from him and tucked them around her sides. "I probably did that to myself when I was escaping."

"Of course you did," Bates replied. He rubbed his hands over his face as though fighting down whatever violent urge had been about to overtake him. "That guy your husband?"

"Absolutely not!" Ellie exclaimed.

"Sorry," he said. "But it happens more often than you'd like to think."

The observation surprised her almost as much as the question had. Ellie gave the man in front of her a more thoughtful look.

"I'm aware," she replied.

Bates pushed back in his chair and turned to a narrow dresser with a chipped finish. The top of it was piled high with letters, some of which were yellowed with age. Most of them looked unopened.

He pulled open a drawer.

"I've got some aloe salve in here," he offered. "Might help."

"Thank you," Ellie replied quietly.

He returned with a battered little tin. He screwed it open and scooped out some of the unguent inside.

Ellie offered him her wrists again. He took them gently and smoothed the aloe over her skin. His fingers were roughly calloused, but his touch was careful.

Bates capped the salve and tossed it neatly into the drawer. He leaned back in his chair and pinned her with a look.

"Time to tell me what all this is about," he ordered.

Ellie's heart rattled uncomfortably in her chest. She rose from the bed and brushed past him to stand by the map that covered the better part of the wall.

In fact, there was more than just one map. Various layers of them were pinned into place and augmented by sketches and notes.

Possible cataracts, one read. *Sinkhole. Cenote. Midden.*

The handwriting matched the loose scrawl in a notebook that lay open on the table.

Ellie ran her fingers along a line inked in blue that meandered across the wall—obviously the course of a river. It had been drawn in by hand.

"Have you been to all these places?" she asked.

"Not all. Just a good few."

Bates had come to stand beside her. Ellie hadn't even heard him move.

"That friend of yours isn't going to wander around forever," he pointed out. "If he doesn't find you where he thinks to look, he's going to come back here on the chance I did more than let you land on me. I'm not sure we have a hell of a lot of time."

He was right, and Ellie knew it. She drew a breath and threw herself into the unknown.

"What do you know about the collapse of the Mayan civilization?" she demanded.

One of his eyebrows arched up.

"As much as there is to know, I guess," Bates said. "They were here—all over the place, if the ruins that keep popping up are any indication—and then five hundred years or so before the Spaniards showed up, something went to hell and the cities were all abandoned."

"And have you ever heard stories of a city in this region that was *not* abandoned when the conquistadors arrived?" Ellie asked.

He moved away from her.

"Like El Dorado," he returned flatly.

"El Dorado is a myth," Ellie countered. "I am talking about an actual city—one that was still flourishing at the time of the conquest."

"No," Bates said. "I've never heard of anything like that."

Ellie could hear his skepticism. It frightened her. In the space of the last few minutes, a very great deal had come to depend upon the outcome of this conversation.

She had to convince Bates to listen to what she was about to tell him. She could think of only one way to do that.

Ellie steeled herself and reached into her pocket to pull out the medallion. The black stone glinted like a jewel as it swung back and forth in the lamplight, dangling from the remnants of her ribbon.

Bates's focus sharpened. He took the artifact from her carefully and carried it over to the desk for a better look.

"Intriguing trinket," Bates declared as he turned it over in his hands.

"The iconography and the style of the glyphs appear to be Mesoamerican, but I can't definitively say anything more than that. Not without access to a proper library," Ellie said, trying not to sound as nervous as she felt.

"It ain't Mayan," Bates replied, picking up a jeweler's lens from the desk and setting it to his eye. He gave the piece a closer look.

"It's not?" Ellie said, unable to completely hide her dismay.

He leaned back a bit.

"I mean—I'm not an expert, but I've been to a fair number of Mayan sites and I've got a pretty good head for images."

"Like these?" Ellie said as she waved a hand to a cluster of drawings on the wall.

Images of birds and the leaf pattern of a tree mingled there with a sketch of a pillar carved with the solemn face of an unknown god.

Bates must have drawn them. He had a good eye and a careful, detailed hand.

"Yeah," Bates admitted a little awkwardly before returning to his study of the medallion.

"Now this guy…" He tapped the figure in the center of the disk. "He's got little pieces of gods I recognize. That line carved across his face—you see that every once in a while. And the snake in place of one of his legs. But they're usually on different guys."

"Schellhas's gods F and K," Ellie replied automatically.

The keys to the Mayan written language had been lost centuries ago when the Spanish conquerors had outlawed the tongue and burned every written example of it they could find. Only a few documents had survived that apocalypse, and they could not yet be read. A German scholar by the name of Schellhas had recently created a systematic catalog of the symbols and figures one could find in those Mayan codices, even though he couldn't yet be sure what names to attach to them.

Ellie had read it, of course. She had ordered a copy from Dresden the year before and devoured it in the wingback chair in her room after work one evening.

She always tried to stay up-to-date with the latest research into the ancient history of various parts of the world. It was something of a compulsion, even though it was highly unlikely she would ever have an opportunity to put the knowledge to use.

"Are you familiar with Schellhas's work?" she asked.

"Nah," Bates replied. "I just know what I've seen."

"It is quite recent and not yet translated from the original German," she continued. "But it is my understanding that the slashed face and serpent leg *are* found combined in the symbology a little further north among the Aztecs—in the god Tezcatlipoca, the master of war, sacrifice, and prophecy. The presence of the disk icon here in the center of the figure would support that identification, as Tezcatlipoca is also strongly associated with the Smoking Mirror..."

"Smoking Mirror?" Bates prompted.

"Oh!" Ellie returned. "Sorry—a mythical piece of flawless obsidian through which the god could supposedly see into the past, the future, or across vast... er, distances," she finished awkwardly.

Bates had gone quiet. He wasn't looking at the medallion anymore. His eyes were on Ellie.

She was consumed by a familiar, uncomfortable fear. She was doing it again—rattling off an instinctive stream of knowledge in a way that usually ended with people looking at her as though she had just fallen out of the sky.

Ellie fought the urge to flinch. In her experience, men were often particularly ungracious when confronted with the reality that a woman might be as well informed as they were on a subject—or better.

She pushed the feeling aside. She could hardly expect to succeed in what she was about to attempt if she had to conceal the fact that she *knew things*.

"Yet this isn't an Aztec artifact," she continued. "The rectangular structure of these characters more closely resembles Mayan script, and the figures are more stylized—less naturalistic."

She waited for Bates's response, brushing a hand uselessly across her skirt. He studied her for a quiet moment before returning his sharp blue gaze to the artifact.

"The glyphs might look like Mayan, but they're not," Bates finally said. "I don't know what they are."

"I suppose we must admit the possibility that it is a fraud." Ellie was unable to keep the disappointment from her tone.

Bates leaned back in his chair and frowned at the surface of the disk thoughtfully.

"Damned clever one, if it is," he replied. "It'd have to have been made by someone pretty familiar with the Mayan language. I mean, a fair few of these symbols look close to stuff I've seen out in the field—like this lollipop."

"What lollipop?" Ellie replied, bewildered.

"This one," he returned, flipping the medallion over and tapping the lone glyph on its reverse side.

Ellie eyed the circle of spiraling, whirling lines skeptically. There was admittedly something just a bit lollipopish about it.

"I am fairly certain that represents some kind of wind or vapor," Ellie cut in defensively.

"But if they knew enough to replicate the lollipop, why not just carve the actual characters?" Bates continued. "Why bother changing them around at all when the real thing would've been more convincing?"

"Yes," Ellie agreed. Her interest sparked again as she returned to his side and gazed down at the medallion with him. "That was my reasoning exactly."

The thoughtful look Bates flashed her was a little difficult to read. She was relieved when he returned his attention to the artifact.

"You can't reach inside a piece of rock and ask it when it was made," he asserted. "In determining the authenticity of something like this, a lot of it's got to come down to knowing where it came from."

He gave her a meaningful look, waiting.

Ellie felt the tingle of rising nerves.

"I can confidently say that it dates back to at least the mid-seventeenth century," she offered carefully.

Bates's tone shifted, taking on a warning note.

"Where'd you get the necklace, Princess?"

She had, of course, stolen it from the archive entrusted with the preservation of the records of the United Kingdom—even if she was quite certain it didn't belong there.

Ellie could hardly tell Bates that. 'I stole it' didn't sound good no matter how one framed it.

She couldn't afford to put him off—not when it looked very much like he might be her only hope of finding her city and getting out of this colony alive.

The obvious solution was a lie. It galled her. She was about to ask the man to help her. Surely she owed him better than that?

On the other hand, she barely knew him. Though Bates seemed honorable beneath his appallingly rough edges, surely it was reasonable for Ellie to err on the side of prudence—at least for a little while longer.

"I found the medallion inside an old psalter," she said. "A family heirloom nobody had ever bothered to open that I picked up at an estate sale."

"A family heirloom," he repeated.

She could hear his skepticism. A bit desperately, she waded in deeper.

"My theory is that the book was confiscated from a Spanish ship by an English privateer," she offered, forcing a bit of cheerful interest into her tone.

"How do you get that from a piece of rock?" Bates returned, puzzled.

"I... don't," Ellie admitted. "I get it from this."

She pulled the map from her pocket.

Bates put down the medallion, took the jeweler's glass from his eye, and accepted the folded packet.

"Map... signifying... location of... habitatur?" he read, squinting a bit at the faded ink on the outside of the parchment. "Damned Ecclesiastical Latin."

"Inhabited," Ellie offered quietly, suppressing a little note of surprise that he could actually read that much of it. She didn't need to look at the words on the outside of the folded map to remember what they said. "The inhabited kingdom."

Bates frowned down at the words.

"You have a treasure map," he said a bit dully.

Ellie stifled an exasperated huff.

"It is *not* a treasure map," she retorted.

He frowned at her and moved to open the parchment.

With a quick, panicked instinct, Ellie plucked it from his hands.

"Hey!" he protested.

She held the map protectively to her chest, her heart pounding.

"Do you want me to look at it or not?" he demanded.

"If I show the map to you, that's it," she countered, the words spilling out of her with all the force of truth. "You'll have everything you need to find the city. You won't need me anymore."

"I can't find it at all if you don't show me the map," Bates countered crossly.

Ellie clutched the parchment, torn with the impossibility of the situation. Bates was right, of course. She had to give him *something* if she wanted him to partner with her on this mad quest. She couldn't possibly expect him to agree based on her word and a lump of stone.

But she knew all too well what would happen if she handed the map over. Even though Bates had proved himself to be a decent fellow—protecting her from Jacobs without a question—he was still a man. He would have been raised all of his life to see women as fragile beings in need of protection... if they weren't simply to be exploited. Centuries of cultural conditioning couldn't be overcome on a whim—not even if he meant her well. *Meaning her well* could easily turn into *sticking her on a boat back to London.*

The solution to the problem crept across her mind. It was simple, really... and it went against her every bone-deep instinct as an archivist charged with a sacred responsibility to *preserve.*

Ellie opened the folded packet of the map and ripped it neatly in half.

"Are you out of your ever-loving—" Bates protested, coming to his feet.

"Here," she cut in as she extended the lower half of the document toward him.

"What about the rest of it?" he demanded.

"The rest stays with me until we're well on our way, as my insurance policy," she replied.

"Insurance against what?" he barked back. "If I was out to steal your map and feed you to the crocodiles, keeping it in your corset isn't going to stop me."

Ellie took a step closer to him, steeling her spine.

"I wouldn't be offering to bring you in on this if I thought you were going to rob me. I am more concerned about being packed back to England out of a convenient sense of chivalry."

Bates put his hand to the bridge of his nose as if fighting a headache.

"For the record, I do think you'd be a hell of a lot better off back in England," he noted.

"No," Ellie replied, an impulsive honesty stripping the words raw. "I am not entirely sure that I would be."

He dropped his hand and met her eyes—considering.

"Where's this city of yours supposed to be? *Approximately,*" he added as her posture quickly turned defensive.

Ellie turned to the sprawling map on the wall. The detail and organization of the hand drawn document stood in stark contrast to the messy chaos of the room that surrounded her. She studied the notes and lines for any sign of the landmarks listed on her parchment. Nothing she could see resembled a *Black Pillar that Draws the Compass* or an *Arch Hollowed by the Hand of God.*

She would have to rely on other means of estimating the place the X on the parchment indicated.

Not to scale, of course, she thought. *The original would have been based on a verbal report by someone lacking modern survey methods... Source would have been traveling by foot. How long could such a man have walked without succumbing to exhaustion or hunger?*

Her mind rapidly made the necessary assumptions and calculations, and she reached out to lay her hand across a swath of topography that included the high, jagged peaks of a distant range of mountains. Only a single, powerful word otherwise marked the area: *Uncharted.*

Bates came to her side, gazing grimly at the spot she had indicated. He stood closer than was strictly polite—all looming, disreputable male, with his suspenders still hanging at his sides. He smelled vaguely of cigars and alcohol. He had left an inordinate number of buttons on his shirt undone, exposing a triangle of skin at his collarbone that was as deeply tanned as the rest of him. The odd implication of that crawled slowly across Ellie's brain. Did the man do most of his surveying without a shirt?

The notion was uncomfortably distracting.

"Let me make one thing perfectly clear," he said as he turned to face her. "If I agree to help you with this insanity, I'm the one who calls the shots. I tell you to duck, you duck. Run, you run—and not after you've asked me thirty questions or called me a patriarchal good-for-nothing. Where you want to go, there are a whole lot of things that would love nothing more than to cut the pair of us down. However many books you might've read, until you've been there, pretending to know what you're doing is a quick way to get yourself killed."

"If I knew what I was doing, Mr. Bates, I wouldn't be asking for your assistance," Ellie tightly replied.

"Well," he returned coolly. "As long as we know where we both stand."

The silence that followed felt like a contest of wills fought across the bare foot of space that separated them. Ellie refused to bend to it. He would meet her in this as an equal or not at all—Jacobs and the threat he posed be dashed.

The tension rose. As it did, something shifted in the tone of it—something that made her mouth go a bit dry. She swallowed thickly, conscious of the slow throb of her heart, the sweat lightly glazing her back, and the way the shadows danced across Bates's jaw with the flicker of the lamplight.

Ellie blinked, forcing the odd sensation back. The tension broke as Bates moved away from her to pluck a battered canvas rucksack from beside the bed. He started tossing things into it.

"How about the story with your friend from upstairs?" he said as he shoved a bundle of mosquito netting into the pack.

"I would say he is a competitor," Ellie replied tightly.

He paused, glancing over at her.

"A competitor who isn't averse to tying up and gagging a lady," he pointed out.

"Er... yes," Ellie admitted.

"Sounds like fun," Bates replied in a grumble.

He unclipped his suspenders and tossed them aside. The bands landed in a haphazard pile on top of the unmade bed.

He yanked open the door to his closet. Something lurched at him from inside in a blur of yellow eyes and rows of wicked teeth. Ellie's throat closed with panic as she recognized the form of a bizarrely upright crocodile.

Bates's hand flashed out and caught the beast by its chest. He pushed it back into the closet automatically, still rifling through the hangers.

With a blink of surprise, Ellie amended her impression. The crocodile was stuffed.

Bates emerged with a sturdy, weathered leather belt. He wrapped it around his waist with an easy, practiced motion as he kicked the dead reptile back into place and shut the closet door.

Ellie recognized the handle of his enormous knife protruding from a sheath attached to the belt. The sight of it made her stomach drop a bit further.

What was she getting herself into?

"Probably best if we avoid going back to your room," Bates pointed out. "And we'll need to travel light. Is there anything you absolutely can't do without?"

The question startled her. Ellie's heart pattered uncomfortably at the sudden *realness* of what was happening.

She flashed her gaze to the equipment hanging from the nails driven into the walls: levels, stakes, theodolites, and spools of masonry string. She had meant to acquire a pick, screen, brush, and shovel in case she decided to dig a small test pit on the site, but as she faced the reality of carrying those items across an unknown span of rainforest, she realized how foolish that had been.

Ellie forced herself to take a breath. This was a preliminary expedition. There was only one thing she needed in order for it to be a success.

"Do you have a blank notebook?" she asked.

Bates's hand moved unerringly to a thin, leather-bound volume that lay among the piles of papers on his desk. He flipped through it quickly and shrugged.

"Mostly blank," he offered as he held it out to her. "Will that do?"

"Yes," Ellie said, looking down at the unassuming book.

She was overwhelmed by the sense of what those ordinary pages meant. They were potential. They were hope.

Bates held out the rucksack.

"Add it to the kit," he said.

Ellie let the notebook slide from her hands into the bag—then quickly darted out to grab a pencil from the desk and throw it in as well.

"Have you a sharpener?" she asked.

He answered her with a grin.

"Sure. It's right here."

He tapped the place where the enormous knife hung at his belt.

Slinging the bag over his shoulder, he paused to eye her figure, eyes roving carefully from her tousled hair to her somewhat dirt-smudged cotton shirt-waist, and finally her feet.

"Those leather boots?" he asked.

"What?" Ellie returned as she lifted the footwear in question. "Er—yes?"

"No heels," Bates commented approvingly. "New laces. How long have you had 'em?"

"About a year?" Ellie returned, confused by the question.

"Do much walking?"

"I do a very great deal of it," she replied as she crossed her arms over her chest and fought a rising note of irritation. "May I ask why it matters?"

"You don't want to be out there in bad shoes," he replied.

Bates paused, his expression going over a bit awkward as he scratched at the side of his jaw.

"Look. I—ah—don't usually much concern myself with this sort of thing, but I should probably make it clear before we do this," he declared awkwardly. "We go out that door, it's going to be just the two of us. I don't usually bring a team with me on this sort of initial expedition, even if that would've made any kind of sense given your current circumstances."

Circumstances like the murderer upstairs, Ellie thought grimly.

"That means you're going to be out in the bush alone with a strange man, possibly for weeks," he went on. "I've never been one to give much of a damn for my reputation, but I've also never been considered a debaucher of proper young ladies. I'm not sure that's a distinction I'd like to earn."

Ellie was aghast.

"Are you telling me that the future of this endeavor depends upon whether or not I am a virgin?" she demanded.

Bates blushed. It was a rather ferocious blush. It had to be in order to make its way through the deep tan of his skin.

"That isn't what I... That's not..." He took a breath and raised his eyes to the ceiling as he tried to gather himself. "What I'm saying is, I'm not in the market for some outraged father or brother to come pounding on my door demanding I make an honest woman of you. Nor do I think you're looking to undertake this expedition at the cost of being hitched to some guy you barely know for the rest of your life. Look... if you just need to get that bastard and whoever he's working with off your tail, there are other ways to do that. I don't exactly maintain friends in high places, but if it's a matter of beating a guy like that out of the idea of wanting anything to do with you or your map—I might find a certain kind of pleasure in that."

There was a rough and delicious edge to his voice. Ellie had little doubt that part of him very much liked the idea of engaging in a bout of fisticuffs with Jacobs.

Bates might even come out on top of such an engagement—but she uneasily found that she could not be entirely sure. For all Bates's virile strength and cat-like readiness, there was something very sharp and wicked about Jacobs that made her warily consider just how dangerous he might be.

No—Ellie could not allow Bates to take that risk. She wondered whether she ought to simply free him of any obligation he felt to lend her aid.

Ellie thought about what she had observed of Bates's character so far, and considered how likely it was that she might convince him to leave the matter alone.

She had as much chance of redirecting a gorilla.

Traveling with him to search for the city was decidedly better than allowing him to barrel off after Jacobs and possibly get himself gutted. Ellie could not let some outmoded concern about social mores and the repressive control of female virtue stand in the way of it.

Besides, no one was going to hear about what she got up to in this place—certainly not her father with his nose in the newspaper and her stepbrother Neil all the way off in Egypt.

What happened in the wilderness could stay in the wilderness.

"That needn't concern you," Ellie informed him evenly. "I am not a virgin."

Bates's eyebrow cocked with surprise.

"I mean that I am a widow," Elle quickly corrected. She extended her hand. "Mrs. Nitherscott-Watby, at your service."

He took her hand. For a moment, he simply held it, as though the imminent shake that would seal their arrangement were suspended somewhere in the air around them.

"Bit of a mouthful there," he commented.

The texture of his skin was weathered and calloused, but he clasped her fingers with an unexpected delicacy of pressure.

"Then you may call me Eleanora," she declared with slightly more firmness than she was feeling.

"Eleanora, huh?"

She wriggled a little uncomfortably. She had never loved her full name. It had always sounded a bit ponderous.

"Maybe just Ellie," she allowed.

He considered it—considered *her*—and Ellie was gripped by the quick and uncomfortable fear that he could see right through all of her prudent fictions.

"What the hell?" he abruptly declared.

He gave her hand a single powerful shake and released her.

Bates plucked the rifle from where it leaned beside the bed. The wooden stock was polished to a gleam, the black barrel neatly oiled. He swung the weapon over his shoulder alongside the rucksack.

"Let's get moving," he announced.

"Are you sure the firearm is strictly necessary?" Ellie demanded, eyeing the gun with distaste.

"This is a Winchester lever-action repeater," Bates protested, obviously offended. "It's the best-made gun in the world. Hell yes, it's necessary."

"I see," Ellie said, quickly sensing that the presence of the gun was not a battle she would win. "And is there anything I can carry?"

"Everything else we need is with the *Mary Lee*," he replied.

"Who is Mary Lee?" Ellie asked.

"My boat."

Bates blew out the lamp and strode toward the French doors that led to the veranda.

"We are going out through the garden?" Ellie blurted as she stumbled into motion after him.

"Where else would we go?" Bates replied. "I gotta steal you some trousers."

TWELVE

$\mathscr{T}$HE TROUSERS BELONGED to Óscar. Adam found them hanging on the clothesline behind the Linares family's rooms, just where he'd expected them to be. He tossed them at Mrs. Eleanora Nitherscott-Watby.

Heading off into the bush with her was almost certainly a bad idea. Adam wasn't sure he'd ever met someone who had 'trouble' stamped across her quite as boldly as Mrs. Nitherscott-Watby. Still, if getting tied up and forced to jump off a balcony hadn't been enough to dissuade her from her purpose, Adam wasn't sure what would. If he didn't help her, she was going to go looking for someone else who would—and probably get herself killed.

Her map and the stone trinket she was carrying were also a damned sight more intriguing than staking out another land grant boundary.

The lowlife from the veranda was another complication. The thought of the red marks on the woman's wrists still made Adam's fists itch.

To say that Adam didn't have much patience for the kind of guy who'd do that to a woman was something of an understatement. Adam had only refrained from beating the daylights out of that lizard-eyed creep because doing so would probably have landed the woman in even more trouble.

He told himself those were the only reasons he'd agreed to her crazy offer as he stepped up onto the overturned wheelbarrow by Diego's shed.

"We can't just steal somebody's clothes," the woman hissed at him.

"Diego'll put it on my tab," Adam assured her as he hopped easily onto the shed roof.

"But how will Mr. Linares know you were the one who took them?" she demanded.

"He's known me for a while now. He'll figure it out. You coming?"

Adam could tell she didn't love his answer by the stubborn set of her mouth, but she kept whatever she was thinking to herself. Lifting up her skirts, she stepped onto the wheelbarrow, climbing from there to join him on the roof.

She slipped a bit on the tiles. Adam caught her. She fit against him nicely.

He set that thought firmly aside and jumped down to the far side of the fence.

"Hold on and I'll—" he began.

He cut himself off as she pushed from the roof and landed neatly beside him, brushing off her skirt.

"Never mind," he finished lamely as he adjusted the weight of his Winchester. "This way."

Adam led her through a familiar maze of garden gates and alleys to the docks that lined the mouth of the river. He kept his eyes carefully peeled for her *competition*. There was no sign of the guy, who must still be looking for her somewhere else.

Adam didn't plan on testing his luck in that department. He kept them to the shadows of his personal shortcuts until they emerged by the water.

The *Mary Lee* was tied up to the sea wall between a pair of larger fishing sloops. The steamboat looked small in comparison. Small was good. The *Mary Lee* had an exceptionally shallow draft, which meant that Adam could navigate further upriver before he had to disembark and continue on foot. The boat couldn't carry much cargo, but that was okay. Adam mostly traveled with what he could carry on his back and acquired the rest of what he needed along the way.

The low, gray deck was begging for a new coat of paint, as were the waist height rails that bordered it. The boat had no cabin—only a canopy, tattered at the edges, which hung in front of the pipe for the steam engine. The coal box in the stern was nearly full, and a quick peek under a pair of loose boards on the deck revealed that nobody had raided Adam's storage hold while the boat was docked.

Most importantly, his lucky rock was just where he'd left it on the shelf by the boiler. Adam gave the lumpy gray stone—which looked a bit like a squatting hedgehog—a ritual pat as he hopped on board.

"Are you quite certain it won't sink?" the woman asked, eyeing the boat skeptically as she hovered on the bank.

Ellie, Adam decided silently—that was how he'd think of her. It was easier than *Mrs. Nitherscott-Watby*.

Or he could simply call her 'Princess.' She obviously loved that.

"The *Mary Lee* has seen a lot more of the bush than you have," he replied as he extended his hand to where Ellie hovered on the bank.

She ignored it and hopped down onto the deck unassisted. The boards echoed hollowly under her sturdy boots.

Adam glanced at his lingering hand and then tucked it into his pocket.

"Welcome aboard," he grumbled and set to work firing the engine.

Adam drove the *Mary Lee* a few miles down the coast from Belize Town before stopping for the night, tying the steamboat up against some of the mangroves that lined the water. He strung a pair of hammocks from the iron poles that supported the canopy, and then draped the frame with mosquito netting, pausing to swat at one of the bugs that whined past his ear.

The woman gave the arrangement a wary look with her hands poised on the hips of Óscar's canvas trousers. The pants seemed to fit her well enough with the ankles rolled up.

She refrained from protesting as she climbed into the hammock, looking only a little awkward as she did so. When Adam peeked at her a few minutes later, she was already asleep, the lines of her face relaxed into an unfamiliar openness.

That black trinket of hers hung around her neck, tucked into the front of her shirt. She had tied the ribbon back together as Adam steamed them south, slipping it over the messy bundle of her hair.

Stretched out in the hammock beside her, Adam took a little longer to find his own oblivion. He wasn't used to sharing the *Mary Lee* with a woman. The canopy wasn't all that big, leaving the other hammock close enough that if he'd reached out a hand, he might've given it a little push.

Or something else.

No pushing, he thought as turned down the lantern and rolled over to face the other way. No *something elsing*, either.

Dawn arrived sooner than Adam would've liked. He packed up the hammocks and mosquito netting, and set the well-tuned boiler to steaming again. Soon, the mangroves were gliding past once more—a sea of vibrant green that bordered waters of a pure cerulean blue.

Ellie sat on the bench in the bow, holding up her face to the bright golden sun. The light of it fell across the spray of freckles that dotted her nose.

"Here," Adam said. He reached under his seat by the rudder, pulled out a battered khaki scout hat, and tossed it at her. "You'll get a sunburn."

She gave the hat a surreptitious sniff before popping it onto her head. Adam couldn't really blame her for that. It had probably been a good idea. The wide brim cast a shadow over her face.

"What about you?" she demanded.

"I'm kinda past the point of sunburns," Adam admitted, leaning back against the rail with his arm resting on the handle of the rudder.

A pair of pelicans rose from a rickety abandoned dock that emerged from the thick mangroves on the shore. The birds sailed over the *Mary Lee*'s wake, obviously hoping that the steam launch was a fishing boat likely to throw out some extra bait.

"Are we going to the mouth of the Sibun River, then?" Ellie asked.

"Yeah," Adam confirmed, a bit surprised. "How'd you figure that out?"

She shot him an arch look.

"Based on the shape of the coast and the positioning of the marked cays, the Sibun is the most likely candidate for the waterway on the map that leads to the first landmark, the *Black Pillar that Draws the Compass*. That's how I knew to come to British Honduras in the first place. I corroborated the mouth of the river and the position of the mission against the historical documentation."

"Course you did," Adam muttered as he adjusted their angle to avoid a sandbar. "Mind my asking how old these historical documentations were?"

Her mouth thinned a bit.

"I can assure you, I took the time to check my calculations against the current map Mr. Linares has mounted on the wall in the lounge."

"That map's not current," Adam replied flatly.

"It was printed less than a decade ago," she returned shortly.

"Things change fast around here."

"Then where does one find the most up-to-date map?" she demanded.

"At the surveyor general's office." Adam flashed her a grin. "Or on my bedroom wall."

That earned him a scowl.

"If you showed me that whole parchment of yours, I might know a short-cut," he offered cheerfully.

"We shall start with the Sibun, Mr. Bates," she sang out in reply as she turned away from him. "The rest will come in good time."

The green-gold line of the mangroves drifted past. Below the *Mary Lee*, the pale sand was clearly visible through the crystalline waters, punctuated by little shells and stones. The woman let her hand fall over the rail of the bow, trailing her fingertips in the water in a way that sent a line of ripples back toward the stern.

Adam watched as a wide shadow flickered across the seabed, the drift of it slightly outpacing the chug of the *Mary Lee*. A moment later, an enormous, whiskered head broke through the surface of the water next to the woman's hand. The gray expanse was punctuated by a pair of small, liquid black eyes.

Ellie let out a strangled squeak of alarm as she lurched back and promptly fell from the bench onto the deck.

"It ain't going to bite," Adam called back lazily. "It's a sea cow. She's just hoping you have food."

After a moment's hesitation, Ellie scrambled up to peer curiously over the side of the boat at the animal, which continued to swim alongside.

"Sailors used to think they were mermaids," Adam continued. "Though that'd be one ugly mermaid."

The woman didn't seem to be listening to him.

"Manatee," Ellie whispered wonderingly as she gazed down at the gracefully moving creature. It wheeled away from them, slipping off toward deeper waters.

Adam felt a smile tug at the corner of his lips as he roped off the tiller and crossed to the boiler to add another load of coal to the box. He set down the shovel and leaned against one of the supports for the canopy as he looked down at her.

"You can put your hands back in the water. I'll let you know when to take them out," he said.

"And when will that be?" she demanded as he dropped back onto his seat in the stern.

"When we get to the crocodiles," Adam replied and flashed her a wicked grin.

THIRTEEN

$\mathcal{S}$HORTLY AFTER THE *Mary Lee* turned from the stunning expanse of blue ocean into the mouth of the Sibun River, Ellie glimpsed the reality behind Bates's warning. She had already returned her limbs to the boat when a rotting log suddenly raised a pair of beady yellow eyes out of the water. The crocodile watched her passively as the steamer chugged past.

Though the creature was significantly smaller than the one in Bates's closet, Ellie still fought the urge to move closer to the middle of the boat.

The world around them had narrowed to a band of muddy brown water framed by a seemingly endless expanse of mangrove swamps. Ellie didn't mind the change. Everything she had seen—from the shocking blue clarity of the sea to the manatee that had startled her that morning—was profoundly, delightfully different from the gray monotony of the world that she had known for the last twenty-four years.

Beyond the coast, the landscape quickly descended into wilderness. There were no farms or villages situated on the banks of the Sibun—only low palms, mangroves, and sea grapes tangled into a wall of brush that extended for miles to either side. Long-legged birds perched in the water along the banks, dipping their beaks into the mud for fish. Insects hopped along the surface of the water, and the sun beat down relentlessly overhead.

As Ellie moved to the shade of the canopy, Bates pulled another hat from the shallow hold under the floorboards of the deck. This one was a battered straw Stetson that had clearly seen better days. He plopped it onto his messy, sun-gilded hair, leaning back against the rail at the stern with the handle of the rudder braced comfortably under his arm.

His eyes were an even more startling shade of blue out here in the wild.

The color rivaled the hue of the clear, open waters that they had left behind.

Ellie brushed the thought aside. She hardly needed to waste any of her attention on that particular aspect of the scenery.

She wished she'd had a bit more time during her escape to examine the notes that Dawson had made on the map—or perhaps to simply steal them. She couldn't know for certain how much of the route the professor had deciphered before she had stolen the parchment back. Ellie comforted herself with the notion that he and Jacobs would need to acquire a boat and likely other supplies before they could hope to come after her. Dawson didn't strike her as the sort to travel light. So long as she and Bates kept making good time, they should be able to stay ahead of any pursuit.

By mid-afternoon, the unrelenting monotony of the palms and mangroves began to give way to the ripple of low foothills. The trees lining the banks grew taller, sometimes reaching out to form a leafy green canopy over the muddy width of the water.

The river was low. The *Mary Lee* handled the sluggish current with ease. By the time the sun began to drift toward the horizon ahead of them, Ellie had not seen so much as a rickety dock for hours. Fat lizards draped across the branches of the trees overhead, accented by the bright flicker of the birds. Thick walls of green served as the boundaries of Ellie's world.

As the sky began to change its blue for purple, Bates rounded another bend in the river and drew the *Mary Lee* closer to the bank. With an echoing rattle, the launch's engine slowed to a stop. The sound raised a cacophonous cry from a flock of birds that startled out of the branches of a massive overhanging oak. They rose up—dark, fluttering shapes calling in irritation to one another against the richly colored dusk.

"Are we stopping already?" Ellie asked, feeling a little jolt of alarm at the prospect.

"Can't pilot a boat in the dark," Bates replied. "Not unless you wanna risk putting a hole in your hull on some stray rock. Don't worry. If your friend is trailing us, he'll have to stop too."

Reassured, Ellie rose and stretched her limbs. Her muscles protested against the long day of inactivity.

As Bates set about banking the fire in the boiler, Ellie moved to the bow.

A break in the foliage ahead of them offered her a glimpse of the mountains. The peaks rose, low and hazy, over the rich green of the trees... and looked far closer than they had from the veranda of the Hotel Rio Nuevo.

Ellie traced the shape of the medallion through the fabric of her shirt. She was so much nearer to the place where it had come from.

If that place is even real, she reminded herself.

Bates hopped up onto the rail and neatly jumped from there to the river bank, carrying a line from the boat with him. He tied it to one of the thick-trunked ceiba trees.

Pulled taut by the current, the rope gracefully swung the *Mary Lee* into a little hollow in the curve of the river, which put them out of the way of any debris that might float past in the night.

"How far have we come?" Ellie asked as he came back on board.

Bates sat down on the deck and pulled his rucksack into his lap. He rifled through it and tugged out a tin cylinder. Unscrewing the top, he shook loose an oilskin.

The waterproof bundle held another map. Unlike Ellie's parchment, this one was obviously modern. It was covered in notations and markings. Ellie studied them over Bates's shoulder as he unrolled it across the deck.

"We've come about fifty miles," he replied. "Which puts us right... about... here."

He dropped his finger to a point on the curve of the river that was not far from the dotted line that marked the edge of the Cayo District.

Ellie knelt down for a closer look as Bates rose to light the lantern using an ember from the box of the boiler.

He pulled a pair of unlabeled cans out of the hold and set about opening them.

"Looks like beans tonight," he concluded as he peered inside.

Bates plucked a tin pan from a hook on the frame of the canopy and set it on the flat top of the boiler. He dumped the beans inside.

Ellie's gaze drifted to the fist-sized gray rock on the shelf beside him. It was shaped roughly like a sleepy hedgehog. She wondered what possible function it could serve.

Before she could ask, Bates plopped down beside her, sitting a bit closer than was strictly polite.

He took his half of the seventeenth-century parchment from the oilskin and laid it beside the modern map. The fine lines at the corners of his eyes crinkled with focus.

"Tomorrow, we'll follow the river up here..." He traced a curve of blue ink. "And then we go off my map."

Bates tapped his finger on a line that broke off from the right side of a fork in the river—and simply stopped.

"Does the water end there?" Ellie asked, confused.

"Nah," he replied as he hopped to his feet to stir the beans. "It just goes through a mountain."

"*Through* a mountain?" she echoed, alarmed.

"Maybe not a mountain," Bates hedged. "More like a big hill."

"How does the river go through a hill?" she demanded. "How do *we* go through a hill?"

"There's a cave." Bates poked his finger into the beans and immediately yanked it out, shaking it off. "Ow!," he muttered. "The river runs through it. The water was always too high for the *Mary Lee* to get inside when I've been here before, but right now, the level is as low as I've seen it. Getting through the tunnel might be tight, and it's probably a terrible idea. Boating through a cave is all kinds of risky. You might hit rock formations under the water and put a hole in your hull. Or get in, only to have it narrow on you so you have to back out again. It'll be chock full of creepy-crawly things. Of course... we might not need to go that way at all if you showed me the other half of your map," he finished casually as he dumped the beans into a pair of bowls and carried them over.

They had only been on the *Mary Lee* for a day. A day didn't feel like quite enough distance from the boat back to England that he might happily stick her on once he knew how to get where they were going. Ellie would show Bates her half of the map *after* they were safely away from town.

"Why should we go off-track when it might be entirely possible to press forward along the map's course?" she offered.

"You," Bates replied, pointing at her with a spoon full of beans, "are stalling."

He ate the beans.

"So what if I am?" Ellie retorted defensively. "You will recall we had an agreement."

"You actually afraid I'm going to drop you in the swamp and go on without you?" Bates challenged. "I told you, if I was out to take advantage of you, your corset isn't about to stop me."

He froze.

"From—uh—stealing your map," he continued. "If I wanted to. Which I don't," he finished firmly and shoved more beans into his mouth.

"I am... mostly confident you do not mean to drop me in the swamp," Ellie offered carefully. "But I would appreciate your patience for another day, if that is not too unreasonable."

He considered it while he chewed.

The night was settling in more thickly. Bates's face was softly gilded by the glow of the lantern. The scruff of his beard had grown more pronounced along his jaw. With his rolled-up shirtsleeves and disheveled hair, he looked decidedly disreputable. Ellie was surprised to realize she found that oddly comforting.

"Why not?" he concluded with a shrug.

They were quiet for a moment as they ate—which didn't take very long. Ellie devoured her humble dinner as though it was the best thing she had tasted in years. Taking part in an expedition through the wilderness was apparently good for her appetite.

After she had scooped out every last legume, she set down her bowl.

"Thank you," she said. "That was very good."

Bates's spoon paused on the way to his mouth.

"The mystery beans?" he prompted with a skeptical glance down at her empty bowl. "Do you need any more of them?"

"Er—no," Ellie assured him. "I'm quite well, thank you."

"We'll have canned grub while we're on the boat," Bates went on as he pushed to his feet and plucked up her dish.

He leaned over the rail, reaching down to the water to give both bowls a rinse. Ellie realized that she was paying more attention to the maneuver than was strictly necessary.

She forced herself to study the dark line of the bank instead.

"I can't imagine it would be sensible to carry tins into the wilderness," she commented.

"I'll bring some dry goods for emergencies, but for the most part we'll have to find what we need," Bates confirmed. "There's usually fruit this time of year. Plenty of tubers. And I'll try to catch us some game, but it probably won't be what you're used to."

There was a note of challenge in his voice.

"How so?" Ellie prompted archly.

"Iguana," Bates replied. "Armadillo. Gibnut. You know what a gibnut is?"

"Large rodent," Ellie replied automatically. "Grows to as long as 30 inches or one-and-a-half stone. Indigenous to Central and South America. The males are known to attract mates by spraying them with urine," she added distantly as her brain popped up another tidbit.

"Uh—right," Bates said awkwardly. He stared at her for a minute before tossing the bowls into the hold and grabbing the pan. "They taste like a greasy rabbit. How about termites?"

He pointed the pan at her.

"I'm not sure I have an opinion on them," Ellie replied with a frown.

"They're all right," Bates conceded as he swished the pan in the river and hung it back up on the canopy. "Kinda minty."

"I see," she returned uneasily.

With dinner settled, Bates set about fixing their hammocks and dropping the mosquito netting back into place. He worked with an easy air of long habit as he tightened straps and fixed ties.

The sight reminded Ellie of the question that had been lurking in the back of her mind since the moment she had seen the glorious chaos of Bates's room, with its stacks of equipment and the detritus of years of explorations. In the casual intimacy of the boat, under the purple sky of a place miles from the nearest outpost of humanity, Ellie found that she had little motivation to resist the urge to ask it.

"How did you come to this?" she demanded.

"What—eating termites?" Bates asked.

"No," she corrected him. "*This.*" She waved her hand over the thick trees arching overhead, the still length of the river, and the chirp of the evening frogs and insects. "Did you always want to end up in a place like this?"

"I mostly just knew where I didn't want to end up," he countered.

"And where is that?"

"Doing what my father does," he returned flatly.

"What terrible thing does your father do, exactly?" Ellie asked.

"Making money," Bates replied as he leaned against one of the poles for the canopy. "My dad makes money."

"Is he some sort of criminal?" Ellie was a little alarmed at the notion.

"More or less." Bates chuckled darkly. "He's in insurance. Robinson, Bates, and MacKenzie of San Francisco. Senior partner."

"But I've heard of them," Ellie blurted out, surprised by the realization. "My father is an actuary. *That's* the terrible fate you were running away from—working for an insurance company?"

"Yeah, well. You asked," he said as he turned away from her.

He tugged the cord to vent the last bit of steam from the boiler. The long, low hiss sent something rustling away through the brush on the nearby shore.

Probably just a gibnut, Ellie thought uneasily.

"Is making money really so terrible?" she asked.

Bates ran a hand through his hair, tangling the cropped length of it a bit more than it was already.

"I don't like pretending to be something I'm not," he finally replied, his tone short. "I don't like looking for ways to take advantage of people. When

I get to the end of my day, I don't want to worry about what connections I should be making or which of my friends might be out to get me. I just want to take off my boots and watch the sky change for a little while."

Ellie hesitated before she replied, thinking of how she had come across Bates in his chair on the veranda that first night at the hotel, looking out over the golden sprawl to the west. The memory tugged at her chest in an unexpected way.

"That all seems entirely sensible to me," she finally concluded.

"Does it, now?" he replied.

His words had a harder edge, and Ellie wondered if this was a topic he was accustomed to battling over.

She raised her head to meet his eyes.

"I know a thing or two about having dreams the rest of the world thinks are madness," she quietly declared.

The tenor of Bates's gaze shifted as he looked back at her.

"Maybe you do," he conceded thoughtfully.

The night air seemed to grow a little thicker. Ellie shook off the sensation as she sat down on the bench in the stern.

"Why British Honduras?" she prompted neatly, pulling off her borrowed hat and tossing it onto the deck.

"I don't know that I really cared that much where I ended up, as long as it was far away from San Francisco," Bates replied. "I heard there was an opening here when I was leaving Cambridge, and I wrote to the Colonial Office to apply."

Ellie straightened a bit.

"I'm sorry, did you say Cambridge?" she asked. "As in Cambridge University, in England?"

"Hinc lucem et pocula sacra." Bates recited the familiar tones of the university's motto automatically. "Et pocula profana—plenty of profane draughts as well. I even strapped an oversized bird to one of the spires of the King's College Chapel with a few of my friends, per tradition."

The husk of a long-neglected memory sparked to life in Ellie's mind.

She had been fourteen, crouched on the stairwell of the house in Canonbury, listening with secret delight as her stepmother's shrill tones had echoed up from the parlor.

And now this! A letter from the dean reprimanding you for behavior unbecoming of a Cambridge scholar!

It was just a harmless bit of fun! It's the sort of thing one does at university.

A written reprimand, Neil Acton Fairfax! A written reprimand over some monstrous stunt with an—

"Emu," Ellie blurted softly.

"Huh?" Bates returned. "How'd you know it was an emu?"

Ellie vividly recalled her quick, whispered exchange with her stepbrother as he had passed her by, pausing briefly to ruffle her hair in that way he knew irritated her.

Eavesdropping—eh, Peanut?
You've really done it this time.
It was the cowboy's idea!

The cowboy.

Neil had occasionally mentioned his university friends during his visits home. Ellie knew there had been a little cohort of them, thick as thieves with each other. Neil had mentioned Lord Scardsale, as well as a charming, well-off Cornishman, Trevelyan Perry. Ellie had heard that Perry had gone to Hong Kong with the diplomatic service.

And then there was the American—the one Neil had habitually referred to as 'the cowboy.'

Neil had spoken of that particular friend with easy affection. He had sounded like a source of both fun and regular trouble.

Of course, Ellie never had an opportunity to meet him or any of Neil's other university friends. She had been too wrapped up at the time with her urgent efforts to excel at her studies and qualify for university.

Perhaps she was wrong. Perhaps there was some hope that she had not inadvertently run off into the wilderness of a remote colony with her stepbrother's old school chum.

"Is that a regular occurrence?" she asked weakly. "Strapping an emu to the spires of the chapel?"

Bates frowned.

"Well, it's something of a gag to stick stuff up there..." he admitted.

Ellie felt the tension in her stomach start to relax.

"...though there was only the one bird," he finished.

"Oh dear," Ellie said.

She leaned forward to rest her head against her knees and hoped the boat would stop spinning.

"You don't need to worry about the emu," Bates quickly cut in, mistaking the cause of her abrupt anxiety. "We didn't hurt it. It was kinda beyond that. Somebody had stuffed it. Badly. Thing looked like an overlarge turkey on stilts."

Neil was going to kill her. Neil was going to kill both of them.

If he ever finds out, Ellie corrected herself silently. As far as Adam Bates knew, she was Eleanora Nitherscott-Watby, a widow from London with no connection to anyone he knew.

There was absolutely no reason it shouldn't stay that way.

Bates was still talking.

"Anyway, I don't think the Colonial Office was exactly overwhelmed with applicants. They couldn't have been, or I can't imagine they'd have given the post to an American who dropped out before graduating."

"Dropped out?" Ellie echoed. Surprise momentarily overwhelmed her horror at discovering that Bates was not, in fact, a total stranger but a dangerously close connection. "Why on earth would you do that?"

"Spite, mostly," Bates replied.

"*Spite?*" Ellie rose to her feet, unable to keep a note of dismay from her voice. "You dropped out of university out of *spite*? Spite for what?"

"Spite for whom," Bates corrected her. "And the answer is—my father."

"I see," Ellie replied—but she didn't, really. Not at all.

She paced away from him toward the bow of the boat.

"You don't approve," Bates noted with a deceptively lazy ease.

Ellie took a breath, trying to be reasonable.

"I can't say that I do," she admitted flatly. "I don't know your situation. It's probably not particularly fair of me to judge, but..." Her hands reflexively clenched into fists. "You must not have had to fight very hard for your education if you could walk away from it for the sake of a grudge."

There was a bitter snap to her words. Ellie closed her mouth and turned away, directing her attention out to the chirping, rustling wilderness around them.

She had to bite her tongue. She needed Bates. She couldn't afford to alienate him... but his casual explanation for leaving university had quietly, thoroughly infuriated her.

"Where did you go?" he asked.

The question startled her.

"Go where?" she returned in a clipped tone.

"University," Bates elaborated.

Ellie blinked at him in surprise.

"I... How did you..." she stammered.

"You read German," he said. "Latin. You rattle off the names of Aztec deities like old friends. You knew where to access a set of historical maps. Casually referenced the collapse of the Mayan civilization. Where did you go?"

"University College, London," she replied.

"And how hard did *you* have to fight for it?" he gently pressed.

Ellie looked back out into the darkness—but she could feel him quietly, patiently waiting for her answer.

"There was little question that I could be accepted. My scores were frankly too high for them to deny me. But I needed a scholarship. We had just finished paying for school for... my brother," she elaborated awkwardly. "There weren't any additional funds left for me. I suppose that even though I'd been talking about going to university since I was a child, everyone simply assumed it was a fantasy."

Ellie kept her voice even, but so much roiled beneath the calm surface of the story.

She remembered looking into her future and watching it narrow precipitously. Feeling the dreams she had nurtured as a child grind to dust under the weight of the reality of her position.

Ellie steeled herself against the old hurt and pressed on.

"I applied for all the funds open to female candidates. Some rejected me immediately by letter despite my examination scores. At several of the remaining interviews, I was asked whether the trustees would be wasting their money on me when I inevitably married and gave up my occupation. Whether I could reasonably be expected to demonstrate the mental fortitude required to keep up with a strenuous course of study. Whether I would be a distraction to my male classmates. One of the committee members told me that university wasn't the place to try to find a *rich husband.*"

Ellie wasn't able to keep that bit calm. Bitterness snapped through her voice. She stopped it by clamping her mouth shut.

"I was finally able to secure funding through a private trust and complete my education," she finished flatly.

Of course, that had been far from the end of it. After the battle for the funds, she had faced the constant, snickering remarks from her fellow students. The flirtations that felt more like threats.

Comments about 'taking up space in the library' that were *meant* to be overheard.

If you're going to be here, you might at least pretty yourself up a bit...

"I'm sorry," Bates said.

Ellie was startled to realize that he had come to stand beside her.

"Why? You weren't part of it." She took another deep breath. "And it is hardly fair of me to judge your decisions based upon my experience, which must necessarily have been very different from your own."

Bates braced his arms on the frame of the canopy and leaned out from it.

The low, orange glow of the lamp gilded his form.

"Naw. Don't do that," he said.

"Do what?" Ellie demanded.

"Let me off the hook that easy," he replied. "It was a stupid move. My old man showed up during my last semester and told me he hoped I'd wised up. Handed me a ticket back to San Francisco for the week after graduation so I could take up my position with the firm. So of course, I told him to go to hell." His mouth twisted into a thin smirk. "My buddy Fairfax never lets me hear the end of it. Says I could've made something of myself."

"But you never wanted to make anything of yourself," Ellie quietly protested, fighting back a wince at his casual mention of her brother again.

"Careful," Bates returned, his eyes flashing darkly. "You might be starting to get to know me."

"What did your father do?" Ellie asked.

"Disowned me," Bates neatly replied.

"Excuse me?"

Bates pushed off the frame and strolled back to the stern.

"With full pomp and circumstance. I am officially no longer a legal descendant of George Bates Jr.," he reported as he plopped down on the bench.

"In a fit of pique over university?" Ellie pressed, feeling a sympathetic outrage.

"I think it was more the culmination of a whole lot of things, but yeah. More or less. My mom still writes. My younger brother, Ethan, is being groomed up to wear the mantle of Robinson, Bates, and MacKenzie. He's not a bad guy, and better suited to the job... though I do wonder how long he'll be able to *stay* decent living in that snakes' nest."

Bates rose.

"We should probably call it a night," he announced. "We've got another long day ahead of us. Once we're past that fork—assuming we actually make it through the cave—you're gonna have to start watching for that *Black Pillar* from the map. And trust me, hunting for a needle like that in this haystack is gonna be exhausting."

"Yes. I suppose retiring early would be sensible," Ellie agreed awkwardly.

They climbed into their hammocks—Bates swinging up into his with the lazy grace of practice, Ellie half-falling into her place. She managed to settle herself after a bit of precarious adjustment.

With her head resting against the rolled blanket that served as her pillow, she looked over at where Bates lay beside her. His arms were behind his head, his eyes already closed. He had turned the lantern down to a bare glimmer, leaving just enough light for Ellie to pick out the dim lines of his face.

"Bates?" she said as she suppressed a yawn.

"Yeah?" he replied without opening his eyes.

"Thank you."

He frowned.

"For what—the beans?"

"For coming out here with me," she corrected him a little irritably.

He looked over at her, but the details of his expression were lost in the gloom of the night.

"Get some sleep, Princess," he said.

Ellie let herself fall into the darkness.

FOURTEEN

*E*LLIE WAS IN EGYPT, and she was dreaming.

A hot, dry sun warmed her skin. The air whispered of dust and time as it pulled at the little tendrils of hair at the back of her neck.

She held a wood-handled brush in her hand. The horsehair bristles were ideal for gently removing debris from stone, or even—if carefully wielded—ancient wood or pottery.

Stratified deposits were visible in the wall of the trench in which Ellie, kneeling, carefully worked to remove the earth from a slab of mud-hued stone.

Looking closer, Ellie realized that the surface of the stone was carved.

She dropped her brush and used a wooden pick to scrape out the delicate lines—the curve of an arch, the distinct angle of a human profile.

Her brain began translating the symbols instinctively as she tried to balance her quick excitement with the necessary delicacy of technique.

Gratitude... sixteen... head... cattle... exchange... four?

Four hundred, she clarified happily as she picked a pebble out of another ridge in the tablet. *Four hundred deben of wheat.*

Wonder rose in her chest, filling her like the sun. Ellie had found a two-thousand-year-old receipt for cows.

The tablet was almost certainly part of a new cache, which meant that there would be more engraved stones hidden under the sand. Such ancient documents were unglamorous, but the mortal transactions they recorded were the stuff of daily life, offering a priceless glimpse into the ordinary world of the people who had lived in this place millennia before.

Ellie had the skills to carefully unwrap those vestiges from the earth, piece them back together, and untangle the ancient threads of what they meant.

One of the local farmers Ellie had hired to assist with her dig called to her from above. Ellie gripped the dusty rungs of the ladder and climbed out of the trench, emerging into the stronger wind of the surface.

It was *too* strong. Canvas flapped against the stiff breeze. An empty water barrel tipped over and rolled across the ground.

Beyond the sprawl of tents stood a diminutive figure that did not belong there.

The woman was not Egyptian. Her rich black hair contrasted sharply with her simple white dress. Even at a distance, Ellie could see that the copper skin of her cheek was marked by the vivid lightning bolt of a scar.

Despite the wind whipping at the intruder's skirts and hair, she remained straight and still as she gazed across the sprawl of trenches to Ellie.

A worker tugged at Ellie's sleeve, pulling her attention away from the immovable woman as he pointed to the west.

Ellie turned to see a black cloud devouring the horizon.

It was a storm—a wind that would pierce like a thousand needles, burying all that she had worked for.

A voice slithered to her through the rising rasp of sand on stone.

Want, it hissed.

The maelstrom flooded across the sky, cloaking the sun. The golden light shifted to a red like blood.

Soon, the dust whispered.

Ellie's stepmother Florence was making a racket again.

The sharp, invasive chatter tore painfully through her veil of sleep. Ellie winced, squeezing her eyes shut in protest. She reached for her blanket to pull it over her head... and grasped the front of her shirt.

Her hands moved lower and found trousers.

Ellie sat up, opening her eyes. The sudden movement toppled her from the hammock.

She landed on the deck of the *Mary Lee*.

"Drat," she muttered, wincing against the impact.

Ellie glanced up at the other hammock and was relieved to find it empty. She could only imagine the look on Bates's face if he had witnessed her throwing herself to the ground.

She climbed to her feet, aching from both her impact on the deck and the unaccustomed angles of sleeping in a canvas sling.

A chorus of parrots squawked at her from the branches overhead. Ellie shot them a rueful look as she deduced where the noise that had awoken her had originated.

"A little more sleep might have been nice," she commented aloud.

The parrots answered with a whistle and fluttered from the tree to swing up the river.

She had been dreaming of something wonderful... and awful. Ellie shook her head, trying to clear her thoughts. The last remaining wisps of the dream slipped away from her, leaving behind only a vague unease.

The *Mary Lee* was empty. Bates was nowhere to be seen. As there were no immediate signs of a jaguar attack, Ellie deduced that he must have gone ashore to forage for something to augment their breakfast.

Her shirt was filthy. Dust and grime smeared the sleeves. Her trousers were a bit better off, but Ellie doubted that she was in any fine fettle, herself. She hadn't so much as splashed water on her face in two days, and the last time she'd had a proper bath was...

Well—a good while before the moment when Adam Bates had kicked through the door to the washroom.

It had been long enough, anyway.

The water of the river looked cool and inviting, especially as the heat of the day was already beginning to rise.

Ellie wondered just how far away her traveling companion had gone.

"Mr. Bates!" she shouted, projecting the call out over the shoreline. "Hellooooo!"

Her voice echoed off the far bank and inspired a renewed racket from the parrots. There was no response from the man himself. It seemed that, for now, Ellie was on her own.

She made a quick scan of the water for any suspicious logs that might turn out to be crocodiles. Satisfied, Ellie tugged off her filthy shirt and trousers, then unlaced the soft pad of her flexible corset. Stripped to her cotton combinations, she grabbed her dirty clothes, swung onto the rail of the boat, and hopped over the side into the water with a splash.

The level of the river rose to the middle of her chest. Her feet sank into the mud of the bottom. Ellie let them squelch there while she squeezed and rubbed at her corset, shirt, and trousers, cleaning them as vigorously as she could in the absence of a bar of laundry soap. She slung the garments back up over the rail, managing to get them there with a little hop and a careful toss. The deck of the *Mary Lee* was nearly level with where her head rose from the water, but the rails rose another three feet above that.

With her laundry taken care of, Ellie pulled the pins from her hair, tossed them onto the deck, and dunked herself below the surface. She gave her scalp a good scrub and took care of the necessary ablutions on the other key areas of her body.

She had reached a satisfactory state of cleanliness, but the water felt too delicious to give up. The temperature was perfect, and the current mild enough that it barely seemed to tug at her, particularly in the sheltered eddy where Bates had tied up their craft.

Ellie kicked loose the mud from her feet and decided to indulge. She laid herself back against the surface with her arms out, going into a float.

The pull of the water turned her lazily. Suspended in perfect comfort, she gazed up at the immense trees rustling overhead. Small, quick birds darted between the branches, chirping softly. Sunlight filtered down through the dancing leaves and sparkled across the surface of the river.

Where would she be now if she hadn't stumbled across that map? Probably staring out her window in Canonbury at the dreary gray skies of London. The thought was surreal.

Ellie closed her eyes as she kicked mildly against the pull of the water and let herself fall completely into the delicious sense of having escaped something dreadful.

A thud sounded against the boards of the deck. A shadow fell across the place where she floated as something came between her and the warmth of the morning sun.

"Sorry I disappeared on…"

Bates's voice trailed off.

Ellie's eyes snapped open.

He stood above her on the *Mary Lee*, gazing stupidly down at where she floated in the water in her eminently practical, currently waterlogged, and most likely all-but-transparent underthings.

Ellie snapped her head up and sank into the water until it was lapping at her chin.

"Turn around!" she ordered.

Bates blinked at her dumbly from above as though words were taking longer than usual to penetrate his brain.

"*Turn. Around!*" Ellie repeated, giving the words an additional threatening emphasis.

Bates spun neatly on his heel and put his back to her.

"I heard you shout for me," he offered awkwardly.

"I was *trying* to see how far away you were," Ellie retorted.

He turned his head just enough that she could make out his smirk.

"You weren't that specific," he noted.

To her horror, he came around lazily to face her again.

Ellie sank herself down a little lower until her nose was just shy of the surface.

"You know, now that I think about it, that looks like a pretty great idea," Bates drawled.

Ellie narrowed her eyes.

"You wouldn't *dare*..." she challenged.

But he had already kicked off his boots. Bates backed up to the far side of the deck, and with a running start, he leapt over the rail.

He soared out over the river in an impressive arc and hit the surface with roughly the force of a boulder.

Ellie spluttered against the tidal wave, which forced her to slightly increase her height in the water.

Bates surfaced, shaking his head like a wet dog.

"Oh yeah," he said with obvious relish. "That feels great."

"You can't just *come in here* like that!" Ellie exclaimed.

"We're outside, Princess," Bates returned easily.

He was taller than her. With his feet in the muddy bottom of the river, the water came roughly to the bottom of his ribcage.

Ellie was able to make this measurement with greater accuracy as he promptly yanked his shirt over his head, exposing an alarming and entirely indecent expanse of chiseled male flesh.

The move was so shocking, Ellie nearly sank.

Bates gave the garment a peremptory shake in the water—clearly constituting his notion of a wash—and tossed it back onto the deck of the boat in a wadded-up ball.

All of him was tanned—the broad line of his shoulders, the rigid planes of his chest, the well-muscled curve of his arms.

The man must not generally bother with a shirt. Restraining himself to merely rolling up his sleeves since they had left town must have been a concession to Ellie's feminine sensibilities.

Sensibilities that he had clearly decided to blow to tiny pieces this morning.

Bates flopped into the water with another splash. He drifted into a lazy backstroke as though their situation did not disconcert him in the least.

"I was in the middle of a bath." Ellie iced her voice with disapproval. "Not that it bloody well stopped you *last* time."

"Trust me, Princess," he called over to her. "If I don't find a place to rinse off every couple of days, I start to offend myself. You'll be glad I did this."

Ellie absorbed this explanation and found it all too horribly plausible.

She pulled herself over to the boat, more than ready to get back into her clothes and out of this mortifying situation… and realized that she hadn't the foggiest idea how to get back on board. The *Mary Lee* had a relatively shallow draft, but the top of the rail was just above her reach.

If she swam around to the far side, she could scale the roots protruding from the clay bank and hop into the boat from there. She'd probably get a bit muddied again in the process, but that was nothing she couldn't fix with a scoop of water—and at least Bates wouldn't be treated to an intimate view of her backside as she managed it.

Ellie started to paddle that way, pushing against the bottom with her toes.

"I wouldn't do that if I were you," Bates called over.

"I am hardly going to climb up this way with *you* here," Ellie retorted.

"Water snakes like close spaces," he replied. "Between the boat and the bank is just the sort of spot you'd find one."

"I assure you, I'll be careful," she shot back coolly.

There was a slosh as Bates dropped from his backstroke and came upright in the water once more.

"They don't care how careful you are," he drawled as he moved closer.

She stumbled back from him a step, but he made no move toward her. Instead, he reached up, and with his longer arms and height, he easily grasped the rail. The muscles in his shoulders bunched as he hauled himself up and swung gracefully over the side.

His wet trousers clung to him mercilessly. Ellie stared with an unwelcome fascination—then dipped back down to chin-level in the water as he leaned over the side, extending his arm.

"Let me give you a lift," he said.

"I don't think that's a very good idea," Ellie quickly replied.

"What if I look away while I'm doing it?" Bates punctuated the offer with a slightly wicked grin.

"Swear it," Ellie shot back. "On that which is most sacred to you."

Bates set his hand to his chest. His face went solemn—except for the glint of mischief in his eyes.

"I swear it," he echoed. "On the bottle of very good rum I have hidden under the deck boards."

"You want me to trust you based on a bottle of spirits?" Ellie burst out.

"It's a really, *really* good bottle of rum," Bates returned gravely.

"You're a cad," she accused.

"A charming one," Bates agreed. "Intelligent. Moderately good looking."

"Oh, blast it anyway," Ellie muttered.

She raised her arms. He took hold of them near her shoulders, braced his leg against the rail, and with a single, mild grunt of effort, hauled her up out of the water.

Bates awkwardly shifted his grip to grasp her around the waist, plastering her to the rock solid mountain of his chest—and then stopped.

Ellie was flush against him with her legs still hanging on the other side of the rail. Only his grip around her torso kept her from tumbling back down again, but the hold left her crushed against a broad expanse of taut male flesh.

The sensation drove all semblance of rational thought from her brain and left her dangling there, speechless.

"You kinda gotta climb in from here," Bates admitted. His voice was just a little tight with exertion.

The curse Ellie bit out in response was not entirely in keeping with her refined character.

She scrambled to pull her legs over the rail as Bates staggered back a step. When she was once more upright on the deck, she pushed herself neatly out of his arms.

To his credit, he turned about the moment he released her, keeping his back to the stern as she snatched up her clothes.

Ellie pulled them on despite the fact that they were uncomfortably damp. Wearing a wet corset was still better than the alternative. She plucked at the folds of her blouse to adjust herself as best she could.

"There," she announced.

Something pale caught her eye near her still-bare feet. She recognized it as the wadded-up, sopping ball of Bates's shirt.

Ellie fought against the roiling feeling in her stomach. She picked up the shirt from the floor and tossed it in the general direction of the canopy.

Bates caught it. She heard him give the garment a squeeze, splattering droplets of water onto the deck. The fabric snapped as he shook it out. When he brushed past her—making her jump at the near contact—he had put the shirt back on again.

"Ready to throw ourselves into a big black hole?" he asked cheerfully.

"Sorry?" Ellie blurted.

"The cave, Princess," Bates replied with just a glint of mischief in his eyes.

"Indeed," she returned tightly.

After all, a tunnel into the unknown could hardly be more dangerous than the waters she had just narrowly escaped.

FIFTEEN

ADAM EYED THEIR options as they reached the fork in the river an hour later. The southern branch—the one he had navigated before—was broader. The tributary to the north—the one that Ellie's map said would lead to their *Black Pillar*, whatever the hell that was—flowed narrower and faster, channeled between high banks lined with lush foliage.

Adam cocked a challenging eyebrow at Ellie, who was perched primly in the bow.

"Still wanna wait to show me the rest of that map?" he prompted. "Remember, that cave's probably full of spiders. Might be I could find us a way around it."

"Stick to the plan, Mr. Bates," Ellie replied firmly.

"*If all the girls were bells in the tower,*" Adam sang cheerfully as he swung the rudder around. "*And I was a clapper I'd bang one each—*"

She gave an awkward cough. Adam grinned as they chugged into the narrower branch of the river.

The wilderness drifted past them, thick and tangled. The motion of the leaves dappled the sunlight as it sparkled against the water.

Ellie tossed aside her hat, apparently determining that it was shady enough not to require it. As Adam watched, she dipped a hand over the side, then smoothed her damp fingers over the back of her neck where the fine tendrils of her chestnut hair curled beneath the mess of her bun.

Adam's thoughts involuntarily flew back to earlier that morning—to the unexpected sight of her softly curved form suspended on the rippling water with her hair loose around her. Those plain-as-toast underthings of hers had left very little to the imagination.

Adam's imagination had charged on regardless. It wasn't one to shy away from a challenge.

He'd deliberately antagonized her with his cannonball off the deck, and maybe it hadn't been strictly necessary for him to strip off his shirt and toss it back onto the boat like a sopping wet missile. But he hadn't been kidding about needing a dip. Give him three or four days in the bush without a wash, and Adam wasn't sure he'd want to keep company with himself—never mind inflict that kind of stink on a woman.

Besides, he had to admit there was a certain kind of joy in getting her mouth to turn into that pretty little scowl.

He'd have to keep a careful watch on those impulses. If the woman was a widow, then she definitely wasn't the kind they wrote the racy songs about—and honestly, Adam had some doubts. In the extremity of the moment back in his room at the Rio Nuevo, it had made sense to buy her story and get them moving before that smooth-faced bastard who'd tied her up came poking around for another look. Now that they were out in the wild, he had no interest in adding *shameless debaucher of ladies* to his resume.

He had best play it safe—enticingly practical underthings aside. And that was what he would do. He would be the safest player that had ever played.

Just watch him.

After three more miles of winding water, the *Mary Lee* rounded a bend and faced the obstacle that lay in their path.

The hill rose up before them, draped in an impenetrable veil of green. The river disappeared into a black mouth at the base of it framed by tangles of falling vines.

Adam cut back on the throttle and lazily looped a line around the handle of the rudder before moving to join the woman at the bow.

Beyond the arch of the cave, the water disappeared, swallowed by a thick darkness.

"Looks a little tight, but I think we'll make it," he concluded.

"*Think* we'll make it?" Ellie echoed, slightly aghast.

"I'll take us in nice and slow," he replied as he moved back to the boiler.

"Are you sure there aren't any additional precautions that might be prudent?" she demanded.

Adam considered it.

"Now you mention it, there is something," he said. "Lemme just rig up the plank."

"Plank?" she said weakly as her eyes widened with alarm.

"It's great," Adam promised her. "You'll love it."

The preparations took only a few moments. First, Adam waded to shore to harvest a likely-looking sapling with his machete. After stripping it of all of its leaves and branches, he was left with a long, slender pole.

Next, he pried a loose board up from the deck of the *Mary Lee* and set it down on the bow rail.

"Hold that," he ordered.

Ellie just managed to catch the plank and keep it from toppling into the water as he walked away.

Adam kicked the toolbox by the boiler in its favorite spot. The lid flew open, just as it was supposed to. He pulled out a hammer and a handful of rusty nails.

"Why are we nailing this board to the bow?" Ellie demanded.

"So you've got something to sit on," he replied.

"You expect me to climb out onto this thing?" she protested.

"How else are you gonna sound our way forward?" he returned before popping the nails into his mouth.

Ellie eyed the chipped gray paint of the plank nervously.

"How old is this board?" she asked.

"Hoff ffould I ffhow?" Adam replied around the nails. He plucked one out and drove it into the rail with an easy thunk of the hammer.

"Are you sure it's entirely sturdy?" she pressed.

Adam drove in another nail and plucked the rest from his lips as he shot her a skeptical look.

"Exactly how much do you think you weigh?" he pushed back.

"I haven't the foggiest idea," she retorted, folding her arms crossly.

Adam eyed her critically.

"I give you a hundred and forty pounds, tops." He shoved the nails back in his mouth. "Bwoard ffhould holw you juss ffine."

Ellie watched him with an expression of muted horror as he knocked in a few more nails, then gave the plank a few rough pushes with his hands. The far end of it bounced a bit, but the near side stayed good and fixed, which was what really mattered.

"Aren't you going to test it properly?" she asked a bit desperately.

"What—do you want me to jump up and down on top of it?" Adam retorted, raising a skeptical eyebrow. "I'm a hell of a lot more than a hundred and forty pounds. I'd snap the damned thing in two. Just get on out there—don't worry about it. Oh, and take the stick."

He tossed the sapling to Ellie. She caught it awkwardly.

"What about crocodiles?" she demanded a little desperately, holding the tree like a weapon.

"You hardly ever see them this far from the coast," Adam assured her.

"Perhaps they will make an exception if I am dangling over the water like a piece of bait," she snapped.

"You wanna do this or not?" Exasperation crept into his tone.

Ellie's mouth firmed into an entirely dissatisfied line—but without further protest, she crawled out onto the board.

Now that Adam could see her out there, he had to admit that it did look a little dicey.

Ellie tried scooting out on the plank while sitting upright, but quickly decided that was less than stable. Instead, she lay flat along it with her elbows and knees on either side for balance.

"Keep the low end of that stick in the water and shout at me if it hits something," Adam instructed as he relit the oil lamp and hung it off the bow near to where she was suspended.

"I am familiar with the concept of a sounding pole," she bit back.

"Great. This should be a piece of cake, then."

Adam untied the line that anchored them to the bank. He set the throttle to a little more than a crawl and eased them forward, resting his hand on the control for the rudder.

The boat crept toward the mouth of the cave. Adam kept a careful eye on the stack of the boiler as they approached it, keenly estimating their clearance.

It was definitely going to be close.

The *Mary Lee* moved against a change in the flow of the current, shifting to the side. Adam neatly adjusted their course—and the tendrils of overhanging foliage brushed against the smoke-stained iron of the boiler as they passed inside.

Gloom settled in around them, turning the bright gold of morning to a dim twilight. The orange glow of the lantern illuminated the place where Ellie was suspended over the water with the sapling in her hand.

The dark, damply glistening walls of the passage were worn smooth almost to the ceiling. The space must fill completely with water at the height of the flood. The only rock formations Adam could see dangling down from above were either minuscule or truncated by the debris that must come flying through when the river was high.

Here and there, the glow of the lantern flickered across quick, shifting forms—the dart of a lizard, the skitter of a fist-sized cave spider.

Adam gave a little shudder at the sight of those. He'd been jibing Ellie about the spiders, but the truth was that the damned things had always spooked him a bit. Something about all those scritchy legs made his skin crawl.

He focused his gaze and worked to penetrate as much of the gloom before them as he could. Occasionally, breaks overhead allowed little spills of light to penetrate down to the water. Those areas were thick with growth. The river below them shifted from black to a startling turquoise.

Adam glanced up to see a log at least fourteen inches in diameter jammed into a crevice of the ceiling. He was uncomfortably reminded of just how hazardous this waterway would become once the rains kicked in and the river rose.

As the slick walls of the cave slid past, Adam considered the wisdom of what they were doing. It was pretty damned close to the start of the rainy season. If he and Ellie didn't make it back through the tunnel before the rains began, they could very well be trapped on the other side. They'd be forced to abandon the boat and try to make their way overland across fifty miles of tropical forest and swamp.

That was not an enticing notion.

But what was the alternative? If they went back to town now—assuming he could convince the woman that was the right move—the guy from the veranda could still be waiting around for her.

Or they might run into him on their way.

If that was the case, it was entirely possible that Adam would have to kill him.

He'd never actually killed anybody before. He was perfectly comfortable with handing out a good, old-fashioned pummeling or two—but outright bloody murder would be a new line for him, and he wasn't all that sure he wanted to cross it.

Of course, he could just demand Ellie get over it and show him the rest of her map. This whole expedition could get a lot simpler if Adam was able to recognize even one of the landmarks on there. Surely by now, she should've realized he wasn't *that* untrustworthy. He was kind of an open book. Not too complicated.

Adam thought of their conversation the night before—of the tight, sharp look of hurt that had come over her when he stupidly let slip that he'd dropped out of Cambridge in what more or less amounted to a temper tantrum.

Ellie would've been going up against the worst sort of idiots from the moment she tried to do something other than sit at home with her embroidery. Adam had seen enough of the world to know how that worked. Heck, he'd even been on the receiving end of it at Cambridge when some of the high-and-mighty types there briefly took it in mind to try to get one over on the new-money Yank. It had been *briefly* because Adam had picked up the worst offender and tossed him ass-over-teakettle into the River Cam.

The Viscount of Whatever-the-Hell had come up with a nice glop of pond weed on his overly pomaded hair, and his crowd had mostly steered clear of Adam after that.

His traveling companion had probably spent most of her life being told what to do by blokes who were half as smart as she was, and she wouldn't have had the luxury of knocking her persecutors into the drink.

Adam found that he didn't really want to be added to the list of men who assumed they knew better than she did. He'd let her keep her map until she was good and ready to share it. What did it matter if it cost them a few extra days? This whole thing was a lark anyway, weird trinkets and shady characters aside. That map was almost certainly just some long-dead pirate's idea of a joke.

It probably had a big old X at the end of it.

"Stop!" Ellie cried from the plank. "Stop the boat now!"

With a quick jolt of fear, Adam threw the throttle into reverse. The engine protested at the quick change. The screw pulled against the *Mary Lee's* momentum but managed to bring them to a relative halt.

Ellie scooted back along her board, tossing the sapling into the boat and plucking the lantern from where it hung. With an air of intense, focused distraction—and a distinct lack of self-preservation—she leaned out over the water with the lamp raised before her.

"Are you trying to end up in the drink?" Adam demanded, slightly alarmed.

"Go back." Ellie waved at him without taking her eyes from the darkness before her. "About twelve feet."

Frowning, Adam eased the boat in reverse. He hoped distantly that he wasn't about to ram the rudder into some underwater obstruction they were lucky enough to miss on the way in.

"Here—right here!" she ordered. "Move in closer to the wall."

"Sure," Adam agreed with just a hint of irritation. "Why not?"

He switched the direction of the screw again and took them carefully forward, nosing the Mary Lee closer to the dark, shining surface of the cave wall.

What he saw there made him start with surprise.

"Hey—there's an opening!" he exclaimed.

"Of course there is!" Ellie returned. "What do you think I've been looking at?"

The narrow crack in the wall of the cave would have been easy to miss. A dark ribbon of water ran into it. The mixed currents made little whirlpool eddies on the surface.

Ellie climbed to her feet, balancing her boots on the plank. She raised the lantern up over her head and strained as though trying to make herself taller.

She was definitely going to end up in the drink.

"There!" she announced triumphantly.

She pointed at a curve of stone near the roof of the cave. Adam squinted at it, curiosity overcoming caution as he moved the boat even closer.

Three divots marred the otherwise smooth surface of the rock—two side-by-side with a third below.

"It's a face," Ellie declared.

"Is it?" Adam returned skeptically as he frowned up at the dots.

"Bates, this is clearly not natural. Look at the depth and the angles of the markings. They were chipped away using a harder material." Ellie gazed up at the rough, almost human visage that gaped out from the wall. Her voice was tight with excitement. "Someone has been here before!"

SIXTEEN

*E*LLIE HOPPED BACK down to the deck and waited in silence as Adam studied the markings above the tunnel. They were clearly man-made... weren't they? Admittedly, she was looking at them from four feet below—but when she shifted the position of her lamp, the hollows deepened, looking even more like a visage challenging them from the stone.

There had to be something worth investigating in the tunnel. The markings were clear evidence of site use, probably ritual in purpose. Why else would they be there?

Ellie itched with the need to investigate it.

Bates's expression wasn't promising. He eyed the divots a little grimly.

Ellie's heart sank a bit, but she rallied against it.

"I know it's risky to enter an unknown cave system without the proper equipment," she hurriedly offered. "At the very least, we should have ropes and chalk, and perhaps a climbing harness. I recognize that there wouldn't be any time for a legitimate survey of the interior—not if we're to reach our own destination before the rains arrive. When I say it all aloud, I can hear that it all sounds a bit foolish, but—"

"You wanna go anyway," Bates filled in quietly.

She did. She wanted to go terribly badly. The need was so intense that she had to take a breath to brace herself against it.

"It's only that I've never actually been so close to something like this before," she admitted.

Bates looked down at her. His expression was uncharacteristically serious.

"I just don't want you to be disappointed."

His words sounded a little bit like a warning... but they also weren't a refusal.

Ellie's hope sparked irresistibly, dancing around in her chest.

"I can assure you, I'm quite capable of moderating my expectations," she promised.

She waited, burning with impatience but holding her tongue, as she sensed that to press him further wouldn't help her cause.

He looked up at the face in the stones like an old acquaintance that he wasn't entirely happy to see.

"Hell with it," he concluded, then killed the throttle and jumped over the side of the boat.

Ellie pressed herself to the rail with a burst of alarm and leaned out after him.

"Mr. Bates!" she cried.

"Toss me the rope," he called back.

Ellie hefted the heavy coil and threw it over the side to where Bates stood chest deep in the black water. The *Mary Lee*, pushed by the current with her engine quietly idling, was already moving away from him.

Bates caught the rope, quickly wrapped it around his arm, and hauled back on it. The line went taut where it was still tied to the cleat at the bow. The boat halted and swung gently into the wall of the wave, bumping against it softly.

"What are you doing?" Ellie demanded.

"We're exploring, aren't we?" he replied. "I need someplace to tie us off."

Bates leaned back against the pull of the boat, bracing his feet against the riverbed.

"Don't you have an anchor?" she pressed.

"I *had* one," he retorted a little crossly. "I lost it."

"How does one lose an anchor?"

"There was this four-foot iguana, and a block of cheese, and—"

"Never mind," Ellie cut in, certain that she did not want to hear any more.

She climbed out onto the edge of the bow where Bates had nailed in her plank, and raised the lantern high.

"Pull us forward—just six yards or so," she ordered.

"Right," Bates grumbled. He turned to slide the rope over his shoulder and across his chest. "Surely you can manage hauling one measly little steamboat upstream in the dark for a while. Can't you, Mr. Bates?"

There was a distinct note of sarcasm to his words.

He dragged himself forward, gripping the wall of the cave with the hand that was not holding the rope in place. The current did not seem particularly strong, but he was still a single man, nearly submerged, trying to move an entire boat.

Ellie pushed herself out onto the plank.

"Would you like me to get in and help you?" she offered from above him.

He jumped as he glanced up at her.

"Jesus!" he exclaimed. "No—you're half a foot shorter than me. The water'd be up to your neck."

"A little more to the right," she ordered instead, pointing out over the water. "I believe you will find a boulder there that will serve."

The boulder was a truncated stalactite, which must have broken off in some other part of the cave and washed down when the water was higher. Bates managed to work the rope around it, then tied it off. The *Mary Lee* pulled taut against the line.

"There," Ellie said neatly as she sat back up on the plank. "That ought to hold us."

"As long as nothing comes floating along to punch a hole in the hull," Bates replied wryly. He extended his arm up toward her. "Gimmie the light."

"Why should you have it?" Ellie replied a little defensively as she handed it over to him.

"Because you're about to go for a swim," he replied and neatly tugged her off the plank.

She landed in the dark river with a splash. The water was colder than she had expected—significantly more so than the sunny bank where she had taken her dip earlier that morning. Bates easily yanked her back up to the surface.

He grinned at her as she spluttered—the utter cad.

"I was perfectly capable of getting into the water myself," Ellie protested darkly.

"Where's the fun in that?" he replied. "Come on."

Without waiting for a further reply, he pushed through the river toward the narrow opening of the tunnel.

The water rose to Ellie's chin, forcing her to use her arms to pull herself forward.

"Shouldn't we at least have taken off our boots?" she protested as she joined him under the arch that held the petroglyph.

"Not unless you wanna risk cutting your foot open," Bates replied. "Here—there's a step up and it gets a bit shallower."

He reached down to grip her arm and half-hauled her the rest of the way into the tunnel. Ellie scrambled up the wet, slippery slope and awkwardly regained her footing. The water now only came as high as her ribcage. The current had softened.

Bates stood close to her. Water dripped down his face from his soaked hair. The limited halo of the lamp cast an intimate circle of pale light around them.

"Are you ready for this?" His tone was oddly serious.

"Why wouldn't I be?" Ellie retorted.

"Never mind." He shook his head a bit grimly and led them on.

Black walls rose up to either side, glistening with moisture. The ground beneath Ellie's feet gradually shallowed until she was wading through water that sloshed at her thighs.

The space around her opened up into a larger cavern dominated by a still, silent pool. The glow of the lantern penetrated only so far, leaving the extent of the space cloaked in shadows. The water she stood in was achingly clear. Little eddies of crayfish darted around her boots and minnows wriggled as they investigated the cuffs of her borrowed trousers.

The lake was punctuated by the smooth pillars of stalagmites, some of which rose to meld with the ceiling roughly twenty feet overhead. To her left, a rippling bridal veil of layered limestone descended almost all the way to the ground, the immense bulk of it impossibly suspended in the air.

The space looked like a fairy Atlantis emerging from the silent waters.

Ellie's breath rose with excitement.

"Which way should we go?" she asked.

Bates frowned as he examined the bed of the lake.

"How about we follow the breadcrumbs?" he replied.

"Breadcrumbs?" Ellie echoed, confused.

Bates pointed down through the water to where little flakes of some dark material rested on the sand under the surface. They formed a path that led toward the nearer shore.

Ellie dropped to a crouch for a better look.

"Are those... charcoal deposits?" she asked wonderingly.

"Pine torches, probably," Bates replied. "They flake off little pieces as they burn."

Alarm burst through her.

"Bates, we are standing on part of the archaeological record!" she burst out.

"How else do you propose we get around?" he replied, cocking an eyebrow at her as he strode forward. "Watch out for spiders."

He sounded as though the notion actually intimidated him.

Ellie hurried after him, doing her best to skirt around the trail of charcoal fragments without losing the lamplight he carried with him. They wove through the elegant pillars of stone.

One of the stalagmites caught Ellie's eye.

"Bates—look!" she exclaimed.

The stone pillar was identical to the others that rose from the water around it, save that its surface had been chipped with the form of a vaguely anthropomorphic figure.

"It's a stela. A very primitive one, but here—arms." Ellie pointed out the roughly hewn lines. "Feet. Torso. And there's the face," she finished, moving her finger up.

"Skull," Bates automatically corrected her.

"Sorry?" Ellie blinked at the simple assemblage of dots and lines.

"Eyes," he said. "Jawbone. Teeth. You see this guy all over the place."

"May I?" Ellie asked as she reached for the lantern.

He released it to her, and she moved closer, shifting the angle of the light to better reveal the rough shapes in the stone.

"Yes," she agreed thoughtfully. "I suppose it could be Schellhas's God A. Of course, the god appears in profile in the Mayan codices, and this figure is facing us." She raised the light to look around the still, haunted atmosphere of the cave. "Perhaps this was used as a ritual entrance to Xibalba, with the Death God serving as guardian."

"I suppose that makes sense," Bates agreed easily.

"Are you familiar with Mayan mythological literature?" Ellie asked hopefully.

It wasn't often she found someone with whom she could discuss Mayan mythological literature.

"Nope," he replied cheerfully.

"Oh," Ellie said a little sadly.

Bates glanced down at her from where they stood thigh-deep in the still, cool water.

"Why don't you tell me about it?" he prompted.

"I wouldn't want to bore you," Ellie returned carefully.

"Think I'm too thick to follow it, huh?" Adam replied, scratching the side of his head.

"What? No—it's not that at all!"

"I'm pretty sure I've actually got some Mayan mythological literature kicking around my room. I try to grab books on local history when I get a chance. I mean—I'm out here stumbling across the stuff all the time. Least I could do is have some idea of what it's all about. I've just never been a great one for reading."

His tone was casual, but he didn't look at her as he said it, squinting at the skull of the Death God instead.

"But you went to Cambridge!" Ellie protested.

"Never said I was particularly good at it." Bates flashed her a deliberately charming grin as he walked away from the pillar. Ellie hurried after him.

"Are you claiming that you made it through Cambridge without reading a book?" she pressed skeptically.

"Didn't say I didn't read *any* of them," Bates countered a little defensively. "I read books. I'm not illiterate. I just..." He sighed and looked away over the lake. "My buddy Fairfax—he can sit down for hours just tearing through pages. Doesn't even need to take a note. It's just all *there* in that weird head of his. I can't do that. I try to pick up a book, and after maybe five or six minutes, I'm thinking about something else—what they're gonna serve for dinner, or that my leg itches, or that I left a lamp lit somewhere. And I'm slow," he added pointedly. "So five minutes of reading doesn't get me very far."

"But you speak Latin," Ellie pressed.

She was having trouble wrapping her mind around it. Books were like breathing for her—an extension of her being. She hardly had to think about the fact that she was reading when she did it. The words melted into a stream of beautiful knowledge pouring into her mind.

"Sure," Bates agreed, pausing shin-deep in the pool to face her. "Spanish, too, and a fair bit of Kriol—though I don't usually speak it. My friend Charlie told me to leave the Kriol to the Creoles or I'd be making an ass of myself. But I can understand everything he's saying when he speaks it. I've even picked up a bit of Yucatec Mayan and a little Mopan. I've always had an ear for things. But you don't learn a language from reading books."

"Don't you?" Ellie countered, confused.

"How would you know what it sounds like?" Bates protested.

"I see," Ellie said carefully.

He laughed a little darkly.

"Look—I can't tell you what a Xibalba is, but I'll keep you from wandering into the wrong snake or eating something that leaves you heaving your brains out for the next forty-eight hours. I might be an oaf, but I'm a reasonably useful one. Afraid you're going to have to live with that. We're a little short on scholars around here."

Ellie had the uncomfortable feeling that she had unwittingly brushed up against one of Bates's soft spots. She was actually surprised to find that he had any. He had always seemed utterly confident in every situation she'd found him in.

There was nothing at all wrong with not being particularly good with books—as foreign as that might be to Ellie. She was grateful that Bates was who he was. She didn't need a scholar nearly as much as she needed someone who understood how the bush worked.

She tried to think of a way to tell him as much, but everything that came into her head sounded a bit patronizing—and so she fell back on the safer topic of Mayan mythological literature.

"Xibalba is the Mayan underworld," she said as she caught up to his longer stride. "It's described as being the underground home of the gods of death, made up of a series of caves with deadly traps designed to separate the worthy from the unworthy."

"What kind of traps?"

Ellie worked to pull up memories of a book she had read five or six years ago on a whim.

"There's... some kind of trial in the council chamber of the gods," she recalled. "Then a cave of razors... a cave of ice. Jaguars. 'The House of Gloom,' which I believe is some sort of room of eternal darkness."

"Sounds fun," Bates concluded wryly.

"Xibalba is supposed to lie beneath the mythological city of Tulan. Tulan crops up in both the Popol Vuh and the Annals of the Cakchiquels—"

Bates stopped walking and gave her a look.

"Er... the mythologies of the K'iche' and Kaqchikel Maya, respectively," Ellie clarified. "As recorded by Spanish scholars in the seventeenth century."

"And Tulan?" he prompted as he sloshed his way out of the lake onto the shore.

"Capital of a mythological city-state that supposedly predates the Mayan civilization. It's described as a shining city of powerful kings where the various Mayan tribes came to gain wisdom, language, the ways of their religion... It was said to be the home of the Chay Abah, a magical scrying stone through which the initiated could receive the wisdom of the gods."

"Sounds a bit like your Smoking Mirror," Adam noted.

Ellie brightened.

"Yes—it does, doesn't it?" she agreed "I should have made that connection myself. I mean, really—of course it must be! The two objects—Chay Abah and Smoking Mirror—serve nearly identical ritual functions in their respective sources—"

"So Xibalba?" Adam cut in, likely looking to head off any further tangents about Mesoamerican religious iconography.

"Right," Ellie conceded. "You see, Tulan is also referred to as the City of Seven Caves—an obvious reference to Xibalba—and under that name, it also appears in the Aztec origin stories, which belong to an entirely different cultural and linguistic group. The convergence speaks to either a genuine common cultural ancestry or an interchange of myths and stories across both geographic and linguistic barriers and… well, it's all rather fascinating," she finished awkwardly and flashed him a smile as she resisted the temptation to delve into her personal theories about cultural transmission.

"So you think maybe the Maya here were trying to build themselves another Xibalba?" Adam offered, waving a hand to take in the vast interior of the cave.

"It is hard to say on the basis of one face petroglyph and a rudimentary stela, but the possibility is… intriguing," Ellie admitted.

As they stepped from the shallow water onto the shore, Ellie turned to glance back out over the elegant cathedral of the cave. The chamber was quiet and still with an air of timelessness about it that felt haunted.

"Yergh!" Bates cried, jumping back.

He stomped down violently with his boot, then repeated the action, grinding his sole for extra measure.

"What was that? A spider?" Ellie asked as she took an uneasy step back.

"Assassin bug," he reported, scraping his sole on the stone floor of the cave. "Definitely crunch those if you see them."

"Are they very terrible?" Ellie pressed.

"I suppose they're not too bad," Bates replied. "If you don't mind feeling like your legs are on fire for the next twenty-four hours."

The notion was somewhat alarming.

"What do they look like?" Ellie asked.

"Like…" Bates's voice trailed off as he raised his hand to point, only to realize there was nothing left to point at except a fat gray smudge on the floor of the cave. "Er, big gray bugs. Shall we?"

He led the way up the slope. His boots crunched on the stones.

"More breadcrumbs," he noted, pointing out a further trail of torch debris.

They followed it along the shore of the subterranean lake until Ellie came to an abrupt halt.

"Oh!" she exclaimed.

The wall ahead of them was marked by a painting executed in thick lines of dark charcoal and red ochre. Angled wings extended to either side of the dark figure. Black smears against the stone framed a snarling visage with pointed ears and enormous, dagger-like fangs.

"Oh hey," Bates said. "It's Bat Guy."

"Bat Guy?" Ellie echoed.

"I've seen him around, though usually when they draw him full size he's got this big pair of..." Bates's enthusiastic explanation trailed off. He glanced over at her awkwardly. "Well, he's definitely a Bat Guy and not a Bat Girl, is what I'm saying."

"I see," Ellie returned as she pinched the bridge of her nose. "Perhaps it's meant to represent Camazotz, one of the guardians of Xibalba that took the form of a giant bat."

She gave the painted monster a closer study. The thick lines of its expression were admittedly a little intimidating.

"Maybe he's guarding this tunnel," Bates suggested. He nodded to a narrow, shadowy gap beside the painting.

"Another tunnel?" Ellie shot back, unable to completely keep the excitement from her tone.

Bates flashed her a grin.

"Only if you insist," he offered.

Ellie crouched through the low opening. After that, the tunnel thinned to the point that she had to crawl after Bates, following the vague shape of his boots. His form blocked the majority of the lamplight as he carried it ahead of them.

They emerged into a slightly wider space, though the ceiling was still low enough that Ellie had to crouch to avoid hitting her head on it.

"Make it through okay?" Bates asked.

"Fine, thank you," Ellie assured him.

She brushed off her shirt, which was now muddy as well as damp.

A fragile film of rippled stone suddenly cracked beside her. It dropped to the ground and shattered.

"Fiddlesticks!" Ellie exclaimed as she stumbled back.

"Fiddlesticks?" Bates echoed incredulously—and then whirled at a sudden eruption of squeals and flapping wings coming from around the bend in the tunnel.

"Down!" he shouted, shoving Ellie to the ground and half-covering her with his body.

A storm of fist-sized black forms roiled out of the tunnel, screeching with alarm and whirling around the cavern like tiny missiles.

"Bats!" he called out, shouting to be heard over the din.

"I can see that!" Ellie retorted, flinching back as a few members of the disturbed colony swept closer.

She knew that bats were not objectively interested in humans. Somehow, the knowledge was less comforting when eighty or so of them were flailing around her head.

The stream of animals poured through the passage that she and Bates had just navigated. The colony moved as one undulating body of tiny claws and fluttering wings until at last the space around Ellie and Bates quieted.

"I believe you can remove yourself from me now," Ellie noted, still pressed to the floor by the bulk of Bates's body.

"Right," he agreed and rolled away from her.

He came to his feet, retrieving the lantern.

"At least we know they've already cleared out of whatever's next," he offered.

"Very comforting," Ellie agreed as she brushed a chunk of clay off the front of her shirt.

They picked their way along a steep, smooth slope that grew gradually higher and broader until they stepped through the entrance to another chamber.

The ceiling was high and lined with dripping rock formations. The floor formed a wide, smooth bowl. The lantern immediately revealed the whole extent of the chamber, which was roughly the size of Ellie's drawing room back in Canonbury.

What she saw there struck her dumb with horror.

The room was a disaster. The ground was covered in a trampled carpet of pottery fragments and other debris. Larger pieces of earthenware lay against the wall where they had been deliberately smashed.

Nor had this destruction taken place centuries before. As Ellie moved closer, she could discern mineral deposits on some of the pot fragments.

The broken edges, however, were clean.

More than broken artifacts lay in the mess. The shards were thickly intermingled with shattered fragments of bone.

A pair of skulls lolled a few feet from her boots. One of them was cracked almost in two.

The sight struck her with both horror and a feeling oddly like grief.

"What happened here?" Shock stripped Ellie's words raw.

"Looters," Bates replied flatly from behind her. He looked out over the room with an expression of grim resignation.

"But they've… they've simply *destroyed* all of it," Ellie protested in a strangled voice.

"Probably looking for amuletos," Bates said as he crouched down and carefully lifted up the curved edge of a skull fragment. "Jewels and trinkets interred with the dead. Jade panels. Masks, polychrome vessels. Anything portable they can hawk on the black market."

Ellie thought back to Bates's oddly solemn hesitance to enter the tunnel. "You *knew*," she accused. "You knew it would be like this."

"I knew it was a distinct possibility," he replied as he set the skull fragment down.

"Because you've seen it before," she filled in.

He met her gaze.

"Yeah."

The ruined remnants of over a hundred vessels were scattered across the floor. Ellie could vividly imagine what they might have looked like had she and Bates arrived here first—a carefully stacked pile of jars, their interiors still glossed with fragments of the offerings they had once held. She might even have discerned a faint whiff of incense or spotted dried kernels of maize. All of it would have been a loving tribute to the dead—to the people carefully interred in the heart of this virtual underworld in order to bring them closer to the gods.

Had the bodies been intact, Ellie could have carefully and respectfully sketched out the arrangements of the bones, noting any indications of the age and health of those who had been left there.

They might have learned *so much*.

Rage rose up in her like a wave, inextricably entwined with a terrible sense of helplessness.

"How often is it like this?" Ellie demanded.

"Most of the time," Bates flatly replied. "And if it's not, that doesn't last. I never know what I'm going to find when I make it back to a site—how much will have been defaced or carried off."

"But that's awful!" she burst out. "Surely someone must find a way to stop it!"

"Like who?" he retorted. "You think the guys at the top care about a bunch of bones? And I don't know that it'd be much better if they did. The only people who do excavations around here are rich types with the connections to pull government strings, and they're all just looking to add to their collections. Maybe if you're lucky, some of the stuff ends up in a museum somewhere on the other side of the world."

Bates's words were tight, sharp, and laced through with frustration.

"Museums are places of public learning," Ellie returned automatically, a bit shocked by the intensity of his response.

"Think Cedric Barrow is ever going to see one?" he pushed back. "Or Ximena and Diego Linares?" He gave a cold shrug. "Who knows? Maybe some of the stuff from right here will turn up in one of your museums. From what I've seen, they're not too particular about how the artifacts they show off in their fancy cases got there."

"You're angry," Ellie noted a bit numbly.

"Yeah—I guess maybe I am!" Bates's tone rose to nearly a yell. "I guess maybe it's occurred to me that if the museums weren't so happy to buy whatever trinkets turned up on offer without asking the right questions about where they came from, there wouldn't be so much of a market for looted antiquities. And maybe I wouldn't have to keep stumbling across places like *this!*"

He waved a hand sharply over the destruction that lay before them, and then caught himself, dropping his arm back to his side. He sat down on the floor at the edge of the sprawl of debris.

"Sorry," he said tiredly. "I'm making an ass of myself."

Ellie knelt down beside him.

"No," she said quietly. "You aren't."

He let his head fall back against the wall.

"I just... think it might be my fault," he confessed.

"*Your* fault?" Ellie echoed with shock.

He turned his head and met her gaze with a look as devastated as the broken pots at her feet.

"I make the maps," he helplessly replied.

Something inside Ellie's chest twisted tightly.

She looked out across the terrible destruction of the cavern. The discovery should have been a moment out of a dream—Ellie's first, real glimpse of the ancient past. She could have learned from what she held in her hands rather than just her endless piles of books.

Instead, all she could feel was loss.

"I stopped adding new sites to my surveys two years ago." Bates closed his eyes as he rested his head against the stones. "I record whatever I can on my own and file the notes back at the Rio Nuevo. I'm the colony surveyor and I'm *lying* about what's out there. And the worst part is, I'm not even sure it matters. *Everything* I do makes it easier for other people to get out into unexplored areas like this one... and everything I find still has a nasty habit of ending up like this."

Ellie had no idea what to say. There was nothing she *could* say—nothing that would put the broken bones back together again.

"Thanks," he said after a little while.

"But I haven't done anything," Ellie admitted awkwardly.

"You listened," he replied.

He pushed back to his feet and held out his hand.

"We should go back," he said.

"Right," she agreed neatly, summoning up her fortitude.

Ellie let him help her up. Once she was standing again, he released his grasp.

It left her feeling oddly like she had just lost something.

They made their way back out of the tunnel and waded once more into the crystalline waters of the lake. The cavern was still and silent around her, its stones glistening with a timeless aura—a false one. The cave wasn't timeless. The world outside had found its way in, and it had left a terrible mark.

Bates was quiet ahead of her as he led them unerringly back in the direction they had come.

As they passed the carved stalagmite they had seen earlier, a change in the angle of the light caught Ellie's eye.

"Hold on," she called out, raising a staying hand as she waded in for a closer look.

There was another carving on the stela. It had been carefully chipped into the opposite side of the stone from the roughly marked, skull-faced god of death.

The single mark took the form of a circle of swirling lines.

The light grew as Bates joined her by the stone, carrying the lantern.

"Hey," he noted a bit uneasily. "Isn't that your lollipop?"

Ellie gazed at the symbol, momentarily quieted by surprise. Slowly, she drew the medallion out from where it hung inside her blouse and brought it into the glow of the lantern. She turned it over, revealing the single glyph that marked the back.

"Smoke," she said a little numbly as her eyes rose from the disk to the roughly carved sigil on the stone. "It looks like smoke."

Bates scratched his head as he eyed the glyph.

"I still say lollipop," he concluded.

"But why is it here?" Ellie pressed.

"I told you I'd seen it around before," Bates pointed out.

"But why *here*?" she repeated stubbornly. "Why in a manufactured Xibalba on the back of the god of death?"

"Maybe he's got a sweet tooth," Bates offered.

"Smoke," she asserted firmly.

"Lollipop," Bates countered, mustering a flash of his usual cheerfulness. "Now how about we go find your magic pillar?"

SEVENTEEN

*A*DAM TOSSED A COMPASS at Ellie as the *Mary Lee* puttered from the gloom of the cave.

"Here," he said.

The instrument was housed in a scratched and battered case of gold. Ellie found an engraving inside when she popped open the lid.

To A—May you always know your path. GB

George Bates. Ellie remembered Adam mentioning his father's name. The case was dented with a bit of rust starting to show on the hinges.

The landscape continued to rise around them. The water narrowed as the territory became more obviously mountainous. The thick, green foliage of the banks began to blur as Ellie's eyes flickered from the shadows between the thick-trunked trees to the instrument in her hand while she searched for the next landmark on the map—*a Black Pillar that Draws the Compass.*

Their progress upriver was slower than the day before. The current that pushed against them grew stronger as they moved higher into the mountains, forcing the engine to work harder. Going too fast might also mean missing an all-important flicker of the compass's needle.

By the time evening began to settle in, Ellie was ready to drop.

Bates tied the boat to the bank. The *Mary Lee* immediately began to tug at her makeshift anchor against the force of the stream. The forest around them had changed from the world of the night before. New birds darted overhead and stranger rustles disturbed the underbrush.

"How can I be this tired?" Ellie protested as Bates pulled more cans out of the hold. "All I did was sit in the bow."

"You were concentrating," Bates replied. She could hear the exhaustion in his voice as well. "That'll take more out of you than you realize."

"More beans?" she guessed tiredly as she eyed the cans.

"No idea. The cans aren't labeled. That's why I got them at a discount." He popped off the lid and gave the contents a sniff. "Beef," he concluded. He peeked into the next. "Tomato soup."

He considered them for a moment, then resignedly dumped the contents into the same pot and gave it a token stir.

Ellie dropped her gaze to the hedgehog-shaped rock on the small shelf by the boiler. She recalled how Bates had given it a tap when they had first boarded the steamer back in Belize Town.

"What *is* that stone for?" she asked.

"It's my lucky rock," Bates replied.

Ellie frowned. The rock was conspicuously ordinary.

"What makes it lucky?" she pressed.

"I didn't crack my head open on it," he returned easily.

"You may need to elaborate," she noted as she leaned back against the rail.

"Right after I started the job, I went out during the rainy season. Thought maybe folks were exaggerating how bad it was." Bates dropped down to the deck beside her. "The ground was saturated and gave way beneath me. I found myself riding a landslide. Just a little one, but even a little one can be bad. When I stopped, I was staring at that rock—which was sitting about an inch from my skull." He shrugged. "So now it's my lucky rock."

"How is it lucky, exactly?" Ellie wondered skeptically.

"As long as it's on the boat, we'll have smooth sailing," Bates asserted confidently.

"How on earth can you expect a *rock* to do that?"

Bates blinked at her uncomprehendingly.

"Because it's lucky," he replied as though the answer should have been obvious.

Ellie had no response to that. Instead, she looked to the peaks that shadowed the violet sky. They were much closer now than they had been the night before.

The air grew cooler and more delicate as the heat of the day broke into twilight, and the world of the *Mary Lee* narrowed to an intimate circle against the gloom.

The memory of her conversation with Bates in the ruined cave chamber earlier that day continued to tug at her. Now that the stillness of evening had replaced the exhausting focus of their work through the afternoon, Ellie thought she ought to say something more about it—but what? Anything that came into her exhausted mind seemed awkward and inadequate... nor was she at all certain that her attempts at consolation would be welcomed.

"Should we have found the *Black Pillar* by now?" she asked instead—and immediately feared how Bates would answer.

"It's hard to say." He let his head fall back to rest against the rail as his legs sprawled out in front of him. "The map's not to scale." He cast a meaningful glance over at her. "Though that might not matter if you let me see the rest of it."

His routine jibe about the map failed to spark the usual irritation. Instead, Ellie unbuttoned the top of her shirt.

Bates's gaze sharpened, but Ellie's thoughts were elsewhere—on the parchment she pulled out from the top of her corset.

His expression shifted from taut focus to a look of dismay.

"Aw hell—were you wearing that when I pulled you into the river?" he moaned.

"It's iron gall ink on parchment, as is typical for the period," Ellie replied calmly. "You can tell by the surface etching and light oxidation. Iron gall ink on parchment is more or less waterproof."

Ellie unfolded the still-damp page and laid it down in front of Bates... and a dark, irresistible laugh rose up from low in his chest.

"What's so funny?" Ellie demanded, her defenses prickling.

"It's got an X on it," he pointed out.

She gritted her teeth.

"The fading of the ink and the quality of the parchment are clear indicators that the age of the document is genuine," she rattled off authoritatively. "You have seen for yourself that it is an accurate representation of the colony, even if not to scale, and the use of Ecclesiastical Latin is appropriate for purported authorship by a Spanish monk in the mid-seventeenth century."

"Great, big ole' X," Bates continued, barely stifling a snort. "X marks the spot."

Ellie fought a wave of both anger and a hot mortification.

"Are you quite done?" she prompted thinly.

Bates coughed back whatever remaining laughter was in his chest and rose to collect his own maps. He spread the lot of them out across the deck and bent over them with concentration.

Ellie went to the stove while he worked. The contents of the pot were already hot. She filled a pair of bowls and rinsed the pan in the river as she'd seen Bates do the day before.

She set his bowl down beside him. Uncharacteristically, he ignored it.

Ellie dug into her own dinner while she waited. Bates's haphazard combination of tinned beef and tomatoes was surprisingly palatable.

"We went the wrong way," Bates announced as he leaned back and picked up his bowl.

Ellie stopped with her spoon halfway to her mouth.

"What?" she blurted.

"See this?" Bates tapped a spot on Ellie's half of the map that lay a little beyond the *Black Pillar* where a few rippled lines had been carefully inked beside the label for one of the other landmarks—*Arch Hollowed by the Hand of God*. "Pretty sure those are cataracts."

Ellie leaned over for a better look, careful to keep her bowl aside so that she wouldn't drip tomatoes onto the precious documents.

"I suppose they could be," she agreed a little uncomfortably.

Bates took a bite of his dinner. His eyebrows went up appreciatively at the flavor. He slurped down another mouthful before pushing the old maps carefully aside and tapping the newer one beneath them.

"And what do you see here?" he probed.

Ellie frowned at the blue line he indicated. The narrower band of it wriggled across the landscape to join up with a far more substantial watercourse—one that ran directly into the center of Belize Town.

"Which—ah—river is that?" she asked, even as her heart sank.

"That's the Belize," Bates replied.

"The river that runs right through the capital?" Ellie's voice came out with just a hint of an awkward squeak.

"Uh-huh." He rapped his finger against the rogue bit of blue ink. "And *this* is a new tributary that a pair of logging scouts reported to me last year. They said this whole section was taken up with rapids."

Ellie pulled both halves of the older map closer and studied them as Bates blithely shoveled more of the soup into his face.

She sat back and looked down at the papers with dismay.

"We went the wrong way," she admitted numbly.

"Sure did," he agreed.

"We should have gone directly up the Belize and looked for the arch. It would have cut..."

"A solid day off the ride," Bates filled in around a mouthful of beef and tomatoes. "And probably two or three days' of trekking through the bush."

Ellie closed her eyes and fought the need to curse.

"Should we go back?" she asked.

"Not at this point," he replied. She heard him carefully fold up the maps.

"We're too far along now for it to be worth backtracking, but it does mean that we don't have to find your pillar to know where we're going. We'll follow the river up another ten miles or so—however far we can get at this time of the year—and then cut overland until we hit the tributary. But…"

He trailed off, and Ellie felt another little jolt of alarm.

"But what?" she prompted.

The look he gave her was unsettlingly sympathetic.

"If we don't find your *Black Pillar*, you might want to ask yourself whether it's worth it," he quietly noted.

"Worth it?" Ellie returned as her sense of dismay grew deeper.

"The location of that tributary on my map is approximate," he said. "I haven't surveyed it myself—I was just going off of what was reported back to me, which isn't always terribly reliable. If we head in the right direction, we'll eventually hit it or some other branch of the Belize… but there's no telling how long we'll have to hack our way through the bush to get there, or what we'll find when we do," he added warningly.

"You still think the map might be a hoax," she pressed. Her throat felt tight.

"I think there's a distinct possibility that even if there is an El Dorado at the end of your rainbow, we're gonna find it in the same state as that cave chamber this morning," Bates concluded bluntly.

His words struck Ellie like a blow.

She thought of the look in Bates's eyes as he had surveyed the devastation in the looted cavern.

Her White City might not be marked on Bates's map on the colony—but that didn't mean someone hadn't already found it and cleaned it out.

For an agonized moment, Ellie considered whether Bates might be right. Did she really want to chance facing that terrible disappointment on an even grander and more awful scale?

She thought of Bates's tense confession that he had stopped adding the new Mayan sites he discovered to his maps. It had shocked her, as documentation was such an essential part of her training—but she could understand what might have driven him to do it.

Ellie would *have* to report their find if it turned out that there really was a city behind that dratted X on the map. She could hardly keep such an important scientific discovery to herself.

Of course, when she did, it would become clear to Bates that she'd been lying to him all this time about her name.

Guilt burst over her at the thought. Thanks to Bates's annoying habit of referring to her as 'Princess,' Ellie had forgotten about her obnoxious alias.

Obviously, she needed to remedy that. Her traveling companion had more than proved that he deserved her trust. The reminder that she had engaged his assistance under false pretenses—and then maintained them long after she had any reasonable excuse for it—made her feel a little ill.

Her name. The truth about how she acquired the map. The teensy little fact that she was related to one of his best friends.

She would fix all of it, she determined firmly. Just… not tonight.

Ellie knew it was weakness, but they were both exhausted by the efforts of the day and the disappointment of discovering the looted cave. She'd find the right time to tell Bates the truth—soon, she promised herself.

Bates's voice startled her out of her reverie.

"Hey—you all right?"

"Yes, of course," Ellie replied quickly. "I am well aware of the various risks of hiking overland. I would still like to try, if you're willing to continue."

Their eyes locked. Ellie felt an unexpected tension build inside of her… and then Bates's gaze dropped to her collarbone.

Her currently exposed collarbone.

Buttons, Ellie thought with a distant alarm as she clamped her hand onto the front of her shirt, which she had neglected to do back up after removing the map.

"Hiking," Bates blurted, snapping his gaze away from her. "Love hiking. Sounds good to me. Best get some sleep."

"Right," Ellie agreed awkwardly. "An eminently wise suggestion."

She rapidly restored her buttons and climbed into her hammock.

"Good night, Mr. Bates," she said, resolutely directing her gaze at the canopy which hung overhead.

"Sweet dreams, Princess," Bates replied, staring up at the canvas from beside her.

EIGHTEEN

$\mathcal{E}$LLIE STOOD IN THE center of Hyde Park amid a sea of women gathered in droves of all ages. Cockney East Enders mingled with Scots, Jamaicans, South Asians and Irishwomen. They waited in noble stillness with their arms linked together.

A stuffy little man in a black suit climbed up to the podium. He cleared his throat and prepared to read from a thick piece of paper.

"Ahem," he began. "The vote on the question of whether the right to participate in elections should be extended to all ladies over the age of twenty-one has been counted. Members in favor: four hundred and eighty-nine. Members against: one hundred and eighty-one. The motion has passed. The franchise of the vote shall be extended to women at the next..."

The rest of his words were drowned out by the cheer that rose up from the crowd—a roar like an enormous tide sweeping over the shore. The women around Ellie jumped and screamed as they hugged one another with tears streaking down their faces.

A dawning comprehension washed over her like cool water. Ellie was consumed by the realization of all that the change would mean—of everything that it would transform.

Women constituted half the population of the nation. With the power of their votes, they could institutionalize fair employment practices. Secure property rights and protection from domestic abuse. Expand the right to divorce. Access safe and reliable forms of birth control.

They could transform Britain's policies in its colonial holdings, liberating countless thousands of other women who struggled, suffered, and fought across the full extent of the globe.

Someone was hugging Ellie, bouncing with happiness at her side. She heard laughter and the wild chatter of resurrected dreams.

The scene stuttered—and changed. Ellie smelled something that reminded her of the aftermath of a brushfire as smoke drifted through the air. The white linen shirtfronts and black silk lapels that surrounded her flashed with crimson splatters.

The world she knew jittered back into place. The stark red stains were gone. Someone passed around a flask of gin. Women flooded the stage to shake the hand of the gentleman at the podium until his dour face split into a grin.

The view contorted with another shuddering transformation. Heat burst over her with a ferocious crack. Pale bodies flew back, tossed like children's dolls.

Her sisters screamed with the savage joy of victory.

Ellie glanced down at the blood covering her hands.

"We've done it!" Constance exclaimed.

Ellie's friend grasped her arms. Constance's lovely face was bright with happiness as tears streaked down her cheeks. Her white lawn dress was spotless as new snow.

Behind her, a terrible smoke spiraled into the sky, stinking of scorched flesh.

Ellie blinked.

No—it was just a cloud, the whisper of an oncoming storm.

A woman stood in the space beyond Constance's shoulder, noticeably still amid the roiling of the crowd. Her figure was delicate, crowned with rich black hair over sun-blessed skin. Eyes like ancient wells gazed at Ellie steadily from above the ordinary gray lines of a proper English walking dress.

Ellie recognized those eyes, just as she recognized the ancient scar that marred the skin of the woman's cheek.

"This is a dream, isn't it?" Ellie called out.

Her sisters danced around her with their arms raised in celebration as ash rained down from the sky.

"This is more than that," the scarred woman replied in a voice like a fall of silk—or a rumble of distant thunder.

Then the world around Ellie exploded, blowing into a thousand scattered fragments.

Ellie woke to a clatter of dishes and bolted upright in her hammock. Bates flashed her an apologetic look as he opened another mystery can for breakfast.

As soon as they had finished eating, they set off once more along the river. Ellie glued herself to the compass as they steamed against the quick-moving current. She desperately hoped that she could find some indication of the presence of the *Black Pillar*, despite Bates's insistence that they could make their way along the path of the map regardless. If she could confirm that just one of the landmarks from the parchment was real, then she would be far more confident that this entire effort wasn't just a risky and terrible waste of time.

The landscape grew wilder. Steep foothills rose up around them, draped in rich, green growth. The boat's engine audibly struggled. Bates took more time to shovel in fuel as he wiped a line of sweat from his forehead.

He looked rough. His clothes and skin were stained with coal dust and mud, while his jaw was darkened by three-days' growth of beard.

Ellie doubted that she was faring much better.

Halfway through the morning, they reached the first set of rapids—a cluster of boulders protruding from the bed of the river. Bates navigated them carefully through the rocks, weaving the *Mary Lee* over the higher spills of water. He took the curves at a wild pace, but Ellie knew he couldn't afford to be more moderate. The steamboat had to overcome the current or else risk losing control of their course.

At one point, the boat swung ominously close to one of the stones. Ellie tensely awaited the inevitable crunch of collision, but Bates swept them past into open water.

A second run of cataracts hit shortly after lunch. They were even more quick and hazardous than the first. Bates's expression grew grimmer as he tightly gripped the rudder.

The *Mary Lee* twisted through a spin that sent Ellie's stomach and nerves into a lurch. Bates wheeled them into the turn and glided them along a spill of water that swirled around one of the larger boulders. The flow spat them out of the stretch of rapids as water splashed up over the place where Ellie clung to the bow.

Once they were through, Bates called to her over the rush of the current.

"We hit another one like that, we might want to think about whether it's worth risking," he said.

There was still no sign of the pillar.

By mid-afternoon, the heat of the day lay over them thickly despite the cool waters under their hull. Ellie wiped the sweat from the back of her neck as the boat rounded a bend... and the river had ended.

The cobalt road stopped abruptly at a thirty-foot cliff veiled by a cascading waterfall.

Disappointment washed over Ellie as she faced the rushing barrier. The steamboat clearly couldn't navigate past this. They had reached the end of the line—with still no sign of the landmark they sought.

The timbre of the engine changed as Bates eased back the throttle until they were barely chugging forward against the swirling current.

"That's it for the boat." He glanced over at the compass in her hand. "Anything?"

Ellie closed the dented golden case with a sharp click.

"It's possible I missed it," she offered numbly.

Bates looked down at her silently for an uncomfortable moment before he turned away to face the waterfall.

"Doesn't matter," he replied. "I can still get us there."

The flat tone of his words left Ellie uneasy. They felt incomplete, and Bates wasn't the type who kept his thoughts to himself.

"What aren't you saying?" she pressed uneasily.

His glance back at her contained a hint of dismay.

"I…" His shoulders sank as he gave in. "Look—this has been the easy part. Trekking through an uncharted stretch of bush on foot is a different bag of worms. We'll have to hunt and forage for whatever we're going to eat—probably not always successfully. Track down safe sources of water. Fix up a place to sleep where we won't find ourselves serving as bait halfway through the night. There are snakes out there that'll kill you if you step in the wrong spot, an absurd quantity of mosquitoes, carnivorous ants—"

"Carnivorous ants?" Ellie cut in, frowning. She did not recall reading about any of those in her natural history books. She wondered if she'd heard him right over the growing rush of the waterfall.

"If you spot them before you step on them, you can just go around, even if it means a detour of a mile or so," Bates continued. "It's only if you've waded into the damned caravan before you realize what's happening that things get hairy."

"How hairy, exactly?" Ellie prodded.

She had to pitch her voice louder to be heard over the rush of the waterfall. They were near enough to the cascade that the light mist cooled Ellie's skin. Little beads of it began to collect on the tips of Bates's hair.

Bates sighed tiredly.

"What I'm saying is—it's not just harder," he replied carefully. "It's risky. A lot more risky."

His eyes flashed with sympathy… and Ellie began to feel a deep, cold fear. "You think we should go back," she filled in numbly.

"I'm just trying to make sure you've got the whole picture," he returned, hedging his tone.

"But what do you think we should do?" she pressed.

Bates didn't answer right away. He looked out toward the shoreline. It was a beautiful, impenetrable wall of green where tangled thatch palms sprouted up beneath soaring trees dripping with vines.

She could not peer at what might lie beyond it. The interior was a mystery shrouded in dangerous life.

Ellie realized that she didn't need Bates to answer. His hesitation told her what he was thinking.

He wanted to go home. And why wouldn't he? He had come out here with her for a lark. They'd had their fun, but now things were going to get hard, and he was far from certain that anything worth finding waited for them at the end of the journey.

Ellie admitted the horrible truth—that she was far from certain of it herself.

They hadn't found the *Black Pillar that Draws the Compass*. She had always known the map and medallion could be a hoax. The fact that Bates had recognized one of the glyphs on it was promising, but anyone who had been poking around the territory centuries ago might have spotted something similar and copied it. The symbol didn't *prove* anything.

They were about to set out into the uncharted wild on the cusp of the dangerous rainy season based on nothing more than a whispered promise of an implausible legend. Was that really worth risking their lives over?

Of course, Bates must risk *his* life like this all of the time. Doing so was quite literally his job. Even if there was no lost city at the end of it all, an excursion like this still gave him more information he could fill in on his maps. So what was different this time?

She was. Ellie was the difference. Bates didn't want to go out into the bush because of *her*—because she was a liability.

And he was absolutely right.

The realization brought with it a wave of anger and shame. Ellie could rattle off the identifying symbols of Schellhas's gods, along with all the latest theories on Mesoamerican archaeology and history, but none of that would keep her alive in a hostile environment. Out here, she was just another piece of baggage Bates would have to cart through the wilderness.

No wonder he was hesitating. Why wouldn't he? It was a perfectly rational position for him to take.

It was also awful.

A terrible sense of frustration and helplessness washed over her. What would be left for her if they did go back to Belize Town?

Nothing but dragging herself back to London to try to gather up the tattered shreds of her old life. She had no job and no prospects—nothing but the wrenching choice between marriage and obscurity lay before her. She would be trapped. All her knowledge, her ambitions, and her dreams would be bottled up like wine left to spoil in the cellar.

Her face was wet. It must be the floating mist from the waterfall. It had nothing at all to do with the burning she felt at the corners of her eyes.

"Fine." Ellie bit out the word even as a piece of her wanted to shrivel up at the sound.

Bates stared down at her, the lines of his face uncharacteristically conflicted.

Water continued to spill down before them. The rush of it drowned out the perpetual rustle of the leaves and the chirps or croaks of any neighboring wildlife. It felt like silence even as it roared incessantly against Ellie's ears.

"Fight with me," Bates abruptly ordered.

Ellie looked up with surprise.

"What?" she blurted.

"Fight with me," he repeated, calling out the words over the relentless cascade. "Tell me why we should keep going."

"I... I'm not sure that we should," Ellie admitted, stammering out the reply.

"Wrong answer," Bates returned flatly.

"You said it was a bad idea!" she accused, rising from where she sat at the bow.

"What do I know about it?"

"A great deal more than I do!" she shot back as her frustration rose.

"Since when has that ever stopped you?" he tossed back.

Ellie's frustration quickly shifted to anger. She narrowed her eyes.

"Excuse me?" she seethed.

"You love telling men when they're wrong about things," Bates returned cheerfully.

"Only when it happens to be true!" she retorted.

Ellie's emotions were a thickening storm that made it hard for her to think clearly. Even through the maelstrom, she sensed that something was off. She didn't know Bates very well, but she felt as though he was deliberately baiting her. But why would he do that?

The roar of the waterfall seemed to be getting louder. The constant, unrelenting noise drove at her ears and made her head pound.

"Why limit yourself? Tell me I'm wrong right now," Bates replied—and then smirked at her. "Or are you admitting you can't hack it out there?"

Fury sparked to life inside of her, and Ellie's hands clenched into fists at her side.

"Unlike some of us, Mr. Bates, I am capable of acknowledging my limitations," she hissed.

"Now, see—that's what's holding you back," he called out easily as the water beaded on his skin.

"What is holding me back," Ellie shouted as she took a step toward him, "is an entire society built on the implied superiority of men! A society that refuses women any sense of agency or competence! What is *holding me back*," she continued as she drove a firm, pointy finger into his sternum, "is a legal and professional system designed to *systematically* exclude women in order to force them into lives of domestic slavery! I can't just walk away from whatever isn't working for me. I don't get to bounce into any job tacked up onto the postings board. I can't just *give up*, secure in the knowledge that there are a thousand other options out there for me. I can't afford to roll through my life like *nothing in it really matters!*"

The words spilled out of her like the water rushing over the cliff above—a seething mass of decades of pent-up, simmering frustration—and yet even as she felt them leave her lips, part of Ellie jolted back in horror at just how *personal* they had suddenly become.

Bates went quiet. That sense of prodding—of someone deliberately riling her up—was suddenly gone.

"You got me, Princess," he replied. "Just a big, dumb lug over here who can't take anything seriously."

His tone was bitter and hard-edged. It slapped up against the wall of Ellie's anger, which refused to entirely give way.

"I never said that," Ellie shot back thinly.

"Pretty sure you just did," he pointed out.

"I was talking about the system!"

The boat spun slowly against the current. The water misted around them as she faced him across a mere foot of the deck. The relentless crash of the falls was an assault against her brain.

"Are you going to make the call here, or what?" Bates snapped.

"Why does it have to be my call?" Ellie pleaded.

"You wanna be in charge, don't you?" he drawled. "Being in charge means *you* make the call."

"I never asked to be in charge!" Ellie returned sharply.

"You hid half the map from me," Bates pointed out.

"That's because I didn't trust you yet!"

"Ahh—I see," he said coldly. "I'm just here because you were *that* desperate for a way out."

"I was not desperate," Ellie countered.

"You were tied up with a psychopath chasing after you," he retorted.

Frustration and anger roiled inside of her, mingling with a colder streak of fear. The horrible tension of it finally burst and spilled out of her.

"You really want to know the truth?" she retorted. "Fine. Of course you weren't what I wanted! You kicked down a door and pushed me into a corner! You tracked me through the city and told me that what I was trying to do was stupid! You were the *absolute last person* I wanted to come out here with!"

Nothing but rushing water answered her.

All of it was true. Ellie recognized that, even as part of her stood back, horrified, at what had just burst from her mouth... but it wasn't *enough* of the truth. There was more, and it was desperately important—if she could just figure out how to pin it down inside of her and speak it into life.

"I'm sorry. I..." She trailed off, struggling. "That's not what I..."

"I get it," Bates replied shortly.

"No," she protested. "You don't understand..."

"I think that's kind of the point. Isn't it?"

Guilt and shame twisted up through the heart of her anger.

"Why did you start this?" she pleaded.

He shrugged. The line of his shoulders was tight and defensive.

"Just wanted to know whether we're turning around," he threw back.

Ellie's fury and dismay rose into a whirlwind.

"You... I... Arggggh!" she yelled.

There were no more words for it. All she could do was act.

She snatched the pan from where it hung on the canopy frame.

"Of all the infuriating—" She launched the pan out over the water.

"Hey!" Bates protested as he whirled back to her. "We needed that!"

She tore the coal shovel from the bin

"Self-important, aggravating things—"

The shovel sailed through the air and disappeared into the current with a tiny splash.

Bates's expression fell, his eyes widening.

"That could be a problem," he noted uncomfortably.

Ellie's hand grasped the gray hedgehog-shaped stone on the shelf by the boiler. A distant part of her mind recognized it as Bates's lucky rock.

"Wait—not that!" he cried.

He lunged for her and succeeded in hooking a wrist around her waist—but Ellie's arms were still free.

She chucked the rock over the side.

The water swallowed it.

Bates stared after it with an expression of blank horror.

Ellie pushed her way free of his hold and jabbed her finger at him.

"I will *not* be manipulated into reinforcing your own unjustified insecurities—"

"You threw my rock," Bates blurted, his eyes still on the water.

Ellie suppressed a growl of frustration.

"I am trying to explain—"

"This is bad," he continued numbly. "This is very, very bad."

"Would you leave off about the bloody rock already?" she burst out.

A thud sounded from above them, followed by a grinding roar. The texture of the spray abruptly changed, arcing much further out from the falls. The wash of it immediately drenched both of them, soaking Ellie to the bone.

She spluttered as she raised her head to look at the source of the water—and found herself staring up at the jagged, battered end of an enormous log.

It wavered at the brink of the cliff. The end of it tipped ever so slightly downward. The current sprayed up around it in misty rainbows.

Bates lurched for the controls. Ellie heard the engine fire back up. The deck shuddered under her boots as the screw whirled back into forward gear.

Above her, the angle of the log shifted... and Ellie realized what was coming next.

"Too late," she breathed—and sprinted for Bates.

She caught him around the waist, using the force of her momentum to shove them both to the deck beside the boiler.

She landed hard. Her shoulder slammed into the boards. Bates's weight pinned her arm—and then the *Mary Lee* leapt beneath her, jolting upwards as an impact like a thunder crack sounded behind them.

Bates instinctively clamped his arms around her shoulders. The deck plummeted, slamming back down into the water with another impact that bounced Ellie's skull against the wood.

"Are you all right?" Bates shouted against her ear.

"Yes!" she called back.

He hauled her upright and turned back to assess the damage. Ellie grasped the pole of the canopy, using it to steady herself as the boat spun, still rocking, away from the waterfall.

The wall at the stern had been crushed into splinters. Near the impact site, the boards of the deck were jolted and uneven.

Bates dropped to his stomach, scooting out over the edge and feeling down beneath it.

The impact of the log had snapped Ellie's anger and frustration. She was left with only a shivering, queasy unease as she watched him assess the damage.

"How bad is it?" she called over to him.

"Well, I don't think we're going to sink," he said. "Hull feels intact. Can't say the same about the propeller."

"What do you mean?" Ellie stumbled over to drop to her knees beside him. "What's happened to it?"

"It's not there anymore." Bates flopped himself back to rest against the remaining portion of the rail.

"Can you fix it?"

"Not unless you've got another prop stashed in that corset of yours," Bates quipped in reply.

Darts of panic leapt to life in Ellie's chest, rattling there like stray marbles.

"So what do we do?" she demanded.

"Float," Bates returned. "Presumably downriver. Until we stop."

Her heart sank as she looked over the shattered transom to the now peaceful waterfall.

"Well," she said numbly. "I suppose that settles our debate."

Bates flashed her a guilty and uncomfortable look.

He kicked out with his boot. One of the boards of the deck popped up in response. Reaching into another of his stashes, he pulled out a tin box, cracked it open, and removed a stick of desiccated meat.

"Tapir jerky?" he offered.

He held it out like a peace treaty.

"I'm... er... quite all right," Ellie replied awkwardly. "But thank you."

He snapped off a bite and chewed it with obvious effort.

"There's plenty here if you change your mind," he said.

"How long will it take for us to make it back like this?" Ellie asked.

"Maybe a week or two?" Bates guessed.

The *Mary Lee* had stopped spinning. The rudderless steamboat settled into a lazy drift down the river. Her bow was pointed back at the waterfall. The craft bobbed stern-first past rows of vine-draped trees.

Ellie looked out over the broken transom as Bates gnawed on more tapir.

Tapir, she thought numbly. *Tapirus bairdii. Herbivorous mammal distinguished by its extended, fleshy proboscis.*

The knowledge anchored her against a wavering, uncertain shock that threatened to swallow her.

They would float back to the mouth of the river for a long, mosquito-swarmed hike to town. If they ran into another boat along the way, perhaps they could get a tow… and then she and Bates would go their separate ways. He would return to his cigars on the veranda between his mud-soaked trudges through the swamp, and Ellie would go back to England… where she probably should have stayed all along.

She would keep the map from falling into Jacobs' hands one way or another. Just because her hopes had been smashed didn't mean she had to hand the parchment over to a batch of criminals. If she had no other options, she could simply burn it. Surely that was better than allowing looters to empty whatever lay at the end of it, leaving it as devastated as the cave from the day before.

The notion of the map's potential curling into ash and smoke made her stomach churn.

Ellie forced back the thought. She wouldn't face that possibility until she had to. Instead, she focused her attention on the shore, where thickly forested slopes were framed by peaks of gray stone.

A fork in the brown current of the river glided past. The two streams were broken by a jagged islet covered in spindly brush and ferns.

The sight unexpectedly jarred her.

"Bates?" she called out without turning back to look at him.

"What?" he returned through a mouthful of jerky.

"We're going the wrong way."

"The river only goes one way, Princess," he drawled from where he slouched against the rail.

"I mean that we've taken some sort of branch." Ellie pointed at the fork, which was now disappearing behind them. "We're not on the same river."

"They all end up at the ocean. Quit worrying about it and sit down," Bates replied.

Ellie dropped onto the remains of the shattered bench. The uneasy feeling lingered in her gut. The landscape around them tugged oddly through her perception of the tangled branches that lined the bank and the clouds that scudded thinly overhead.

She realized that the nagging concern was centered on the way the rushing water echoed back from in front of her.

"That's funny," she said distractedly.

"What is?" Bates replied.

"The waterfall," she clarified. "We're moving away from it, but it seems to be growing louder."

"Sounds travel in weird ways up here in the mountains," Bates returned lightly and popped the last bite of tapir into his mouth.

Ellie gazed over the rippling water in front of them. The branch they had inadvertently taken was narrow and quick. The steamboat bounced gently along the rush of it. The water frothed here and there at the surface with the strength of the current. The white caps on the ripples were more apparent a little further ahead of them where the trees lining the banks opened into a wider vista over a deep, thickly overgrown valley.

An instinctive dart of fear quickened Ellie's pulse.

"Bates?" she said as she jolted to her feet.

"You should lay back and take a nap," he returned easily. "We'll tie off and look for more grub whenever we bump into the bank."

"But something is wrong with the river," Ellie pressed back.

Bates reluctantly peeled himself from the deck and strolled over to her. "What could possibly be wrong with—" he began. "*Oh hell!*"

His eyes locked on the place a hundred yards ahead of them where the river disappeared into a low wall of mist. He grabbed Ellie's shoulder and swung her toward him roughly.

"*Waterfall!*" he shouted, pointing out over the water.

Ellie stared forward blankly, panic driving the thoughts from her head.

Bates sprang into action. He yanked the Winchester and his canteen and swung them across his shoulders. He snatched up the rucksack as well and skidded across the deck. Whipping his machete from his belt, he jammed the blade under another board and pried it up with a pop. He yanked out the map tin—and hesitated for a breath.

"Heck with it," he muttered.

He grabbed out an unlabeled bottle of dark golden liquid and tossed that in the stuffed bag as well.

"What did you just pack?" Ellie demanded.

"How well can you swim?" he shot back, ignoring the question as he threw on the rucksack.

"Tolerably well, I suppose," Ellie replied. "Though I haven't really—"

"Deep breath," Bates interrupted and yanked her over the rail.

Ellie plunged into cold, rushing water. The river swirled around her violently as the current swept her forward with terrifying speed. Only the anchor of Bates's grip on her arm kept her from being utterly disoriented by the maelstrom of it.

He hauled at her in a direction that she hoped was up. She broke the surface and gasped in a desperate breath. The force of the river shoved her forward as water splashed against her face.

Bates tugged at her. His hair was plastered to his scalp.

"There!" He waved a hand at the bank ahead of them. "Swim with the current. Don't fight it!"

Ellie forced her shocked limbs to move. Every instinct screamed for her to swim directly for land. With Bates's words fresh in her ear, she resisted, and instead let the river propel her forward as she pulled ferociously for the shore.

Her flailing hand brushed against a slick, protruding root. Ellie grasped it. The force of the water pressed her up against the wood.

Bates slammed into place beside her, hitting the extended roots of the tree with a thud. He hauled himself up and reached back to pull Ellie after him.

They fell against the leaf-strewn earth of the bank and lay there, breathless.

Ellie stared up at the flickering green leaves of the trees overhead. The rush of the water still sang in her ears. Slowly, she forced herself to stagger back to her feet and look out over the river.

The waterfall was just ahead of them. Through the cool, damp mist, Ellie could see just how far away the ground below it lay.

The drop was dizzying.

As she watched, the *Mary Lee* reached the edge, spun in a lazy half-circle—and then toppled over the brink.

A sickening crunch sounded from below.

She looked down at where Bates lay on the ground with his eyes still closed.

"That was my boat. Wasn't it?" he asked quietly.

"I'm afraid it was," Ellie replied.

She waited for his reaction, wondering whether it would be anger or dismay.

Bates laughed.

He sat up with the force of it, coughing, and pounded a hand to his chest.

The laugh was contagious. Ellie fought back a bubbling, wild hysteria—and then succumbed to it. Tears leaked from the corners of her eyes.

"How are we going to get back?" she demanded, forcing the words out through the spasms in her chest.

"I have absolutely no idea," Bates replied, wheezing.

Laugher consumed her in another helpless fit until she slumped down against the trunk of a nearby tree, sprawling her legs out in front of her.

"Are we going to die out here?" she asked mirthfully.

"Naw," Bates replied. "I've been in worse scrapes. We'll figure it out." He frowned. "Well. Maybe not *worse...*"

That threatened another outburst of hysteria.

"Come on," he said at last. He hopped to his feet and crossed over to her. "Let's see what we might be able to salvage..."

His voice trailed off. His eyes locked on the space beyond Ellie's tree. Ellie quickly rose and whirled with alarm as she wondered whether a jaguar was in the process of sneaking up on them.

She saw only the place where the river fell away and, far below it, the cloud of mist that covered the rocks where the *Mary Lee* had been smashed to splinters.

When she turned back to Bates, his skin was looking distinctly clammy.

"Is something the matter?" she demanded.

"Nope," he mumbled. "Just great."

"Did you hit your head in the current?" she pressed. "You look as though you might be showing signs of a concussion."

"Head's fine. Everything's fine," he numbly and unconvincingly assured her. "Just going to... sit on down here for a minute. Look at some trees."

He promptly dropped to the ground and flopped onto his back again.

Ellie stared down at him in surprise.

"Are you ill?" she demanded.

"No. Nope. Just great."

"Then why are you on the ground?" she pressed, exasperated—and an unexpected suspicion popped into her mind. "Bates—are you afraid of heights?"

"Nope. Not me," he returned thickly. "Not afraid at all. Just sensibly cautious." He paused and then blurted out the rest, still looking a bit green. "They might also make me feel like I'm gonna puke on my boots."

Ellie knelt down beside him.

"Perhaps we'll set up our camp a little further inland," she suggested.

"Great idea," he agreed. "Setting up. Gotta get ourselves organized before..."

His voice trailed off as his hand moved automatically down to the sheath of his machete—and then continued. He groped along the length of the blade as his features creased into a frown.

"Knife's gone a bit..." he started.

He lifted his head to gaze down across his torso. Ellie followed the direction of his look, and her own eyes widened with surprise.

The leather sheath danced away from his thigh, pulling out toward the dense foliage.

Bates poked at it curiously, shoving the blade back down an inch. As he removed his hand, it sprang back up again.

"That's awkward," he commented.

Ellie had already leapt to her feet. She pushed into the tangle of palms and vines.

Shoving aside a stand of ferns, she revealed a tall, glittering pillar of night-black stone.

Bates scrambled up beside her. He gazed at the monument in wordless surprise. He took the machete from his belt. Slowly, he extended the blade out before him, stopping an inch or so from the fierce visage of the figure carved into the surface of the black monument.

He let go.

The knife snapped across the remaining space and stuck to the stone with a clank.

"Well, Princess…" he said wonderingly. "It looks like you found your rock."

NINETEEN

$\mathscr{E}$LLIE RAN HER FINGERS over the carved surface of the monument. Suffused by amazement, she brushed a bit of moss off the stone.

The towering pillar was a stela—a rectangular block that had been set up to commemorate some lost ruler or great event.

The stela was dominated by the bas relief carving of a single, powerful figure—a man in the prime of life, draped in elaborate finery. He wore a headdress of jeweled feathers. His cape was carved with the spots of a jaguar pelt. A line of skulls danced at his feet.

The borders of the stone were covered with square symbols.

"Bates, some of these signs are identical to the ones on my medallion!" Ellie's skin danced with an electric sense of potential. "Do you realize what that means? On its own, the medallion might have been a clever hoax—but this? No one could possibly have come out here and forged *this*."

She moved closer to the stela. Her thoughts raced in time with the pounding of her heart.

"Look at this marking." Ellie pointed to an anthropomorphic glyph. "That's another deity related to God K. These carvings over here look similar to the dots and bars of the Mayan number system. And this..." She stopped, her fingers hovering over the surface of a polished black circle, which was framed by the hands of the king. "The Smoking Mirror, if I am not mistaken."

"Princess..." Bates began.

Ellie barely heard him. Her mind was spinning with the possibilities.

"The iconography and the language glyphs don't match up with Mayan or Aztec characters," she concluded firmly. "The symbolism here combines elements of *both* civilizations. It could belong to a descendant culture, of course—but then, why wouldn't the Spanish have heard about it? Either way, the implications are clear. This means… This is…"

Wonder choked off the flow of her words.

"Something new," she finally blurted.

Something new. The stela was clear evidence for the existence of a previously unknown Mesoamerican culture… and Ellie had the map to the heart of it tucked into her corset.

"Hand me my pencil," she ordered.

"Pretty sure it's my pencil," Adam countered lightly.

"And the notebook. I need to make a complete record of all this—" Ellie stopped. "The notebook! It was in the rucksack! It will have been soaked through. How am I going to document our finds if I don't have anything to write in?"

"We'll dry it out." Bates tugged her back from the monument. "But first, we need to set up camp. We've only got about three hours before dark, and we do not want to get caught out here unprepared when the sun sets."

Ellie bit back the curse that leapt to her lips. She cast one more longing look at the feathers and bones that punctuated the carving, enraptured by the conjunction of the elegant and the brutal. An unknown language whispered to her of as-yet-undreamed knowledge.

She tore her gaze away.

"What do we need to do?" she asked.

"*You* need to collect any dry wood you can find," Bates replied. "I'll do the rest."

"Surely, there is more that I might do in addition to picking up sticks," she insisted.

"Nope." Bates peeled his machete off the stela. "Get a whole lot of sticks. Pine is great. Don't touch anything with thorns. Keep your eye out for snakes—and ants. Great big lines of carnivorous ants."

"What am I supposed to do if I see one?" Ellie protested as he moved away.

"Walk the other way!" Bates called back to her.

Ellie did not see any snakes, or ants. She did disturb some sort of oversized brown rodent—it moved too quickly for her to identify it clearly—as well as a nest of hurrying little spiders.

Finding fuel turned out to be more of a challenge than she had thought. So many of the branches that she stumbled across were damp. She finally discovered that she could gather dryer wood if she managed to scramble up the trees a bit and kick loose any dead branches.

She also dragged a few yellowed, curling palm fronds to the fire pit that Bates had scraped out of the earth, deducing they might make for decent kindling.

Ellie was rapidly acquiring a greater appreciation for Bates's excessively large knife. The machete was a remarkably versatile tool. He used it to neatly whack down thin saplings, which he laid across the branches of two adjacent trees to form a platform safely suspended above the ground. He lashed these supports together with strips of shaggy bark that he peeled off another tree, and then layered a small mountain of palm fronds on top of it all.

Bates used the blade to trim a branch into a flexible wand that he fashioned into a trap by the river. The snare snapped to life an hour later with an enormous wriggling iguana suspended from it.

The machete also neatly dispatched the iguana.

"Do we have enough wood now?" Ellie demanded as Bates ignited a pile of dry grass and pine shavings with a match.

"Nope," he returned without looking at her. "Bring me big stuff now. Doesn't matter how wet."

Ellie dragged logs across the uneven ground. Sweat dripped down her face as she cursed and swatted at the annoying buzz of a mosquito. As she returned with the better part of a small tree, she saw Bates spear the gutted corpse of the lizard on a pointed stick with one practiced tug.

The sight made her feel a bit ill.

Bates glanced up at her as she dropped the log beside him... perhaps because she opted to do it rather closer than she had before.

"Have some water," he ordered. "And use this."

He pulled a small tin canister from the rucksack and tossed it at her.

"What is it?" Ellie opened the container and gave the jelly-like substance inside an experimental sniff. It smelled of herbs and citrus with bitter undertones.

"Rub it on any exposed skin," Bates said. "It'll help keep the bugs off."

Ellie scooped a little of the salve out with her fingers and rubbed it onto her neck and wrists.

"You need a break?" Bates asked.

"Certainly not," Ellie returned a bit defensively.

"Great." He drove the pole with the dead lizard into the earth by the fire. "Grab us another couple logs."

By the time Ellie dropped a final pile of slimy wood on the stack, Bates had finished constructing their shelter. It looked surprisingly sturdy and comfortable. He had added a simple frame of saplings to the platform. The mosquito net hung over it, covered with more palm fronds to keep off both the bugs and the damp.

The platform was not particularly large. Ellie would be sleeping quite close to Bates. Of course, the hammocks on the *Mary Lee* had hardly been much further apart. Ellie reminded herself that in practice, there had been nothing terribly indecent about that. Besides, they were in the back country now. Survival obviously took precedence over any silly social constraints.

Bates sat on a rock by the little blaze and gave the coals a stir. The skin of the spitted iguana had gone black and crackly.

He shoved a few more sticks into the earth around the fire. They were speared with chunks of a thick white vegetable.

"What are those?" Ellie asked as she plopped down beside him.

"Palm hearts," he replied.

He plucked the spit with the iguana from the ground and dropped the cooked lizard onto a pile of plantain leaves.

"Hot hot hot..." he cursed, shaking out his fingers.

The iguana tasted better than it had any right to. Ellie devoured it, along with the grilled palm hearts.

She had just drained the last mouthful of water from the canteen when she was struck by a terrible realization.

"We can't refill this from the river!" she blurted. "The water might not be safe."

"Nope," Bates agreed.

"And we have nothing in which to boil water," she pointed out urgently.

He raised an eyebrow at her.

"You really think I made it this far in my life without knowing how to find water out here?" he prompted. "I can get you some now, if you're thirsty. Or... you can help me drink this."

He reached into the rucksack and pulled out a bottle, which he gazed at with an appreciation that looked almost loving.

Ellie recognized it as the mysterious item that Bates had wasted precious seconds adding to his bag when their boat was about to plummet over a cliff.

"Please tell me that's medicinal," she commented flatly.

"It'll cure what ails you." Bates set the blade of his machete to the wax-covered cork. "Veni, Sancte Spiritus," he recited and neatly popped it loose.

"*Come, Holy Spirit?*" Ellie automatically translated, both impressed and slightly aghast. "Did you just apply the Pentecostal liturgy to your whiskey?"

"It's rum." Bates took an indulgent sniff at the top of the bottle. "The best rum in the world, and thank all Sanctis Spiritibus, it made it ashore in one piece."

"It's just 'spiritūs' in the accusative," Ellie replied automatically, using the longer 'u' to indicate the plural.

"Us, ūs, uī, um, u, ūs, uum, ibus, ūs, ibus." Bates cheerfully rattled off the Latin fourth declension, then lifted the bottle and took a generous swig. "Carpe diem."

"This is the rum you swore on," Ellie quickly deduced. "When you—ah…" She trailed off with a flush.

"Promised not to look at your underwear," Bates filled in cheerfully. "And I didn't, did I?"

He extended the bottle to her.

"Oh, I don't think so," Ellie quickly countered. "I don't partake in spirits."

Bates's expression grew serious.

"This is—beyond all doubt—the finest rum in the world," he pronounced solemnly. "For all I know, it may very well be the last bottle of it. I had it off a grandma in Jamaica who kept a still in her barn. Tried my damnedest to pry the technique out of her, but she swore she'd take it to the grave. She was ancient then—and that had to be six or seven years ago—so I'd be surprised if she's still bootlegging."

"You've had this bottle for *seven years?*" Ellie asked.

"Been saving it for a special occasion." He took another sip, obviously relishing the taste. His eyes closed with an expression of pure pleasure.

"You are drinking it now," Ellie pointed out. "This hardly seems like a special occasion."

"Sure it is." He raised the bottle in a salute. "To not being dead."

He took another sip as he leaned against the tree behind him.

"You should at least give it a taste," he urged. "Can't be any harm in that, can there? Unless you're one of those hellfire-and-damnation temperance types." He cracked a wary eye at her.

"I am not a *temperance type*," Ellie returned neatly. "I have simply never seen the appeal of spirits."

"Some spirits are terrible," Bates agreed. "And some spirits are sancte. This is the sancte-est of spirits."

Ellie eyed the bottle warily. The golden liquid inside of it shimmered in the firelight.

Dusk had settled thickly around them as the tropical forest dimmed into gloom. When Ellie looked back in the direction of the river, the pieces of the sky that she could see were streaked with purple and rose.

What harm could there be in one little taste?

Before Ellie could think better of it, she snapped out her hand for the bottle. She tipped it up to her lips and took a sip.

Her mouth flooded with gold. The liquor was all warm spice, caramel, vanilla, and fruit. It tasted like sunshine on Christmas morning.

"Dear God!" she exclaimed wonderingly.

"Gloria in excelsis Deo," Bates comfortably agreed. "Have another."

She shouldn't. Ellie was not a teetotaler, but she had always believed that spirits were generally best avoided. What could they offer, really, that a bracing cup of strong tea could not?

She was a hundred miles from civilization with a belly full of lizard. Ellie took another sip. It was most certainly not tea, and it was wonderful.

Reluctantly, she handed the bottle back. Bates took a swig of his own, and then planted the rum on the ground between them.

"How did you learn to do this?" Ellie asked.

"What—roast an iguana?" he replied.

"No. *All* of this," she countered, waving her hand around the camp. "I frankly wouldn't have known the first thing about how to keep us alive out here."

"Why the hell would you?" he returned easily.

Ellie tried not to be stung by his reply, but some part of her reaction must have shown on her face.

"I don't mean it like that," Bates quickly corrected. "I meant, this isn't stuff you *can* find in books. I had no idea what I was doing when I first got out here. I learned from other people who were nice enough to teach me how *not* to kill myself. Like Cedric Barrow, who you met back in town. Andy Gordon—he was a great guy. Passed away a couple years ago. I got some of my best tricks from Tadeas Chan, a K'iche' Maya grandpa who went on a couple excursions with me. A few things, I figured out on my own by doing something stupid and getting lucky enough not to die. Every now and then, I keep that fine tradition alive—like today, when I threw our boat over a waterfall."

"Your boat…" Ellie began with a pang of guilt. "Had you had it very long?"

"Pretty much since I got here," Bates replied.

"I'm terribly sorry it went over the waterfall." Ellie amended her words with a quick burst of guilt. "I mean that I am sorry that *my expedition* led to your boat going over the waterfall. You would not have been out here at all, if it weren't for me."

Bates watched her quietly as the firelight flickered across his features. He picked up the bottle of rum and handed it to her.

Ellie had another drink. This time, she didn't have to think about it quite so much.

"You didn't have to twist my arm too hard to get me out here, Princess," Bates noted.

"I landed on you whilst bound and gagged," Ellie retorted skeptically.

He chuckled lowly.

"Yup," he agreed. "You sure did. Dropped right out of the damned sky."

Ellie's mouth firmed as she struggled to hold back the bubbling urge to laugh at the absurdity of it.

Instead, the stifled impulse came out in the form of a snort. Horrified by it, she clamped her hand over her mouth.

At the sound, Bates let out a clear, happy bark of laughter.

"Gimmie back my bottle," he ordered, grinning at her.

Ellie realized that she was still clinging to the rum. She handed it over, and he took another generous swig.

"I would've been back out here on my own one way or another," Bates continued. "I *like* it out here. And it's always been a matter of sheer, blind luck that I avoided disaster to this point."

Ellie thought of how he had easily, confidently built their camp out of nothing but a machete and a piece of mosquito net.

"I don't think that is quite an accurate assessment, Mr. Bates," she said quietly.

"Adam," he corrected her. His eyes were a bit shadowy in the gloom that was deepening around them.

"Adam," Ellie tried carefully.

The name felt strange on her tongue… but not unpleasant. It reminded her of the taste of the rum.

He proffered the bottle. Ellie took another drink.

Her insides were beginning to feel nicely warm. The temperature had dropped with the falling of the sun, making the air around them more comfortable. The smoke and Bates's salve kept most of the bugs at bay.

Adam's salve, she corrected herself inwardly.

"And as it turns out, it's starting to look like there might actually be something to that treasure map of yours." Adam nodded back in the direction of the black pillar.

The monument was lost in the shadowed darkness. The visible world had shrunk to the circle cast by the orange glow of their fire. Beyond it, strange hoots and chirps rose to fill the silences between their words. Leaves rustled and insects buzzed as the dense tropical growth came to a darker, richer life.

The setting was both intimate and intimidating, though Ellie still felt reasonably safe here by the fire with Adam. She was a little surprised to realize that she trusted he would know if there was any real danger. He wouldn't have been comfortably sprawled out and drinking his rum if there was.

That feeling—*trust*—was quite foreign. The enormity of it made Ellie feel a bit solemn, even as the rum still danced in her veins.

"I know we… discussed this earlier," she said carefully. "But would it be a mistake for us to press forward? Now that we've more or less been shipwrecked."

"If anything, that makes a pretty good case for going forward," he countered.

"But all of your things went down with the boat!" Ellie protested.

He raised an eyebrow.

"Just how much do you think I cart with me into the bush, Princess?" he asked.

Ellie looked around their primitive campsite.

"More than this?" she awkwardly offered.

"I mean—a little," he admitted. "But not by *that* much. The more you have, the more you carry. If we were planning to camp out here and conduct a proper survey for the next four weeks, maybe I'd have brought some more gear along—but we'd still be sleeping rough. We're not exactly swimming in funds at the surveyor general's office. The guys who come out here with tents, cots, and afternoon sherry are privately funded, and they're looking for stuff they can make a whole lot of money off of. I've always been a man of relatively simple needs."

He punctuated the declaration with another sip of his rum and then passed her the bottle.

"That is an understatement," Ellie retorted before once more filling her mouth with the rich, golden taste of the rum.

She felt a little happily loose in her limbs. Her thoughts, too, ran easily—lightly dancing from one thing to another. Ellie was carried along in a current that smelled of spice and vanilla. Her attention skipped from the big, capable knife at Adam's belt to his hands, which were roughened from the work she now knew he did when out in the back country.

He was still talking. Ellie only half listened to it as her eyes settled on the way that the firelight flickered along the strong angle of his jaw.

"It makes more sense to try to cut our way overland to the Belize River," he said. "There'll be some traffic there even at this time of the year, where the Sibun's likely deserted for the next fifty miles. We could build a raft, if we had to, and try to float our way back—but I'd sure as hell rather catch a lift, if we can. And if we're heading that way anyway, what's an extra day or two detouring to check out this city of yours?" He took another swig.

"Why aren't you married?" Ellie asked.

Adam spat the rum into the fire. The flames roared up in response.

"Where the hell did that come from?" he spluttered.

In truth, the question had been the sort of rogue thought that Ellie would normally have judiciously kept to herself... as was the next one, which spilled out of her mouth just as easily as the first.

"I mean, you're reasonably good-looking..." she began.

Adam gaped at her, then snapped his mouth shut.

"You aren't indigent, despite your unorthodox lifestyle," Ellie continued. "You are well-educated, with good overall career prospects. You must be rapidly approaching thirty..."

"I'm twenty-seven," he said back. He pressed his fingers to the bridge of his nose, and then took another deliberate swig of rum.

Part of Ellie's brain watched the whole scene unfold with a sense of horrified embarrassment, but it seemed to be walled off from the neurons that were actually making her mouth move.

"Surely some woman has set her cap at you by now," she rambled, "and most men of your position would've at least been thinking of settling down. I hardly expect you've been remaining celibate—"

Adam choked.

"—but there are other features of a marriage which most men seem desirous of acquiring." Ellie's mouth firmed into a grimmer line. "After all, the relationship has been structured to accrue all the possible benefits to them at the expense of the women involved."

"You—ah—speaking from experience there?" he prompted tentatively.

Ellie recalled with a start that she was supposed to be masquerading as a widow. She was reminded—very uncomfortably— that she still wasn't being completely honest with him.

She needed to remedy that... and yet the thought of doing it now—of how it would so quickly and thoroughly shatter this quiet camaraderie by the fire—made her chest feel tight.

"Sorry," he went on without waiting for her answer. "I'm not looking to pry. But... to answer your question, since you *have* asked it—I am not married because I don't *want* to be married."

"But why not?" Ellie demanded, guiltily latching on to the change in subject.

"It just... wouldn't work out."

"I should think it would work out very nicely for *you*," she grumbled.

"No woman is going to want to put up with me running off into the wilderness for the better part of the year," Adam protested. "She might say she doesn't mind, but that wouldn't last. Couple kids come along, it'd change."

"Children," Ellie echoed darkly. The word sounded like a curse.

"You, ah... not fond of kids?" Adam offered carefully.

"Children," she asserted as she warmed to the topic, "are another weight added to the chains of marriage. They trap a woman in the most intolerable of circumstances, depriving her of any slim hope she might have had of intellectual freedom or achievement. Do you know that as soon as a woman even becomes engaged to be married, she is dismissed from the civil service? It's one thing to be removed because you were arrested—"

"Arrested?" Adam cut in as his eyes sharpened with interest.

Ellie clamped her mouth shut.

"Oh, no. No, you don't," he pressed, leaning forward. "You don't drop a juicy tidbit like that and get away without elaborating. Did you get yourself arrested for something, Princess?"

"I... may have... chained-myself-to-the-gates-of-Parliament," Ellie finished quickly and snatched the rum from his hand.

A low, rumbling chuckle rolled out of him.

"Do you have any idea," he offered darkly, "how much I would've paid to see that?"

Ellie shot him a glare.

"It was hardly the most edifying spectacle," she pointed out crossly.

"You telling me you regret it?" he prompted.

"Absolutely not!"

His grin widened devilishly.

"The police only held me for a few hours," Ellie finished thinly. "And they agreed not to press charges if I signed a statement promising good behavior in the future."

Adam cocked up an eyebrow.

"And you signed it?" he asked with obvious disbelief.

Ellie raised her chin defiantly.

"It is possible that I wrote down the name of the Right Honorable William Gladstone instead of my own," she admitted stoutly.

Adam burst out laughing.

"It's their own fault if they didn't bother to read it," she cut in scathingly over his hysterics. "Surely, the prime minister of a nation which continues to systematically oppress the rights of half its population is more in need of 'good behavior' than I am."

Adam shook his head. His eyes were watering with mirth as he looked up at her again.

"They really broke the mold with you, didn't they?" he said wonderingly.

At the affectionate humor in his words, Ellie's skin began to warm.

The sensation slipped along her limbs, tingling into her fingers and toes— then shifted, turning wilder and more electric. It buzzed through her as her attention sharpened on the details of the man before her.

The fine, joyful creases at the corners of his eyes. The lazy, powerful line of his shoulders.

Rum heated her veins. Her tongue still tasted of sweet vanilla fire. The firelight caressed his skin, dancing along the elegant angle of his stubble-roughened jaw.

Ellie's gaze locked onto the place where the curve of his well-muscled forearm was revealed by the rolled-up sleeve of his shirt. There was something deeply, wildly appealing about that forearm.

Her mouth was dry. She needed... she wanted...

She wanted.

The realization struck her with all the force of a blow to the head.

She wanted *him.*

Ellie was in the throes of a primitive, overwhelming, and undeniable lust.

Her mind burned with the possibilities. Recklessly disobedient brain cells sparked to life with the image of Adam's bare torso from after Ellie's disastrous swim by the *Mary Lee...* and then her wretched thoughts shifted to vividly imagining what it would feel like to trace her fingers over every delicious angle.

She wondered how the scruff on his face would feel scratching against her cheek... her lips...

Mortification rolled over her. Everything the temperance people said about drink was true. Here Ellie was, just partway through that bottle of liquid gold, and she had turned from a rational, modern woman into a savage beast.

If she climbed onto Adam's lap and kissed him right now, he would taste like more of that rum.

It was abominable. These were not the thoughts of a rational mind. Adam's *spiritus* was transforming her into an animal... and there was nothing to stop her from acting on her terrible impulses.

The realization set Ellie's heart pounding. She and Adam were alone in the back country, miles from even the most remote outpost of civilization. What happened between them here need never find its way back to Neil or her parents—to the rest of the world.

She could unleash her wildest desires without any fear of the social consequences.

Ellie leaned toward Adam, drawn like the needle on his compass. A lingering shred of her rational mind marveled at it wonderingly.

I'm going to do it. I'm going to put my hands on him—and I'm not going to stop.

Adam's expression shifted—first to curiosity, and then to something that radiated both surprise and a sudden heat.

The silence of the night was shattered by a roar.

The sound echoed through the trees, echoing eerily off the river nearby. A primitive instinct drove Ellie to her feet. Her pulse pounded as she looked around helplessly, but her eyes refused to penetrate the velvet darkness that surrounded them.

"Jaguar," Adam said as he rose gracefully beside her.

"Are we in danger?" Ellie demanded.

Her gaze flew to his belt, where his machete remained sheathed.

"No," he replied evenly. "It won't come near the fire."

"Right, then," Ellie announced awkwardly. "I suppose I should be getting to bed."

The word—*bed*—seemed to linger mercilessly in the air. It recalled, in painful detail, everything Ellie had been about to do before the jaguar had interrupted her.

Her face flushed. She hoped the ruddy firelight would disguise the change until she could make her escape.

"We do have a long day ahead of us tomorrow," she finished stiffly.

"Go on ahead," Adam replied. "I'm going to build up the fire a bit more."

Ellie nodded awkwardly, then pivoted and stalked quickly to the shelter. She crawled under the mosquito net. The thick bed of palm fronds rustled beneath her.

Over by the blaze, Adam easily tossed an enormous log onto the fire. The sparks whirled up around him, illuminating his figure in a way that sent another uncomfortable and unwelcome jolt through her.

Ellie lay down on the platform and deliberately put her back to him as she scooted as close to the far edge as she could.

She knew, in theory, that the strict standards of virtue imposed upon the women of England were yet another tool of oppression. Still, she had assumed that as a scholar and a suffragist, she could choose her own noble principles… and then *actually stick to them.*

Now, she knew that to be nothing but an illusion. All it had taken was a few sips of rum to send her moral fiber shrieking into the abyss. She had very nearly thrown herself at a man whom she had only known for a matter of days.

A few minutes later, Ellie felt the shelter shift with Adam's weight as he joined her. She kept carefully silent, curled up into a ball on her side of the platform. He didn't try to speak to her. He simply lay down beside her, decently arranged with his head at her feet. A reasonable few inches of space kept them separate.

Ellie didn't move. She barely breathed as that coiled, ravenous beast inside of her hissed its low demands until she was finally graced with oblivion.

TWENTY

$\mathcal{E}$LLIE MOVED BLINDLY through the trees, brushing through the smooth, damp leaves. Vines caught at her feet. She pushed past them as she coughed on the acrid taste of the smoke that filled the air.

Someone was crying nearby. The sound carried to her like a ghost through the still, hot air.

She ought to go find whoever it was. They needed help.

The leaves parted, and she stepped into the city.

It rose before her in gleaming white tiers and columns. The shapes were softened by the ever-present haze of the smoke.

A buzzing rose into her awareness. The hum came from somewhere nearby. Ellie turned to look for it—and realized that she was standing at the edge of a pit full of the dead.

The bodies that had not yet rotted displayed the terrible scars of a disease she knew through books and public health notices.

Ellie staggered back from the pile. She turned instead to the pale facade of an enormous pyramid. It loomed over an alabaster courtyard framed by rows of night-dark stelae.

Someone waited for her in the center of that open space. It was the small, scarred woman whom Ellie had dreamed of before.

The woman was dressed in a spectacular gown of feathers, which mingled bright hues of red, green, blue, gold, and black. The feathers rose behind her head, framing her noble face like the halo of a saint.

"Can you hear it?" she demanded. Her voice was rich and strong.

"Hear what?" Ellie replied.

"The voice of the god."

Ellie listened.

Silence pressed in around her, as thick as the humid air.

Something slid through it. It crept along the space between words, whispering with a hush like the murmur of a thousand long-dead dreams.

The hairs rose on the skin of Ellie's arms as an uncanny fear crawled through her.

"I don't think that's what God sounds like," she slowly replied.

The space around her shuddered. The pale ghosts of the palaces and temples lining the courtyard jolted and shivered behind the smoke, flickering like the flame of a candle on the verge of guttering.

Shadows twisted in the corners of Ellie's vision. The way they moved reminded her of the beating of black wings.

"It is waiting for you," the woman continued. "You must prepare yourself."

The color of her eyes spoke of earth and trees. Her slight figure was still and resolute.

"How?" Ellie asked.

It began to snow. Pale flakes spun gently down onto the courtyard, forming little drifts and eddies. A few of them landed on the woman's warm brown skin.

The skin burned, turning to red, and then a crackling black like the lizard Ellie had eaten the night before.

"Answer the question," the scarred woman said as the smoke curled up from her charred arms and her crown of feathers smoldered into flame.

"Which one?" Ellie demanded as terror tightened her voice.

The ash fell closer. Delicate flakes of it brushed against Ellie's hands, sparking bursts of scorching pain.

"*What do you want?*" the woman replied.

Ellie opened her mouth to scream.

She woke with a jolt.

Her guts immediately revolted against the precipitous movement. Ellie stumbled upright, almost falling from the platform, and then shoved her way out the mosquito netting. She lost the remnants of last night's lizard behind a fledgling palm as she leaned against the trunk for support.

Her head pounded in time with her own heartbeat as the horror of the dream receded, the pieces of it dissolving like smoke.

Ellie tried to cling to the details, but the remnants slipped away at another roil from her stomach.

She staggered out of the brush a few minutes later to find Adam crouched in front of the fire. More hearts of palm were staked there to grill, along with the carcass of a large catfish.

"Hey, you're up!" he called over cheerfully without looking at her. His eyes were still on the fire he was tending. "I was starting to think I'd have to shake you out of there. It's fish and palm hearts for breakfast. Not exactly eggs and bacon, but it'll get us going."

As the last wisps of the dream faded, Ellie was forced to acknowledge the obvious. The headache, the nausea, the awful dryness of her mouth… all of it clearly indicated that she was suffering from the legendary after-effects of an overindulgence in spirits.

Adam had consumed at least as much of the blasted stuff as she had. He appeared perfectly, infuriatingly fine.

He finally glanced up at her as she staggered over, and immediately winced.

"Why don't you sit down, Princess?" he suggested carefully.

"This is your fault," Ellie muttered thickly as she dropped herself onto a nearby log.

The movement made the pounding in her head intensify.

"Just hang on there a minute," Adam ordered.

He hopped to his feet with all his usual ease, and then plucked a large green orb from beside the fire. He hacked at it with his machete, pieces of husk flying into the air around him, until he finally chopped open the fibrous exterior.

"Drink," he ordered as he handed it to her.

"What is it?" Ellie asked blearily.

"A coconut?" he replied, eyeing her a little skeptically.

Ellie frowned at the big, heavy fruit in her hands.

"Why isn't it brown?" she demanded.

"Because it's fresh," Adam returned carefully.

"Yes." Ellie mustered an authoritative tone. "Of course. Just slipped my mind for a moment."

'Slipped my mind' felt like a better excuse for failing to recognize the obvious shape of a cocos nucifera drupe than *you have burned away half my brain with your demon drink.*

"Take that down while I cut you another," Adam said. "It'll help with… er, everything."

Ellie lifted the drupe to her lips and sipped.

She had tasted coconuts before, when Florence carried one of the brown, hairy things home from the exotic grocers in Islington. This was entirely different. The liquid that poured into Ellie's mouth was cool, sweet, and ever-so-slightly viscous.

"That's nice," she concluded and slumped back against the trunk of a nearby cohune palm.

Adam offered her another.

"You know, what'd really help with that hangover is taking the last couple swallows of the rum," he suggested.

"If you bring that bottle near me, I will beat you with it," Ellie calmly replied.

"More coconuts then," he concluded with a cheerful toss of his machete.

Adam set a slow, careful pace as they started out into the wilderness. Ellie wondered whether he did it based on the assumption that she wasn't capable of going faster, but soon came to appreciate why he'd chosen not to rush them. After a few hours of shoving through the underbrush and scrambling over rocks, her limbs began to ache.

The heat of the day thickened as the sun rose, even though the glow was barely visible through the thick canopy overhead.

Adam kept the machete in his hand. He used the enormous blade to push through brush or point out things that he instructed Ellie to avoid.

"Poisonous spikes," he said as he aimed the knife at a spiky-trunked tree. He swung it to another target. "Deadly frog. Definitely don't touch that."

"I wasn't planning on it," Ellie countered tiredly.

She half expected Adam to whack their way straight through the brush with his knife, but quickly realized the impracticality of that. Instead, he led them down the thin threads of game trails, and only wove them through the thick underbrush when the trails disappeared or veered off in the wrong direction.

He had taken back his compass, which had thankfully survived its plunge into the river. He checked it regularly as they walked, adjusting their course in order to keep them on track. The art of navigation seemed to come naturally to him.

Adam also introduced Ellie to water vines. He grinned like a schoolboy as he severed one with a neat chop and revealed how cool, fresh liquid dripped from inside. Ellie had enjoyed the decidedly strange experience of drinking from a hanging vertical straw.

The day was exhausting but largely without any dramatic incident, save for a brief run-in with an angry herd of javelinas.

Adam had managed to extricate them from *that* encounter without any major injuries... though the bit where they had nearly plummeted into a sinkhole had been admittedly nerve-wracking.

Ellie had a new appreciation for the threat posed by diminutive wild pigs. When there were eighty of them on one's tail, it didn't matter quite so much that the animals were only eighteen inches tall.

As the sun finally dipped toward the horizon, Ellie's muscles began to voice their protest in a loud chorus. She eyed the deeper angle of the light.

"Shouldn't we be stopping to set up camp soon?" she asked, recalling Adam's urgency the previous afternoon.

He flashed her an awkward look and rubbed a line of sweat from his face.

"Yeah," he admitted.

"Then why haven't we?"

"Because I'm deciding whether or not to make a gamble," he admitted.

Ellie narrowed her eyes skeptically.

"What sort of gamble, exactly?" she prompted.

"Smell that?" Adam asked.

Ellie took a surprised moment to tune into her nose—and caught at a distant, wafting note of smoke.

"Fire," she blurted. "It smells like fire."

"I'm pretty sure that's a milpa burn," Adam said. "It's the right time of year for it."

"You mean there's a Mayan farm nearby," Ellie filled in carefully.

Ellie recognized the word—*milpa*—as a term specific to the modern Mayan communities that peppered British Honduras, Guatemala, and Mexico.

"They use the fire to clear the forest for planting, then let the field go fallow and come around a few years later for another burn," Adam explained.

"So what's the gamble?" she pressed.

"On the one hand? We get a damned good meal and a comfortable place to sleep for the night," he said.

"That doesn't sound terrible," she returned tentatively. "What about the other hand?"

"Getting threatened with knives and chased across the district?" Adam offered back with an awkward smile.

Ellie stared at him.

"It's a really small other hand," he hurried to assure her.

"How small?" she pressed.

"The Mayans who choose to stay out here in the Cayo instead of moving closer to the coast usually aren't looking for visitors," Adam explained. "They tend to make their settlements deliberately hard to find. But if there's a milpa here, then there's a village nearby—and we might be able to talk them into letting us stay the night. It'd be a damned sight more comfortable than sleeping rough in the bush again, and the food's usually amazing."

"Do you expect talking them into that to be very difficult?" Ellie pressed cautiously.

"Well… last time I was at one of their villages, I was with a Mayan," Adam admitted. "Can't be entirely sure how it'll go showing up on our own unannounced. Most of the Mayan folks who live out this way came here in order to get away from being hijacked into forced labor over in Guatemala. Somebody trying to enslave you or your family can make you a little skittish."

He pushed his way through another stand of brush.

Ellie stopped walking.

"Should we really be bothering them, then?" she demanded.

Adam paused to consider it.

"Maybe not," he allowed. "But it's also possible they'll know something about this city of yours. How about if we feel like we're not welcome, we make a graceful exit?"

Ellie realized that he was waiting for her to answer. She gave him a careful nod.

He led them into the brush, and the scent of a recent fire grew stronger. A short while later, the trees parted to reveal a broad clearing of freshly charred ground. Some of the stumps were still smoldering.

As they reached the milpa, a figure slipped from the brush to Ellie's right—a reedy stick of a boy. He dashed up a barely perceptible game trail that she could now see lined the edge of the field.

No, she corrected herself. It was not a game trail. It was a path to the village.

"Should we follow him?" Ellie asked cautiously.

"If he didn't want to be followed, he would've made sure we didn't see him," Adam replied confidently.

He set off after the boy. The trail wound along the milpa, and then crawled up the side of a steep, forested hill. Ellie's legs had just begun to ache from the climb when the foliage parted, and the village revealed itself.

A scatter of houses sat along a ridge that clung to the steep hillside. A creek ran beneath the settlement, fed by a low waterfall to the north. The buildings were palm-thatched and neatly whitewashed, set behind little fenced yards with colorful, abundant gardens.

The game trail Adam and Ellie followed widened into a road. Chickens wandered around in the middle of it, squawking and fluttering in alarm at their approach. There was no sign of the boy they had followed, but other children materialized from the houses and yards as they drew closer. The young people were dressed in light, undyed cotton shirts, with leather sandals on their feet. They formed little clusters at the verge of the road, staring and whispering. Their eyes were bright with curiosity.

A rooster crowed out a warning, and a trio of women—two middle-aged and one older—poked their heads out of one of the houses. Their gazes were slightly more tinged with suspicion than those of the children.

"Buenas días," Adam said. "¿Dónde está el alcalde?"

The women's eyes narrowed. Ellie tried to make out Adam's Spanish. She was only peripherally familiar with the language.

"What's an alcalde?" she asked quietly.

"It means mayor. It's what they call the village leader," he explained in a low mutter. "Maybe I should try Mopan..."

"Do you speak Mopan?" Ellie asked with surprise, recognizing the name of one of the other Mayan languages used in the region.

"Er—sort of?" Adam hedged. He turned his attention to the women again. "Tub'aj yan alcalde?"

His efforts earned him a flash of surprise, but didn't entirely banish the women's suspicion. The trio ducked back inside and whispered furiously.

"Hope I didn't just ask them how to sail a fish or something," Adam grumbled awkwardly.

The children looked far more comfortable with their presence. A little scattering of them had drifted out of their hiding places to form a cluster at Ellie's back. The group grew as Adam gave the house of unfriendly women an awkward wave, and then guided Ellie deeper into the village.

The road widened until it formed a rough square of beaten earth that surrounded a well. At the far end of the bare plaza stood a slightly larger thatched roof building with a cross hung over the door—clearly the local church. Ellie hadn't read a very great deal of Mayan ethnographic literature, as there wasn't an awful lot of it to begin with—but she did know that most of the Maya were practicing Catholics, albeit with a few local variations on the faith.

A dozen or so men were gathered in front of the building. They sat on low stools or hovered in the shade. The members of the group wore simple shirts and trousers. Some shaded their faces with hats woven from dried palm fronds.

None of them looked very friendly—or surprised. Ellie guessed that the boy from the milpa had already spread the news of their arrival.

As a welcome, it did not seem very promising.

"Don't worry," Adam said quietly from beside her. "I've talked my way out of worse."

His comment was far from reassuring.

The train of children dissolved to take up positions around the square. A few of them climbed into the trees while others peered from behind rocks or fences.

Adam slapped a deliberately friendly smile on his face. He raised a hand in greeting as he approached the men.

"D'yoos b'o'tik," he said. "K'aat janal, naj'a ak'a."

Ellie guessed that he was using Mopan again. She could hear how awkwardly the words fell from his tongue.

The men continued to glare at them suspiciously.

"What did you say?" she asked in a whispered hiss.

"Just whether there's a place where we could stay for the night," he countered defensively. "I think."

"Are you sure they're Mopan speakers?" Ellie pressed. "There are quite a few distinct Mayan languages..."

"Well, it's not like I know all of them," he retorted, and then took a breath. "Lemme try something else. Bix a beel! Tu'ux u alcalde?"

One of the oldest fellows clustered by the church raised his head. His lean, weathered face was marred by a pale scar on his forehead—a jagged line that ran into the white fringe of hair under his straw hat. A wooden cross hung around his neck alongside another rough pendant that looked like a fang from some large, hungry animal.

"Is that supposed to be Yucatec?" the older man asked in accented but clearly fluent English.

Adam shuffled a little awkwardly beside her.

"Er... yes?" he offered.

"Padre Amilcar Kuyoc," the older man said, introducing himself. "Your offense against my language is forgiven—but we don't have an alcalde here. You are looking for a place to stay for the night?"

"If it isn't too much trouble," Adam replied, brightening.

"You married?" Kuyoc pressed crisply.

Ellie startled at the unexpected inquiry from the man, whose title revealed him to be the village's priest. She flashed an alarmed glance at Adam.

"You mean, like... to each other?" Adam asked tentatively.

Kuyoc raised a wry eyebrow. "Are you married to somebody else?"

"No," Adam replied quickly.

"I'm a widow," Ellie blurted instinctively, even as she inwardly winced at the discomfort of the continued fiction about her marital status.

"She's a widow," Adam confirmed. "I'm not."

"Not a widow?" Kuyoc repeated carefully.

"Not married," Adam clarified. "To anyone. Including her."

Kuyoc blinked at them.

"I see," he said flatly. "Are you here to convert us?"

"To what?" Adam returned dumbly.

"I don't know," the priest returned a bit impatiently. "Methodism?"

"Er... no," Adam said.

"We're not missionaries," Ellie added neatly.

An awkward pause followed—one where some statement about their actual business should have gone. Ellie flashed Adam a look as she struggled to think of a way to describe their mission that wouldn't see them get chased back into the bush.

Adam shrugged—which was singularly unhelpful.

"Riiight," Kuyoc said with a bit of a sigh. "Welcome to Santa Dolores Xenacoj. Why don't we get you sorted?"

"We're staying?" Ellie exclaimed.

The priest threw her another skeptical look.

"Would you prefer to go?" he asked.

"No," she quickly replied.

"We're very grateful for your hospitality," Adam added helpfully.

Kuyoc gave them a longer study—one that made Ellie feel distinctly aware of just how painfully awkward their introduction had been. She flashed him a smile, hoping that might help make up for it.

The priest shouted a few lines of Mopan back toward the men by the church. They made an easy reply, and the atmosphere of the square shifted as everyone went back to what looked like normal life.

"Follow me," Kuyoc ordered. He set off up the road.

The track switchbacked steeply up the hillside. Ellie quickly found herself sweating again at the effort of the climb. Her legs had already been aching.

The priest didn't seem to have any trouble with it at all, despite the fact that he was clearly a man in his seventies.

"Keep up!" he called back from ahead of them.

"He has a great deal of energy for someone his age," Ellie commented a bit breathlessly.

"He probably didn't hike through fifteen miles of bush today," Adam grumbled in reply.

TWENTY-ONE

*A*DAM SUPPOSED THEIR introduction to the village could've gone worse... though maybe not much worse.

The priest, Kuyoc, led them up the hill past tidy houses lush with growing herbs, and the odd pen of clucking chickens. Adam tried not to huff openly as he followed. The old timer set a hell of a pace for a guy who looked like he could be someone's great-grandpa. He was unnaturally nimble.

Ellie trudged beside Adam. He could see that she was tired, however much she tried to hide it. It had been a grueling day, especially after that whole business with the javelinas.

Damned pigs.

Kuyoc's questions about the nature of Adam's relationship with Ellie had been more awkward than they should've been... probably because last night, Adam had come damned close to doing something incredibly stupid.

For an alarming moment by the fire, Adam had been sure Ellie was about to kiss him. He had seen the tell-tale gleam in her eye right before the jaguar cried out—assuming, of course, that he hadn't just dreamed the whole business up through a rum-soaked haze.

It wasn't that he wouldn't have liked it. Heck, Adam had spent the last two days trying to shake the image of Ellie floating in the river in her underwear.

But the woman was *trouble*. Ellie was exactly the sort of girl who came with all sorts of complications—complications that Adam had studiously avoided for the last twenty-seven years.

He had every intention of continuing to avoid them—no matter how cute she looked with mud smeared over her freckles and her hair all curled with sweat at the back of her neck...

"Are you trying to tell me something?" Ellie whispered conspiratorially as she leaned in a little closer.

"What? No!" Adam returned with a jolt. "What'd you think that for?"

"You keep looking at me," she returned with obvious confusion.

"Heat. Tired. Chickens." Adam waved a hand at the fowl who watched them pass with beady-eyed indifference. "Probably hungry."

"I see." Ellie flashed him an odd look before quickening her pace to keep up with the priest.

Adam searched for something that would take his mind off of underthings and freckles. He found it in the sight of a low, squat building that sat on an isolated reach of the hillside. While all the rest of the structures in Santa Dolores were clearly part of some household plot, this one stood alone and apart. It was accessed by a narrow path that Adam could just make out skirting the ridge.

"What's that for?" he called out toward the spry old priest.

"That?" Kuyoc echoed, looking to where Adam pointed. "Ah! That is where we keep the dynamite."

Adam stiffened.

"Dynamite?" he repeated urgently.

"For removing stumps," the priest cheerfully explained. He flashed them a grin. "Keep up!"

"Is that normal?" Ellie hissed beside him.

"Sure?" Adam replied awkwardly. "I mean, who doesn't need a stump removed every now and then?"

Ellie cast another thoughtful glance at the building before it slipped from view.

Adam hauled his weary bones the rest of the way up the slope of the hillside to where a larger plot perched above the rest of the village. As they reached it, he glanced back the way they had come. From this higher vantage, he could see over the break in the trees to a low valley—and beyond that, the misty green contours of rolling, forest-covered hills.

It was a great view. Adam took an extra minute to decide whether it was the sort of great view that might make him want to lie down in the road with his eyes closed.

It was close, but the presence of all those nice, solid houses just below him took the edge off.

The plot that they had climbed to contained a pair of houses. They were framed by a substantial yard stuffed with flowers and plots of herbs.

A young boy squatted on the threshold of the larger of the two buildings.

He clutched a hen to his chest like a sleeping cat and watched them approach with wide brown eyes.

"This is Paolo." Kuyoc waved a hand at the boy, and then the bird. "That is Cruzita. He named it after his mother, who is not pleased that her son chose a good meal as a pet."

Kuyoc rattled off a line in Mopan that Adam couldn't hope to keep up with, and the boy dashed around the side of the house with the hen still clutched in his arms. His small bare feet picked out a habitual path through the newly raked vegetable plots and bushy cilantro.

A smell wafted to Adam from across the evening air—the enticing aroma of roasting corn and chili. Somebody was already making dinner.

His mouth started to water.

"You will owe your hospitality tonight to Na'chiin Feliciana. Her husband was the alcalde of the village," Kuyoc explained.

Na'chiin—Adam recognized the Mopan word for grandmother. It spoke to the woman's status in the household—and likely the village as well, if her husband had been alcalde.

Adam ducked to enter the doorway behind the priest. Kuyoc and the other men in the village were all a few inches shorter than Adam, and the houses here had been built accordingly. Thankfully, the roof was peaked enough that he could stand back up once inside.

The house was dim, and cooler than the outdoors. A few hammocks were tucked into the corner, flanked by the baskets and hollow gourds that the family used for storage. A handful of wooden stools surrounded a low table.

The family altar stood in a place of obvious importance on a shelf by the far wall. The wood was draped with a beautifully embroidered cloth. The carved figures of a handful of santos flanked the wooden cross at the center. A clay vase stuffed with bright, fresh blooms stood before them.

A woman stepped through a doorway at the back of the room. She was accompanied by Paolo, who had been relieved of his chicken. Her silver-haired head came no higher than Adam's armpit. Her dark brown face was richly lined around eyes that looked as sharp as glass—and about as friendly.

Kuyoc rattled off a stream of rapid Mopan. Adam managed to pick out a word or two.

The priest seemed to be telling the na'chiin—Feliciana—something that Adam was pretty sure meant 'lost idiots' and 'not married.'

Feliciana arched an eyebrow in response, and then flashed a skeptical look at Adam and Ellie.

She replied to the priest in more Mopan. Kuyoc shrugged, and with a sigh,

Feliciana graciously nodded.

"Ustedes son bienvenidos aquí," she announced in clipped, formal Spanish. She obviously wasn't very comfortable using the language. Adam couldn't blame her. Spanish speakers probably hadn't treated her and her people very well.

"Venga conmigo, jovencita," Feliciana finished. She gave Ellie a perfunctory wave and turned for the back door.

Adam shot Ellie an uncomfortable look.

"She—ah—wants you to go with her," he filled in.

"Yes, of course," Ellie said quickly. Adam could practically see her mind whirring. "Because Mayan societies largely divide their daily activities by gender."

"Lemme guess," Adam offered. "You read a book about it."

Ellie glared at him. Adam raised his hands defensively.

"Probably a really great book," he added. "Because books are great."

"You have books about us?" the priest cut in. His eyes glinted a little wickedly. "How very interesting."

Ellie's cheeks flushed. She turned to the older woman, who was still waiting in the doorway.

"Sí, Doña," Ellie said, making courteous use of her limited Spanish. "Gracias."

She flashed Adam a look that distinctly said *you had better not do anything stupid* and then followed the na'chiin outside.

"How do you feel about javelina?" Kuyoc abruptly asked.

Adam startled.

"You mean in general?" he prompted.

"In a tortilla," the priest patiently replied.

"Great!" Adam's thoughts immediately turned to the pleasant prospect of dinner.

Roasted javelina would go very nicely with tortillas. It would probably taste a bit like justice.

"Let's get you settled in," the priest concluded neatly.

Two hours later, Adam leaned back from the low table. He was pleasantly and completely stuffed with chili-spiked beans, smoky meat, and a seemingly endless pile of hot corn tortillas. One of the women of the household came to clear his plate. She looked to be aged about thirty. Adam had heard Kuyoc address her as Cruzita, which meant she must have been the one whom the chicken was named after.

"¿Habla usted español?" he asked as she approached.

She shook her head.

Adam nodded to the priest, who sat across the table from him.

"Could you tell her to please extend my thanks to the other ladies for the food?" he asked.

Kuyoc flashed him a thoughtful look, then spoke a little Mopan to Cruzita. There was a distinctly wry tone to it.

Cruzita snorted, but gave Adam a pleasant nod and a half smile before leaving.

"Why'd she laugh?" Adam asked.

"I told her I knew you really liked it because you ate the better half of a pig," Kuyoc returned blithely.

"I walked a lot today," Adam grumbled in reply. "And it was good."

The other men at the table—a collection of Feliciana's sons and sons-in-law, as best Adam could tell—rose from their stools, chatting together comfortably as they made their way out into the night.

Kuyoc popped up behind them like an unfairly energetic cork.

"We should clear the way for the women to eat. Want to share a little k'uutz?" he asked.

Adam definitely recognized the Mopan word for tobacco.

"Don't mind if I do," he replied happily.

Outside, evening had settled in over the village. Kuyoc settled them on a pair of wooden stools in front of the house. The seats were perfectly positioned to take in the expansive view, which was still just gradual enough to be nice instead of nausea-inducing.

Adam extended his legs out comfortably as he leaned against the whitewashed wall and enjoyed his cigar.

The sun drifted toward the line of the mountains that lay to the west. The sky above it was falling into shades of breathtaking orange and purple. Even the mosquitoes weren't as bad up here—though the cigar smoke also helped with that.

Adam took another puff. The spicy, rich taste of the tobacco pleasantly filled his mouth.

"Hell of a nice place you've got here," he commented.

"Thank you," the priest replied evenly.

"Have your people been here long?"

"The first settlers came about forty years ago," Kuyoc said.

"From the Peten or Izabal?" Adam casually asked.

JACQUELYN BENSON

There was a pause the length of a breath before Kuyoc replied.

"You know your history," the priest noted carefully.

Adam knew enough of it. The Spanish-descended elites in Guatemala had been grabbing lands and enslaving the Maya for generations—whatever nicer terms they might use for the latter. The men and women forced to labor on the coffee plantations were paid abysmal wages and subjected to all manner of abuses, including beatings and starvation. Disease was also a problem, as workers compelled to labor in the lowland areas returned home with malaria, parasites, and other ailments that then spread through their villages.

Things had only worsened in the 1870s, when the government got in on the game as well and began drafting unwilling Mayans into massive—and massively underpaid—public works projects.

Based on what Kuyoc said about the timing of their exodus, the people of Santa Dolores had at least been spared that.

"If you folks got out forty years ago, then whoever was in charge deserves an award," Adam commented darkly.

"Felciana's husband." Kuyoc took another slow drag on his cigar. "Right after the local governor sent him the first mandamiento."

The word translated as *order*, but Adam knew what it really meant—a draft for more involuntary workers. Any alcalde who didn't offer up the right numbers could be jailed, or else fined and forced to work on one of the plantations himself.

There was an awful relief in knowing that the old alcalde of Santa Dolores had been principled and insightful enough to see the writing on the wall before things really got bad. So many of the highland villages in Guatemala had been devastated by the mandamientos, which transformed them from thriving communities to impoverished, ragged ghost towns.

But making the choice to run—to leave behind lands that might have been farmed by your ancestors for generations—wouldn't have been easy either.

"I'm sorry you had to go through that," Adam said.

The words felt inadequate, but they were the best he had.

"I didn't go through it," the priest replied coolly as the smoke curled up from his cigar. "But the sentiment is appreciated."

The reply surprised him.

Adam took a better look at the scar on Kuyoc's face and the curved fang that hung beside the crucifix around the priest's neck.

"You recognized my Yucatec back at the church," Adam noted tentatively.

Kuyoc snorted.

"Barely."

"And there aren't a hell of a lot of people speaking English in Guatemala," Adam pointed out.

Kuyoc leaned back against the wall. He gazed out over the quiet sprawl of the village, where candles were beginning to wink to light in the windows against the growing gloom.

"I am not from Guatemala," the priest finally replied.

"Sorry," Adam said. "I didn't mean to pry."

Kuyoc took another draw on his cigar. Adam did the same. He decided to keep whatever other questions he might have to himself.

"I came from San Pedro Siris," Kuyoc finally offered.

Adam went still as the significance of the name—*San Pedro Siris*—sank in. "The San Pedro Siris up by the Mexican border?" he pressed carefully.

"Mmm hmm," the priest confirmed, still looking out over the sunset.

"I heard some bad things went down around there thirty or so years ago," Adam continued cautiously.

"You could say that."

Adam could've said more than that.

He'd had the story in pieces from a few different sources over his years in the colony, but as he understood it, the village of San Pedro Siris had been burned to the ground by the British Army's West India Regiment.

Adam knew a bit of the context. In the 1860s, Mexico, the Republic of Yucatán, and British Honduras had been wrangling over where to draw the borders of their respective lands.

Right in the middle of the areas under dispute were a few Mayan communities... communities that insisted on staking their *own* claims to some of the territory. Probably because it was territory that their ancestors had been living on for the last few centuries or so.

The big players in the game didn't really love the idea of ceding any of their land to a bunch of natives. Some of the Maya had been smart enough to figure out how to play the colonists off of each other. They made alliances with Mexico or the Yucatán, who offered to confirm their land rights in exchange for help keeping the British out of it—or vice-versa.

San Pedro Siris had been caught right up in the middle of it. The alcalde there had claimed to be an ally of the British, but rumor had it that the village was secretly supporting the Ichaiche Maya revolutionary leader Marcus Canul.

It had all fully gone to hell in 1867, when some civil servant on his way to San Pedro Siris was attacked by Canul's men. Nobody really knew for sure whether the village had been complicit in the raid, or whether Canul had simply turned up at an opportune moment.

The colonial authorities didn't care. Burning the village sent a message... and what was one less Mayan settlement to worry about?

If Kuyoc was from San Pedro Siris, Adam wasn't surprised that he had run. Most likely, *everybody* had run when the army was approaching the village... but most of the rest of them had eventually gone back. Adam knew that the town had been rebuilt a couple of years after the burning.

Kuyoc was a priest, which would've made him an important part of the community. So why was he still here in Santa Dolores and not back home with the rest of his people?

The question itched, but Adam was pretty sure it wasn't his place to ask it.

"Sorry you were caught up in that," he said instead.

"Are you?" Kuyoc returned mildly.

Adam met the priest's eyes.

"I don't have much time for people who burn down civilian homes and call it..." He paused and rubbed his face tiredly. "Hell, I don't even know what they call it. But it ain't right."

The priest studied him with narrowed eyes.

"An unusual point of view for a gentleman of your extraction," he pointed out.

"I've never had much time for my extraction," Adam admitted wryly. "But how'd you end up all the way out here?"

Kuyoc's expression subtly shuttered.

"That is a longer story," he replied.

"Well, I appreciate that you took a chance on us," Adam offered. "The lady and I had a bit of a... complicated time getting here, and I'm glad she has a shot at a decent night's sleep tonight."

"Mrs. Nitherscott-Watby is your...?"

Kuyoc let the question hang.

"Uhh..." Adam started awkwardly.

The priest continued to wait, arching an eyebrow.

"Partner?" Adam finally suggested.

"¿Compañera o socia?" Kuyoc returned.

Adam knew the difference between those two possible translations of the word *partner*. The first implied that Ellie was his sidekick or companion. The other was used for a business associate.

"Er... little of both?" he tried.

The priest shook his head tiredly and took another puff of his cigar.

"So what brings you to our corner of the mountains?" he asked.

"Actually, we're looking for a set of ruins," Adam admitted.

Kuyoc stilled.

"Oh?" the priest casually prompted—maybe just a little *too* casually, Adam thought.

"Maybe you've heard about them," Adam continued. "They'd be about three days' walk from here. You head north toward the next tributary of the Belize, and then dogleg to the west. There's something about a... *River of Smoke* being nearby," he filled in, pulling up the memory of the final landmark on Ellie's map.

"So you are on a treasure hunt," Kuyoc returned.

Adam suppressed a wince as he thought of the looted cave that they had passed through earlier.

"No," he replied firmly—firmly enough that Kuyoc looked over at him with a little surprise.

"Ellie's a scholar," Adam continued purposefully. "She thinks whatever's there could be important for understanding the history around here."

He stopped again as he realized how that might sound to a man whose ancestors could very well have been part of the *history* he and Ellie were looking for.

"She's not going to take anything," Adam quickly declared. "She's... she's not like that. Whatever she finds there, she'll want to protect it."

Kuyoc's response was uncharacteristically serious.

"Protect it from whom?"

Adam opened his mouth to answer—and realized he didn't have one. Of course, he was sure that Ellie meant to protect her finds from guys like the ones who had rifled that cave... but what about the colonial authorities, or the academics who wrote all those fancy journal articles? Those were the people who'd end up coming here to excavate everything... and then carry it all back to some storage room under a London museum.

At least in the storage room, any artifacts would be safe from the black market, Adam reminded himself... and yet somehow— as he looked out over a village of actual, living Mayans—that didn't feel like enough.

Still, finding out if the people here knew anything about the ruins could save him and Ellie a hell of a lot of time wandering around in the bush. It'd also minimize some very real risks.

"You—ah—heard anything about a place like that?" Adam pressed awkwardly.

Smoke bloomed over Kuyoc's head like a fading ghost.

"I know of the area you are describing," he said at last.

Adam perked up.

"You do?"

"Sure," the priest replied easily. "It's the realm of the k'ak'as ba'alo'ob."

"I'm afraid I don't know that one," Adam admitted.

"It means evil spirits," Kuyoc said cheerfully.

"Evil... huh?" Adam echoed dumbly.

"The hungry spirits of the restless dead and their monstrous servants," Kuyoc explained. "They suck the living souls out of anyone foolish enough to trespass on their land."

Adam was momentarily speechless. He'd pegged the priest for more of a rationalist, but here the guy was casually sharing stories of soul-sucking evil dead as though they were talking about lousy weather.

"Right," Adam returned carefully.

"We've all heard the stories, of course," the priest continued with a casual wave of his cigar. "How there are great, black beasts that haunt the night, driving their fangs into the skulls of anyone reckless enough to go wandering there."

"That's... vivid," Adam said.

His gaze involuntarily dropped to the finger-length, wickedly pointed tooth that hung from the other cord around the priest's neck.

"Is that where you got your—er..." he began.

"This?" Kuyoc replied, lifting the pendant. "Naw. This is just a bit of antler."

It didn't look like a bit of antler.

"It is all a load of superstition," the priest continued. He hesitated as he took another puff. "Probably. Of course, none of my people are willing to go there."

"Yeah. Sure," Adam replied. "Makes sense."

"But I am sure you are perfectly qualified to wander into an unknown and potentially dangerous area of the forest with nothing more than a lady scholar, a machete, and a reasonably nice Winchester," Kuyoc neatly concluded.

Adam bristled a bit.

"It's a great Winchester," he retorted. "And I kinda am, actually."

"Oh?" the priest prompted as his gaze sharpened. "And how is that?"

"I'm the assistant surveyor general for the colony."

"Ah," Kuyoc replied. "So you are *that* Mr. Bates."

"You've heard of me?" Adam blurted in surprise.

Kuyoc shrugged.

"I mean—a little. A very small amount. Mostly just your name in passing," he noted dismissively.

The priest pushed nimbly to his feet.

"Well, then," he continued. "If you will excuse me, it is getting late. I should be getting my rest. Old bones, you see."

Adam thought of how energetically the guy had practically danced up the hill a couple of hours ago.

"Sure." Adam forced back his skepticism as he rose as well. "Thank you—for all of this. It's very much appreciated."

"What is it you Yankees say? Don't mention it." Kuyoc flashed him a smile. "Good evening to you, Mr. Bates."

"K'a'ak'ate, Padre," Adam replied, using some of his more reliable Mopan words.

Kuyoc gave him a nod, and then was gone.

TWENTY-TWO

$\mathcal{E}$LLIE WOKE TO THE sound of giggles. She rolled over in her hammock to see Lupe and Itza's dark heads bent together beside her as the two girls whispered conspiratorially. As the pair noticed that Ellie's eyes were open, they brightened and chattered to her cheerfully in Mopan.

Lupe and Itza were two of Feliciana's several granddaughters. The girls lived with their mother and father in the smaller of the two houses on Feliciana's plot. Ellie guessed that Lupe was around fourteen, with Itza perhaps two years younger.

She had slept very comfortably in their house, and upon waking, was feeling more refreshed than she had in quite a while. Perhaps that was simply due to the good food and lack of mosquitoes—but it was also true that Ellie didn't recall having any dreams the night before.

The absence of any nighttime visitations was a surprise. Ellie's dreams had come so regularly since she had arrived in the colony that she had grown to expect them.

As she sat up, Ellie's gaze fell on the painting of a saint, which was mounted on the wall across from her hammock. The figure was clothed in robes like those of the Holy Virgin—but instead of the Virgin's placid face, the layers of fabric framed an elegant white skull.

The small, framed card tugged at Ellie strangely. By all rights, the image should have seemed a bit gruesome, but instead, it felt oddly benevolent—as though an old friend had been watching over her as she slept.

A little shelf in front of the icon held offerings of flowers and cigarettes. Ellie put her limited Spanish to use to try to ask about it.

"¿Quién es ella?" she asked.

Lupe and Itza offered her a quick explanation in Mopan, and then remembered that Ellie couldn't understand it. After a glance at each other, they attempted a bit of Spanish.

"Santa Muerte," Lupe said.

Ellie managed to translate the words—*Saint Death*.

"Santa Muerte," she echoed.

The girls smiled with approval.

As she washed up at the basin that the two young women had brought her, Ellie thought back to the rest of her evening in the village. After being separated from Adam, she had been shuttled into the kitchen, where Feliciana's daughter Cruzita and the girls had been busy pressing out tortillas.

Feliciana had deposited Ellie there, pointing her to a stool in the corner, and then left. Ellie had managed to sit quietly and watch the other women work for about five minutes before—with a great deal of hand waving and pointing—she convinced them to give her a try at patting out the little circles of maize.

Her abject failures had resulted in a general hilarity.

After the men had been fed, the women took over the table for a leisurely and social meal. Feliciana had rejoined them. She had towed along the skinny ten-year-old Ellie had seen yesterday by the milpa. He turned out to be Héctor, another of Feliciana's grandsons. Feliciana plopped him down on the ground beside Ellie's stool and charged him with translating.

Héctor had been learning both English and Spanish from the priest, Kuyoc. Though his skills were still a bit rough, they were sufficient to allow the women of the household to mercilessly interrogate Ellie.

They had been *very* curious to know the nature of her relationship with Adam. Was he her husband? Her brother? Her lover? (The latter query had been delivered only after a great deal of protesting by Héctor and another outburst of laughter from the women.)

"We are colleagues," Ellie had asserted neatly.

The women had made a smattering response to that in Mopan.

"They say that is too bad for you," Héctor had automatically translated, and then immediately turned pink with a blush.

After dinner, Feliciana had rolled herself narrow cigarettes while she reclined in a low slung hammock. The other women took out their spinning and weaving. The projects were simply a way to keep their hands busy as they continued gossiping.

Impertinent questions aside, it had been a lovely evening. Ellie had even been treated to the local version of a hot chocolate—a piping hot, bitter concoction generously spiced with chili.

It was possible she had consumed three cups of it.

Lupe and Itza waved at Ellie from their doorway as she crossed the garden. Back at Feliciana's house, she found Adam waiting outside beside Padre Kuyoc. Her traveling companion already had his rucksack and the Winchester slung over his shoulders.

Feliciana stood regally in the doorway.

Ellie mustered up a bit of Spanish as she approached the older woman.

"Adios, na'chiin," she said. She tried to infuse the awkward words with as much significance as she could. "Gracias por todos."

"De nada, mija." Feliciana's voice was warm with a hint of genuine affection.

Apparently, Ellie's failed attempts at making tortillas and her indulgence of the women's gossip the night before had earned her a little approval from the matriarch.

"And did you enjoy your stay with us?" Kuyoc prompted.

"Very much so," Ellie returned. "The village is beautiful, and you have a wonderful community here. I'm very grateful to you for sharing it with us."

"Did it live up to what you read in your books?" the priest pressed as his eyes twinkled mischievously.

Ellie's cheeks flushed a little.

"I should say that the books were rather incomplete," she carefully returned.

"That is not surprising," Kuyoc replied. "I am sure they were written by self-important Englishmen."

"American men, actually," Ellie blurted in response—not that it sounded much better.

"Americans, English... Do not feel too bad about it," the priest easily assured her. "They write all of the books."

Ellie narrowed her eyes.

"That is something I hope to change, Padre Kuyoc," she asserted sharply.

The priest cocked an eyebrow.

"You think it will all be better if Englishwomen also write books?" he challenged.

"Oh boy..." Adam muttered from beside her.

Ellie ignored him, meeting the priest's eyes.

"I think it will be better when the purview of academic knowledge is open to the entire globe instead of just a single class and gender in a tiny corner of it," she declared firmly.

"Probably," Kuyoc agreed with a playful shrug. "And who knows? Maybe we will even see it."

"*I* certainly mean to, Padre," Ellie returned forcefully.

Kuyoc gave her a quietly considering gaze.

"I wish you well in that endeavor," he finally said. "God be with you both."

With much waving and a great deal of shouted Mopan from Feliciana's horde of grandchildren, Ellie and Adam made their way back down the road through the village.

"The padre said if we're heading to the river, we should follow this trail for the next two miles—then cut west and make our way overland," Adam explained as they left the cheerful clusters of houses behind and followed a pale track into the dense green of the forest. "And Cruzita packed this full of tamales before she sent us off."

He patted his rucksack, obviously pleased by the idea.

"Won't that mean extra weight?" Ellie pointed out.

"Worth it," Adam declared.

The day was still early. The air wasn't yet as thick and humid as it would become by midday. Well-fed and rested, Ellie found the pace comfortable as Adam wove them through the bush, occasionally consulting his compass.

"Were you able to learn anything about our city?" Ellie asked.

"Just that the padre thinks it's a cursed realm full of the hungry spirits of the damned," Adam replied as he shouldered though a stand of wild plantains.

Ellie stopped short.

"Sorry—what?"

Adam flashed her a grin.

"Didn't take you for the type to get spooked by a few ghost stories," he challenged.

Ellie frowned at him.

"I am hardly one to indulge in gross superstition," she countered. "But there are times when local folklore can reveal clues about lost portions of the oral historical record."

"He said there are monsters that bite people's skulls," Adam cheerfully elaborated.

"Wonderful," Ellie grumbled crossly. "What did you think of the old fellow, anyway?"

"I'm pretty sure he's a revolutionary," Adam replied with a swing of his machete.

"He did seem to be a tad iconoclastic," Ellie acknowledged.

"No—I mean a literal revolutionary," Adam corrected her. "The kind that revolts against things."

Ellie felt a distinct burst of alarm.

"Is that why he has dynamite?" she demanded nervously.

"You mean the stuff in that shack on the hill?" Adam replied. "Naw, he said that was for stumps."

"And you believe him?" Ellie pressed.

"Have you ever tried to pull a stump out by hand?" Adam countered. "Ain't gonna happen. Dynamite makes way more sense."

"I didn't realize it was in regular circulation," Ellie noted.

"It's not," Adam returned. "They probably stole it from somewhere, or else it's old stuff the loggers won't use anymore. Honestly, I kinda hope they *did* steal it. Dynamite gets damned tricky if you leave it lying around for too long."

"If by 'tricky' you mean 'highly unstable and prone to spontaneous combustion,'" Ellie returned uneasily.

"Well, now you know why they built a special shed for it," Adam concluded.

She followed him under a veil of low hanging vines.

"Is he still at it, do you think?" she asked.

"Who?"

"The priest," she clarified.

"Blowing up stumps?"

"Revolutionizing," Ellie retorted a little impatiently.

"Pretty sure he's retired." Adam held a thick veil of brush back for her. "But I think he got tangled up in something dangerous in his old village. The alcalde there was trying to make peace with the British, but I'm wondering if maybe Kuyoc had other ideas. It'd explain why he never went back."

"How very interesting," Ellie mused, her mind already whirring. "I wonder how he ended up in Santa Dolores, of all places?"

She paused as a less comfortable thought occurred to her.

"It wasn't on your map, was it?" she asked.

Adam came to a halt in the path ahead of her.

"What wasn't?" he said.

"Santa Dolores," Ellie replied.

Adam leaned his arm against a tree. His shoulders slumped a little tiredly.

"No. It wasn't," he confirmed.

"Are you going to add it?" Ellie quietly demanded.

"I don't know," he admitted. "Do you think I should?"

Ellie was surprised by the genuineness of the question.

"I... Well," She struggled to find the right response. "If the village was on your map, I imagine it would mean more trade. Better communication with the other settlements. It might make it easier for the people there to resupply when things run short."

"None of that's wrong," Adam carefully allowed.

"But..." Ellie continued hesitantly. "I can't help but feel..."

Her words trailed off.

"Feel what?" Adam prompted gently.

"It just reminds me of the cave," she burst out. "And how you said that you stopped putting the new Mayan sites you found on the map because everything always ended up being looted. I think... I think I'm afraid if you share Santa Dolores with the world, there is a very good chance that the world won't appreciate what it has to offer."

"Or that they'll appreciate it too much," Adam added grimly.

Silence lingered for a moment as they considered each other across the close, green space of the forest.

"What will you do?" Ellie finally pressed.

"I didn't come out here to draw any maps," Adam concluded bluntly.

He pushed back from the tree he'd been leaning against. His tanned face cracked into a grin.

"Besides, you've got the only pencil," he pointed out.

"I do not!" Ellie protested. "It's in your rucksack."

"Yeah, but it's *yours*," Adam easily countered.

"I took it off your desk," Ellie reminded him.

"Stolen fair and square," Adam agreed.

He tossed up the machete. Ellie watched the blade spin, glinting, through the air until the grip landed neatly back in his palm.

"What if I lent the pencil to you?" she offered.

"Oh, I'm pretty sure you need it for stuff," Adam lightly returned.

He hopped up onto an enormous fallen tree that blocked their way forward. Pausing at the top, he turned back to offer her his machete-free hand.

"It's slippery," he warned.

His shirt was stained with dirt and his face was rough with four days' worth of stubble. The gesture still made Ellie think of stories of knights errant rescuing maidens.

Slaying dragons, she thought distantly.

She wondered what sort of dragons a man like Adam Bates might be called to slay.

His hand was still extended. Ellie grasped it and let him lead her into what came next.

TWENTY-THREE

$\mathcal{B}$Y THE TIME SHE and Adam stopped for lunch, Ellie was willing all manner of blessings on Cruzita. Hiking through a rainforest was hard work, with a great deal of scrambling over obstacles and pushing through thick growth. The stash of tamales would've been a godsend even if they hadn't been possibly one of the most delicious things Ellie had ever eaten.

"Have another," Adam encouraged her with his mouth half full of masa. "They won't keep."

By mid-afternoon, the land had grown more rocky, signaling that they were heading higher into the mountains. The notion sent an electric thrill across her skin.

The forest around Ellie buzzed thickly, while the heat continued to rise— until suddenly a cooler breeze brushed over Ellie's skin, rich with moisture. The change in the air was accompanied by a soft rushing that rose through the constant rustling of the leaves as she and Adam pressed their way forward.

"What's that sound?" she asked.

Adam grinned back at her.

"Come find out," he said and ducked under a branch, forcing Ellie to hurry after him.

They followed the line of a vine-draped cliff of pale limestone that rose overhead and curved raggedly to the left. A few minutes later, the forest parted to reveal the course of a quick-rushing stream. Water leapt over the rocks, churning up white foam.

A wonderfully refreshing mist filled the air. Ellie relished in the cool feeling of it against her skin.

"Looks like we're back on the map," Adam commented. "And would you look at that?"

Ellie's relief was replaced by an awed surprise as she saw what loomed over the place where they stood.

The cliff jutted out across the river in the shape of a massive bridge thickly covered with moss, orchids, and ferns. Life clung to every crevice, thriving thanks to the constant damp of the cataracts.

"The *Arch Hollowed by the Hand of God!*" Ellie burst out wonderingly.

They had found the next landmark.

Ellie grinned up at Adam. He grinned back—his eyes crinkling warmly at the corners—and she was suffused with the knowledge of how completely, utterly happy she was.

"What happens now?" she asked, pitching her voice louder to be heard over the rapids.

For just a moment before Adam responded, it felt as though the answer drifted to her through the warm air and the droplets of water that danced on her skin.

Now you kiss him.

The impulse rang through her like a bell. Ellie caught her breath against it. She shouldn't. They were colleagues. Colleagues didn't kiss each other.

Her heart didn't seem to care about that logic. It continued to bounce around inside her chest like a child whacking at a drum set.

Adam glanced out over the rapids.

"Let's find someplace a bit dryer to take a better look at that—" he began.

He stopped. His eyes widened as the brush at Ellie's back audibly rustled.

Ellie froze as something hard poked into the space between her shoulder blades.

"I have a better idea," said an unfamiliar voice from behind her. "How about instead you both put your hands up in the air where I can see them?"

Adam's hand flew to the Winchester slung over his shoulder—but stopped there as the stranger behind Ellie spoke again, punctuating his words with a further prod at Ellie's back.

She felt uncomfortably certain that the object jabbing at her was the barrel of another rifle.

"Uh-uh," the stranger warned. "You really don't want to do that. Kohn ya, Flowers!" he called out.

The branches behind Adam shifted, and someone else stepped onto the bank of the cataract. The new arrival topped Adam by at least two inches in height and probably three stone in weight. His cheeks, hued a rich mahogany, were round and friendly under a wide-brimmed straw hat.

He leveled the Enfield rifle in his hands and greeted them in cheerful Kriol. "Weh di gaan an?"

"Tek ih shatgan, Flowers!" snapped the voice behind Ellie.

Ellie still hadn't dared to turn around and see what the fellow looked like. He spoke his English and Kriol with a sharp, Spanish-inflected accent.

"Cho, Mendez," Flowers replied. "I'm getting around to that. You mind?" He addressed the last bit to Adam.

Adam's gaze moved from Flowers' rifle to the man's face, and then shifted over to where the other fellow—Mendez—stood behind Ellie's shoulder. With a smooth, resigned movement, Adam swung the Winchester off his back and handed it over.

"The bag and the knife, too," Mendez ordered.

Adam handed over his pack and—with an obviously pained look of regret—parted with his blade.

"This is a nice machete," Flowers commented appreciatively as he accepted it. He pronounced the word the Kriol way, leaving off the final 'e.'

"Thanks," Adam replied grimly.

"We were just passing through..." Ellie began lamely.

"Well, now you are passing through to the boss," Mendez cut in.

He prodded her again with his gun.

Ellie's temper blazed with an abrupt, volatile heat. She whirled in place and found herself glaring at a fortyish man of roughly her own height. He had sun-weathered olive skin and a thick black mustache.

"If you touch me with that rifle again, I will rip it from your hands and knock you soundly with it," she seethed.

Mendez's eyes widened a bit with surprise. Flowers chuckled.

"This one got a little pepa," he noted.

"Princess..." Adam warned from behind her.

Ellie gritted her teeth as she fought back the ferocious urge to throw something at the man in front of her, knowing it would be utterly foolish.

He was lucky she didn't have a towel rack.

"Walk," Mendez ordered.

Ellie flashed him a glare, but stalked the way he indicated.

"Mind your step!" Flowers extended an arm to catch her elbow as she started down the trail. "The rocks are slippery."

Startled, Ellie glanced up at the big man—but he had already moved on with a smile.

The path led down a steep slope. Ellie's view of the way forward was blocked by both Flowers' broad back and the slick green leaves that slapped at her arms and face.

Adam's grim silence gave her a clear, unpleasant sense of just how serious their situation must be.

The path opened onto a broad, flat bank beside the river where it calmed below the cataracts. The area would be flooded during the rainy season, but for now, it was a relatively dry plateau of packed earth and scraggly grass... all seething with activity.

Ellie counted three steam barges floating on the calm brown water. Each of them was easily four times as big as the *Mary Lee*.

The shore itself was a hive of tents, hammocks, and piles of crates. Roughly two dozen mules brayed from within a rigged-up corral under the ceiba trees. Men shouted to each other across the camp.

Ellie counted at least thirty of them.

"I thought you said nobody mounted expeditions this close to the rains," she muttered to Adam as Flowers moved a few steps ahead of her.

"They don't," Adam countered.

"Then who are they?" she demanded.

"Guess we'll find out," Adam returned grimly.

"Move!" Mendez barked from behind them.

Adam was uncharacteristically quiet as they were marched across the sprawling camp. Ellie saw his hand flex irritably at the empty sheath for his machete. He was obviously feeling the blade's absence.

Ellie felt a pang of sympathy for him. He was clearly very attached to that knife.

Most of the men that she saw were busy working—except for the ones with the guns, like Flowers and Mendez. Those fellows lingered at various points around the camp, quietly smoking or more loudly socializing.

Ellie's mind whirled over the puzzle of what their presence meant. An unlicensed logging operation might employ some hired toughs to keep an eye on their perimeter. Perhaps she and Adam had stumbled onto a band of timber poachers.

Surely, they could talk their way past a few loggers. Adam would figure it out. Ellie would just follow his cues—and pick up as much information as she could on her own in the meantime.

She made a study of the workers as they passed. The men had a mix of Creole and Mestizo backgrounds. There was also a group of young South Asian fellows sitting around one of the campfires, chatting comfortably among themselves. Their Bhojpuri melded with the Kriol, English, and Spanish that clamored through the air.

The poaching operation—or whatever it was—carried far more equipment with it than Ellie and Adam had… though that bar was admittedly low. Most of the men appeared to be sleeping in hammocks with mosquito nets. A few tents were also scattered about. As they passed one, Ellie peeked inside to spot both a cot and a desk.

Burlap bags of dried maize and coffee were stacked in piles beside crates of tinned beef and lamp oil.

Her captors stopped outside of a larger tent on the far edge of the camp. Mendez tossed back the flap and strode inside. Ellie heard the sharp bark of his voice from within.

"We found a couple bakras up on the ridge," he announced.

He had spoken English rather than Spanish or Kriol. That told her something about whoever the 'boss' must be.

Any reply was drowned out by a crash from behind them as the men felled one of the trees.

Mendez emerged.

"Inside," he ordered with a jerk of his head.

Ellie glanced over at Adam for guidance. His eyes were on the tent. He stepped forward to enter it, leaving Ellie to follow.

"This the woman you were looking for, then?" Mendez demanded as he came in behind them.

The interior of the tent was dim compared to the bright afternoon of the sunlit riverbank. Ellie's eyes took a moment to adjust—and so she heard what waited for her inside before she saw it.

"It is indeed," Jacobs replied.

Ellie's stomach dropped. Her vision finally settled, revealing Jacobs' lean, dangerous figure standing at the far end of the canvas enclosure. His gaze shifted from her to Adam.

"And you have brought a friend," he commented. "How surprising."

Jacobs did not sound the least bit surprised.

"How are you here?" The words spilled from Ellie's lips as her mind spun with a rising fear.

"In a rare example of foresight, the professor made several useful annotations about the map in his notebook before you took it," Jacobs replied. "Enough, at least, to get us here once we corroborated them against the latest documentation from the colony survey office." He gave Ellie a considering look. "I wondered whether you would recognize that the tributary might serve as a shortcut. I half expected we would run into you on our way here, especially if you had managed to convince him to come along with you."

He waved a hand casually at where Adam stood beside her.

"So this is an ambush," Ellie fumed.

"An expedience," Jacobs calmly corrected her. "It made far more sense to simply continue with an expedition once we had caught you, rather than returning to the city to collect the requisite men and equipment."

The tent flap was thrown back again, and Dawson entered.

"What's she doing here?" the professor spluttered, pointing a nervous finger at Ellie.

"Miss Mallory was just about to return our map," Jacobs smoothly replied.

Ellie felt the ground begin to slide from beneath her feet.

"Mallory?" Adam echoed carefully.

Jacobs went quiet. His gaze shifted to Ellie, and he lifted a single, terribly expressive eyebrow.

Shame drained the blood from her cheeks as fear twisted her gut.

Jacobs made no further answer. He seemed entirely content to wait. The terrible silence stretched until it felt as though it must break her.

"That's my name," Ellie finally said. "Eleanora Mallory."

Adam didn't reply. His expression shuttered, locking away whatever he was really thinking.

Fear thickened in Ellie's throat.

"But who is *he*?" Dawson demanded as he waved an ineffectual hand at Adam's imposing figure.

"This is Mr. Adam Bates of the surveyor general's office." Jacobs shifted his cool, impenetrable gaze to Adam. "We neglected to make proper introductions during our previous encounter."

"Guess we did," Adam returned thinly. "Curious how you figured that out."

"I was informed that you had disappeared from the hotel at the same time as the girl. The conclusion was logical enough," Jacobs returned.

"But what are we going to *do* with them?" Dawson protested.

The professor was sweating. Ellie wondered how much of it was the heat, and how much was his discomfort with the idea of once again being potentially party to murder.

Not that she expected his discomfort would make him do anything to stop it.

"I suppose that depends on Mr. Bates," Jacobs said.

"Oh?" Adam replied with deceptive ease. His hand flexed near the empty sheath of his machete. "And how's that?"

"You are the assistant surveyor general," Jacobs elaborated. "As I understand it, you are responsible for the maps we consulted to get here. You are by far the most adept navigator we have in this camp."

"What?" Dawson spluttered indignantly. He fumbled the pen he had been holding, dropping it to the floor.

Jacobs ignored him. His eyes were on Adam.

"Use those skills to direct us to the city, and perhaps we can avoid more… unpleasant consequences," Jacobs said.

Ellie's fear sharpened, growing colder. Jacobs would kill Adam without a second thought. Did Adam realize that? Would it matter if he did? He was hardly the most diplomatic personality at the best of times. Ellie could tell that he was barely refraining from attacking the man now, even with Mendez still pointing his rifle at the pair of them.

Her stomach twisted.

"I am entirely capable of reading a map!" Dawson retorted, obviously offended.

"Not as capable as he is," Jacobs countered neatly.

"Need I remind you that this is *my* expedition?" the professor exclaimed.

Jacobs turned to look at him.

"Is it?" he asked mildly.

Dawson shut up.

"And what happens if I tell you to go straight to hell?" Adam asked.

Jacobs didn't smile or gloat. He looked a little tired.

"Then I start cutting the woman, Mr. Bates," he replied.

Ellie forced herself to breathe. Her head spun as the tent seemed to grow smaller around her.

"You enjoy that sort of thing? Mutilating women?" Adam's voice seethed with threat.

Jacobs' response was level.

"I am here, Mr. Bates, because I do whatever needs to be done."

Silence lingered. Mendez scratched uncomfortably at his ear as he avoided looking at Ellie. Dawson pouted over by the desk. The threat to Ellie was obviously of far less concern to him than the fact that Jacobs had impugned his scholarly capabilities.

Adam was a tense, untouchable presence beside her. Ellie couldn't tell what he was thinking. For all she knew, he might have been a thousand miles away.

"Is your concern for the woman sufficient motivation to secure your cooperation?" Jacobs demanded.

"What happens if it's not?" Adam replied.

Listening to these men casually discuss her fate over her head would normally have filled Ellie with a righteous rage. Instead, she felt as though the room was tipping away from her.

Adam hadn't looked at her since Jacobs' revelation. Ellie might as well have turned invisible beside him.

She had lied to him about her name. She had lied to him about a fair bit more than that, even if he didn't know it yet... but perhaps he'd already begun to suspect.

How much worse would it be when she told him the rest?

Because she would have to tell him, just as she should have done a long time ago... if she got the chance.

"Then Miss Mallory becomes a liability," Jacobs replied. "I do not need to tell you how we must deal with liabilities."

"No. I don't suppose you do," Adam returned, his voice tight and cold.

"Then answer the question," Jacobs ordered as he locked his gaze on Adam's face.

Ellie looked as well. She couldn't stop herself, even though she knew it was almost certainly a mistake—that what she saw in Adam's expression would only twist the knot in her chest even tighter.

"It's sufficient," Adam said flatly.

His eyes were as cold as his tone.

Another of the armed guards stepped into the tent. He was a slender Creole man who stood a couple of inches shorter than Adam. His hair was combed into place with an indulgent smear of pomade.

He held Adam's map canister in his hand.

"Here you go, boss," he said.

"Thank you, Mr. Staines." Jacobs accepted the canister, popped open the lid, and glanced idly inside before extending the tube to Dawson.

The professor snatched it and clutched it to his chest possessively.

"Mr. Bates will stay here and plot the remainder of our route on the map," Jacobs announced. "The professor will review your work. If there is any indication that you are doing less than your utmost, I will reinforce my instructions on Miss Mallory's skin. Mr. Staines will remain here to monitor the situation. Mr. Mendez?"

"Yes, boss?" Mendez replied.

"Secure Miss Mallory in the foreman's tent for the evening. She will need to be kept under watch."

"Claro."

Mendez hooked his hand under Ellie's elbow and yanked her toward the exit.

"Hold," Jacobs cut in.

Mendez stopped. Jacobs stepped near enough to Ellie that she instinctively pulled back from him. Only Mendez's grip on her arm kept her in place.

"The artifact?" Jacobs prompted. He extended his hand, waiting.

Shame and frustration burned through her. Ellie put her hands to the ribbon and lifted the medallion over her head.

She set the black disk down in Jacobs' palm.

Jacobs tossed it across the tent. Dawson fumbled his catch and was forced to pick the object up off the ground. The professor clasped the relic in his hands and studied it greedily. A moment later, he remembered himself and fumblingly tucked it into his pocket.

"That will be all." Jacobs waved dismissively.

Ellie stumbled after Mendez as he hauled her from the tent.

Panic choked her. It had all happened too fast. Surely, there had to be a way out of this.

She glanced over her shoulder at Adam. He turned to watch her go, but his expression was as unreadable as a shuttered window.

Mendez propelled her through the camp. Flowers fell into step behind them, frowning a bit as he slung the rifle over his shoulder.

Some of the scattered workers glanced over at Ellie uncomfortably as she passed. They quickly looked away again.

A few of the ones with guns watched her progress with a distinctly more threatening glance.

Mendez shoved her through the entrance to a tent in the middle of the camp. The space was perhaps twelve feet square, and was furnished with a cot, a field desk, and a chair.

"Pacheco!" Mendez shouted. "Clear this out and tell Bones to find another place for his stuff."

Ellie glanced down at the surface of the desk as her escort momentarily turned his back. Her eyes fell on a round, heavy magnifying lens. Instinctively, she shoved it into her pocket just as Pacheco—a slender young Mestizo man—hurried inside.

He cast her an uncomfortable look from under a fall of dark brown hair, and then scrambled to collect the papers. On his way back outside, he paused to give her a sympathetic nod.

"Señorita," he said.

Another bark from Mendez had him scurrying out again.

Mendez jabbed a finger at Ellie from the entrance to the tent.

"Stay here. Don't cause trouble," he instructed her bluntly.

He walked back outside, impatiently waving Flowers around to guard the back side of the tent.

Ellie scurried over to peer out through the slight gap in the canvas flaps.

Mendez had plopped himself down on the ground just outside. He lit a short cigar and puffed at it, obviously settling in for a boring afternoon.

Ellie's fists clenched at her side as some of her fear gave way to a more comfortable anger.

How *dare* they? Did Jacobs really think he could use her like a pawn with no mind or will of her own? Ellie was the one who had escaped him back in London, and who had beaten him to British Honduras. *She* was the one with the skills and qualifications to properly assess and document what they had come to find.

She was a university-trained scholar, a professional archivist, and a political agitator. She was *not* a chip for someone to push around on their table.

Fury rose, swelling up into her skull until she thought it must crack from the sheer pressure... but there was nowhere for it to go.

There was nothing she could *do*.

Ellie gave the metal cot a ferocious kick. It leaped and rattled alarmingly in response.

Thankfully, her boots held up to the impact. Otherwise, all she would've gained herself was a stubbed toe.

Frustration bloomed up to match her rage... and then fizzled into something more unsettling.

Ellie slumped back against the post at the rear of the tent as she fought a rising sense of despair.

She had well and truly mucked this up.

"Fiddlesticks," she breathed with soft dismay.

Ellie pressed the heels of her hands to her eyes, willing back the tears that threatened to overwhelm her defenses. She would *not* cry. They would think she was weak if she did—and she was *not* weak.

She was clever, resourceful, and determined—and she was damned well going to act like it.

Her thoughts shifted to Adam as though by force of gravity. They stopped on the memory of the look on his face as Mendez had dragged her out of Dawson's tent.

It wasn't a look that she had seen before. Ellie was accustomed to looks that spoke of respect and camaraderie—looks that made her feel important. Appreciated.

She wondered if Adam would ever look at her like that again.

Ellie *had* to talk to him. She had to find a way to get him alone so that they might figure out how they were going to get out of this mess... and so that she might come clean about the rest of what she'd been hiding.

Even if it meant that those looks would get even worse.

Ellie slowly lifted her head from the post and turned her thoughts to how she might make that happen.

TWENTY-FOUR

*A*DAM WATCHED MENDEZ drag Ellie from the tent. An unnamable tumult of emotions roiled in his chest at the desperate, scared look she threw back at him.

He gritted his teeth with the effort of not allowing any of it to show on his face—not here. Not in front of the men who'd just captured them.

They already held all the cards. They hardly needed any extra advantages.

"Report the results to me when you are finished, professor," Jacobs ordered as he moved to leave the tent.

Dawson spluttered a protest.

"Are you just going to leave me here with this... him?" he said, waving an uncomfortable hand in Adam's direction.

"Mr. Staines will stay with you," Jacobs replied dismissively.

"I should think we would need more than that!" Dawson retorted. "What if he runs off or... or attacks me!"

Jacobs swung his gaze to Adam. It locked there with quiet confidence.

"I don't believe we'll need to worry about that," he concluded.

Then he left.

Adam forced himself to unclench his fists and breathe. Pounding the nearest person into a puddle wasn't going to solve any of his problems. He needed to be smart about this.

Setting aside his very real need to hit something, Adam took a better look at his situation.

Dawson's gaze moved nervously from Adam to the remaining guard. Staines was eyeing the neatly made cot like he very much wanted to plop down onto it and do his guarding from a more comfortable position. After a glance at the red-faced Dawson, Staines obviously determined that the more prudent course was to stay on his feet. He adjusted his grip on the rifle, looking bored and uncomfortable.

The guard wasn't the only uncomfortable one. The professor was clearly furious.

Adam hadn't met the guy back at the capital, like Ellie clearly had. Still, he could easily deduce that Dawson must've been involved in whatever had got her tied up and jumping over balconies into Adam's lap.

The man's tent was ridiculously over-furnished. There were actual *carpets* on the floor, and a tin dinner service sat on the table where a plantain leaf or coconut shell would've done perfectly fine.

A trunk of books was open on the floor by the desk. Dawson had apparently brought a library into the bush with him so that it could get infested by termites or turned to a pulp by the damp. From where Adam was standing, he could just make out some of the labels on the spines. They were mostly bound journals and historical tomes on Mesoamerican civilizations, but he also spotted what looked like a novel alongside a well-thumbed volume of the poetry of Robert Burns.

Pleasure reading, Adam deduced.

Every ounce of it would have to be packed up each time they stopped for the night, and then carefully loaded onto the mules in a way that ensured an even distribution of weight... only to be unpacked and set back up again at the end of a long day's march.

It was crazy.

The disdain Adam felt was clearly mutual. The professor was eyeing him like something foul he'd just realized he had stepped on. Apparently, the thought of having his work corrected by a filthy, unshaven guy in shirtsleeves got the professor's goat. The notion might have brought Adam a little burst of satisfaction, if he hadn't also been burning with fury at how he'd been violently blackmailed into doing this.

Ellie. They were going to hurt Ellie.

Miss Mallory, he corrected himself. His mind shied away from the name. He didn't want to think about the fact that she'd lied to him about who she really was. He wasn't sure whether it said something about her... or more about what she thought of him.

Maybe she still hadn't really trusted him—or maybe she just hadn't felt like he was worth giving her real name to.

Adam squirmed away from all the unanswered questions. He wasn't going to think about them right now. He had bigger concerns—like trying to figure out how he was going to get both of them out of this alive.

And it *would* be both of them. Adam wasn't sure what he'd say to the woman when he finally spoke to her again… but he sure as hell wasn't going to leave her to the tender mercies of a guy who threatened to cut her up for what more or less amounted to *just business.*

Adam couldn't do much about any of that while he had a gun pointed at his back, no matter how bored the guy with the gun looked. Until he had a chance to make a plan, he needed to suck it up and do what Jacobs had ordered him to do, however much he hated the idea.

He had no doubt that if he didn't, Jacobs would start hurting Ellie.

"Show me what you've got," Adam ordered.

The professor bristled. He was red-faced from the heat—probably because he was dressed like a Sears catalog advertisement in his khaki field jacket and pith helmet. All of it had blatantly been purchased for the sake of this expedition.

Dawson didn't wear it well. He looked uncomfortable and kept itching at the skin around his collar.

"I really don't see how this is necessary." Dawson glared at Adam from across his desk. "I am a Professor Emeritus of Ancient History at the University of Saint Andrews. I am entirely capable of reading some blasted map!"

Adam didn't bother honoring that with a reply. Instead, he plucked his map canister from Dawson's hand and turned to the table, which offered more space than the desk once Adam shoved the professor's excessive dinner setting off to the side. He unrolled the maps across the surface, weighing down the corners with a fork, a knife, a tin mug, and a salt shaker.

At least the idiot hadn't brought a wine glass.

"Pencil," Adam ordered, extending his hand.

Dawson gaped at him with outrage, unmoving. Adam sighed and reached back to the desk, snatching a writing implement from the box on the surface. He returned his attention to the maps.

He could feel the professor seething behind him. Eventually, Dawson stomped over to the other side of the table and glowered down at Adam's work.

The glower turned to an outraged stammer.

"You—you can't just write all over it!" he protested as he waved his hand over the modern map that Adam had taken from the cylinder.

"It's my map," Adam returned easily.

"It is not!" Dawson retorted. "It says it came from the survey office, just like ours. We were expressly told that the map needed to be returned in the exact condition in which it was taken out."

Adam raised his head to meet Dawson's eyes.

"It's my map," he repeated flatly. He pointed to the unrolled sheet. "I drew it. I can keep drawing it if I want to."

He scratched another mark on it with the pencil.

Dawson made a strangled sound of outrage.

"You aren't even following the line on the parchment," he protested.

"Yeah, well. They were a little short on modern survey methods in the seventeenth century," Adam returned without bothering to look up. "It's safe to say the line's an approximation."

"Surely an approximation is better than making it up off the top of one's head!"

Adam straightened.

"You wanna try?" He held out his pencil.

The professor hesitated, clearly torn between his desire to be too self-important to take the bait and his need to prove himself superior to Adam.

The latter won.

Dawson snatched the pencil and took Adam's place at the table as Adam stepped back to make way for him. Dawson thanked him with a glare.

The professor began to scribble onto a piece of notepaper. Adam took the opportunity to glance over at Staines. The guard suppressed a yawn, and then peered out the flap of the tent as though jealous of the men out there sweating through the work of unloading the barges.

Adam drifted closer to Dawson's desk and took a moment to eye the professor's things. The surface was cluttered with more books and papers. His eye caught on a slender wooden case carved with words in a language Adam didn't recognize. After making sure no one was looking, he lifted the lid.

He'd been hoping for a letter opener he might pocket—hardly as useful as a machete, of course, but better than nothing. Instead, he found a small, slender bone resting on a lining of moth-eaten velvet.

Adam frowned down at it. The bone was maybe six inches long. It looked like a wing bone from something roughly the size of a turkey.

What the hell did Dawson have a wing bone in a special case for?

Adam carefully closed the lid of the bone box and turned his attention to the rest of what lay on the desk. A battered, leatherbound notebook looked promising. Adam opened it to a random page.

Dawson's handwriting was abominable, but Adam still managed to make out bits of it.

Prospects under consideration, location unknown:
Armor of Örvar-Oddr
Babr-e Bayan of Rostam
Ring of Gyges

It sounded like a load of nonsense except for that last bit. The *Ring of Gyges* was vaguely familiar. Adam's brain coughed up something about a Greek myth of a guy who turned himself invisible and caused all kinds of trouble.

He flipped to another page and kept reading.

Received another update from the Unas South Cemetery excavation at Saqqara. Site evidence indicates identification with Horemheb's tomb may be correct. If confirmed, will require immediate investigation to explore possible connection to the Staff of Moses...

Adam blinked. He'd definitely heard of the Staff of Moses—what with all the plagues of locusts and parting the Red Sea.

Dawson had some weird interests, but none of what Adam had seen so far had a damned thing to do with British Honduras.

He took another careful look at his guard and involuntary captor. Neither Staines nor Dawson were bothering to pay him the least bit of attention.

Adam flipped neatly to the last page in the book with any of Dawson's abominable scribble on it. He squinted as he tried to translate it. Dawson's handwriting had grown worse once he got out into the Cayo. The professor must find it harder to hold a pencil when he was sweating.

Adam repressed a chuckle.

A few words made themselves discernible from the mess—*Popol Vuh... annals... gifts of prophecy...*

Adam frowned and risked leaning down for a closer look.

Two words leapt out at him amid the scrawl.

Smoking Mirror.

"There," Dawson announced, straightening.

Adam took a quick step back from the desk and did his best to look innocent.

Staines fixed him with a quick, suspicious glare.

"Have a look," Dawson continued, waving a hand over the maps.

There was a hint of a self-satisfied smile on the professor's face as he took a step back and hovered there.

Adam braced himself over the table and picked up the pencil. He made another mark on his modern map, which elicited a wince from Dawson—but not a protest. Maybe they were making progress.

"You brought a lot of stuff," Adam commented as he worked.

Dawson stiffened a bit beside him.

"This sort of travel is hardly pleasurable," he retorted. "The heat gives me the most dreadful rash, and the mosquitoes! They are incessant. I don't know how anyone can pretend not to be affected by it. I am quite within my rights to make myself as comfortable as possible while I endure it."

Adam was quite aware that Dawson's rights meant the guys outside wrangling a bunch of extra gear through the bush.

"Uh-huh," he said instead, trying—but not entirely succeeding—in keeping the disdain from his tone.

Dawson managed to stay quiet for maybe another minute while Adam worked before he broke into an uncomfortable stream of chatter.

"I copied the route from the parchment precisely," he asserted. "I'm sure you'll see that it's—"

Adam made another mark. This time, he moved to Dawson's sheet of notes and firmly crossed out a line.

"Nope," he declared flatly.

Dawson made a stifled sound of outrage behind him.

Adam crossed out another line, and then a third. He scribbled in a new annotation.

"Remind me again just how you are qualified for this?" Dawson demanded.

Adam paused and looked up at him.

"Are you forgetting I made the map?" He pointed to the document on the table with his pencil.

"How did you even gain a position at the survey office?" Dawson pressed. "You're an *American!*"

He made the word sound like a venereal disease. Adam resisted the urge to throw the pencil at him.

Trying not to get killed, he reminded himself.

"There was an opening. I applied," he returned thinly.

"How would an American even hear about an opening in the civil service of a British imperial holding?" Dawson protested.

"The Cambridge postings board?" Adam suggested as he made another note.

"*You* went to Cambridge?" Dawson exclaimed. "As in the university? In England?"

"That's the one," Adam dryly confirmed.

"But did you actually *study* there?"

"Yup." Adam made another note on the map.

"I... well. That is unexpected," Dawson said blankly.

The professor was obviously shocked to find that the unshaven guy in his shirtsleeves currently taking up space in his tent was an intellectual peer.

"You covered at least some geography, obviously," Dawson continued as he flapped a hand at the map. "What about history?"

This line of conversation was starting to irritate Adam.

"Some," he replied tersely.

"Theology?"

Not if I could help it, Adam thought. He set down the pencil and looked up.

"Does it matter?" he demanded.

Dawson stiffened.

"Hardly."

Adam worked in welcome silence for another minute before Dawson broke it again.

"Have you traveled over very much of this territory, then?" the professor asked.

The man's tone had changed. It sounded just a bit more... *interested.*

Adam's alarm bells rang.

"You could say that," he answered carefully.

"I see," Dawson returned.

Another silence. Adam's pencil scratched on the paper.

"I noticed that there are quite a few Mayan sites marked on the map," Dawson noted from behind him.

He had moved closer. Adam resisted the urge to flinch.

"Most of them are small," Adam replied without looking back at him. "Petroglyphs. Foundation imprints."

"But you *have* seen them, then?" Dawson prompted.

Adam's pencil paused on the paper.

"Some," he said again.

The word felt a bit thinner this time as Adam endured a barrage of memories of shattered pottery and scattered bones.

"And do you have any theories about the city we are seeking on this expedition?"

Dawson's question caught Adam off guard. He set his pencil down on the map with a flat snap and looked back at the professor.

"What?" he demanded.

"You are a Cambridge scholar. You have visited a number of other ruins. Do you have a theory?" Dawson repeated impatiently.

"I'm not much on theories," Adam returned evenly.

He turned back to his work. A distinct sniff sounded from behind him.

"I thought as much," Dawson noted stuffily.

Adam fought the urge to respond. The man didn't deserve it. A few moments later, he set down the pencil.

"There's your route," he announced.

Dawson hurried in, casting Adam a sideways look as he passed. He peered down at the pages on the table.

Adam put his finger on the modern map and traced a line.

"Your route had us going through the middle of this mountain... and then back through it again. Which makes not one damned bit of sense," Adam finished neatly.

Dawson bristled but managed to contain himself.

"My route goes through a mountain?" he pressed.

Adam answered by tapping his finger on the mountain in question.

Dawson pulled the papers toward him for a quick, furious examination, and then straightened awkwardly.

"Oh," he said.

"We gotta follow the line of this ridge." Adam waved his hand over the entirety of the region. "None of this territory has undergone a formal survey beyond a straight-line expedition to the border with Guatemala a dozen or so years ago. We can be pretty confident about the locations of the various peaks, but that's about it. Our route's actually got to run more directly south. It almost doubles back on itself." He crossed his arms and considered the line against the path that he and Ellie had taken to get there.

The most direct route to the X on the map would've required heading west from Padre Kuyoc's village. Adam honestly should've figured that out himself, once Ellie had finally shown him the whole of the map. He'd been so focused on getting them to the next landmark alive and intact, he hadn't taken the time to plot further.

He burned a bit at the mistake. If he had, they never would've bothered hiking to the cataracts—and Jacobs might've sat out here waiting for them for weeks.

Which would've been just fine with Adam.

"You should be able to make it as far as here tomorrow," he said and tapped the map. "After that, I'd look for an open stretch of the ridge to see if you can spot this *River of Smoke*. Whatever that is."

"Yes, well," Dawson said stiffly. "Thank you for your assistance."

"Don't mention it," Adam replied thinly.

Assistance. Was it really assistance if he gave it on the threat of Jacobs carving Ellie into pieces?

"You can go now." Dawson waved a hand dismissively before greedily gathering up the maps.

Adam fought against the urge to tell the professor exactly what he was thinking.

Don't get killed, he reminded himself again. The phrase was becoming something of a mantra.

Adam pivoted for the door of the tent. Staines snapped to attention behind him.

"Where am I supposed to take him?" Staines demanded.

Dawson looked up, flustered, as Adam paused at the threshold.

"How should I know?" the professor exclaimed. "Ask Mr. Jacobs."

With a flap of his hands, he dismissed them.

TWENTY-FIVE

$\mathcal{A}$S THE GLOOM of the deepening evening settled in, Ellie sat inside the tent and plotted furiously.

She needed to talk to Adam Bates. It was absolutely essential that they coordinate their plans for escape.

The thought made her stomach twist uncomfortably. Ellie had no doubt that Adam would still be willing to save her from Dawson and Jacobs. He would never abandon her to a pair of thugs... no matter how poorly he thought of her after learning that she'd lied to him.

The interior of her canvas prison was sadly short on potentially useful supplies. Dropping to her belly at the side wall of the tent, Ellie took advantage of the growing gloom to lift the canvas ever-so-slightly and peer out.

Mendez still slouched by the front flaps, holding his rifle. He looked desperately bored.

She tilted the little gap she'd made in the tent flap and twisted to get a peek at the back.

Flowers gave her a cheerful wave from where he sat on a stump.

Ellie pulled herself back into the tent, cursing softly.

She might be able to slip past her guards once it was truly dark. After all, two men couldn't possibly keep their eyes on every angle of the tent at all times. If Ellie waited long enough—and used a less noticeable spying gap—she could probably find an opportunity to slide out and escape... but then what?

The camp was crawling with men, and it was madness to think that Adam would be left conveniently unguarded.

Ellie needed a way to make sure that she wouldn't be spotted before she reached him—and that she would find him alone when she did. She needed a distraction.

The obvious solution lay in the steam barges that she had seen floating on the river a short distance from the shore.

The temperature at which water converted into steam changed based on atmospheric pressure, and steam engines were pressurized. Were that pressure to drop precipitously—perhaps from a fracture in the boiler caused by overheating—the remaining water in the system would instantaneously convert to gas.

Gas took up more space than water. In a confined environment, a rapid increase in mass had to find a way out—ergo, explosion.

An explosion would be a perfectly adequate distraction.

Ellie pressed her face to the canvas tarpaulin covering the floor. Through a much smaller gap in the side of the tent, she peered out at the watercraft.

"Maybe if I drained some of the water from the cooling system," she muttered to herself under her breath as her mind worked furiously, "then added a few paraffin canisters to the firebox…"

"Added paraffin to what?" a voice behind her demanded with obvious alarm.

"Bates!" Ellie cried out as she whirled around.

He was just visible across the shadowy interior of the tent where he stood by the entrance. His expression was slightly aghast.

"Hold on—cooling system? Firebox?" he said. "Sweet hell—are you talking about blowing up a boiler?"

"Well, not anymore," Ellie retorted as she climbed to her feet. "Not now that you're here."

"What a relief."

Adam did not sound the least bit relieved. He rubbed at the bridge of his nose as though fighting a headache.

"Please promise me you'll stick that plan on the shelf," he said. "No—burn it. Just erase it from your brain. Pretend it never existed."

"The plan was perfectly sound." Ellie crossed her arms in irritation. "Entirely based on hard science."

"Blowing up a steam engine?" Adam shot back as his voice rose.

Ellie stepped closer, dropping her own words to a fierce whisper as she glanced at the tent flap—beyond which Mendez was almost certainly trying to eavesdrop.

"I would have had at least six minutes to get to shore before the system overheated," she insisted.

"*After* you threw the explosive stuff onto the fire," Adam filled in flatly.

"In a sealed tin!" Ellie protested, still working to keep her volume down. "I have calculated it would take at least four minutes at the standard ambient temperature of an idling steam boiler to melt."

Adam leaned against the tent post tiredly.

"And why were you planning to blow up a boat, Princess?" he asked patiently.

"To create a distraction, of course! I needed to talk to you," she replied.

"Well, here I am," Adam said, spreading his arms.

Ellie eyed him skeptically.

"How *are* you here?" she demanded, and then brightened. "Did you overcome Mr. Dawson and tie him up in his tent?"

"I just asked," Adam replied. "Jacobs didn't tell anybody I couldn't, so they let me in. Apparently, he doesn't see the two of us talking to each other as any kind of threat. Probably because he's got this camp surrounded by a dozen or so guys with guns, and all I've got is a match tin."

Ellie narrowed her eyes thoughtfully.

"A match tin, did you say?" she prompted.

"No," Adam countered flatly. "Don't even think about it."

He dropped down into the chair by the empty desk and rested his head in his hands.

"So what'd you want to talk about?" he asked.

Ellie's stomach sank. She knew what she should be talking about.

"How did things go with Dawson?" she asked instead.

"He stood around and complained while I fixed his route," Adam replied. "Presumably, they'll want me to keep doing it until they find whatever's at the end of that map."

"Yes, I see," Ellie said.

She sat down on the edge of the cot. Though only a few feet of packed earth separated them, it felt like miles.

"You should escape," she declared.

Adam stiffened in his chair. He raised his head to glare at her.

"Excuse me?" he demanded angrily.

Ellie lifted her chin, refusing to flinch.

"You should slip away as soon as you have a chance. You can simply disappear. You're entirely capable of it."

"And what will you be doing while I'm disappearing?" Adam shot back darkly.

"I'll figure something out," Ellie asserted with a wave of her hand.

She had meant for it to sound confident. It didn't.

"You really think I'd do that?" Adam retorted fiercely. "You really think I'd run off and leave you here with a guy who's threatening to cut you to pieces?"

"No," Ellie admitted glumly. "I don't. But it would have been the reasonable thing to do."

"I guess it's a good thing for you that I'm unreasonable, then."

"Honorable," she returned automatically. She closed her eyes for a moment against a well of emotion that rose up inside of her. "The word you are looking for is *honorable*."

Adam went quiet. She could still feel the weight of his gaze through the near-darkness.

Ellie took a breath.

"If I had trusted you with the entirety of the map from the beginning, we would have been here days ago," she spilled out. "We might have found the arch and moved on before Dawson and Jacobs ever arrived."

Adam rubbed his face. "Yeah, well... if I'd hazarded more of an educated guess about where the rest of your landmarks might be once I *did* have the whole thing, I might've saved us the trouble anyway."

"I suppose Dawson and Jacobs would simply have caught us in the city, then," Ellie mused awkwardly.

"I dunno. That guy Dawson is godawful at reading a map," Adam returned dryly.

A smile pulled at her lips involuntarily at this hint of his old humor—and then died fairly quickly.

"I... owe you an apology for the rest of it as well," Ellie said carefully.

Adam's silence had weight. Ellie forced herself to push past it, knowing that it was the right thing to do.

"There might have been some sense to it in the beginning—concealing my name," she continued. "Before I really knew who you were. I should have corrected it long before now... along with everything else."

"Everything else?" Adam echoed a little dangerously.

"I stole that map," Ellie blurted out. "The circumstances were admittedly unusual, and I told myself I was only really borrowing it... but borrowing something without telling anyone about it is stealing. Dawson and Jacobs *are* thieves as well," she hurried to add. "Jacobs was trying to purchase the map and the medallion off my supervisor, Mr. Henbury, who had absolutely no right to sell them. When Mr. Henbury no longer had the items to sell, Jacobs tried to throw him through a door."

She forced herself to say the rest.

"But I haven't any more right to it than they do. I took it with me because I knew it shouldn't belong to *them*, but I could quite easily have turned it over to a reputable authority. I kept it for myself, and I was far from transparent about that with you when we agreed to undertake this expedition together. I was afraid if I told you the truth about where the map had come from, you'd decide the whole business was more trouble than it was worth."

"Princess... you fell on me from a balcony with a gag on," Adam pointed out. "I'm pretty sure I knew how much trouble I was getting into."

"You helped me," Ellie countered firmly. "You came to my aid, and I repaid you with falsehoods. You deserved better than that."

She could see his shrug through the gloom.

"You wanted to follow your map. I had an opening in my calendar. Don't see that you owe me much for that," he replied flatly.

The reply stung, even as it offered Ellie a convenient way out. She could accept it, and the matter would be settled. They were more or less strangers—their relationship one of convenience. What else should it be?

"*No*," she burst out roughly. "You protected me from Jacobs. You took a chance on my map. You—you lost your *boat*, and you never once made me feel like it was my fault. You treated me like an equal partner—like... like a *colleague* when you were the one with all the knowledge of how to get where we were going, and all I brought to the table was... well, a respectable knowledge of current scholarship on Mesoamerican civilizations... but you hardly required that. Perhaps I was simply an opening in your calendar, but you have been a *very* great deal more than that to me."

Ellie uttered the words in the same low tones that she had used since Adam had entered. They still seemed to ring in the silence of the tent in a manner that left her feeling terribly exposed.

"The least I could have done in return was grant you the truth," she finished.

"It would've been nice to know who I was really traveling with," Adam finally said. His voice carried to her softly through the shadows that cloaked them.

There was nothing of accusation in his voice. What Ellie heard there sounded more like hurt.

She winced against it, knowing what must come next.

"Yes. Well. About that..." she began awkwardly.

Adam slumped back in his chair.

"Awww hell," he said. "What is it? You're actually an escaped felon? You've got a trigger-happy maharajah for a boyfriend?"

"Not exactly," Ellie returned carefully. "It is rather that I am... er... *related*, in a manner of speaking... to Mr... ah, Fairfax. I mean... Neil. I'm related to Neil."

Adam's head shot up with alarm.

"You're *what?*" He blinked as his focus sharpened. "Ellie... Eleanora. Fairfax's sister is an Eleanora. But your name is Mallory!" He shook his head. "Except Fairfax's dad passed when he was a kid. His mother remarried. Some nice insurance clerk... Daniel?"

"David," Ellie corrected him weakly as she forced a grimace into an approximation of a smile. "David Mallory."

"Your dad," Adam filled in bluntly. "Because Fairfax is your brother."

"Technically my stepbrother," she hedged in return.

Adam stared at her, paling.

"Because you're Peanut," he said numbly. "You're Fairfax's Peanut."

Ellie's irritation flared.

"I will not endorse that wretched nickname," she pronounced.

"You're Fairfax's Peanut," Adam repeated stubbornly. His expression shifted to one of deeper dawning horror. "And I've ruined you."

Ellie's jaw dropped. She snapped it closed again.

"You most certainly have not!" she protested.

Adam pushed to his feet, agitation animating his frame.

"We've been alone in the bush together for a week. You think anybody is going to believe I kept my hands off you?" He laughed a little madly as he pushed his hands through his hair. "I mean, for all anybody knows we might've been—" He caught himself, choking back the words as he flashed Ellie an uncomfortable look. "Just... things. Extremely inappropriate things."

A bolt of indignation straightened Ellie's spine.

"I am not ignorant of the conditions required for sexual congress, Mr. Bates."

Adam made a strangled noise, and then dropped back into his chair, lowering his head. He raised it a moment later, looking stricken.

"We're gonna have to get married," he declared.

Panic drove Ellie to her feet as the response spilled out of her.

"Absolutely not!"

Adam jabbed a finger at her.

"Word of this gets back to London, what do you think is going to happen?" he demanded.

"Maybe word of it doesn't need to get back to anyone," Ellie suggested uneasily.

"So—what? We just lie to everybody for the rest of our lives? One of my best friends? Your *brother?*" he emphasized.

Ellie ground her teeth against the conundrum.

A falsehood would certainly be easier. They were on the other side of the world. The chances that anyone would ever find out about it were practically nonexistent... as long as she didn't mind living a lie for the rest of her life, and obligating Adam to do the same.

She let out a growl of frustration and fell back onto the cot, sprawling out her arms. She stared up at the blank canvas roof of the tent.

"I don't want to be married," Ellie protested. "To *anybody.*"

There was an alarming wobble to the words.

"I'm not exactly crazy about the idea myself," Adam retorted.

His reply stung... and then a less logical response bubbled up inside of her. A laugh slipped out of her, edged with hysteria.

She heard Adam shift across from her. The cot jolted as he sat down on the ground beside her and leaned back against the frame.

A head of unruly sun-stained hair rested by her right hand. It would be the simplest thing for Ellie to reach out and run her fingers through it.

The impulse was wildly inappropriate. Ellie resisted it. After all, she had no reason to think it would be welcome. Instead, she continued to stare up at the ceiling as the sounds of the camp filtered softly through to where they sat. The low conversation of the men by the campfires mingled with the snorting and shuffling of the mules in their pen.

"I swear I didn't know," Ellie quietly confessed. "Not until you told the story about the emu when we were on the boat."

"I thought you were worried about the bird," Adam replied.

"If I had just told you then, you would certainly have made us turn back," she said. "All of this could have been avoided."

"Maybe," Adam agreed. "We would've missed out on a lot of fun, though."

"Fun?" Ellie sat up and looked down at him. "Nearly going over a waterfall was *fun?*"

"Don't pretend you didn't enjoy it," he retorted as he glanced up at her with a wicked glint in his eyes.

She flopped back down and shook her head at the ceiling. "You're impossible."

"I think the word you're looking for is *right,*" he countered.

Ellie didn't reply. For a moment, she let herself simply *be*, soaking up the rumble of laughter, the soft rush of water from outside the tent, and the easy presence of Adam leaning beside her.

She took a breath as she steeled herself for what must come next.

"Please don't take this the wrong way. You're a very nice person—" she began.

"I'm a *what?*" Adam sounded offended.

"…But surely there must be some way out of our situation that doesn't involve legally binding ourselves together for life!" Ellie finished.

She felt his sigh through the frame of the cot.

"I am a suffragist!" she continued. "I have been arrested. I went to university, for goodness's sake! It's not as though I have any reputation worth speaking of."

"This is different, and you know it," he replied. "Look—I'm the last guy to lecture someone on sexual mores—"

"Are you?" Ellie asked, suddenly curious.

"But this isn't about you," he pressed on, deliberately avoiding her question. "It's about everybody else. Your dad. Your stepmom. Your brother. I know how the world treats people who don't follow the rules. It's why I got out. They don't just go after you. They punish everyone you care about like it's contagious."

He was right, and Ellie knew it. She hated that she knew it, but that didn't make it any less true. Raising a spinster was one thing, but a whore…

Ellie perseverated over it in grim silence until Adam finally spoke again.

"Why didn't you fix it?" he asked.

The words were unusually tentative.

"I mean the… things you hadn't been completely honest about," he added awkwardly. "Once you realized I wasn't the kind of guy who'd just leave you in the wilderness over them." He frowned and turned toward her, resting his arm on the cot. "You did realize I wasn't the kind of guy who'd leave you in the wilderness, right?"

"Of course I did," Ellie replied. She kept her gaze on the ceiling. It was easier than looking at him.

He turned away again. "Never mind. It's none of my business."

Ellie's heart clenched inside her chest. She came upright and swung her legs over the side of the cot so that she sat beside him, albeit at different levels.

"Ask the question," she ordered gently.

He took a breath as though gathering himself before he answered.

"Why didn't you tell me?" He swallowed, obviously uncomfortable. "You knew I wouldn't ditch you in the swamp over it, and you keep saying you felt like you owed me, so…"

There were things he wasn't saying. Somehow Ellie sensed that those things were what really mattered—and that they were fragile. That if she answered wrong, something desperately important might simply break.

There was only one way to respond to that. She had to tell the truth.

"I didn't want the way you looked at me to change," she quietly confessed.

Adam didn't move... and yet it still seemed as though the air of the tent had shifted.

"How did I look at you?"

His voice was soft and deep. It carried to her through the darkness as though it could've crossed a hundred times that distance, even at a murmur.

Ellie let the answer fall from her lips, even as her voice broke a bit on the words.

"Like I was your friend."

Birds called softly through the night air. Footsteps crunched beyond the walls of the tent, blending with the crackling of a campfire. Someone laughed a little distance away.

"Ah hell, Princess," Adam replied softly.

The cot jolted again as he moved. He rose from the floor, and then plopped down beside the place where she sat. The springs creaked under his weight.

His arm came around her. Ellie let it. She leaned into his side, and her head fell to his shoulder.

His chin came down to rest on her hair.

Emotions tripped and thundered inside of her... and then stilled. A warm, solid sense of calm moved through her. It was all wrapped up in the steady rhythm of Adam's breath, which Ellie could feel rising and falling through the place where her cheek rested against his chest.

"I'll find us a way out of this," Adam declared. "I'll need to get my hands on a knife—it'd be nuts to try to slip away without one—but I can work on that."

"Bates, there are a lot of armed men running about," Ellie cautioned.

"I've gotten out of worse scrapes before."

"Have you?" she pressed.

"Er... maybe not, but it can't be that different. It's all about waiting for the right opportunity and then improvising."

Adam's cheerful reply sparked a flash of concern.

"What about a plan?" Ellie countered urgently.

"Sure," Adam agreed with a shrug. "We can make one of those too."

The way he said it gave Ellie the distinct impression that Adam's regard for plans fell significantly short of her own... but it was not his alarming faith in his own improvisational skills that made her go quietly still under the weight of his arm.

"What is it?" Adam asked, sensing the change.

Ellie hesitated.

"Princess," Adam pressed warningly.

"I'm not sure that we should go," Ellie blurted in reply. The rest of it spilled out of her. "I just keep thinking of that terrible rubble in the cave on the way here. If we run, there will be no one to stop Dawson and Jacobs from doing exactly the same thing to whatever is at the end of that map. When think of how much might be lost..." She looked up to meet his eyes. "But it's madness. Even if we did stay, how could we possibly expect to stop them There's just the two of us."

Adam went quiet beside her.

"Staying would be dangerous," he finally said.

"More dangerous than running off into the bush with only a machete for equipment?" she retorted.

"Yeah," Adam replied flatly.

Ellie's heart sank.

"Definitely life threatening," he added.

His tone made her look back up again. His eyes glinted dangerously at her in the near darkness.

"Probably incredibly stupid," he said.

His mouth split into a grin.

Ellie's nerves jolted uneasily in response, but the feeling was mingled through with something warmer... something that felt like hope.

"Sounds like my cup of tea," he finished.

Her own smile rose in answer, beaming out through the gloom of the tent

Adam's expression grew serious again.

"The only part I don't like about it is that there's a guy out in that camp who's made it clear he's got no problem cutting you up if he thinks we aren't playing along," he cautioned.

"Then we'll play along," she concluded. "Trying to lead them astray wouldn't work anyway. Jacobs will be watching for that. I have an... *uncomfortable* feeling that he has an uncanny ability to see through a deception."

Ellie's resolve firmed.

"We will simply have to find a way to stop them once we have reached the city," she determined.

"You and me," Adam replied. "Against ten guys with guns. A murderous bastard with an infallible nose for lies."

"An imminent monsoon," Ellie added, barely fighting back a giggle.

"And one really sweaty professor," Adam added wryly.

The giggle burst out. Ellie clamped her hand over her mouth to contain it, conscious of the men just outside the tent.

"No problem," Adam whispered confidently.

Ellie rose from the cot and brushed off her trousers.

"I shall start making a plan," she declared.

Adam rose as well.

"You do that." His expression shifted, going over a bit cautious. "Just... promise you won't try to blow anything up without checking with me first."

Ellie frowned.

"What if the circumstances are such that an explosion is very clearly called for?" she demanded.

"Maybe... try to plan your way *around* any circumstances like that?" Adam suggested.

Ellie considered it.

"I suppose that is fair," she allowed.

She looked up at his face. It was familiar even through the deep shadows, and at the sight of it, something in her chest started to glow warmly.

Without further warning, the tent flap flew back. Ellie startled as Mendez stuck his head inside with a lantern in his hand.

"Oye—you!" he said, waving a hand at Adam. "Boss had them rig a hammock for you."

Adam paused at the threshold to glance back at Ellie. The look he gave her made the hairs on her arms tingle.

"Try to get some sleep, Princess," he said.

"You as well, Mr. Bates," Ellie returned evenly.

And then he was gone.

TWENTY-SIX

*T*HE NEXT MORNING, the caravan set out far later than it would have on one of Adam's expeditions. Of course, Adam's expeditions usually involved no more than four or five guys. This was easily seven times that size, with a couple of dozen mules to boot.

You needed a lot of mules if you were going to drag books out with you into the middle of nowhere.

When the long line of animals and men finally did get moving, it wove into the bush at a crawl as it followed the route Adam had mapped out. Adam ground his teeth against the urge to move faster. Breaking off to make his own more efficient way along the trail would probably have raised a ruckus. After all, he did have an armed guard trotting along in his wake.

It seemed Staines, the pomaded guy from Dawson's tent, had been assigned to monitor Adam. Staines looked like the last thing he wanted to do was hike at a snail's pace through the uncharted wilderness behind an unshaven, grumpy bakra.

Adam glanced along the snaking line of the caravan until his eyes stopped on Ellie's figure. She was mounted on a mule and looked damned uncomfortable with the position. Flowers and Mendez flanked her to either side.

Adam still wasn't sure what to think about their conversation the night before. A small, terrible part of him had feared that Ellie had lied to him because he simply wasn't worth telling the truth to. He'd been relieved to know that wasn't the case... maybe a little *too* relieved.

Feeling *too* relieved meant that what the woman thought of him had become pretty damned important to him—that it was something he cared about.

Aw, hell. Who was he kidding? He cared.

Well, he could enjoy knowing she cared as well for a little while longer... until their forced marriage solidly killed that dead.

Adam didn't waste any time being offended that Ellie wasn't excited about the idea of being stuck with him for life. He knew it wasn't personal. Even if Ellie hadn't been dead opposed to the entire idea of matrimony, Adam certainly wasn't the kind of man she would have chosen for herself. She'd probably want some nice, mild guy in a waistcoat who shaved regularly and never once caught himself smelling a bit like a rotten lizard. Someone who could read books with her and chat about Aramaic semantics over dinner. He'd probably be a professor of something.

That made Adam think of Dawson. He quickly amended the theory—not a professor. Maybe a nice school teacher. Yeah, that felt right. He'd be from one of those girls' schools that actually taught them things besides balancing books on their heads.

And he'd definitely be the kind of jerk who took on a bunch of extra charity students on the side.

Instead of that, Ellie was going to get Adam. It kind of made him feel awful for her, even as he also imagined himself socking that schoolteacher right in the waistcoat.

Adam startled. Why was he fantasizing about beating the schoolteacher? The guy had never done anything to him. He didn't even exist.

The conundrum of that left him with the creeping and uncomfortable sensation that he was missing something important... something that stalked him like a jaguar in the fog.

Well, whatever that was, he'd worry about it later. Right now, he needed to focus on more practical concerns.

British Honduras was a small colony, and the community of men who did expedition work there was even smaller. Adam knew most of them, so he hadn't been surprised when he started picking familiar faces out of the crowd at the camp once it was light enough for him to actually see everybody.

He had figured out Nigel Reneau was manning the cookfire when he tasted last night's dinner. Adam could have recognized Nigel's hudutu, a mouthwatering Garifuna fish stew, just from the smell.

Then there was Arturo Velegas. The old Mestizo fellow looked a bit like a gray-mustachioed grandpa who should be dozing on someone's porch. He was actually one of the best hunters and trackers in the business.

Aurelio Fajardo was handling the mules, which figured. Aurelio looked like the less friendly kind of grandpa—or maybe he saved that glowering air of disapproval just for Adam. After all, Adam had an unfortunate habit of coming back from his expeditions a few mules short of the full contingent he'd rented from Aurelio. Adam had managed to talk his way around that problem the first two times it happened, but he figured he was probably on some damned thin ice as far as Aurelio was concerned.

The two guys from Caulker Caye, Pacheco and Lopez, were new to him. They couldn't have been more than eighteen. The pair spent most of their time chatting with each other incessantly, flipping from Spanish to Kriol based on which language was less likely to be understood by whoever was within earshot.

There were also four East Indians fresh out of their indentured service contracts over in Jamaica—if they hadn't just run off. There were Indians all over the various British colonial holdings in the Caribbean. Most of them were from the Bhojpuri region. They were treated pretty miserably once they arrived. Adam wouldn't have blamed Ram and the other guys if they'd decided to take off, contract be damned, and build a new life for themselves in a different port.

He didn't recognize any of Jacobs' armed men. There were ten of them altogether—more than enough for him to feel unpleasantly surrounded.

Adam had spotted two other faces in the crowd that he was particularly interested in catching up with. When the caravan stopped for lunch, he finally got his chance.

The mules brayed with irritation as Nigel handed out dry rations from the expedition's supplies. The forest around them had already started to include more of the tall pines that would dominate the landscape of the mountains.

Adam's guard, Staines, shifted uncomfortably from one foot to another as Adam crunched down some hard biscuit and dried goat. As the day progressed, the guy had managed to look even more bored and put-upon by his assignment.

Staines jumped as a troll-like figure popped up at his back. The new arrival's pale skin was permanently ruddied from years in the sun—at least, the little of it that could be seen past the mass of an unruly reddish-brown beard. He was built as solidly as a brick wall, for all that the top of his head was maybe level with Adam's biceps.

"Eh niaiseux," the troll announced as he gave Staines a poke in the ribs. "The boss is asking for you."

His *the* was dulled into *de*, while *asking* drew itself out into *hasking*. One didn't often hear the distinctive tones of a Quebecois accent in the colony of British Honduras.

Staines managed to look both annoyed at the interruption and hopeful at a possible reassignment.

"And who's gonna watch this bakra here, then?" he demanded.

"I'm going to watch him," the Quebecois replied.

"But you don't have one of the guns," Staines pointed out.

The squat Canadian plucked a wicked, gleaming length of machete from the sheath at his belt.

"This good enough for you? Or do you want a closer look?" He punctuated this with a slightly terrifying grin that showed off his three missing teeth.

"Good enough," Staines agreed. He swung his rifle to his back and stalked off.

"Salut, Lessard," Adam said easily once Staines had gone.

"Bonne après-midi, Anglo," Lessard replied. He punctuated the traditional Quebecois insult by loosing a stream of tobacco-stained expectorant.

It nearly hit a lizard. The lizard scampered away in alarm.

Adam had known Martin Lessard for years. Lessard had been a logger in Canada for decades before coming to British Honduras. Adam still wasn't entirely sure what had brought him there, as there were still plenty of trees to cut in Canada. The ways of Lessard were a mystery you didn't really want to get close enough to solve—but the hairy Quebecois was a hell of a hunter with a keen sense of direction. He also came in pretty handy in a brawl.

"It's nice to see you," Adam offered genuinely.

"It will be nicer to see you when you learn how to speak like a man instead of forcing me to use your ugly bastard language," Lessard replied casually.

Lessard, like most of his countrymen, had decided opinions about the superiority of Quebec's particular variety of French.

They were joined a moment later by Charles Goodwin. The lean, well-muscled Kriol man kept his hair close-cropped and natural above a neat beard. He swung himself onto a boulder and rolled a cigarette as he watched Staines stomp across the camp.

"You got your hand in the tiger's mouth this time, bali," Charlie commented blandly.

"It's not my finest moment," Adam admitted.

Charlie was a regular on Adam's expeditions. He'd grown up in the bush trailing his father, who had made his living as a mahogany cutter. Charlie was wickedly resourceful and generally unflappable. He had gotten Adam out of more than one tough pinch in the past.

"And with a woman," Charlie added pointedly. "Can't wait to hear about that."

He flicked a match to life against the stone, lit his smoke, and took a satisfied draw.

"It's complicated," Adam replied.

"C'est une femme," Lessard returned flatly as though the connection between *woman* and *complicated* should have been obvious.

"Any particular reason you're being marched around here with a gun at your back?" Charlie asked mildly.

Adam rubbed his face tiredly. "It's a long story."

Lessard frowned at the empty sheath on Adam's belt.

"Where's your knife?" he demanded.

"Your bosses took it," Adam replied. "Got my Winchester, too."

"My condolences, mon ami," Lessard replied.

It sounded like he actually meant it. Then again, it didn't surprise Adam that Lessard might consider losing one's machete to be a bit like the death of a beloved aunt.

Adam couldn't entirely blame him. He'd had aunts he cared less about than his knife.

"Lessard and I thought we best check in," Charlie said with another puff on his cigarette. "Won't be long before our boy Staines finds out nobody was asking for him, so we'd best check quick."

"Who's running this line?" Adam asked.

Charlie pointed across the camp with his cigarette. The ember picked out a tall, lanky Jamaican with a precise mustache.

"That's Bones," Charlie said.

"Haven't heard of him," Adam noted.

Adam's lack of familiarity with the man was worth noting. He had been pretty sure he knew everybody in the colony who might run a caravan like this. After all, there were only about six of them—himself and Charlie included.

"He's former West India Regiment, fresh out. Knows his business well enough, but not much for a joke," Charlie explained.

"How about these guys with the guns?" Adam pressed.

"Company men," Charlie returned flatly.

There was only one company that mattered around here—the British Honduras Export Company. Run by a board of executives who did their decision-making from cushy chairs in a London office, the Company owned the vast majority of the land outside Belize Town and claimed a monopoly on logging rights. Most of the local colonial officials were solidly in the Company's pocket—and it didn't shy away from using less-than-scrupulous methods to expand its land claims or remove obstacles to timber harvesting...

obstacles like some of the local Maya.

The Company's hired guns weren't chosen for their high morals. They got the job because they didn't ask questions, and because they said yes to whatever needed to be done.

"Great," Adam grumbled.

"Except for the bakra," Lessard added helpfully.

"What bakra?" Adam demanded.

"What bakra do you think?" Lessard shot back. "The one that looks like somebody dropped him a few times when he was a baby."

Adam scanned the camp. His gaze locked onto one of the only other white men in the vicinity. He looked to be around twenty. He was a few inches shorter than Adam, with a scraggly blonde mustache and blue eyes that bulged a little.

"That guy?" Adam asked.

"Pickett," Charlie filled in with a tired sigh. "Boy falls a little short of Company standards."

"Probably because he spawned from all your Confederates marrying their cousins," Lessard cheerfully offered.

Adam was familiar with the local Confederates. A contingent of them had landed in British Honduras after the war. They set up new plantations in the Toledo district. Though slavery had been against the law in the colony for about a hundred years, Adam figured the rebel sons had been drawn south by a combination of cheap land, lax indentured labor laws, and a general terror of sleeping just down the road from the justifiably angry people whom they and their ancestors had once owned.

A bunch of people who'd used skin color as an excuse for putting others in chains weren't likely to intermarry with the local population in the colony. That had left them with a somewhat limited courtship pool.

"How the hell did you two end up involved in this?" Adam demanded.

"The bosses offered triple rates," Lessard replied. He took a piece of jerky off of the plantain leaf that Adam was using as a plate and shoved it in his mouth.

Charlie shrugged. "Laura wants a new shed. And how do I know the old boss is gonna show up on the wrong end of a rifle?"

"You got a plan, then?" Lessard asked from around Adam's jerky.

"I'm still working on it," Adam replied.

"You won't get far without a knife," Lessard warned.

"I don't suppose I could borrow either of yours?" Adam tried.

Lessard spat. The look that Charlie flashed Adam would've withered fruit on the vine.

"Yeah, I thought as much." Adam sighed. "What're the chances you could steal me one?"

"No chance," Charlie retorted flatly.

"Aww, come on," Adam countered. "It's not like the pair of you aren't capable of swiping a knife without getting caught."

"Maybe without getting caught," Charlie returned crossly. "But not without somebody noticing their knife is gone. And who you think they gonna figure took it?"

"Probably the guy without a knife," Lessard pointed out helpfully.

"The Frenchman and I are not the ones with the guns out here," Charlie protested. "We get caught taking some boy's knife for you, you think they going to keep us around for decoration like your bakra self?"

"Lessard's a bakra," Adam protested with a wave at the ruddy-faced Canadian.

"Lessard's not a bakra," Charlie returned. "Look at him."

Lessard flashed Adam a gap-toothed, tobacco-stained smile.

"When they're about to drag you out into the bush and shoot you, maybe I'll get you a knife." Charlie took an irritated puff on his cigarette. "*Maybe.*"

"Our boy here still has that favor," Lessard noted. His eyes glittered with dark mischief.

Charlie's head swiveled. He pinned Lessard with a glare.

"That's right," Adam said slowly as a grin spread irresistibly across his face. "You said you owed me one when I got you out of that trouble with your wife."

"After this idiot tried to climb the lighthouse when he was drunk as a rat and broke his arm," Lessard added with a dark chortle.

"It was a protest," Charlie shot back.

"You were going to hang your underpants from the flagpole," Lessard retorted. His eyes began to water as he snorted at the memory.

Charlie straightened and looked down his nose at his smaller, more grizzled companion.

"I am a sixth generation Belize man, and I have no vote in the elections," he retorted, jabbing his cigarette to make the point. "How does that Union Jack do me any good? Maybe we'd all be better off with the underpants."

"Sure. Tell that to Laura," Lessard returned with another wheeze.

Charlie glowered at Lessard, and then shifted the glower to Adam.

"Aarait," he snapped. "You still got your favor. You wanna use it for a knife, what do I care? But when you do, your raass better be ready to run."

Adam began to feel the distinct beginnings of a headache. "Fair enough. Anything else I should know?"

Charlie gave his cigarette an irritated flick.

"The professor acts like he's in charge, but everybody knows Jacobs is the real boss," he said. "Jacobs does all the work, while the professor sits around and reads those books he brought with him. He's got a real fire lit under his feet about finding some big thing when they reach the city."

Adam frowned.

"Some big thing like what?" he asked.

"What do I know?" Charlie took another drag, tapping his foot. "I'm just the help."

Being *just the help* gave Charlie the chance to quietly soak up every bit of useful information from what was going on around him. There was a reason Belize Town's nascent anti-imperialist movement had quickly recruited Charlie into its ranks. He was very good at noticing things.

Not that this particular piece of information was all that enlightening. It only made things even more confusing. Adam fought against his own exasperation.

"How can he be after something at the end of this trail when we have no idea what the hell we're going to find there?" he protested.

"You tell him about the crazy candle?" Lessard demanded, looking to Charlie.

"What candle?" Adam asked.

Charlie rolled his eyes a bit.

"You tell him about the candle," he shot back. "You're the crazy Frenchman saw it."

"It was in the professor's cabin on the boats—all of a sudden this light blazing out the windows like somebody lit up a bonfire," Lessard filled in with obvious relish. "And then—pffft!—it goes out."

"That's... odd," Adam commented, trying not to sound too skeptical.

"Bah, what do you know? The whole room was glowing like a comet, and not so much as a piece of charcoal the next morning." Lessard emphasized the point with another hock of tobacco spit.

"Here comes Staines." Charlie nodded across the camp to where Adam's bodyguard trudged toward them, looking even more grumpy than he had when he'd left. "Looks like he figured out nobody wants him."

Lessard let out a wicked chuckle.

"That's a good one, Charlie," he said happily.

"Keep your head on, bali," Charlie finished with a pointed look at Adam.

He flicked away the butt of his cigarette, crushed it under his boot, and moved away.

"Try not to get yourself shot," Lessard added with another slightly terrifying grin before following after him.

TWENTY-SEVEN

$\mathcal{A}$S THE DAY SHIFTED toward afternoon, Ellie adjusted her position on the mule and thought about how much her rear end hurt.

She would have preferred to simply walk with the caravan as it set out from the riverbank toward the mountains—but when she'd started to protest, Mendez had barked at Flowers, who then picked her up and plopped her down on the beast.

Ellie had been jolting along on the animal now for the better part of the day. Muscles she didn't know she had were starting to ache. Ellie was a Londoner. She'd never been on a horse in her life. She was sure that a mule was significantly less comfortable.

The environment around her had changed as they wove their way higher into the mountains. The surrounding trees turned from lush hardwoods to soaring Caribbean pines. Despite the increase in altitude, the air was still hot. Plenty of mosquitoes buzzed around. Ellie slapped at one and thought longingly of the tub of salve in Adam's rucksack. The bag holding their few supplies was likely shoved into one of the myriad bundles that hung to either side of the mules.

The wilderness through which they passed was oddly quiet. When Ellie had hiked through the lower forests with Adam, the air had been alive with bird calls and the movements of both large and small animals. Perhaps those sounds were conspicuously absent here because she was traveling with such a large, groaning mass of men and mules. Still, the difference was stark enough that when the odd rodent did startle out of the brush, it surprised her.

Ellie had been keeping a careful eye on the landscape. Though she hadn't specialized in geology, the shape of the hills suggested more karst geography—limestone bedrock that might be riddled with caves like the one they had passed through on the way here.

Another cave could be useful. If Ellie did see one, perhaps she could drive her mule into it and flee deep enough to conceal herself before anyone could come after her. Caves were also excellent sources of both bat guano and sulfur. If a university-educated woman with a knack for chemistry combined refined bat guano and sulfur with charcoal from one of the fires in the right quantities, she might find herself with a substance approximating black powder.

Ellie halted that enticing train of thought. No explosions, she reminded herself—not until she'd cleared them with Adam… but then again, he hadn't said anything about simply concocting a few explosive *materials*, had he?

She was still working on her plan for how she and Adam could possibly stop Dawson and Jacobs from looting whatever they found at the end of their route. In the meantime, she had set herself to swiping every potentially useful item that she managed to get her hands on.

So far, Ellie had the magnifying lens from the foreman's desk, as well as a broken pencil, a needle with a bit of thread in it, a pair of nail scissors, and a flask of moonshine, which she had absolutely no intention of drinking. She had opened the bottle for a single sniff and nearly burned her nose hairs off.

It was important to be prepared. One never knew when some unexpected piece of equipment might prove to be the difference between defeat and success.

Ellie was contemplating how she might pluck a hand spade from the gear strapped to the mule in front of her—and where she might conceal it on her person—when she realized that the caravan had stopped moving.

Whispers slid through the men around her in a mix of languages, threaded with an uncomfortable urgency.

"What's going on?" Ellie demanded.

"Who knows?" Mendez retorted impatiently.

Ellie shifted in the saddle. There was really no position she could find that didn't irritate her.

With a spark of inspiration, she stood up in the stirrups.

The mule grunted unhappily beneath her, but the change lifted her just high enough to see over the heads of the men in front of her.

The expedition's leaders were gathered in a tight knot at the top of the caravan line, where they gestured at some object she couldn't yet make out.

Throughout the morning, Ellie had taken time to familiarize herself with more of the men working the expedition—at least, those that didn't simply glare at her over their rifles. It was common courtesy... and one never knew who might prove an ally rather than an enemy. Flowers had aided her efforts with casual introductions, while Mendez had glowered irritably and marched her on as quickly as possible.

The men who held the expedition's more menial positions had been relatively friendly with her. After all, they were simply here for a paycheck. They had little sense of any difference between their current employers and the other white wealthy people who usually hired them.

Ellie had contemplated trying to sow the seeds of an outright revolt, but she had no illusions about how disposable fellows like Ram and Aditya, two of the young East Indian gentlemen recently escaped from their indentured servitude in Jamaica, would seem to someone like Jacobs if they caused any trouble.

The gathering at the front of the halted caravan included Bones, the Jamaican foreman, as well as Velegas, the grandfatherly-looking tracker. Jacobs and Dawson were with them—as was Adam, Ellie realized as his familiar frame became visible through a shift in the bodies ahead of her.

"Get back on the mule," Mendez ordered and gave her belt a tug.

Ellie landed in the saddle with an uncomfortable thud.

"We need to go up there," she declared.

"No chance," Mendez retorted flatly as he shifted his rifle to the other shoulder.

Ellie looked to Flowers, who struck her as the more sympathetic party.

"Sorry, Pepa," he said with a shrug.

She turned her face forward again, burning with frustration. The whispers around her had grown into an outright murmur as the men shuffled awkwardly, wondering what had caused the delay.

Something was going on up there, and she was being left out of it.

Ellie couldn't afford to be left out. She had no way of knowing what piece of information might give her the advantage she needed to stay alive.

The afternoon sun beat down on her through a break in the canopy overhead. The heat of it against her shoulders gave her a little spark of inspiration. Ellie hesitated, as the inspiration would certainly earn her Mendez's ire... but then again, Mendez wasn't in charge. Jacobs had made it clear that he was reserving the threat of violence against Ellie as a means of keeping Adam in line.

She supposed that meant she could afford a little ire.

Surreptitiously, Ellie slipped the magnifying lens out of her pocket. Holding it low against her thigh, she turned it carefully back and forth until it winked at her as it caught the light.

She carefully directed the focused beam toward the back of Mendez's trousers.

He shifted his footing uncomfortably and frowned under his mustache.

The olive fabric of his pants began to turn slightly darker in one perfect, round spot.

Mendez jolted with pain and whirled around.

"¡Ay! ¿Qué pedo?" he exclaimed.

Ellie had already dismounted. She darted up the line.

She heard another curse from Mendez behind her, followed by a chuckle from Flowers, as she pushed her way through the caravan.

"Pardon me, Aditya. Hello, Ram," she noted as she darted between a trio of mules and the four East Indian fellows.

"Miss Mallory," Ram replied with a glint of amusement in his eyes.

"Good morning, Mr. Fajardo," she added as she flashed a smile at the taciturn muleteer, who waved her on with an air of impatient indulgence.

She gave a cheerful wave to Nigel Reneau, the cook, and the two charming young builders from Caulker Caye, Pacheco and Lopez.

Finally, she skidded to a halt at the front of the line where Dawson and the others were clustered around something thickly veiled by greenery.

"I can't be entirely certain..." Dawson began—and then Adam's well-muscled forearm grasped hold of one of the vines and ripped it out of the way.

A rustling pile of foliage collapsed with a hiss and revealed what had brought the expedition to a halt.

It was another stela. The block stood perhaps five feet tall. It was carved in elegant bas relief from the same night-black stone as the monument that she and Adam had found by the waterfall.

The stela was dominated by an imposing, handsome figure ornamented with beaded necklaces, calf bands, and bracelets. His head was crowned with a spectacular headdress.

Smaller figures knelt at his feet. Their bodies were bent in supplication as their hands rose with offerings of tribute. There were seven of them.

"Ah—yes. Very helpful, Mr. Bates," Dawson said uncomfortably.

Ellie realized that she had stopped just behind Adam's shadow, Staines. The shorter, slightly fussy-looking guard seemed like the sort who would try to show off for the ladies when he wasn't out in the middle of nowhere. Right now, he appeared sweaty and unhappy as he shifted his rifle awkwardly in his grip. He startled as he realized that Ellie lurked at his back.

Ellie took that as an invitation to move closer. She peered over his shoulder and studied the carving more closely.

"It is obviously a tribute to some ruler of great importance," Dawson announced authoritatively.

"No, it isn't," Ellie countered. "It's Kukulkan."

The professor startled and nearly dropped his pencil.

Jacobs turned more slowly and pinned Ellie with a curious gaze. It made her distinctly uncomfortable. She looked away from it to where Adam stood instead.

He grinned at her.

It felt like a vote of confidence. Ellie squeezed past Staines to point at the stone.

"See?" she prompted. "Feathered cloak, snake mask... and yet there's a throne here. There are symbols here for both a god *and* a ruler. Oh!"

The exclamation escaped her as Velegas, the grandfatherly tracker, stood from where he crouched at the base of the monument. His movement revealed what lay beneath the pillar.

Like most Mayan stelae, a flat stone had been set in the ground before it to serve as an altar... and it held an offering.

The golden pelt of the jaguar was smooth and beautiful—where it hadn't been ripped to shreds. The animal was brutally mutilated. Torn flesh revealed pieces of cracked bone.

Ellie uncomfortably recalled what Adam had told her of Padre Kuyoc's warnings back in Santa Dolores.

The padre thinks it's a cursed realm full of the hungry spirits of the damned...

She shook off the thought. This was hardly the time to indulge in superstition.

"This was an animal kill," Velegas concluded as he carefully wiped his hands on a scrap of cloth. "But I cannot tell you what animal."

"Surely, it must have been another jaguar," Dawson protested. He looked slightly ill as he eyed the crimson violence.

Velegas flashed the professor a glare laced with tired contempt.

"This is a female. Male jaguars may fight, but a female?" The tracker shook his head. "Something else killed her."

"Some other animal just happened to kill a jaguar on a Mesoamerican altar stone?" Ellie retorted skeptically.

"Not here," Adam cut in from where he stood a few feet away. "Somewhere else. There's a blood trail."

The knot of men by the stela shifted, allowing Velegas to push through. The old tracker crouched down in the underbrush and sharply studied the dried leaves.

"It was dragged," he concluded.

"By what?" Dawson exclaimed nervously.

"Or who," Jacobs cut in smoothly.

"You think a person put this here?" Dawson stammered. "What, as some sort of... threat?"

Ellie's gaze drifted once more to the stela as she picked out more details of the beautifully engraved image.

The hands of the king-or-god were extended toward the people who bowed as his feet. In one hand were more of those square, not-Mayan characters. Ellie felt as though she could almost tease out the meaning of the glyphs—a bow, a shield, a staff.

His other hand was pierced by a sharpened spear of bone. Blood dripped from the wound.

An uncomfortable recognition sparked through her.

"This is the story of Tulan!" she blurted.

"I beg your pardon?" Dawson spluttered. He looked at Ellie as though she had just started spouting Sumerian.

"The City of Seven Caves?" Ellie clarified. "As referenced in the Popol Vuh and the Annals of the Cakchiquels? The kingdom that was the origin point for both Mayan and Aztec culture, according to their own myths and stories. Or perhaps you aren't familiar with it."

"Of course I am familiar with it," Dawson retorted stuffily. "I am quite a bit more than merely *familiar* with it, though I fail to see how some slip of a—"

"University College, London graduate," Adam cut in. His gaze shifted to Ellie. His eyes were warm. "I believe that's the term you were looking for."

Dawson gaped from Adam to Ellie. He reminded her a bit of a beached fish.

"The bas relief is depicting Tulan's gifts to the seven tribes," Ellie continued as she pointed out the symbols on the stone. "War. Kingship. Sacrifice."

Ellie studied the figures that knelt before the king. They were far smaller and more humble in their ornamentation, but there was still a sense of grace and respect to how they were depicted.

She wondered who was telling the story depicted on the stone. If she was right, and it was an account of the gifts of Tulan, then those kneeling figures would have been the heroes—the founders who came to receive Tulan's blessings and carry them back to their people.

The man who dominated the carving had human features, for all that his feathers and accouterments were clearly those of one of the more well-established Mayan deities—Aztec as well, she quickly recalled. Quetzalcoatl and Kukulkan shared much of their symbolism.

"But why build it here?" she mused aloud as her mind spun. "Why leave the story of Tulan in the middle of the forest?"

"Because it's a boundary stone," Dawson snapped. He drew himself up self-importantly as he tugged on his field jacket. "Because we are on the borders of Tulan."

"We are *what?*" Ellie whirled to him as the significance of his comment cut through her fascination with the stone.

"I should hardly expect someone like *you* to understand," Dawson sniffed stuffily.

Ellie didn't bother to respond to the very obvious and deliberate slight. She was too busy putting the rest of the pieces together.

"You think the city at the end of the map is *Tulan*." She paced away from the gathering before turning back. "But Tulan is a myth! Of course, even myths can be rooted in truth... and the annals never *do* say that Tulan was conquered or collapsed. Only that the founders of the great Mayan city-states received their gifts there. That it was the place where kings were made."

She raised her eyes to Dawson.

"But if it existed, Tulan would have had to predate the earliest vestiges of Mayan civilization," she added pointedly. "For it to have survived until the time of the conquest would have made it thousands of years old!"

Her mind reeled. Tulan, the City of Seven Caves—a Mesoamerican Eden populated by a people with the wisdom of eons—*that* was what Dawson believed lay at the end of her map.

If it was true, the implications were more than revolutionary. They were staggering.

"We've delayed long enough," Jacobs declared, interrupting the wild spin of her thoughts. "Dispose of the animal, and let's get going."

He stalked away without waiting for a response, obviously confident that he would be obeyed. Dawson glared at Ellie as though her knowledge of Tulan was vaguely reprehensible, and then hurried after him.

The foreman, Bones, shouted an order over the line. The mass of mules and men creaked and complained their way back into motion.

Velegas tugged a spade from the baggage roll on the nearest mule and swung it over his shoulder. He grasped the jaguar by its hind legs and dragged it off behind the ferns.

Adam stepped aside to let the tracker by, and then shifted his gaze to Ellie. He looked worried.

"Form the line!" Bones called. He repeated the order in Spanish.

"Go on," Staines snapped as he waved the barrel of his Enfield at Adam.

Adam gave the gun a look—and then lifted the look to Staines. The guard cleared his throat awkwardly and took an instinctive step back.

"You know, like the foreman said," he added more moderately.

Adam gave Ellie a nod.

"Princess," he said.

"Mr. Bates," she replied.

He moved away, with Staines hurrying after him.

Ellie felt an odd flush of heat as she watched him go. Was she fighting off a fever?

The thought was alarming. She certainly couldn't afford to get ill at the moment.

"Are we going to stand here and look at the blood all day?" Mendez complained from where he and Flowers had come to a stop behind her.

"Come along, Pepa," Flowers offered more gently, and then guided her back toward her mule.

TWENTY-EIGHT

$\mathcal{T}$HE EXPEDITION SET up camp on the banks of a small stream. The atmosphere around the various fires was more strained than it had been back at the river. The dead jaguar hadn't gone unnoticed by the men, and some of them were clearly feeling a little superstitious about the country that they were headed into.

The tree cover had started to thin a bit. Through the gaps in the foliage, Adam could see the peaks of the mountains rising to the south.

All day, he had scanned the baggage loaded onto the mules for some sign of his gear—without any luck. If he'd been able to spot where his rucksack and rifle had landed, he might've been able to work on snatching them back.

That Adam *hadn't* managed to find any of his stuff made him wonder whether Jacobs had just tossed it all in the river... including his machete.

The thought made his gut lurch with a terrible sense of loss. *Not my knife...*

One of the men approached the place where Adam glowered out at the camp. Adam recognized him as Pacheco, one of the young guys from Caulker Caye.

"Mr. Bates? They want you to look at the maps again," Pacheco announced a little nervously.

Adam couldn't entirely blame him for being wary. After all, as far as Pacheco knew, Adam was a filthy, unshaven, grumpy-looking bakra getting marched around camp at the wrong end of a gun.

The kid obviously had no idea who the real bad guys were around here.

"Sure. Be right there," Adam replied flatly.

He finished the last few bites of his stew. Nigel had worked a small miracle with dinner, given that all Velegas had managed to drag back to camp had been a pair of iguanas.

"No game," the tracker had announced as he had tossed the dead lizards down by the fire.

Adam didn't doubt it. He'd barely caught sight of anything larger than a lizard himself since they'd passed the stela.

He was probably looking even grumpier than usual as he followed Pacheco through the camp. Why wouldn't he be? He was being summoned to put his skills to use for a couple of thugs who were threatening Ellie.

The notion made him want to hit something.

Adam was so focused on not hitting anything that he almost missed the subtle flash in the corner of his vision. It was just a quick reflection of the late afternoon light—but there was something achingly familiar about it.

Adam whirled toward the glare, and his eyes locked onto the place where Braxton Pickett, the fish-eyed Confederate son, sat on a fallen log.

A machete twisted in Pickett's hand. The eighteen inch blade curved at the perfect angle and was sharp enough to split a blade of grass. The well-oiled handle had been custom carved by an old Mayan guy in town out of pest-resistant cocobolo wood before being wrapped in flexible, comfortable strips of leather.

The knife would fit Adam's grip like it had been made for it—because it damned well had been.

Adam realized that he'd grabbed poor Pacheco by the front of his shirt.

"Is that my knife?" he seethed as Pacheco gaped up at him in terrified surprise.

Pickett slowly lifted the tip of the blade to his mouth—and inserted it between two of his teeth.

The bug-eyed Confederate pulled the knife out a moment later. He studied what he'd mined, and then wiped it on the leg of his trousers.

Adam choked back a strangled cry of outrage.

"Uh... Hey, bali? Maybe let go of the boy?" Staines offered carefully from behind him.

Adam looked down. He'd nearly lifted Pacheco's feet off the ground.

He quickly released his hold on the kid's shirt and forced himself to take a breath.

"Sorry," Adam said as he squeezed Pacheco's shoulder awkwardly. "It's just... That's my knife."

Staines scratched the side of his nose awkwardly. He looked a little shame-faced. Pacheco patted Adam's arm.

"You have my sympathies," he said, and then dashed off across the camp.

"You, ah… ready?" Staines jerked his head in the direction of Dawson's nearby campfire.

Adam didn't answer. He just turned and stalked toward the professor, hating everything about his life.

Dawson's tent was up again. Inside, Adam could see the carpet spread across the tarpaulin. He wondered how many more spiders would be living inside of it by the morning.

The professor had set up his field desk under the front awning in order to take advantage of the light.

He was alone. Most of the men were wisely gathered near Nigel's cookfire, waiting hopefully for seconds. A few others clustered around a game of dice.

Ellie stood near the game, with Flowers and Mendez flanking her.

Since they had been captured, Ellie had sported two escorts against Adam's one. When Adam puzzled over why, he recalled Jacobs' easy confidence back in Dawson's tent on their first night with the expedition

When Jacobs had told Dawson that Adam wasn't a risk, he'd sounded entirely sure of it. But how could he be? Jacobs had no notion of just how far Adam's relationship with Ellie might stretch—and he didn't seem like the kind of guy who'd throw all his chips onto a half-assed bet.

Jacobs hadn't been gambling. He had *known* that Adam wouldn't risk Ellie's safety… and even after a day of mulling over it, Adam couldn't think of a single damned way in which that was possible.

Ellie's words from the night before came back to him.

I have an uncomfortable feeling that he has an unnatural ability to see through a deception.

Adam forced his attention away from the conundrum of Jacobs. He plopped himself down on a rock beside the professor, who was looking a little worse for wear. Dawson's graying, gingerish hair tufted out in odd places, and there were dark circles under his eyes.

It didn't look as though he'd been sleeping very well. Somehow, Adam doubted it was guilt keeping the guy up at night—even though he *should* feel bad for the mules and men charged with carting around his small mountain of books and unnecessary gear.

"Oh. You're here," Dawson announced with a distinct lack of enthusiasm as he scratched uncomfortably at the skin under his collar.

"Sure am," Adam agreed flatly. "What've you got?"

"I believe they are hives," Dawson answered in a bit of a whine. "It's this relentless, ungodly heat. Perhaps I simply lack the robust constitution of these natives, but I am most put out by it."

Adam glanced back at Staines and caught the guard rolling his eyes.

"I meant your map," Adam returned.

Dawson made a face like he'd just sucked on a lemon, but he handed over what he'd been working on. Once again, it was all scribbled onto a piece of notepaper. The professor was still apparently afraid to put marks on his map.

Adam took the page with a sigh. He glanced over it for a few seconds before tossing it back to the professor.

"Nope," he concluded and moved to the table.

Dawson scooted away as though Adam were carrying something contagious.

"That was an interesting find we came across this morning," the professor said carefully as Adam worked. "I mean the monument, of course."

"Uh-huh," Adam replied without looking up. He made another note on the map.

"It certainly seems to indicate that we are on the correct path—a fact which I must concede we owe to some degree to your labors," Dawson added with a thin note of cheer.

Adam frowned. The remark had sounded suspiciously like a compliment… a compliment for the work that Adam had been extorted into doing for the men who were currently marching him around at the wrong end of an Enfield.

Adam reined in a threatening flash of anger. He couldn't afford to lose his temper—however tempting it might be. Not with Ellie's skin on the line.

"Glad to be of service," he retorted.

Dawson appeared to be oblivious to the sarcasm.

"Yes—It seems that despite appearances, you are rather a useful fellow!" the professor mused. "I have been giving the matter a bit of thought, and I am forced to acknowledge that really, your particular combination of talents is quite rare. I mean, I have come across university men with pretensions of thriving in the wilderness, but it has always been quite clear to me that their capacity for survival in the wild depended entirely on the skills of their hired hands. That is certainly not the case with you!"

The last remark sounded a bit chummy. Adam paused in his work and slowly turned his head to give Dawson a better look.

The professor smiled back at him with an expression that managed to look both bland and nervous… but it was the avaricious glint in Dawson's eyes that really set Adam's alarm bells blaring.

Dawson wanted something from him. Nothing about that sounded promising to Adam.

"Hired hands have kept me from doing something extremely stupid more times than I can count," Adam returned bluntly.

Dawson chuckled awkwardly. "Yes, well. We all have things to learn, don't we? As Socrates said, the wise man knows what he does not know."

"'I know that I know nothing,'" Adam corrected.

"Sorry?" Dawson said.

"That's the quote. 'Ipse se nihil scire id unum sciat.'" Adam made another mark on the map. "Not saying I agree with it."

Dawson blinked at him again before forcing another smile.

"Right, right—of course," he easily agreed—a little *too* easily. "Personally, I am happy to admit that *I* know far less of navigating through uncharted areas than you do." He finished with an awkward little chuckle.

Adam's pencil stilled.

Dawson was trying to get on his good side. The professor clearly resented the notion that a filthy, half-dressed guy from the woods was better at navigating than he was, so there had to be a reason for that... one that had nothing to do with lines on a map.

Adam decided to stay quiet. In his experience, people like Dawson would keep talking for as long as they could get away with it. Dawson would probably spill the beans about whatever he really wanted if Adam simply let him ramble for a while longer.

Sure enough, after a few seconds, the professor continued blabbing.

"I wonder what a man with your unique combination of talents might be able to accomplish if he were granted more resources than those available to you in this backwater colony?" Dawson mused.

Adam wondered if Dawson had any idea that what he'd just said was actually an insult.

"My resources are fine, thanks," Adam replied.

Dawson gave a more genuine laugh.

"Perhaps you would feel a little differently once you have seen what a great deal of money can offer you!" Dawson said.

Adam had seen it. He'd seen it, and then turned around and walked away from it the first chance he got. In his experience, a great deal of money sent you scrambling for as much more of it as you could possibly acquire, and to hell with anyone who got in your way in the process.

He didn't bother voicing this to Dawson. The guy wasn't worth the conversation.

"You know, I have been considering asking Mr. Jacobs to secure your services for a further bit of work once we reach our destination," Dawson said thoughtfully.

Adam set the pencil down.

"Oh?" he said.

His tone came out more threatening than he'd intended. Behind him, Staines took a step back and shifted his grip on the rifle.

Dawson didn't seem to notice. He was frowning down at a bit of dirt on his cuff.

"Our expedition is of a unique nature," the professor continued. "We have a particular goal once we reach the ruins, and I for one am interested in accomplishing it as quickly and efficiently as possible! It occurs to me that you might be quite useful in that regard."

Dawson said it as though Adam's cooperation weren't dependent upon Jacobs threatening to inflict violence on Ellie.

"Might I," Adam returned flatly.

He forced himself to swallow back the rest of what he wanted to say—which more or less amounted to telling Dawson exactly where he could shove his request for further cooperation. He could hear Ellie's voice in the back of his head. If she was here, she'd absolutely be telling him to play along and get as much information as he could out of Dawson so that they could learn more about exactly who they were up against—and what they really wanted.

Adam hated playing along with things. It was one of the main reasons he had walked out of his old life. He was also flat-out bad at it. Adam was the sort of guy who said whatever he was thinking. He'd always kinda liked that about himself.

But imaginary Ellie was right. As satisfying as it would be to tell Dawson to shove it where the sun didn't shine, Adam probably had more to gain by trying to draw the professor out.

It wasn't going to be pretty—but to hell with it.

Adam focused his full attention on Dawson, who looked startled to find himself on the receiving end of it.

"At our destination—what would you be looking for from me?" he demanded bluntly.

Dawson perked up.

"Ah! Well—I'm afraid I can't tell you *too* much about it at this point in our venture," he noted coyly. "Suffice to say that our interests in the ruins of Tulan are more... *focused* than a simple survey or excavation."

Adam sighed. He had a pretty good idea of what 'focused interests' in an archaeological site meant.

"Right," he replied. He rubbed the bridge of his nose as his frustration and dismay rose. "So you're collectors."

"My, my!" Dawson returned. "You are more clever than you let on, Mr. Bates."

Adam dropped his hand and treated Dawson to a flatly bewildered stare. Did the man have any idea how condescending he was?

"We are indeed collectors," Dawson continued, and then raised an abrupt hand. "I will say no more. The nature of our collection is... rather unique in a manner that I am not at liberty to share. But there is a particular artifact that we believe may reside at Tulan, which you might aid me in securing—and that would be aid for which both I and my organization would be very grateful."

Adam wondered if Dawson's gratitude meant a good goddamn to Mr. Jacobs—who was obviously the boss here, whatever pretensions of authority Dawson might have. The professor made it sound like he was part of something elite and desperately important... but desperately important people didn't get bossed around by murderous street thugs.

More likely, Dawson was a minion, Adam thought as the professor slapped angrily at another buzzing mosquito. The professor wasn't overly enamored with his current assignment, and he thought maybe Adam could get him out of it a bit faster.

Adam knew the type. They were usually a type that he threw his drink at. He didn't have a drink at the moment, which was probably for the best.

He crossed his arms and pinned Dawson with a look.

"How am I supposed to help you find your special thing if you won't tell me what it is?" he demanded.

Dawson gaped at him, and then snapped his mouth shut. The professor was clearly weighing his commitment to secrecy against his very real desire to get the hell out of the back country as quickly as possible.

The latter apparently won out—at least enough to shift the balance a bit.

"It is something which is almost certainly secured in the ritual heart of the ruins," Dawson carefully offered. "Or in a location that would not have been accessible to the general populace, but only to the religious and political elites. And it will be... black," he added awkwardly. "Black and flat."

Adam frowned. He'd been expecting more of the usual stuff collectors lusted for—like pornographic vases or things made of shiny important metals.

Adam didn't know any shiny important metals that were black.

"How big is it?" he asked.

Dawson was starting to look nervous.

"I... Well, I'm not sure I can say precisely."

"Like—a little teeny something?" Adam held apart his fingers to demonstrate. "Or hand sized? Maybe a dinner platter?"

"Mirror sized," Dawson blurted. The professor was starting to sweat more than he routinely did. He glanced around the camp as though looking to see who might be able to hear them. "It would be—ah—mirror sized."

"What the hell is mirror sized?" Adam retorted.

"Shhh!" Dawson urged, slightly panicky. "Please! I... Just... That's all I can say about the matter. Really, I should think it would be quite sufficient."

And abruptly... it was. A connection zipped to life in Adam's brain as he recalled a phrase that he had seen scrawled in Dawson's notebook on the night he and Ellie had been captured.

The Smoking Mirror.

Ellie had rattled on about the Smoking Mirror. It was the meaning behind the disk icon on her medallion—the one that Jacobs had stolen off her when they arrived at the camp. She'd described it as some magical artifact through which people had supposedly been able to see the past and the future. She'd mentioned it being associated with the legendary city of Tulan.

Apparently, Dawson had read the same books.

But Ellie had described the mirror as a myth. Dawson wouldn't need Adam to help him dig up a myth.

The implication was obvious. Dawson didn't think the mirror *was* a myth. He thought the damned thing was real—and he'd just asked Adam to find it for him.

"Hell," Adam blurted.

"I beg your pardon?" Dawson said, stiffening.

Adam scrambled for a recovery. He slapped at his neck and wiped his hand off on his filthy shirt. "Botfly," he lied.

Dawson's eyes widened with alarm.

"Isn't that the one that lays eggs under your skin?" he demanded as he scrambled to his feet.

"Er... Now that you mention it," Adam replied with a spark of wicked inspiration.

Dawson looked around himself wildly.

"Are there more of them?" he pressed.

"Probably."

Dawson scampered for his tent.

"Thank you, Mr. Bates. You've been most helpful," he called back over his shoulder.

"But I..." Adam looked back down at the map. "Ah, hell with it."

He made a final mark along their projected route, rolled the page up, and tossed it after the retreating professor.

"That should take us to this *River of Smoke*," he said. "Whatever that turns out to be."

"Marvelous. Excellent. Good evening," Dawson retorted, and then yanked shut the flaps.

Staines frowned at Adam with the rifle held loosely in his hands.

"The botfly doesn't put eggs in you. He gives them to the mosquito, and the mosquito puts them in you," Staines said flatly.

"Yup," Adam confirmed.

Staines shook his head.

"Crazy bakra," he muttered and marched Adam back across the camp.

TWENTY-NINE

*E*LLIE WOKE UP feeling sticky. Her tent-prison had been closed up since she'd been deposited in it earlier that evening. The canvas had relentlessly held on to the day's thick heat.

She supposed she should be glad it was simple discomfort that had dragged her from sleep, instead of another nightmare. Ellie had actually slept dreamlessly for the last two nights—ever since Jacobs had caught them and confiscated the black medallion from the psalter.

Her hand brushed over the empty place under her blouse where it had once lain.

Ellie supposed she ought to be grateful for the change. Who wanted to be regularly woken by nightmares? Still, a small part of her felt oddly as though she were missing something important by indulging in simple oblivion instead.

She sat up on her cot. Through the canvas walls of the tent, she could just make out the glow of one of the campfires and the murmur of voices from those keeping watch.

It would be cooler outside.

Giving up, she swung her legs out of bed and pushed through the tent flap.

The more temperate air outside was an immediate relief. A soft breeze whispered through the branches of the surrounding pines. There was no other sound from the forest. Not so much as a chirp or hoot disturbed the quiet—only the low buzz of insects.

Flowers sat on a stone by the entrance to the tent with his rifle leaning beside him, whistling tunelessly. The lantern at his feet had been turned down to a glimmer.

"Bad dream?" he asked.

"I just needed a little fresh air," Ellie mumbled in reply.

"Everybody's having bad dreams," Flowers noted authoritatively. "This place has got the bad wind."

He waved a hand which took in the camp and the oddly silent woods around it.

"Can I just… sit out here a little while?" Ellie asked.

"There's plenty of rock." Flowers scooted over to make room for her.

Relieved, Ellie plopped down beside him. She would need more rest in order to have the energy for the next day's trek—especially if their captors once more insisted on sticking her on a mule—but she couldn't bring herself to go back into the stuffy atmosphere of the tent just yet. Sitting outside in the dark with Flowers was surprisingly agreeable. The big man wasn't like the other guards Jacobs had hired for the expedition. If Ellie had to guess, Flowers had been picked out for the job purely on the basis of his size.

She could almost pretend that Flowers was there to guard her *from* things, rather than to hold her captive.

Someone flopped over in the hammock which hung nearest to them. His form was obscured by the pale fall of a mosquito net. A frustrated grunt from the vicinity sounded distinctly of Mendez.

"Bad dreams for you too, bali?" Flowers asked.

"None of your business," Mendez retorted.

A scream broke the silence of the night.

Mendez shot upright in his hammock. Flowers rose instinctively, drawing the rifle into his arms. Ellie stood with him, grabbing the lantern as she rose. Her pulse jumped at the terrible urgency of the sound.

The scream came again, sounding from the shadowy trees to their left—and then stopped abruptly.

Too abruptly.

Ellie and Flowers exchanged a look.

"Don't you two even think about it," Mendez barked at the pair of them as he flailed to get out of his mosquito net.

"Stay here, Pepa," Flowers ordered, and then ran into the darkness.

Ellie hesitated for only a breath before bolting after him, with Mendez's curses echoing behind her.

The lantern provided her with a halo of golden illumination as she raced through the trees after Flowers. She could still clearly recall the direction from which the sound had come. The source of it could not be far.

Flowers slowed, holding the rifle ready in his hands. That in itself was unusual for Flowers, who usually treated the gun more like a casual accessory.

He glanced over to Ellie as she arrived with the lantern. He shook his head in disapproval, but didn't try to order her to go. Instead, he shifted the rifle to one hand and pulled his machete from its sheath.

The knife was a bit longer than Adam's, and had obviously been well cared for… though it was not quite as nicely formed, in Ellie's admittedly inexpert opinion.

"Know how to use this?" Flowers asked.

"Um…" Ellie eyed the enormous blade as she weighed her well-justified feelings of intimidation against a deep curiosity about what it would feel like to carry it. She extended her hand. "Yes."

Flowers passed her the knife and steadied his grip on the gun, continuing quietly and carefully through the forest.

Ellie followed. The weight of the machete was strange in her hand. It was heavier than she'd thought it would be. How did Adam toss his own knife around so easily?

She considered what she'd seen of his well-muscled, constantly exposed forearms and supposed she had her answer.

Her companion stopped a few steps later. He tilted his head, carefully focused and listening. Ellie did the same, tuning her ears to the layered sounds of the night which surrounded them.

There weren't many. The air had gone uncomfortably still. Not even the pines were whispering. There was only a very distant murmur of the water from the stream back at camp, and something else that just scratched at the corner of Ellie's awareness. Her mind identified the sound a moment later—as a ragged, uneven breath.

Ellie whirled toward it. She pushed through some scrubby underbrush with her lantern held up before her.

The glow spilled across the source of the scream that had brought them there.

One of Jacobs' guards lay spread-eagled on the ground, starkly revealed in the light of her lantern. His eyes were wide and white in his blood-splattered face as they stared blankly up at the motionless pine branches overheard.

Flowers muttered a curse and made a quick sign of the cross.

"Who is it?" Ellie asked, instinctively lowering her voice in the face of what lay before them.

"Rhynie," Flowers said darkly. He picked up the man's discarded rifle and swung it across his back.

There were wounds in both of Rhynie's shoulders. The rents in the fabric of his shirt revealed the torn skin beneath… but it was the two puncture wounds in his forehead that had clearly been the reason he had stopped screaming.

The twin holes were each about an inch wide. They were terribly deep and red.

"What could possibly have done this?" Ellie whispered roughly as her stomach twisted.

The answer slid into her mind in an echo of Adam's joking voice as he reported Padre Kuyoc's words from the night before.

There are monsters there that bite people's skulls.

The memory—coupled with the horror that lay before her—sparked a quick, cold fear.

But there is no such thing as monsters, Ellie reminded herself firmly.

"He didn't shoot," she pointed out, swallowing thickly.

The sound of a rifle discharge would certainly have been audible from where she and Flowers had been sitting.

"No," Flowers agreed, scanning the darkness around them with his rifle ready in his hands. "He did not."

Something whispered against the back of Ellie's neck—an abrupt breeze which tickled the fine hairs there. A strange sound brushed at her ears from beyond the shadowy undergrowth behind her. It was a familiar sound, and yet so out of place that she struggled to fix it in her mind.

Her attempts to do so were quickly drowned out by the crashing, hurried arrival of more men from the camp.

Jacobs appeared first. He moved far more quickly and quietly than the companions who emerged from the shadows behind him. Ellie recognized Bones, the expedition foreman, with two more of the armed guards. Dawson trailed along at the rear, looking around himself nervously with his shoulders hunched.

The professor startled with a barely contained squeak as Adam stepped silently from the trees beside him.

Staines hurried in his wake, carrying his rifle in his hands.

"I told the bakra to stay in the camp, but he doesn't listen to me," Staines complained. "How do I know if I'm supposed to shoot him for that?"

Jacobs ignored him. His eyes flashed thoughtfully from Ellie and Flowers to the corpse.

"Coming through. ¡Abran paso!" Velegas ordered. The tracker pushed past the two guards who had arrived with Jacobs and now gaped at their fallen colleague with drained faces.

Velegas knelt down at the dead man's side. He whipped a clean handkerchief from his pocket and touched gently at the wounds.

"More light," he ordered.

Ellie realized that she was the one with the lantern. She moved in closer, turning up the wick to provide him with more illumination.

Velegas frowned under his gray mustache.

"This was not a cat," he concluded firmly.

"Then what the devil was it?" Dawson demanded. He was half-hiding behind Jacobs' two nervous-looking guards.

"I cannot say," Velegas concluded as he pulled aside the man's shirt to study the wounds in his shoulders.

In the greater glow of the lamp, Ellie could see the injuries too. They looked as though they had been torn by thick claws.

A silence followed, heavy with unspoken dread. Jacobs broke it.

"Where is his partner?" He looked impatiently back at the blank stares that answered him. "These men patrol in pairs."

Ellie thought of the odd sound she had heard a moment before. Following an uncomfortable instinct, she turned and pressed through the thick green leaves toward it.

In the clearing on the other side, another man lay on the ground. His face was gruesomely injured.

Blood soaked his shirt around another pair of those terrible puncture wounds which marked the center of his chest.

He blinked up at the intrusion of the light. His eyes rolled toward her as he took in another gurgling breath.

Adam moved quickly to the man's side and dropped to his knees. He yanked his shirt over his head, stuffing it at the wounds on the victim's chest.

Ellie swallowed thickly.

"I think he's punctured a lung. I can…" Her voice caught. "I can hear it."

Jacobs and the others joined them, forming a ragged circle around the fallen man—Ramos, Ellie thought as she looked down at him. She had heard someone in the camp call him Ramos.

His eyes fixed on Adam.

"Salió de… la noche," he rasped. He blinked, and his eyes focused as though he was just realizing who he was speaking to. "Out of the night," he repeated, choking the words out in English twisted by pain.

"What did?" Adam demanded, his voice low and urgent.

Ramos coughed. A spray of blood splattered across Adam's chest and face. He flinched back from it as Ellie took a step forward, propelled by the need to help—to do *something*… even though it was abundantly clear that there was nothing any of them could do.

"El ángel de la muerte," Ramos rasped.

The words ended on a desperate, choking pull for air. Ramos's limbs twitched.

It looked as though he were drowning... and then it was over.

Adam reached down and gently closed the dead man's eyes.

Dawson's face glistened with nervous sweat in the lamplight.

"What did he say?" he demanded. "What did this?"

"He said it was the angel of death," Adam replied.

He stood. His tanned chest was speckled with Ramos's blood. His gaze locked onto Ellie across the fallen man's body.

She could read the lines written in it clearly enough.

Escape might have been an option for them before—but not anymore. Not when something was hunting in this forest... something big enough to bring two armed men to the ground.

Something that looked very much to Ellie as though it had somehow attacked from above.

She thought of the odd noise she had heard a few moments before as an impossible breeze had brushed the back of her neck.

Wings, she realized with a distant and terrible shock. It had sounded very much like wings.

THIRTY

*A*s ADAM SET BACK out with the caravan that morning, the atmosphere was decidedly grim. Word had spread about last night's attack. Bones, the foreman, had ordered Pacheco, Ram, and three of their companions to dig a pair of graves for the bodies of the slaughtered men.

It had been tough work. The ground was root-bound and rocky. Adam had picked up a pickax and strode in to help, Staines's muttering complaints be damned.

He'd spent another ten minutes after that trying to scrub the blood from his shirt, and failing. He'd finally just thrown the ruined garment in the river and let the current take it.

It had been Aurelio Fajardo, of all people, who had given Adam a replacement. The muleteer tossed a spare at him as Adam walked past the corral. The shirt was a bit short in the arms—but since when had Adam bothered to wear his sleeves down?

Aurelio had answered Adam's thanks with a disapproving grunt as he turned his attention back to his animals.

The delay imposed by the burials meant that the caravan didn't get rolling until nearly half past nine. Bones drove them at a harder pace to try to make up some of the time. The men endured it in taciturn silence.

The ground grew steeper and rockier, wending along the ridge as they progressed. The air was thick, and the sky grayed with haze. The air remained thick and humid, despite the fact that they were gradually working their way to higher ground.

As the expedition halted for lunch, Adam eyed the rocky ledge that rose beside them and curved toward the south.

"I'm going to climb to the ridge," he announced.

Staines startled.

"What do you want to do that for?" he protested. "There is perfectly nice ground right here."

"I know," Adam agreed—with feeling—as he eyed the high, steep slope. "But I should probably make sure we're actually going where I think we are." He shot a wry glance over at the guard. "Didn't say you had to follow me."

"Of course, I don't have to follow you, you crazy bakra," Staines retorted. "I could just shoot you instead."

"That won't be necessary, Mr. Staines."

Adam turned toward the source of the reply.

Jacobs stepped from the trees.

Unlike Dawson, Jacobs hadn't purchased a special wardrobe for their trip into the bush. He wore sturdy boots and plain trousers with a shirt and waistcoat that would have looked perfectly acceptable on a London street.

Also unlike Dawson, Jacobs was not perpetually covered in sweat.

"Your rifle," Jacobs ordered, extending his arm to Staines without taking his eyes off Adam.

Staines handed Jacobs the gun without hesitation, eyeing him a bit like he might look at a tiger on an unreliable leash.

Jacobs swung the rifle over his shoulder and let it hang there. That he didn't bother to point it at Adam felt remarkably like an insult.

"Lead the way," Jacobs said, gesturing them up.

They climbed in silence. Adam supposed it was better than being forced to maintain a conversation. He focused on the landscape instead, picking out the most likely path up the steeply rising ground.

Which was fine—as long as all he did was look up.

Jacobs was barely breathing any harder, even when Adam's route required them to scramble over the rocks, using both hands and feet to haul themselves upwards. The real boss of the expedition was clearly nothing like the soft, red-faced Dawson. Wherever Jacobs had come from, it was a place that bred men of a different ilk than his complaining, hive-stricken partner.

The man wasn't doing a damned thing but following in Adam's wake, and he somehow still made it feel threatening.

"I gather you agreed to assist the professor with securing the artifact," Jacobs said.

The sound of his voice startled Adam—and immediately grated on him.

Had he? Adam cast his thoughts back to his conversation with Dawson the night before. He didn't actually remember agreeing to anything... but then, he didn't put it past Dawson to have stopped listening and simply assumed that everything was going the way he wanted it to go.

"What can I say?" Adam returned flatly as he found another handhold.

"I believe we may both agree that your assistance will be granted to the utmost of your ability without any additional complications?" Jacobs offered. He set his boot to the stones and followed adeptly.

Adam paused with his hands on the next boulder. He cast a slow glance back over his shoulder at where Jacobs climbed below him.

"Or you start cutting up my friend?" he returned coldly.

"Good," Jacobs replied, easily pulling himself up another step. "I see we understand each other."

Adam contemplated kicking Jacobs in the face. It would have felt great— but he had no doubt that Jacobs was carefully watching his every move, and the man still had the gun. Adam didn't doubt that Jacobs knew perfectly well how to use it.

Adam might be prone to occasionally rash decision-making, but even he could see that those were lousy odds... and if he got himself shot, there wouldn't be much reason left for Jacobs to keep Ellie around.

No kicking for now, Adam decided. He gritted his teeth and pushed on.

"I believe the professor may be considering whether you could be of longer-term use to us," Jacobs continued.

Adam halted in his tracks to stare down at the other man in surprise.

"I'm sorry—What?" he blurted.

Jacobs didn't stop. He stepped neatly up the rest of the winding trail, only stopping when he had come parallel to Adam.

"Dawson is looking for a way to avoid the aspects of his own duties he considers less appealing, of course." Jacobs was not the least bit out of breath. "He dislikes enduring the outdoors—nor is he much good at it. I don't believe anyone would be averse to replacing the professor in that capacity. Were you to show an interest in such work, it would certainly extend your usefulness. I am sure you have realized by now that your and Miss Mallory's continued health depends on how long you remain... *useful.*"

Adam's jaw clenched as he absorbed Jacobs' revelation. It certainly made some sense of Dawson's weird conversation with Adam the night before.

He recalled how the professor's attitude toward him had shifted when Adam had first revealed that he'd attended Cambridge. He wondered if it would shift again if Dawson learned that Adam had walked out without a degree.

But Jacobs wasn't bluffing. Adam knew perfectly well that he was only alive because Jacobs needed him. The minute that changed, both he and Ellie would be in serious trouble.

If Adam had been smart, he would have pummeled Braxton Pickett, reclaimed his machete, and made off into the woods with Ellie days ago. Sticking around in the hopes that they could find a way to prevent Jacobs and his companion from destroying whatever lay in this mysterious city was a hell of a lot more risky.

It might be slightly *less* risky if Jacobs believed that Adam was interested in taking over Dawson's job.

Adam suppressed a groan. He was still fighting the urge to grab Jacobs by his waistcoat and start pummeling him—even though he was pretty sure he'd get stabbed someplace vital as soon as he tried.

But he also knew an opportunity when he saw one.

"You asking if I'm interested?" Adam said. He hopped down from the boulder he'd just climbed, landing solidly beside Jacobs in a dry streambed.

"Are you?" Jacobs returned.

"Sure," Adam replied neatly.

As lies went, Adam thought it was a pretty good one—even for him.

Jacobs smiled. His dark eyes were unreadable.

"Thank you," he said evenly. "That is most informative."

Jacobs sounded a little bit like someone who had just confirmed something which he had already suspected. That should've been a good thing. An uneasy lurch in Adam's gut said otherwise.

Jacobs turned away to continue up the trail with the rifle still slung casually over his shoulder... as though he knew that Adam wasn't a real threat.

"Ah," Jacobs announced from ahead. "I believe we have found your River of Smoke."

He had stopped on the flat, truncated edge of a high rock outcropping. Adam climbed up to join him there—and then promptly wished he hadn't.

Rows of dark green pines fell away from beneath the spit of rock, along with the ground. The trees and the meandering line of the caravan unwound far beneath Adam's boots. Beyond that lay the broad, rolling sprawl of the mountains.

Adam's head was floating. The distance from his brain to the ground seemed to grow, lengthening like a tunnel.

That wasn't good.

In the back of Adam's mind, some rational sliver of his brain was hollering at him—loudly and vociferously—to throw himself down to the ground and cling to it until the world stopped threatening to go into a spin.

Adam settled for taking a single, careful step backwards. The move brought the edge of the stones on which he stood back into view. That was slightly better, if still far from great.

The change in position at least allowed Adam to *look* at what lay before him, instead of succumbing to the urge to drop to his gut on the stones and hold on for dear life. He forced himself to study the view, even as a burst of queasiness jolted through his stomach.

The mountain range curved to the east in a thick barrier of dark forest punctuated by the occasional sliver of a tumbling stream. Directly to the south, a high cliff of pale gray stone broke through the wall of green.

The surface of the cliff was marred by a sinuous line of coal-black stone which spilled down the face of it like the frozen imprint of a long-dead waterfall—or a river.

Jacobs was right. They had found the last landmark on the map—the gateway to a lost world.

"Aw hell," Adam exclaimed as he fought the urge to puke.

They rejoined the caravan at the base of the ridge. Adam carved an unerring route back to the slow-moving line of men and beasts.

Jacobs stayed with him until they passed the place where Staines shuffled along with the others. Then he tossed the rifle to the startled guard, tipped his hat politely to Adam, and strode up to the front of the line to confer with the foreman.

Adam watched his back uneasily the whole way.

Staines shuffled his gun. He jumped away from a nippy nearby mule, muttering a curse.

Charles Goodwin stepped neatly into his place. His lanky stride made it easy.

"I can't tell if you look like you want to strangle a man or throw up on your shoes," Charlie commented. "Go that well up on the hill?"

"We found it," Adam reported bluntly.

Charlie glanced over at him.

"You don't sound too happy about that," he noted.

Adam caught sight of Ellie through the shifting bodies of the pack animals and men. She had turned on her mule to glance back at him, frowning as her gaze shifted between him and Jacobs.

She was almost certainly counting the minutes until the time when she could ruthlessly interrogate Adam about whatever had passed on the ridge.

Oh, not much, Adam imagined himself telling her. *Just me guessing that Jacobs can somehow read minds and plans to kill us both the minute he and Dawson have what they're looking for.*

With effort, he tore his gaze from Ellie to return his attention to the friend who walked beside him.

"I'm afraid I gotta call in that underpants favor," Adam declared flatly.

"Raass," Charlie swore with a groan.

THIRTY-ONE

$\mathcal{E}$LLIE WAS TRAPPED near the back of the caravan when the trees parted before her, revealing a soaring gray cliff split by a twisting ribbon of black stone. The sight sent a wild thrill chasing through her.

The River of Smoke.

"I'm going up there," Ellie announced.

"¡Ay, mierda!" Mendez groaned.

Ellie whirled in the saddle to pin him with a glare.

"Did Jacobs specifically order you not to allow me to approach the cliff?" she demanded.

"I do not believe he did," Flowers helpfully replied.

Mendez glowered over his mustache.

"Then I am going." Ellie declared, and neatly hopped down from the saddle. "Mr. Pacheco! Would you mind my mule, please?"

Pacheco flashed her a charming smile.

"Of course, cariño," he replied.

"Thank you." Ellie tossed him the reins. "That is most kind of you."

She set off without waiting for any further debate, pushing her way through the brush at the edge of the caravan. The line was already disintegrating into a muddle as more men shuffled their way toward the base of the cliff.

At last, Ellie fought her way through a mess of palms to gaze up at the soaring wall of limestone. A narrow, shadowy crevice split the length of it right where the unusual line of black stone marred its surface.

The expedition's leaders had gathered by the opening… along with Adam and his guard, Staines. Ellie slipped and apologized her way toward them through the uncertain men and mules. Mendez elbowed his way in her wake as Flowers followed more easily behind him.

The break in the cliff was perhaps six feet wide. Ellie could see into it a little way before her view was obscured by the shadows of the ravine.

She shouldered between some of the onlookers and popped out to Dawson's left. The professor gave a little start of alarm as he realized that she was there. He took an uneasy step away from her.

"Shouldn't you be under guard?" he demanded.

"Oh, they're coming," Ellie cheerfully assured him.

She caught Adam's eye across the black gap of the opening. He looked uncharacteristically worried.

Velegas emerged from the gap.

"The way appears to be clear," he announced. "I can scout the rest of it if you would like."

The tracker took off his hat and wiped the sweat from his forehead with a careful handkerchief.

"Surely a few of us should go forward as well," Dawson objected.

The professor was clearly itching with his eagerness to pass through the crevice and get his hands on whatever lay on the far side.

"Dawson, myself, Velegas," Jacobs declared. He cast a sideways glance at Adam. "And I suppose we had best include Mr. Bates."

"And me," Ellie declared, stepping forward.

Dawson huffed with outrage.

"I should think not!" he exclaimed.

Jacobs shifted his cool, impenetrable gaze to her—and then back to Adam again.

"The woman comes," he smoothly ordered. There was a hint of a smile on his face as he said it.

Adam's expression went grimmer.

Perhaps Jacobs only wanted Ellie there to better threaten Adam into compliance. That was fine. At least she would be going along, rather than moldering back here with the mules where she stood no chance of protecting whatever lay on the other side.

Jacobs flicked a hand at Mendez, Flowers, and Staines.

"You three stay with them," he ordered, and stepped into the dark mouth of the cliff.

The air inside the crevice was strangely cool. The walls rose dizzyingly to either side, and then narrowed to frame a line of hazy blue sky. The light that filtered down to where Ellie and the others walked was dim and otherworldly.

The wall to her right was all jagged gray limestone. On her left, the limestone mingled with threads of the thick vein of obsidian which ran through the mountain.

Verdant life surrounded her. Plants clung to the stones, sending tentative tendrils down toward the ground. They were framed by patches of jewel-green moss and bundled orchids.

The clamor of the caravan faded. In its place was only the soft crunch of boots against the packed earth and the uneven breathing of the men who surrounded her.

The way broadened ahead of them. A wider patch of sky overhead spilled light down into a slight opening in the ravine, revealing something that brought the entire scouting party to a reverent halt.

On the wall before her, all the remaining limestone had been chipped away to expose the gleaming obsidian beneath. The black mineral had been carved into an elegant mural which rose at least twenty feet up the face of the cliff.

The bas relief depicted an assemblage of gleaming figures. Each of them was elegantly ornamented with ear plugs, wrist cuffs, and necklaces. They were crowned with feathers and elaborate sculpted headdresses.

It was a dynasty—an awe-inspiring conclave of kings, queens, and priests. As Ellie studied it, details leapt out at her from the scene.

A feathered serpent. A foot of lightning. Jaguar teeth and sprouting maize around falling drops of rain.

Ellie knew those symbols. They were the signs which other scholars had used to identify the gods of the Mayan and Aztec pantheons.

An idea crept to life in her mind.

The portrait clearly depicted the great nobles of Tulan—perhaps even the city's founders.

How might those awe-inspiring leaders have appeared to the less powerful people who had come to them seeking wisdom? How might they have been transformed in the stories those petitioners carried back to more distant lands?

Perhaps... they might have sounded like gods.

With a jolt of surprise, Ellie wondered if she was looking at the birth of a faith.

The assemblage of nobles was gathered around a circle inscribed at their feet. Each of their hands was pierced by a blade. Blood dripped down from their wounds.

"It's here," Dawson uttered with quiet awe as he gazed up at the image.

Ellie startled beside him.

"What is?" she demanded.

Dawson snapped his mouth shut. He treated her to a mulish glare before he stalked away.

Ellie lingered to study the black disk over which the divine figures were gathered.

She didn't need Dawson to answer her. She knew what it had to be. It was the Chay Abah—the prophecy-granting obsidian stone said to lie beneath the heart of Tulan.

The Smoking Mirror.

"We are losing daylight!" Velegas's authoritative tones cut through the stillness of the ravine.

"Keep moving," Jacobs ordered.

Ellie didn't want to take her eyes away from the dark relief of the mural. A firm but gentle hand on her arm finally caught her attention.

"Come on," Adam said, gently guiding her after the others.

The passage narrowed once more, winding past spills of rock over which the scouting party had to climb... and then Ellie looked past the shoulders of the men before her to a sliver of green trees and the golden light of late afternoon.

She scrambled down the rest of the crevice and spilled out onto a ledge which overlooked the broad bowl of a valley.

The view was framed by the majestic rise of the mountains, which were now fully upon them. The land below was a rich and vibrant green—a perfect, sheltered paradise framed by tall black peaks and the curving line of the ridge.

White stone towers pierced through the canopy. Ellie's heart pounded as she gazed out at them.

The low gray clouds to the east shifted. Sunlight spilled out across the scene. The warm rays fell over the crowns of the temples and painted them a startling gold.

"It's real!" Ellie breathed.

She closed her eyes, half convinced that when she opened them, she would find herself back in the wet gloom of the Public Record Office, staring down at a stack of crumbling tax assessments.

The gilded temples greeted her instead. A flock of tiny birds burst from the canopy to wheel over the ruins.

No—she was not in London.

This was not a dream.

Adam moved to her side. The falling sunlight highlighted his rugged profile.

"Congratulations, Princess," he said. His voice was flattened with wonder and shock. "Looks like you found El Dorado."

As he spoke, the clouds shifted, swallowing the sun's warm rays. A breeze brushed against the back of Ellie's neck and then stirred the leaves of the trees below her. Ellie turned toward it to see that the sky beyond the peaks had turned thick and gray with the promise of a storm.

"Looks like rain," Velegas warned. His voice rang out clearly over the ledge.

"Go back to Bones. Tell him to bring the gear and set up camp," Jacobs ordered flatly. "Let's get what we came here for."

He stalked toward the path that led down into the ruins.

The trail descended from the ledge to a thick, verdant forest. The aromatic mountain pines were mixed with trees which Ellie had become more accustomed to seeing in the lowlands. Many of them were fruit-bearing, their boughs heavy with cashews or ripening sapodillas.

Ellie's mind spun as she wondered whether the people of Tulan had deliberately brought them here.

This was not the same wilderness that Ellie had passed through on her journey. The landscape around her looked more like a long-abandoned garden.

Vines tumbled down from the boughs, some of them as thick as Ellie's arm. She could hear the rest of the caravan shuffling out onto the ledge above them. Bones's voice rang out as the foreman organized the movement of mules and gear through the narrow pass.

Beyond the creaking ropes and the quick shouts of the men, the wood around her was eerily quiet. A lush, fertile region like this one should have been crawling with birds, monkeys, and tapir—not oddly deserted. When Ellie spotted the undulating form of a snake hurrying after a quick-darting mouse, she was almost surprised.

Even the ever-present hum of the insects was lessened here, which Ellie would have thought impossible.

Adam walked beside her. She bit back the urge to grab his arm and drag him over to examine every thrilling discovery she made, like the divots in the earth alongside their path which likely indicated the presence of cellar holes for wooden dwellings. She was conscious that anything she said would be overheard by Flowers, Staines, and Mendez, who trudged along at their heels.

Ellie dropped her gaze to the remarkably even path on which she walked. The ribbon of land was slightly raised up from the ground around it as it curved away ahead of her.

She grabbed Adam by the elbow.

"Bates… I think we are walking on a road!" she exclaimed.

Adam cocked an eyebrow at her, and then kicked thoughtfully at the forest debris under his boot.

"You'll disturb the layers!" Ellie protested with a squeak of panic.

"If it's a road, there's a hell of a lot of it, Princess," Adam returned. "I think you'll still have plenty of layers to play with."

Ellie dropped to her knees in order to give the area Adam had cleared a closer look.

The toe of his boot had exposed a surface of pale, mud-stained stone. She shoved more of the debris aside with her hands and revealed a long, straight line where two blocks had been joined together. Their edges were perfectly matched.

"They're pavers," she said. Her voice was strangled with wonder. "Cut, quarried pavers. They *paved* the road. Bates, do you have any idea what sort of engineering prowess would have been required to—"

"Let's keep moving, Princess," Adam cut in. He gently tugged her back up with an uneasy look at where Jacobs walked ahead of them.

The landscape around them shifted. The cellar holes gave way to moss-grown piles of tumbled stone which peered at Ellie from between the trees in every direction.

They had to be houses—*actual* houses, where everyday people had lived rather than the elites of the city. There would be room layouts for her to discern, along with hearths and sleeping areas that hinted at the local kinship structures.

And there would be middens.

The thought of an ancient trash heap between those buildings waiting to be discovered filled Ellie with a wild and impatient joy.

"Bates," she exclaimed. "This one is intact!"

Ellie didn't wait for him to follow. She dashed over to the building that she had spotted not far from the road ahead of them. Parts of the walls were still standing.

Mendez grumbled out a curse behind her.

Ellie stopped on the threshold to study the interior. The roof had rotted away long ago, and the ground was thick with fallen leaves and debris.

She let out a strangled squeal.

"Pots!" she gasped as her heart pounded with the enormity of what she was looking at. "*Intact* pots!"

There were four of them, each roughly three feet in height, standing in the corner of the structure. Hints of colorful glaze peered through the verdigris which discolored them.

Ellie's desperate desire to get closer to the objects warred with her fear of damaging something within the house if she walked into it.

She took a breath, steadying herself. The bases of the pots were buried at least four inches into the ground. There was two hundred years of sediment in here. Ellie wasn't going to break anything by walking on that.

She dashed inside, crouching down to give the artifacts a better look.

"Oh God," she groaned. "I think there's still wax around the lids! Bates, do you have any idea what that means?"

"Pretty sure you're going to tell me," Adam replied as he made a quiet, thoughtful examination of the rest of the room.

"It means they might still be *sealed*," Ellie emphasized, buzzing with the joy of it. "Sealed! The implications are... I'm not sure I can even... Bates?" she finished less certainly.

Adam had gone silent. He crouched in the opposite corner, looking down at something he had carefully exposed by brushing away a few layers of dried leaves.

Ellie noticed the unusual solemnity of his focus and rose to join him. She found herself looking down at the jumble of a skeleton half-buried in the sediment. Only parts of it were visible—but one of those pieces included what was very obviously the eye socket of a human skull.

"Oh," she breathed softly as she carefully brushed a bit more of the debris away. "The bones are still somewhat articulated. That's odd for a body left above ground like this. One would have expected the local wildlife to have done more damage to it." She frowned. "Why wouldn't it have been damaged? And why leave the body here at all? Surely a city with such extensive resources had procedures for the ritual disposal of the dead, and this clearly isn't a deliberate excarnation. It's as if there was..."

"...nobody left to bury her," Adam finished, looking down at the place where the missing eye was now filled with soft brown earth.

Ellie felt a chill that defied the thick, hazy heat. A breeze rustled through the tall, elegant trees overhead. The canopy swayed gently as wind whispered through the leaves.

"Can we be done, please?" Staines complained from the doorway. "The others are getting ahead of us."

Adam pushed the leaves back over the bones, carefully covering the body before he rose to go.

The road continued to unfurl in wide, well-planned curves past structures that grew gradually larger and more complex until Ellie had to crane her neck in order to look up at them.

Here and there, three-story complexes of columns and balconies were more or less intact. Others had fallen into nothing more than vine-draped facades.

Ellie's skin buzzed with excitement. She'd read about all the major Mayan cities which had been found so far. These ruins were nothing like them. Certainly, there were familiar elements—the shape of an elegant tower, or a colonnaded facade—but the architecture here was both grander and more graceful.

The sheer scale of it was like nothing she had heard of.

The wild, seemingly impossible dream that a lost city lay at the end of Ellie's map had compelled her to grab it from her desk and race off to corroborate it against the records. Even so, she would never have dared to dream of something like *this*. This wasn't just another ruin. It was an upheaval of everything the world had known about Mesoamerican history—and Ellie was standing in the middle of it.

Every one of the magnificent structures they passed demanded investigation. Ellie's hands itched for a notebook and pencil—for string, stakes, and measuring tape. They should have been embarking on a thorough survey of the entirety of the ruins, identifying potential sites, digging test pits—and documenting, documenting, documenting.

Instead, Jacobs and Dawson led them past archaeological wonders as if they were merely lumps in the landscape. It took all of Ellie's willpower not to shout the whole expedition to a halt so that she could start making some measurements... and yet at the same time, the gorgeous question of what might still lie ahead of them tugged at her as hard and sure as a fishing line. Even as her mind spun to organize a responsible approach to examining the ruins, another part of her wanted to race through it all like an overeager puppy.

The rest of the caravan sprawled along the road behind them. The line of men and mules was setting a better pace than usual, aided by the flat surface of the ancient road.

The mules' ears lay back flat along their necks as the animals hurried along. Ellie wondered whether the animals had sensed the significance of the thick gray clouds which rose over the ridge to the east through breaks in the trees.

The buildings around them had grown even more elaborate—a signal that they must be approaching the center of the city.

Ellie's attention was arrested by a glimpse of something through the thick-leaved flowers to her right. She veered from the road, pushing through the blooms as Mendez grumbled another complaint behind her.

On the far side lay a verdigris-covered basin measuring at least forty feet long. A staircase descended along the inner wall to a layer of green water which was perhaps six feet down from the surface.

Ellie eyed the periphery, noting the places where small notches had been cut into the top of the walls. They led to stone-lined channels which wound into the overgrowth around her.

The stone head of a feathered serpent protruded from the higher wall to her left. A trickle of water dripped from its gaping jaw, which was easily big enough for Ellie to have crawled inside it.

She leaned forward for a better look. The throat of the sculpture was a black tunnel leading into darkness.

As Adam arrived beside her, Ellie whirled toward him.

"Bates, do you realize what this is?" Ellie demanded.

"A half-empty swimming pool?" he replied, frowning down at the murky water.

"It's a reservoir!" she countered. "Look—there are aqueducts carrying water to other areas of the city. They wouldn't be using this for irrigation in the middle of a population center. It can only be some sort of municipal water system." She gripped his shirt, beaming up at him with excitement. "*A municipal water system*, Bates!"

Ellie released him to scramble along the edge of the pool to the serpent statue.

"I think the water must be coming through this—but from what source?" Ellie stuck her head inside the sculpture's mouth and shouted back. Her own voice echoed wildly around her. "I can't see where it goes. There must be some sort of underground source."

"Princess..." Adam cut in carefully.

Ellie pulled her head back out into the daylight to glance back at him.

Their guards lingered at his back—Staines looking uncomfortable, Mendez tapping his foot, and Flowers seeming mildly amused.

"Er... right. We should probably keep going," Ellie reluctantly declared.

She couldn't entirely hide her disappointment. The discovery of a municipal water system was revolutionary. It overwhelmed her with the awareness of how very much there was to *learn*... but this wasn't a normal archaeological survey. It was a crime in the making, and she was a prisoner within it.

The truth of that tore at her as she gazed at the murky water of the reservoir.

Adam gave her shoulder a squeeze. "I know," he said quietly.

He guided her back through the tangles of overgrown flowers to the road—and Ellie realized that it had ended.

The broad path stopped at the bottom of a wide staircase. Bits of white stone showed where the debris had blown aside rather than rotting in place. Voices rang out from above them in tones of greedy excitement.

Ellie mounted the steps into the heart of Tulan.

She stood at the edge of an open plaza longer than a cricket pitch. The space was paved entirely in gleaming white stones. The structures that bordered it had to be the most important buildings in the city.

A sprawling palace complex lay to the west, punctuated by towers that reminded her of church belfries. Colonnaded passages lined the way between shallow ornamental pools and broken fountains.

Stelae dotted the perimeter, carved in a familiar night-black obsidian. Their surfaces were inscribed with some of the same figures Ellie had seen honored on the bas relief in the passage.

The altar stones at their feet still held fragments of broken offering vessels.

Looming over all of it was the temple. The pyramid was by far the tallest structure in the city. Its white stone tiers rose to a height which Ellie thought might rival that of Westminster Abbey—and that was frankly astonishing. She knew of no other pre-Colombian monuments that could even come close to it.

Nature had tried to reclaim the enormous, graceful structure. Here and there, it had succeeded in gaining a foothold. Roots had worked their way into small cracks between the stones, while little shrubs and vines marred what must otherwise have been a mind-boggling feat of engineering.

A squat temple structure crowned the top of the pyramid. Five elegantly arched portals fronted it, leading to an interior swathed in shadows. A narrow ledge in front of the entrance offered space for more public rituals.

Behind it all rose the steep, ragged face of the mountain. A waterfall glittered against its surface, trickling down to some unseen place behind the temple.

There were other pyramids as well. A smaller one lay to the east, and the peaks of a cluster of others emerged from further out in the canopy.

The last gasp of afternoon light slipped out from between the mountains and the bank of charcoal clouds which hung threateningly against the horizon. It turned the whole of what Ellie was looking at to a sun-blessed gold, giving her a heart-wrenching glimpse of what must once have been an astonishingly beautiful and powerful nation.

She took it in with wonder… and then with an uncomfortable sense of recognition. The white pyramid, the rows of waiting gods embodied in black

stone, the broad stones of the plaza, and the graceful palace in the distance...
it all seemed *familiar*.

Ellie shook the feeling off. Most Mesoamerican cities boasted a central
temple district organized around a ritual square or plaza. She had probably
just read about the arrangement so many times that it had taken up residence
inside her mind.

The sunlight slipped away in a breath. The stones turned to a cooler gray
as the wind picked up once more. It rustled uneasily through the leaves of
the nearby trees.

"Foodstuffs, hammocks, fuel, and ammunition—inside!" Bones called out
as the mules began to clomp noisily up the stairs. The foreman's attention was
focused on the encroaching clouds rather than on the wonders of the lost
city. "Clear the most secure structure for quarters. We are preparing for rain."

The word—*rain*—rang out like a curse, shivering down Ellie's spine.

A quick gust of wind broke through the waiting stillness of the ruins,
sending the trees into a restless sway.

The men hurried to their work, elbowing each other out of their open-
mouthed gaping at the ruins. They loosed the crates and bundles from the
mules, and then formed quick lines to shuffle the gear into some of the low,
open structures that bordered the plaza.

None of the buildings had been properly cleared. There could be historical material under the debris layers inside. They certainly shouldn't be used
as camps.

Ellie bit back her protest. No one would listen to it anyway... and she
was consumed by a rising, irrational feeling that there was something *strange*
about this place—something that went beyond the mere shock of a remarkable discovery.

"Hey," Adam said, frowning down at her. "Everything okay?"

Ellie looked around the pale plaza, from the black sentinels of the name-
less ancestors to the imposing, glimmering bulk of the temple—and then
firmly shook the feeling off. She was a scholar. She approached the unknown
with the twin weapons of knowledge and rationality. She knew better than to
pay heed to something as illogical as a hunch.

"It's nothing," she asserted.

Adam looked concerned—but before he could respond, a call rang out
across the stones.

"Mr. Bates! With me, if you will."

Dawson waved imperiously from the foot of the pyramid.

Adam glanced down at Ellie again—this time with all the sharp focus of a promise.

"I'll be back," he said, then left her alone in a field of white stone.

THIRTY-TWO

$\mathcal{H}$ALFWAY UP THE steps of the pyramid, Adam stopped to wait for Dawson to catch up. The professor climbed slowly, pausing frequently to wipe sweat from under the band of his hat and mutter complaints about the weather.

Staines shifted awkwardly behind Adam. He held the rifle, but didn't look particularly ready to use it. Adam's guard was becoming a bit complacent—the sort of thing that was bound to happen after days of guarding someone who refrained from doing anything worthy of being shot for.

That was good, because Adam was pretty sure the time was coming for him and Ellie to cut their losses and make a run for it.

Ellie was going to hate the idea. God knew, Adam hated it too. Now that he'd seen the jaw-dropping extent and complexity of the ruins, the idea of leaving it all to the likes of Dawson and Jacobs made him want to break something... but his conversation with Jacobs on the ridge had left him with a bad feeling in his gut.

Adam had a lot of respect for his gut. Listening to it had saved his skin more times than he could count.

Jacobs didn't buy that Adam was interested in taking over Dawson's job. Adam wasn't sure how Jacobs could be so certain about it—surely he wasn't *that* bad a liar—but he hadn't made it this far in life by ignoring his instincts.

Dawson and Jacobs needed him to help find the artifact they were after. Once that was done, he and Ellie would be toast.

Adam had already set the wheels in motion for an escape. He just had to play the game for a little while longer, and then seize the first moment he could to get the pair of them out of there. Ellie would be furious with him—but he'd take her being mad at him over being dead.

The two Caulker Caye kids, Pacheco and Lopez, lingered behind Dawson as he caught his breath. Adam caught the pair of them exchanging whispered commentary behind the professor. Pacheco rolled his eyes.

"On we go, then," Dawson finally said, casting another greedy look up at the temple.

At the top of the pyramid, Adam made the mistake of turning around.

The city sprawled out below him in wild, overgrown luxury. Columned houses and towers flashed through the gaps in the trees as far as he could see. The settlement had to fill most of the low, flat bowl of the valley which lay between the ridge and the mountain that rose up at his back.

The place was a miracle—and it was possible that he was going to be sick.

Adam pressed himself back against one of the columns which lined the facade of the temple, hoping that the solid feel of it under his back would stop his head from spinning.

Why exactly had the people of Tulan decided that the most important place in their damned city needed to be so high off the ground?

The ground was perfectly nice as far as Adam was concerned.

Staines frowned at him with concern. Adam hoped his guard couldn't tell that he was about to either lose his lunch or fall over.

He could try turning around, but knowing that there would be just a little ledge of stone and then a whole lot of very high nothing behind him was even worse. Instead, Adam stuck himself to the column like a barnacle and waited for a well-dressed looter to haul his way up the stairs.

The very steep, very long stairs.

Dawson finally reached the top, pausing to pant.

"My," he exclaimed breathlessly. "Quite a climb. Shall we?"

He didn't wait for Adam to answer. Instead, he stepped between the columns to enter the shaded interior of the temple.

Adam followed and immediately felt some relief.

The arches he had been clinging to framed a long, shallow chamber, backed by a wall of the same pale stone that made up the rest of the city's structures. The broad, flat surface was covered in another bas relief mural. Adam recognized some of the same god-like figures that he had seen on the carving in the pass. They were depicted standing on the platform in front of the temple. Smaller people knelt below them in positions of worship.

One of the rulers held out an offering of maize. Another clasped running threads of water. A third extended a clenched fist that dripped with blood.

The carvings were richly detailed and full of life as though at any moment, they might step off the stone and expose themselves to the dying sunlight.

Dawson glanced quickly up and down the chamber.

"There's nothing here," he concluded. "But it looks like there's another room."

He hurried toward a gap between the stone mural and the far wall.

Adam's irritation flashed. Dawson clearly expected him to follow along in his wake like an obedient dog.

Usually, someone expecting Adam to do something was all the reason he needed to do something else—but Adam wasn't quite ready to make that move. Not yet.

He turned through the narrow opening after Dawson.

The second chamber was long, like the first, but slightly broader. Soft illumination glowed through five narrow windows which looked out the back of the temple. The pyramid on which the temple stood had been built almost flush with the steep face of the mountain. The waterfall that ran down the rocky surface was visible through the openings in the wall. The flow was currently a trickle, but it likely turned into an impressive rush during the rains.

The air inside was cooler. It smelled of stone and old wood. The shelves lining the walls were packed with objects.

Dawson hurried closer, his eyes darting over the assorted artifacts.

Curiosity drew Adam after him.

The shelves held a collection of seemingly ritual materials. There were masks—one made from a jaguar skull, another from chips of jade—beside an elaborate feather headdress. The colors of the feathers had barely faded, though some of the leather which bound them together looked rotten. Small, beautifully glazed pots likely held perfumes or paints.

There were jewels as well—gold cuffs and ear plugs. A few glints of silver flashed from among the jumble—platinum, Adam recognized with surprise. Silver would have been tarnished.

Platinum was a tough metal to shape, and Adam didn't know of any sources of it in British Honduras. The nearest platinum mine was in Colombia.

That meant the people of this place had been trading, even as they kept the truth about their city secret enough to turn it into a myth.

Adam stepped deeper into the room, glancing out of one of the windows as he passed. The face of the mountain was startlingly close. He followed the trail of the waterfall with his gaze until the narrow wash of it disappeared into the plants at the base of the structure. He couldn't see any stream leading away from it.

A shelf on the far wall drew his attention. It was covered in folded bundles of stiff, slightly yellowed paper.

They were books, he realized with a jolt—a whole wall of books.

Adam was no expert on Mayan culture, but he'd certainly picked up enough to know that damned few books had survived the conquest.

It looked like the people of Tulan had left an entire library behind.

Insects should have chewed any paper apart out here several centuries ago. Adam guessed that the scribes here must have known some way to treat their documents in order to protect them. He was pretty sure he shouldn't even be breathing near something so delicate, but he couldn't resist a peek at the covers. They were vibrantly painted like the medieval manuscripts in the Cambridge library. Illustrated scenes intermingled with lines of the square characters that made up the language of this place.

If Ellie were there, she'd probably be grabbing the front of his shirt and shaking him right about now, Adam thought with a smile.

Behind him, Dawson coughed.

Adam stiffened as reality crashed back in. He was here with someone a hell of a lot less fun than Ellie.

Staines wide-eyed gaze flickered to the more obvious treasures that glittered from among the less shiny artifacts. Pacheco and Lopez lingered in the doorway.

"Has to be here somewhere..." Dawson muttered to himself. He crouched down, studying the lower shelves with uncomfortable haste.

Another mural decorated the inner side of the wall which divided the two chambers. This one had been carved into the city's other favorite material of night-black obsidian.

The bas relief was dominated by the feathered serpent king whom Adam had seen on the stela they'd passed on the way there. He stood in the corner of the image, looking down at a round opening in the ground connected to the long neck of a tunnel. It led to a series of chambers which were depicted more or less as round bubbles on the wall.

In each of the bubbles, the king struggled against some adversary—an army of nasty-looking insects, a whirlwind of daggers, a pack of jaguars. There was another room that followed, but Adam couldn't tell what it might have held. A piece of the obsidian facing had fallen off and shattered on the ground.

In Adam's admittedly inexpert opinion, the carving looked a heck of a lot like the way Ellie had described Xibalba, the Mayan underworld which was supposed to lie beneath Tulan.

Ellie would go wild over that, too.

The last chamber depicted on the mural was by far the largest, but Adam couldn't make out much of it beyond the fact that it showed the serpent king surrounded by a group of odd-looking figures looming over something that lay on the floor. The shadows in that part of the room were too deep—and there was a corpse in the way.

The body was a humble pile of bones and rotting fabric slumped into the corner between the mural and the wall. The bones had mostly collapsed into a loose jumble within remnants of desiccated leather and a pile of jade beads which must once have been an ornate necklace. The skull, aged to a rich brown, gazed sightlessly up at him.

It was another case of someone who had been left to decay where they fell. Based on the richness of the person's attire, they had clearly been some-one of importance. Adam wasn't an expert, but he was pretty sure important people weren't left lying where they died unless something had gone real wrong, real fast.

What the hell had happened in this place?

A glittering, wickedly sharp obsidian blade lay among the bones, jammed between a pair of ribs.

Some of the corpse's fingers still clung to the handle, with just enough dried tissue remaining to keep them articulated.

Had they been pulling the knife out, or driving it in?

The question put a deeper chill into the atmosphere of the room.

Whoever the body on the floor had been, someone had either killed him right here in the ritual heart of Tulan—or else he'd done it to himself.

Or *herself*, Adam thought uncomfortably, noting the diminutive size of the bones.

There was a clatter behind him. Adam turned to see Dawson rifling through the objects on the shelves. The professor peered under the delicate pots and pushed aside ancient garments that cracked and collapsed at his touch.

"Whoa—hey!" Adam cut in. "Watch how you're handling that stuff."

"But it has to be here!" Dawson shot back. He stomped his foot with frustration.

"What—your Smoking Mirror?" Adam retorted irritably.

Dawson's eyes widened. He looked anxiously toward Staines, Pacheco, and Lopez—and then back to Adam again.

He narrowed his gaze thoughtfully.

"You three," the professor said, waving dismissively at the others. "Go out on the platform. No, wait!" he quickly corrected himself. "Give me that first."

He flapped a hand at the rifle Staines was carrying.

Staines cast him a surprised look, but handed the gun over before he left.

Adam wondered if he was about to be shot. Dawson didn't seem like the kind of guy who shot people. He probably had no idea where to put the bullet.

Adam debated whether that was a good or bad thing.

Dawson skipped over to the doorway and peered out at the departing men.

"My apologies," he said. "I needed to make sure we weren't being overheard."

Adam raised an eyebrow. Did the professor not want to be overhead murdering him? Or was something else going on here?

The way the man held the rifle was all wrong. It was obvious he barely knew how to use it, if at all.

An idea sparked to life inside Adam's mind. It was probably a bad one— but Adam was going to consider it anyway.

"I am aware you are not particularly fond of me, Mr. Bates," Dawson began.

"That's one way of putting it," Adam replied automatically, still distracted by his bad idea.

Dawson hardly seemed to notice. He rolled on into a monologue.

"...but there is far more at stake in this than personal regard. You may be a bit... rough," Dawson said awkwardly as he eyed Adam's filthy borrowed shirt and unshaven jaw. "But I do not believe you to be a man completely lacking in *principles*."

"I didn't realize you could tell a guy's principles by his wardrobe," Adam dryly returned.

"Entirely correct, Mr. Bates," Dawson agreed obliviously. "Sometimes, appearances can be quite deceiving! But if I am right, and you are a man of principle, then perhaps you might like to know that the very future of our civilization might depend upon our efforts in this place."

That sure as hell hadn't been what Adam expected to hear, and Dawson looked damned earnest about it.

"I'm sorry, but you're going to have to explain that a little better," Adam replied.

The professor shifted his grip on the rifle as though it were a bit too heavy for him to comfortably hold.

"I told you that my colleague and I had been dispatched to this place to retrieve a single artifact," he went on. "You were clever enough to deduce that the artifact in question was the Smoking Mirror."

After you told me it was mirror-sized, Adam thought, resisting the urge to roll his eyes.

"But did it not occur to you to wonder why we would go to such trouble and expense for just a *single object*?" Dawson added significantly.

"How the hell should I know?" Adam retorted with a flash of irritation. "Why do collectors raise all sorts of hell for anything? Some rich guy got fixed on it and threw a bunch of money at you to bring it back for him."

Visions of all the looted sites he had stumbled across flashed through his brain—broken pots, defaced walls, torn up foundations, and bones scattered like refuse.

Adam's hands clenched.

"But I do not work for a single individual, Mr. Bates," Dawson returned meaningfully. "I am employed by... an *association* of individuals. Tell me— what collector who simply seeks to satisfy his greed has ever agreed to share his spoils with others?"

It was as if Dawson had flipped over a table. He worked for a group?

The professor was right. Adam didn't know of any collector who cheerfully shared his stuff—not unless it was going to a museum that'd put his name in big letters all over it.

"What unites a group is *purpose*," Dawson continued pointedly.

The room in which they stood was growing more gloomy. The increasing darkness was due either to the onset of evening, or to the thickening clouds overhead. Adam couldn't see the sky through the narrow, mountain-facing windows cut into the wall, but he could feel the tingling drop of pressure in the air, which promised a turn in the weather.

"I have not yet told you our true purpose here," Dawson said. "I have kept it from you because I have been strictly sworn not to reveal it, even upon the pain of death. But I will tell you that a single, overarching goal indeed unites the association I am privileged to call myself a part of, and it is one that no man of morals and logic could fail to support... once he acknowledged the shocking truth that underlays it."

Dawson spoke like a preacher firing up for a sermon. The tone set Adam's nerves on alert. In his experience, men got more dangerous the more fervently they believed in something—and Dawson was still the one in the room with a gun.

"What truth is that?" Adam asked carefully.

"What do you know of the Smoking Mirror?" Dawson demanded.

"Not much," Adam admitted bluntly.

"But you are aware that the mirror is both the name of a god and a mythological artifact of reputedly immense power." Dawson's eyes were bright with fervor. "A disk of polished obsidian in which one is said to be

313

able to see across both time and distance—deep into the past, or far into the future. An object through which one might look with the very eyes of the gods themselves! Think on that, Mr. Bates—think what that would *mean*. The movements of any enemy could be laid out before you without relying on the vagaries of scouting or the terrible risk of observation balloons. The wisdom of our ancestors might simply unlock itself for our perusal. The unimaginable technology which our descendants will dream into life could be within our grasp even *now*—requiring the most rigorous investigation to understand and replicate, of course, but think how much progress might be achieved were we merely able to *see* where the end result is destined to take us."

"You're talking like you think this thing is real," Adam carefully noted.

"An alliance of highly educated, influential, *well-bred* individuals has gone to a very great deal of trouble and expense to acquire the mirror, Mr. Bates," Dawson countered. "Tell me—why on earth would they have done so if there were not a very good chance that it is, in fact, *real?*"

"Look, professor... I dunno who put this notion in your head, but I think maybe you and the rest of your highly influential people are getting conned," Adam replied.

In response, Dawson tucked the rifle under his arm awkwardly. With his free hand, he reached into the inner pocket of his field jacket. He took out a slender wooden case—one Adam recognized from the moments in which he'd been able to make a brief snoop of the professor's desk. Dawson opened it and removed the delicate bird bone from inside. He held it up like a trophy with a slyly triumphant expression.

"This is the humerus of a firebird," he announced grandly. "It was recovered by one of our agents in the beechwood outside Vihorlat in Austria-Hungary. It is only a minor arcanum—a feather, I am told, would have a more immediate and impressive effect. This one takes a hair more effort, but I find it to be quite useful."

Dawson proceeded to shake the bone vigorously.

For the first time, Adam wondered whether the man in front of him might not be a self-important academic but rather a complete and utter lunatic.

That would not bode well for his and Ellie's prospects... which hadn't been great to begin with.

Then the bone bloomed with a wild and fiery light.

THIRTY-THREE

A few minutes earlier

$\mathcal{A}$s THE CLOUDS thickened overhead, Ellie watched the urgent buzz of the camp from her perch on a fallen column.

Her fingers itched where she clenched them uselessly in her lap. Mendez hovered at her back and shifted from foot to foot as he looked restlessly from the ruins to the sky. Ellie wasn't sure whether he was dreaming of taking off to explore the mysterious structures for gold… or worrying that the ghosts of the place were going to jump out at them.

The imminent threat of the weather had also sobered the mood in the camp. Many of the men glanced nervously toward the encroaching clouds—though not Braxton Pickett. The fish-eyed Confederate stomped across the plaza, interrogating anyone he came across.

He grabbed Ram by the collar and gave him a shake.

"Which of you made off with my knife?" he shouted, pitching his voice out over the tired assortment of men.

"What do any of us want your knife for?" Ram retorted in his clear, Bhojpur-accented English. "We already have our own, thank you very much."

"Well, somebody made off with it!" Pickett protested.

He released Ram and stalked away to continue his search.

Ram straightened his shirt, and then treated Pickett's back to an emphatic gesture that Ellie was fairly certain meant *sod off.*

Someone had lit a campfire on the stones of the plaza. Ellie choked on her protest at the sight of it. Activities such as establishing campsites and building fires should have been happening well outside of the settlement area, ideally in a location that had been carefully reviewed to ensure there was no evidence of habitation which they might be disturbing.

Jacobs didn't care about disturbing evidence of habitation.

Ellie had seen little of the true leader of their company since she had arrived. Dawson had dragged Adam up into the temple at the top of the pyramid, and Jacobs had moved off. Perhaps he was stalking the perimeter of the camp to ensure that greed didn't get the better of his guards and send them off treasure-hunting in neglect of their other duties.

Another gust of wind stirred the hairs at the back of her neck. Aurelio's mules shifted and brayed uncomfortably in their corral.

Ellie burned with the urge to explore the city. From her spot at the edge of the plaza, she could see clear indications of how organized urban planning had shaped the natural growth of the settlement by way of water and sewage systems, bath houses, road networks, and community spaces.

She could vividly picture what Tulan might have looked like when still inhabited, with the soaring temple free of growth and debris, and the bas relief murals painted in vivid colors. Cloth banners might decorate the buildings while flowers adorned the figures of the ancestors on the stelae.

The details of the vision were so rich and familiar, Ellie could almost imagine that she had really seen them.

She looked up at the temple where Adam and Dawson had disappeared. The building was clearly the major ritual center for the city. If it had remained as untouched as the rest of what they'd discovered, its contents could offer earth-shattering revelations about the people of Tulan... and Ellie had been left out of that exploration because Dawson found it impossible to comprehend that a woman might also be a competent scholar of the antiquities.

Ellie's frustrated thoughts were interrupted by the arrival of a squat fellow with an enormous ginger beard.

"Hey weasel," he said by way of announcing himself. He jerked his head at Mendez. "The boss wants to see you by the temple."

The man spoke with a noticeably French Canadian accent.

Mendez glanced at the enormous structure across the plaza.

"Not that one, niaiseux. The small one." The Canadian pointed to a white peak just visible through the dense trees beyond the city center.

"What does he want?" Mendez demanded crossly.

"He didn't tell me," the Canadian replied flatly. He loosed a stream of tobacco-stained spit through a missing tooth. "You want me to go back and ask him?"

The remark was casual enough, but even Ellie could hear the threat in it.

Mendez shuffled uncertainly, and then set off with a muttered curse.

"Stay with the woman!" he shouted back at Flowers, who remained comfortably positioned behind Ellie with his rifle resting on his shoulder.

Flowers acknowledged this with an easy wave.

A moment later, another of the workers sat down beside Ellie on the column—a lanky Creole fellow with well-muscled arms and a close-cropped beard that showed off his fine cheekbones.

"Weh gaan on, Charlie?" Flowers said amicably. "Lessard," he added with a nod at the squat Canadian.

"Aarait, cousin," Charlie replied easily.

He took out a cigarette, obviously preparing to light it.

Ellie frowned.

"You do realize that's a dreadful habit," she noted.

"Laura tells him that all the time," Flowers cheerfully added.

Charlie looked at the cigarette a little mournfully, and then put it away with a sigh.

"Your boy Bates asked me to acquire something for him," Charlie said. His Kriol accent warmed the words. "I acquired it into the coffee."

"Don't dig too far," Lessard added with a terrifying grin. "It bites."

"And maybe don't find it until you are well and ready to disappear," Charlie added pointedly as he locked his sharp brown gaze on her.

Ellie glared at them. "How am I supposed to dig through anything if I am constantly being watched?" she demanded. "Unless I am meant to go right now?"

The three men exchanged a look.

"She goes now, it will fall on this one here," Lessard pointed out as he jerked his thumb at Flowers.

"She needs a distraction," Charlie concluded.

He looked up at the temple. Ellie suspected he must be thinking the same thing that she was—that Adam was still under guard up there, and any distraction down below might not be enough to get him loose as well.

"I might have an idea," Ellie blurted.

Charlie cocked an eyebrow. Behind her, Flowers chuckled, though he still maintained every appearance of guarding her.

"Oh?" Charlie prompted carefully.

Ellie felt a little burst of excitement at his invitation to elaborate.

"There is a box of ammunition in that pile of equipment over there, which they haven't yet moved into one of the structures," she explained. "I happen to have a bit of strong liquor in my pocket as well as a magnifying lens—which as a convex lens is quite useful for focusing light. Were we to douse the dry debris under the crate with the alcohol, and then focus the remaining light there with the lens, generating sufficient heat to spark a blaze—"

"You want to blow up the bullets?" Charlie cut in with a look that managed to be both horrified and vaguely impressed.

"I like this woman," Lessard announced happily.

Ellie's shoulders slumped as she thought of the flaw in her plan.

"Of course, I cannot know what sort of danger any shrapnel from the rounds might cause," she admitted, "and Mr. Bates was quite insistent that I not make any explosions without clearing the matter with him first."

"Did you want to make *more* of them?" Charlie prompted.

Ellie brightened and leaned in as she whispered a little wickedly. "I had the most wonderful idea for overheating the boiler on one of the steamers back at camp..."

Flowers snorted behind her.

Charlie pinched the bridge of his nose in a gesture that struck Ellie as rather Adam-like.

"Baas gat di regyula papshat ya," he muttered in Kriol.

"What's a *papshat?*" Ellie demanded, looking to Lessard and Flowers.

"Like a firework," Lessard replied and illustrated with a gesture. "Hssss—pow!"

Charlie raised his head, looking a bit tired.

"Lessard, bali—You still good for throwing your fists around some?" he asked.

Lessard shifted his tobacco to the other side of his mouth. "So long as I get seventy percent," he replied easily.

"Seventy percent of what?" Ellie cut in, confused and mildly alarmed.

"The bets, Pepa," Flowers replied cheerfully. "Who you gonna pick a fight with then, Frenchman?"

"Maybe that bakra Pickett," Lessard offered with obvious relish.

"Pretty sure that one is fool enough to try stabbing you," Flowers noted.

"Good thing somebody took his knife, then," Lessard said with a laugh.

A sharp cry rose up from across the camp. It sounded of both alarm and interest.

The noise was followed by a distinct wave of chatter, which emanated from somewhere behind the ruins of the palace.

"C'est quoi ça sacrament?" Lessard demanded with a pointed look at Charlie, providing Ellie with a lovely example of the Quebecois habit of using sacred terms as profanity.

Charlie sighed.

"Suppose we better go find out," he concluded and set off across the plaza.

Ellie leapt up as well and fell into step behind them. With a shake of his head, Flowers followed, slinging his rifle over his shoulder.

Mendez jogged up to meet them, flustered and out of breath.

"The boss wasn't at any temple. I don't know where he's gone," he said with a note of panic.

"He wants you, he'll come and find you," Flowers assured him, waving it off.

"What's all this?" Mendez demanded.

"I think maybe somebody found something," Flowers replied and nodded to the thick cluster of men ahead of them.

The crowd had gathered in a circle. Ellie scurried around the edge of it, with Mendez complaining at her heels. She picked out a less thickly packed spot and nudged her way in.

The men were clustered around an open hole in the ground. It dropped perhaps ten feet down. Ellie recognized the general form of it as a sinkhole.

There must be more caves under the city, which meant that Tulan likely sat at the edge of the place where the limestone karst met the harder stone of the mountains.

Between the clouds and the encroaching sunset, it was getting darker. A pair of lanterns flared to life at opposite sides of the gap. The light spilled across the pit and revealed what had sparked that shout of surprise.

The sinkhole was full of bones.

They were browned with age, jumbled into a pile, and twisted through with vines. Moss grew from them in places. Ellie could pick out faded remnants of tattered cloth and old leather.

Scattered throughout the debris were distinct hints of gold, which glinted in the light of the lanterns.

It was a grave—a mass grave where the bodies of the people of Tulan had been tossed as though there had been no time to do anything better for them.

With a cold shock, Ellie realized that she had seen it before... that she had seen *all* of it before.

The white road that led to the city. The plaza with its palaces and temples—and this, the grave that lay before her.

She had *dreamed* it as a scarred woman spoke of the voices of gods and ash rained down from the sky.

Ellie staggered back a step as the impossibility of it washed over her.

Thunder rumbled in the distance. The sound brought the men clustered around the sinkhole to a hush. Wind gusted through the trees again, ripe with the promise of rain.

Bones arrived and pushed his way through the crowd.

"Back to work!" he ordered. He clapped his hands for emphasis as he herded the men away from the sinkhole.

They went slowly, glancing back with either fear of the dead or greed for those hints of gold. Ellie didn't doubt that some of them would slip back here tonight, seeking to climb down and rifle through the bones.

She wondered if anyone would bother to stop them.

A flash of light caught her eye. It winked from the temple at the top of the pyramid… from where Adam and Dawson had gone. The glare was unnaturally bright—a star-like illumination that blazed out from between the columns.

Then it was gone.

An instinctive panic tightened at Ellie's chest. She looked to the far side of the sinkhole, seeking out the place where Charlie stood.

He was also staring up at the pyramid. He lowered his gaze and met her eyes from across the pit. Ellie could read the question in them.

She nodded.

Charlie nudged Lessard with his elbow.

"Eh! Slaver pig!" Lessard shouted.

The harsh call of it shattered the hushed quiet of the scene.

Braxton Pickett whirled toward the sound, and Lessard threw a meat-handed punch into his jaw.

Pickett's head snapped back as the blow sent him reeling—and the crowd burst into a roar.

"Is he crazy?" Mendez demanded behind Ellie. He took a few steps closer to the edge of the sinkhole as he angled for a better view.

Flowers shrugged—and then easily knocked Mendez over the side.

Mendez landed on a pile of bones and barked out a ferocious curse.

"You aarait there, bali?" Flowers called out.

He turned and gave Ellie a pointed wink.

A cheer rose up from the crowd gathered around Lessard and Pickett as Charlie called out stakes. Ellie cast them only a glance before looking back to Flowers.

Thank you, she mouthed and darted off into the bush.

She bolted through the ruins. A shout echoed through the trees a moment later—Mendez's cry of alarm as Flowers pulled him out of the pit and he realized that Ellie wasn't there. His protest was largely drowned out by the roar of the men gathered around Lessard's brawl.

Ellie dodged through the deepening shadows around the ruined buildings, stumbling over roots and tumbled stones. She paused for a breath to orient herself. Her lungs burned from the sprint.

The central plaza must lie somewhere to the right ahead of her. Through the distant leaves, Ellie could just make out a faint glimmer of light from the campfire there.

Crashing footsteps and voices sounded from behind her, far closer than she would have liked. Ellie stumbled forward through the thickening gloom as quickly as she dared without raising a racket or twisting an ankle.

Her boot came down—then slid on a hard, round surface. As she fell forward, something under her foot let out a sharp crack.

She found herself kneeling on the shattered remnants of an excellent example of Mayan urn manufacturing. Her hands itched to gather up the pieces even as she winced against the echoing racket of her misstep.

That echo was abruptly answered with the thunder of a rifle shot. A bullet smacked into a tree beside her.

Her pursuers were on to her—and Ellie could think of only one way to elude them.

Wincing against her archaeological sensibilities, Ellie grasped the neck of the broken urn and chucked it out into the forest.

The artifact burst with another crack. The men behind her murmured before setting off in pursuit.

Ellie picked her way more carefully forward, ducking to keep to the growing shadows that cloaked the overgrown, moss-covered ruins. Voices continued to sound from various points around her, but the deepening dusk and the towering rubble of the once-palatial residences made for ample cover.

Silently, she crept toward a jumble of fallen stones that sat right at the edge of the great plaza.

A handful of men still lingered around the campfire there, uninterested in the brawl. The light of the flames looked small amid the ghostly grandeur of the city.

None of Jacobs' guards were with them, but Ellie knew they could still be nearby.

She risked inching out of her hiding place for a better look at the roofed structure where Bones had chosen to store the company's supplies.

The front wall of the building was missing, leaving it open to the broad plateau—probably because it was some sort of ceremonial structure for public rituals. The men had built their campfire just in front of it. Ellie couldn't hope to get inside that way without them seeing her.

She glanced up at the pyramid. The strange light was gone, but she could just make out the silhouettes of three men lingering on the platform at the top of the steps. She couldn't be sure through the gloom and distance, but she felt certain none of them were Adam.

What was going on up there?

Worry tore at her, but she couldn't give in to the impulse to rush up there—not until she'd done what she had come here for.

Ellie slipped back onto the overgrown path behind the buildings that lined the plaza, listening carefully for more patrols. She reached the back of the structure that housed the supplies, hoping her hypothesis would prove correct.

Ceremonial architecture had to include a way for the figures in ritual pageants to get inside and await the moment for their appearances—like a back door

The rear entrance to the storehouse was half crumbled to rubble, but as Ellie had hoped, it led not to the main chamber but to a smaller annex within the building.

She climbed carefully over the loose stones into the shadowy passage. Soft light glimmered from around the corner. Ellie followed it and found herself looking through an opening cut into the wall.

Through it, she could see the piled crates of the expedition's dry goods, stacked beside sacks of maize, rice, and beans. The case of ammunition had been moved inside as well.

Ellie looked at it longingly, thinking of the magnifying lens in her pocket... but the sun was gone, and an explosion would do her little good in her current circumstances, even if she hadn't made that dashed promise to Adam.

At last, she spotted the coffee. The burlap sack of beans leaned against a pile of crated excavation equipment.

She risked peeking a little farther through the opening. Just beyond the open threshold of the chamber, the men still sat at their fire. Ellie recognized Ram and his friends there, along with Nigel and Aurelio.

None of them struck Ellie as a threat—but even an alarmed cry of surprise when they spotted her would draw the interest of any of Jacobs' patrols that happened to be nearby.

It didn't matter. She would have to chance it.

Thunder rumbled, and a flash of lightning brightened the clouds overhead. In the quick glow, Ellie spotted two more figures standing just beyond the range of the firelight.

It was Jacobs and Bones, holding a quiet consultation.

She tucked herself neatly back into the shadows. How could she even *think* of trying this with Jacobs standing right there?

Ellie took a breath and forced herself to calm. He was just one man. He had no idea she was there. She didn't know what was happening with Adam up in the temple, but every instinct told her time was running out.

With her eyes locked on the coffee bag, Ellie dashed for it.

She slid into place behind the crates and made herself small. The murmur of conversation around the campfire was unchanged. Nothing had alarmed Ram and the other men.

The top of the burlap bag was open. Ellie couldn't reach into it without making herself visible to those outside—as well as to Jacobs, if he happened to glance her way.

She peeked around the crate. Nigel stood by the fire, stirring his big pot with a spoon. She tried to look past him to see if Jacobs still lurked there in the darkness, but her eyes refused to penetrate the deeper gloom beyond the glow of the blaze.

Blast it anyway, she determined fiercely. Ellie rose and plunged her hand into the smooth, dark beans—then bit back a curse at a quick sting on her finger.

Lessard's warning came back to her. *It might bite.*

She pushed her hand deeper more slowly—and brushed against something that was most certainly *not* coffee beans.

Ellie grasped it carefully, and then drew it out of the bag as the beans rustled softly around it.

She found herself eyeing the familiar, gleaming shape of Adam's machete.

There was a new clamor of voices from outside the storehouse. Ellie dropped back and pressed herself against the crates as Jacobs' voice cut to her from just outside the building.

"What is this?" he snapped.

"We found this old goat lurking outside the camp," another voice replied. It belonged to one of Jacobs' armed men. Ellie worked to place it and pictured a shorter man with an unpleasant smile—Price, perhaps? He usually patrolled with Buller, who was larger and had a noticeably big nose.

"But is he... *from* this place?" she heard Buller ask, sounding uncomfortable.

"Nobody is from this place," Price scoffed.

"Why are you here?" Jacobs demanded coldly.

Ellie shivered at how *close* he sounded as she clutched Adam's machete to her chest.

"I came to deliver a warning," a familiar voice replied.

Ellie risked a peek around the corner of the crates... where she saw Padre Kuyoc looking up at the taller figure of Jacobs with an expression of cool defiance.

But what on earth was the priest from Santa Dolores doing *here?*

Kuyoc was dressed like a diminutive Mayan Don Quixote. Over his plain shirt and trousers, he wore a bizarre homemade breastplate made of clattering rows of hollow reeds woven together with wiry cords.

"A warning from whom?" Jacobs dryly pressed.

"From the dead," Kuyoc replied and flashed him a knife-sharp grin.

A few of the men by the fire exchanged looks at his reply, shifting uncomfortably.

"They know why you are here," the priest continued relentlessly with his gaze locked onto Jacobs. "They know what you seek. And they have charged me with telling you that if you try to take it from this place, all the beasts of Hell will be unleashed upon you."

Kuyoc raised his voice, pitching it out over the scattered men.

"I have seen Death sweeping down from the sky to claim the blood of the damned," he called out boldly. "And none shall escape its wrath if the secrets of this place are profaned!"

Ellie blinked with surprise. Adam had warned her that Kuyoc had expressed some fantastical beliefs about the region of the wilderness in which Tulan was concealed, but the priest had also struck her as decidedly rational and clear-thinking.

Had she been mistaken in her impression... or was something else going on here?

"Tie him up and leave him with the mules," Jacobs ordered flatly, and then walked away.

Price bound the priest's hands behind him with a length of rope. The man's bizarre breastplate clunked as the guard jerked him into position. The tenor of the sound was odd. Dry, hollow reeds should have given off a noise more like a clatter than a dull thunk.

Ellie set the thought aside. There were more immediate things to worry about.

With another peek to ensure that the attention of the men was still focused on Kuyoc, she darted back into the ruined hallway and crept through it until she hopped out into the overgrown alley. Ellie picked her way behind the looming structures, rounding the courtyard until she reached the place where they had deposited the priest.

The mules shifted uneasily in their nearby corral as she slipped back up to the plaza, which was bordered on this side by a low stone wall. One of the animals brayed, and Ellie ducked back behind the barrier, keeping her head below the stones until the beasts had settled.

Slowly, she peered over the wall. The men by the fire had gone back to quietly talking among themselves. A few of them glanced up nervously at the occasional gusts of damp wind that unsettled the leaves of the nearby trees. Behind them, Jacobs gave low, authoritative orders to Buller and Price as more of the men filtered back from the now-concluded fight by the pit of bones.

Kuyoc sat on a sack of feed in front of Ellie, whistling tunelessly to himself.

"Padre!" she hissed.

"Ah," he replied with quiet ease. "I was wondering when you would turn up."

"But why are you here?" Ellie demanded.

Kuyoc's eyes narrowed as his gaze locked on the pale, looming shape of the temple.

"To do something I should have done a long time ago," he replied grimly.

With a glance to make sure the men on the far side of the courtyard were otherwise occupied, Ellie scrambled over the wall and slipped to Kuyoc's side.

"Never mind. We need to get you out of here," she asserted, hefting the awkward weight of Adam's machete. "Hold still while I cut these ropes."

"I think not," the priest returned quickly as he shuffled his hands out of her reach. "I need those."

"Why?" Ellie replied with surprise.

"Well, I can hardly get where I'm trying to go without them, can I?" Kuyoc retorted.

"But where are you trying to go?"

"There," Kuyoc replied with a determined nod toward the temple.

"You *wanted* them to catch you," Ellie burst out, barely remembering to keep her voice down.

Kuyoc shot a disgruntled look at her over his shoulder.

"What—you think this bunch of lead-footed noisy fools could've found me if I didn't want them to? I am Maya," he asserted fiercely.

"I don't understand," Ellie protested.

The priest cast her a look edged with disdain.

"I should hardly expect you to," he replied.

"Then tell me how I can help you," she pressed back.

"What you should do is collect Mr. Bates and leave this place. Get out of here before it's too late."

Outrage hummed through her.

"Before Death sweeps from the sky?" she retorted skeptically.

The priest let out a dark, slightly unsettling chuckle.

"You're *trying* to scare them off," Ellie accused. "Just like you tried to scare me and Adam. But we were never coming here to steal. We just wanted to learn about this place. If you're here to protect it, then we're all fighting on the same side!"

Kuyoc slowly shook his head.

"I know you do not mean to harm, mija," he said tiredly. "But I have told you what you need to do. Now get behind that rock."

"Why?" Ellie pushed back as her temper flared.

The priest's mouth quirked into a dangerous smile. "Because I am about to call that murderer over," he neatly replied. "¡Oye! ¡Patrón! How is your search for the glass going?"

A jolt of surprise nearly exposed her. Ellie scrambled to the right and skidded into the makeshift corral for the mules. A few of the animals snorted with irritation as she tucked herself in behind the forest of their legs.

She hoped none of them were in a kicking sort of mood.

In the flickering light of the campfire, Jacobs' eyes narrowed thoughtfully.

Ellie's mind spun. What glass had Kuyoc been talking about?

Abruptly, she knew the answer. It was the Smoking Mirror.

The iconography of the mirror had been haunting her ever since she had first picked up the medallion back in London. Ellie knew the mythological glass was associated with the legends of Tulan in both Mayan and Aztec cultures. Apparently, Jacobs and Dawson were aware of that as well.

And so was Kuyoc.

Jacobs strode across the plaza to loom over the smaller man.

"Which glass would that be?" he said evenly.

The sound of his voice from so close by sent another shiver over Ellie's skin.

"The one your men are up in that temple hunting for," Kuyoc returned just as calmly, meeting Jacobs' icy gaze. "The one that is worth more than all the rest of the riches of this city combined."

Jacobs tilted his head thoughtfully. "And how do you know about it?" he quietly demanded.

"Because I have been here before, obviously," Kuyoc retorted blithely.

Ellie clenched her teeth against a gasp, even as the pieces began to shuffle into place. Kuyoc's warnings and threats back in Santa Dolores hadn't been bizarre superstition. He'd been trying to scare them away from Tulan... because he had known exactly where it was and why it mattered.

But why had he followed them here? Was he trying to save the ruins from looting? But then, why insist on getting himself captured?

None of it made any sense.

"Why don't you send me up to the temple?" Kuyoc suggested. "I might know a thing or two that could help you find what you're looking for."

"Is that right?" Jacobs returned smoothly.

Ellie felt an instinctive sense of danger flare, as it did anytime Jacobs asked a direct question in that same easy, dangerous tone.

The small, weathered priest met Jacobs' gaze unflinchingly as his eyes glittered with dark intelligence.

"It is," he replied. His words resonated with certainty.

Something in Jacobs' eyes shifted, moving from challenge to an unsettling interest.

"Well," he mused quietly. "That does change things."

A new voice cut through the wind-tossed gloom, echoing clearly from across the plaza.

"Boss!"

Ellie risked a better peek through her fence of mules and saw Braxton Pickett striding toward them. His lip was split, and an angry bruise marred his cheek.

He was dragging Mendez by the collar. As he neared, Pickett shoved the smaller man toward Jacobs' feet. His words rang out clear and bold across the shadowed stillness of the city.

"This idiot has lost the woman!"

THIRTY-FOUR

A few minutes earlier

𝒜DAM GAPED AT THE glowing bone in Dawson's hand, shocked speechless.

"Yes, well—I think that's enough of that," Dawson concluded and popped the thing—an *arcanum*, he had called it—back into the wooden box. He snapped shut the lid, cutting off the unnatural, blazing light.

It took Adam's eyes another minute to adjust. The darkness had grown deeper.

Dawson returned the box to his pocket. He seemed to have forgotten the rifle, which hung loosely from his shoulder.

"The only other thing I will say on the subject for now is that *our* side, Mr. Bates, seeks the arcana for noble purposes," he concluded.

"You mean, there's more of them?" Adam burst out.

Dawson straightened self-importantly, though the weight of the gun still dragged him down a bit on one side.

"Of course!" he confirmed. "As an educated man, you must be familiar with the stories of powerful artifacts scattered through the historical and mythological record. We presume that the rest of what those old texts tell us holds at least a shadow of the truth of what passed in ancient times, yet we dismiss the more fantastical elements as fiction—but why should they be any different? It is only because our imaginations cannot expand to acknowledge the truth, even when it is staring us right in the face... and what potential that truth holds! Think of some of the objects you must have read about during your time in Cambridge—the death ray of Archimedes, which burned the ships at Syracuse. The spear of Cú Chulainn, which must strike and kill every target at which it is thrown. These are the powers of gods!"

Adam's mind was reeling. He would've laughed Dawson out of the room...

if he hadn't seen that damned glowing bone for himself.

Dawson's voice grew both lower and more intense as he plunged onward. "We live in a time when the British Empire has spread its peace and prosperity across the globe, and yet those very imperial holdings are the places where such artifacts are most likely to emerge. Simply imagine what chaos might result if they were to fall into the wrong hands, like some ignorant batch of farmers or... or *revolutionaries.*"

Dawson made the word sound like a disease.

"My fellows and I would see the arcana used to uphold the principles of law and order," he continued, "of enlightenment over ignorance. I am sure you must agree that order is preferable to the sheer chaos that must result if such powerful objects are left scattered about the world willy-nilly!"

"Your fellows?" Adam echoed carefully.

"All in good time, Mr. Bates," Dawson returned. "Should you prove your utility, then perhaps I might gain permission to reveal it all to you. For now, I am afraid you must proceed with me on trust."

Adam's temper flared, cutting through the haze of his shock.

Sure. *Trust.* Why wouldn't Adam take the word of a bunch of guys who'd coerced him into helping them by threatening to cut up somebody he cared about?

"You there!" Dawson called.

Staines poked his head into the room a moment later, carrying the lantern.

"Summon those other two fellows, if you would. We are going to find our way inside this pyramid!" Dawson declared cheerfully.

"What do you mean—inside?" Adam returned.

Dawson blinked at him with surprise. He handed Staines back the rifle as Pacheco and Lopez returned.

"Into the interior of this structure, of course," he explained. "That is where the most holy sanctum must be—and that is where we shall find what we are looking for!"

"Nobody's ever found anything inside these pyramids except rubble," Adam retorted.

"But why else would the people of Tulan have built them?" Dawson pushed back.

"Maybe they liked the view?" Adam said as his exasperation rose, driven by his already frayed nerves.

Dawson paled a little.

"No," he concluded as he paced across the floor. "That can't be right. If not within the pyramid of their greatest temple, then where else could they have possibly concealed the mirror? Why…" he paused and gave a nervous giggle. "Why, it could be absolutely anywhere if it isn't here! Anywhere in this entire city complex. It could take *months* to search the whole of it." His tone shifted to one of obvious panic. "We can't possibly stay out here that long!"

"You could always go home," Adam helpfully suggested.

Dawson flashed him a narrow, angry look. Clearly Adam had touched a nerve.

"That is not an option, Mr. Bates," Dawson shot back thinly. "Which you would do best to remember if you wish to get out of this place alive. Search this room!" he ordered, waving a hand at the other men. "I want to know if you see any hint of a possible opening."

Pacheco and Lopez exchanged a look before setting themselves to the task, peering carefully into corners and poking at the stones.

Adam stood back and watched.

Dawson studied the black mural, and then stalked back to the front chamber, muttering to himself as he tested every edge and corner. After a minute he came back and shot Adam a glare.

"Need I remind you that your continued value to this expedition depends upon your *usefulness*, Mr. Bates?" Dawson snapped. "Shall we see what happens when you are no longer of value?"

Adam was supposed to make himself useful by finding an entrance that didn't exist. There was no secret chamber in this pyramid. As far as Adam had ever seen, Mesoamerican pyramids didn't conceal chambered tombs like their Egyptian counterparts. Dawson was mixing up his continents.

He ground his teeth against the inanity of it. *This* was what he was being pushed around and threatened for?

Staines stood at Adam's back with the rifle. He looked bored.

Could Adam do it? Could he pretend to hunt around the chamber like Pacheco and Lopez, who were currently exchanging low, dry whispers about *el gringo loco*? Would he play Dawson's game in order to buy himself and Ellie a little more time?

Adam's patience felt like the burnt end of a cigar. His mind still reeled with Dawson's revelation that the magical gizmos of history might be more than just bedtime stories—and what the hell was he supposed to do with that?

He'd been playing this game for days now, and there had only ever been one way it was going to end.

He turned his gaze to the mural. The final panel of it was easier to see, now that Pacheco had brought the lantern. The figures that flanked the serpent king in that last great chamber weren't the elegant nobles of the bas relief in the pass or the worshipers from the stela.

They were monsters.

Adam picked out the faces of lizards, jaguars, and insects—the rotting visage of a corpse and the stripped bone of a skull.

They were the same monsters he'd seen honored on carvings in Mayan ruins across the colony. Adam didn't need to have read a bunch of books to recognize them for what they were—the gods of Hell.

The king held something in his arms. Adam knelt down for a closer look.

It was a child—a small, skinny little girl.

The guy had thrust a knife into her heart.

Blood poured from the wound, dripping onto the object that lay at the feet of the gods—a round, black disk.

The scene made for a hell of a contrast with the grace and beauty of the art Adam had seen in the pass.

His gaze dropped to the corpse on the floor. Maybe she had been some kind of priestess. The description felt right. He looked at the knife she still held in her hand.

What here would've been worth dying to protect?

A buzz built in the back of Adam's brain.

The mural was bordered by a row of carved stone blocks inscribed with the characters of Tulan's language. Adam studied the ones closest to the dead priestess. The symbols there reminded him of parrots, monkeys, ears of corn, and a grinning skull.

One in particular caught his eye. Adam realized that he had seen it before.

It was the damned lollipop.

Well—he knew it wasn't a lollipop. The familiar swirling pattern was far more likely to represent the wind… or maybe smoke, Adam thought as he looked at it. There was definitely something a little smoke-like about it.

What he did know for certain was that the same symbol adorned the back of Ellie's medallion.

The glyph sat in the border of the mural, directly below the carved image of the mirror at the feet of the king. Before time had withered her away, the dead woman's back would have been covering it when she fell.

Adam ran his fingers along the edges of the block.

The stone popped loose, revealing a cavity in the wall.

He peered at it, getting as close to the corpse as he could without disturbing her.

Inside the opening in the wall hung a rope.

Driven by the sheer puzzle, Adam grasped hold of the loop—and pulled.

The paving stone on the floor beside him dropped, sinking three inches into the ground with a thunk that captured the attention of everyone in the room.

It hung there... looking for all the world as though it had been built to slide neatly out of the way.

Dawson whirled toward him. Pacheco and Lopez looked up with surprise as Staines's eyes went wide.

"Aw hell," Adam blurted.

Dawson ran over.

"You found it. *You found it!*" He burst out with a slightly hysterical laugh. "Must be something more than just rubble in there—eh, Mr. Bates? You—boys!—move this out of the way."

Dawson flapped a hand at Pacheco and Lopez, and then waved dismissively at the crumpled corpse of the priestess as though the body were a mere inconvenience—as though the woman who had died to conceal the secrets of her people was nothing but debris to be swept out of the way.

Adam's fury snapped to life. The feeling was as clear as the winter air... and it was going to make him do something irreversibly stupid.

Something like stepping between Dawson and the dead woman on the floor.

"I don't think so," Adam said flatly even as another, saner part of him groaned in the back of his head.

"Excuse me?" Dawson stammered as his eyes went wide with surprise.

At that moment, a voice rang out from the plaza below, breaking through the silence of the temple.

"This idiot has lost the woman!"

The words were a catalyst.

Adam realized that Ellie was gone... which meant that nobody could hurt her for whatever Adam might take it in mind to do with himself.

And Dawson realized exactly the same thing.

The professor's eyes locked on Adam, sharpening with a well-justified panic.

"You—*you!*" Dawson shouted urgently as he waved his hands at Staines. "The gun! *Point the gun at him!*"

It should have been the end of the line for Adam. And it would have been... had Dawson ever bothered to actually learn the names of the people who worked for him.

It took Staines a crucial extra second to realize that Dawson's 'you' meant 'Mr. Staines.' By then, Adam had already launched himself from his crouch on the floor.

His shoulder took Staines in the ribs. The guard's breath whooshed out at the impact, and the rifle fell from his hands. It skidded across the floor as Staines himself slammed into the wall.

Pacheco and Lopez watched with gaping mouths from over by the shelves of artifacts. Pacheco's hands loosened on the fragile mask he was holding. Lopez darted down instinctively to catch it before it hit the ground.

Dawson stumbled back into the corner of the room, pressing himself against the stones as though he hoped they would swallow him.

"Get Jacobs!" Dawson shouted. "Go! *Now!*"

Since Dawson hadn't bothered to specify, both Pacheco and Lopez happily bolted from the temple.

Adam wondered whether the pair of them would actually fetch Jacobs, or just high-tail it into the bush—and then forced himself to focus on what the hell he was going to do with Staines.

Shock and nerves had dulled the guard's reaction, but that didn't last. Staines slammed his clasped hands down onto Adam's spine, and Adam hissed with pain.

Staines was smaller, which gave Adam an advantage—but what really mattered was who got their hands on the rifle on the floor.

Adam grasped Staines's arms and pivoted, using the momentum to toss the guard across the chamber.

Dawson squeaked and pressed himself further into the corner. Staines's impact made the artifacts on the shelves rattle. The mask that Lopez had hurriedly shoved back into place slipped loose, crashed to the ground, and shattered.

Adam winced. Ellie was gonna kill him for that.

Survive first. Get chewed out later.

He yanked his attention from the broken artifact and lunged for the rifle.

Staines was already scrambling upright. He launched himself toward the weapon as well, forcing Adam to settle for kicking the gun out of reach.

The Enfield spun across the floor, hit the wall, and fired.

The round cracked against the obsidian mural, splintering off a chunk of it, and then ricocheted to the ceiling. The sound of the discharge was like a thunderclap.

Staines snapped his gaze to the gun.

Adam threw himself at the guard, neatly shoving both of them through the doorway into the forward chamber, where they rolled across the floor.

The arches that lined the facade of the temple looked out over an increasingly violent twilight of thick purple storm clouds that flickered with lightning.

Adam's back slammed into one of the columns, breaking him loose from Staines. He scrambled to his feet on the platform at the pinnacle of the temple as the wind tugged at his shirt and hair.

The plaza was illuminated by the orange sparks of a flickering campfire below him... *way* too far below him.

Adam's head spun as shouts rose, echoing up to the temple.

Somebody had noticed them up there... which meant that the clock was ticking.

He swallowed a wave of queasiness and forced himself to focus. He had to get rid of Staines. Then he could worry about the rest of his problems—like Dawson, or the possibility of tumbling to a painful death.

Staines stood a few steps away. He looked torn between throwing himself into another attack or simply running away.

To his credit, he chose the former.

Adam twisted to deflect the force of Staines's impact. As the smaller man hit him, Adam grasped him around the waist. He used the momentum to complete the turn—and then let go.

Staines flew from Adam's arms and hit the stairs of the pyramid.

The guard rolled, shrieking in high-pitched panic, until he managed to snag his hands on one of the tiers. He hung there, scrabbling his boots against the stone until he managed to kick himself up onto a solid perch.

The guard pressed himself against the stones like a man who knew that he had just nearly been chucked off the top of a three-hundred-foot pyramid.

Still feeling uncomfortably light-headed, Adam whipped around—and then froze as Dawson stepped from the temple with the rifle held unsteadily in his hands.

The professor looked disheveled. His eyes were wide and panicked as he hefted the gun up and pointed it at Adam.

"Not another move, Mr. Bates!" he barked.

The gun barrel wavered a bit.

Adam raised his hands as he skidded to a halt.

He kept his eyes on the Enfield. After all, the barrel of a gun was nicer to look at than the long, terrifying drop that awaited him in every other direction.

"You even know how to use that?" Adam demanded.

"Of course I know how to use it!" Dawson exclaimed a bit wildly.

He shifted his sweaty-handed grip on the weapon as he set the stock to his shoulder.

The professor's grip was terrible, but he did have his finger on the trigger, and Adam knew that the safety was already off.

Adam had accidentally discharged one round inside the temple. Did Dawson know enough to have chambered another?

If he hadn't, then Adam could probably jump him before he had a chance to shoot.

If he had, then jumping him would probably earn Adam a bullet in the chest… and there was no way that he could tell the difference just by looking.

Time ticked past as the stalemate froze him. Jacobs had to be on his way, and he'd undoubtedly be bringing more guns and more bullets. As soon as he arrived, Adam would be toast. And if Adam was toast, then there was no way Ellie was getting out of here alive, no matter how brave and resourceful she was.

In the end, that left him with only one option… spinning the wheel of fortune and hoping it didn't kill him.

Another wave of uneasy vertigo crawled up the back of his brain. Adam fought it as he faced Dawson across the windy gloom… and readied himself to leap.

A familiar voice blazed across the silence.

"Remove your finger from that trigger, Professor Dawson, or I shall drive this excessively large knife through your throat," it called out boldly.

A figure stepped from the archway at Dawson's back—holding a beautifully familiar blade to the professor's neck.

"Ellie?" Adam blurted in surprise.

THIRTY-FIVE

*T*HERE WAS A NEW scrape on Ellie's cheek. Her hair was tumbling from the perpetually messy bun in which she kept it. The knife in her hand—Adam's knife, he realized with a bolt of joy—was steady as a rock.

She looked gloriously furious.

Dawson removed his finger from the trigger of the rifle, making a clear and obvious show of it. He couldn't see the blade that Ellie held to his throat, but he must have been able to feel it well enough to take it very, *very* seriously.

"Now place the weapon on the ground, please," she ordered.

Dawson slowly moved to obey—with his eyes locked on Adam's—and then tossed the gun over the side of the pyramid.

Adam instinctively dropped. The rifle hit the next tier of stones, and another shot cracked through the night, pinging off one of the carved archways.

Chips of debris peppered Adam's arm.

He heard a distinct clatter as the rifle continued to tumble down the side of the pyramid before coming to rest somewhere in the shadows below.

"Of all the lunatic, *irresponsible* things to do…" Ellie raged.

"I couldn't let him take it!" Dawson stammered wildly. "He would have killed me with it!"

"The hell I would have," Adam shot back, still lying on the flat, safe-feeling stones. "There were four rounds in there, tops. I've got much better things to do with four rounds than waste one of them on you."

The machete flashed as Ellie pulled it away from Dawson's throat, and then set her boot to his rear end. She kicked, sending the professor sprawling down the top steps of the pyramid.

"Come on," she urged as she grabbed Adam's arm and hauled him up off the floor.

She tugged him toward the temple. Adam resisted, waving toward the place where the rifle had fallen.

"Four rounds!" he said urgently.

"No time!" she retorted and ducked behind the archway.

Another bullet pinged off the stones uncomfortably close to Adam's head, as though to emphasize her point.

He lurched behind one of the columns, and then peered down at the foot of the pyramid. Jacobs stood a quarter of the way up the stairs, balancing another Enfield expertly on his shoulder as he took aim.

"Point taken," Adam called over to where Ellie hid against the inner wall.

"You nearly hit me!" Dawson screamed at Jacobs from where he crouched abjectly on the stairs.

"I don't think he cares," Adam pointed out loudly, unable to resist.

A few steps farther down the pyramid, Staines shifted from cowering to bolting around the corner of the structure to get out of range.

Ellie darted from her cover. She grabbed Adam by the front of his shirt and yanked him into the temple. They raced into the inner chamber, where she slapped the machete into his hand.

Relief washed over him at the beautiful sensation of having his knife back where it belonged.

"Did somebody *break* that?" Ellie blazed.

The outrage in her voice snapped Adam out of it. She was glaring down at the shattered jade mask on the floor, where it had fallen when Adam threw Dawson into the shelf.

"Uh—let's worry about that later. How are we going to get out of here?" Adam demanded.

"The same way I came in," Ellie replied. She pointed to one of the narrow windows. "Out the back—but Bates..." She caught his sleeve and held him back. "Padre Kuyoc is here. I don't know how—or why—but Jacobs has him. It sounded like Kuyoc might be trying to *help* them. But why would he do that?"

Adam's gut lurched with unpleasant surprise.

"Live first. Deal with the crazy priest later," he declared.

Angry voices echoed up from the front of the pyramid. Jacobs barked at people, cold and authoritative, while Dawson complained loudly in between his commands.

Adam yanked Ellie to the window. "Lead the way, Princess," he ordered.

Ellie scrambled onto the ledge, slid through the opening, and lowered herself down awkwardly until she dropped from view.

Adam followed, turning sideways to squeeze himself through the narrow gap in the stones. It was just wide enough to accommodate his chest.

Good thing he hadn't been able to carry more of Cruzita's tamales.

The drop from the window to the nearest tier of the pyramid was about six feet. Adam managed it easily.

The mountain rose up before him, cloaked in long, deep shadows. There were no stairs on this side of the structure—only the enormous tiers. Each rose perhaps seven feet from its base... or was it further?

It looked further, Adam thought as he wobbled dangerously and abruptly sat down.

Ellie scrambled ahead of him like a cat, shimmying over the side of each layer until she could let go and safely drop.

"Are you coming?" she demanded from a few tiers below him.

"The rocks aren't moving," Adam muttered to himself. "It only *feels* like they're moving."

"Bates!" she called impatiently.

Adam forced himself into motion, sliding to the edge of the tier and dropping over it.

His body accomplished the move gracefully. It seemed to know what to do even as Adam's thoughts were consumed by something like a silent, high-pitched wail of protest.

It got easier as the ground got closer. He even managed to pull ahead of Ellie. At last, he cleared the final tier, landed solidly, and turned around to extend his arms.

"Come on. I'll catch you," he offered, mustering up a bit of his signature charm.

"I am entirely capable of—"

Another bullet snapped off the stone nearby. Adam's gaze shot up to see Jacobs' dark silhouette emerge from the window of the temple.

"Drat," Ellie declared—and jumped.

Adam caught her with a grunt and nearly lost his footing. He pulled both of them up against the base of the pyramid, pressing closer for cover.

"Now what?" Ellie demanded.

Thunder cracked overheard. A damp gust of wind blew against Adam's neck. Ellie flinched in his grip as another bullet cracked somewhere nearby.

"How about we get the hell out of here?" he suggested.

He grabbed her arm, swung her in front of him, and pushed her into a run.

They plunged into the deeper shadows of the brush, sprinting blindly through the gloom as more bullets snapped down at them from above. Ellie flashed a narrow-eyed glare back at him as she ran.

"Why are you behind me?" she demanded as she caught herself against a stumble.

"Does it matter?" Adam shot back, flinching as another bullet cracked off a tree trunk beside him.

"It had better not be out of some misguided, chauvinistic attempt to use your person to shield me from the bullets!" Ellie pitched the words back at him as she bolted across the tumbled stones, her boots skidding for purchase.

"Can we worry about this later?" Adam retorted as he caught her arm and steered her around the obstacle of a fallen wall. He yanked her down into a crouch behind the crumbling barrier as another quick cluster of gunshots flashed at them from behind.

"They are *shooting* at the structures!" Ellie protested. Outrage strangled her voice.

"They're shooting at *us*," Adam countered as he made a quick, sharp study of what lay around them. "They've come from around the front of the pyramid as well. Jacobs must have ordered them to try to flank us."

"Well? What does that mean?"

The sun had already dipped below the mountains. It would set soon, sinking the entire place into complete darkness rather than the shadow-swathed gloom in which they currently hid.

Another scattering of gunshots splintered the tree trunks to Adam's right. To his left rose the mountain. The face of it was far too steep for them to climb in the dark without equipment.

"It means we're going straight," he concluded and tugged Ellie into another sprint along the crumbling path.

They dodged through the slender trees as more shots rang out behind them. Adam heard pounding footsteps and calling voices as Jacobs and his minions coordinated their chase.

The road ended at a broad stairwell, which led down to a long, overgrown rectangle of ground framed by massive, sloped tiers of stone.

"It's a ball court," Ellie said. Her voice managed to mingle both urgency and wonder.

At the far end of the structure was a circular annex framed by more stone tiers. It looked almost like an amphitheater. Beyond that loomed the dark shadow of a thicker, wilder forest—a forest they could easily lose themselves in.

"Let's cut through," Adam ordered.

Ellie gave him a tight nod, and they hurried down the tumbled steps.

The tangled brush that grew on the old game field was thick and tall. It provided them with a modicum of cover. Adam shoved through it quickly, heedless of the thorns that scratched at his arms. Speed was what mattered now. No amount of foliage would save him from a bullet in the head if their pursuers managed to catch up from behind them.

The thicket ended, and Adam stumbled onto a paved court that surrounded a big, black hole in the ground.

It was the amphitheater he'd seen from above. The tiers of seats circled the dark gap. The space looked as though it had been deliberately constructed to frame the opening.

Probably another sinkhole, Adam thought.

They would need to skirt it. He picked a side and tugged Ellie with him. He kept his eyes on their goal—the darkly promising trees that rose on the far side of the seats, rustling with the uneasy wind.

A dark silhouette rose from behind the time-stained stones. Jacobs stepped into view and leveled his rifle neatly at Adam.

"Best step back down now," he ordered calmly.

Adam whirled to see Mendez, Pickett, Buller, and Price burst from the tangled growth of the ball court. The four guards quickly took up positions around the amphitheater, blocking any other possible route of escape.

Dawson jogged out a few minutes later, red-faced and breathing heavily. He carried a lantern. The light of it illuminated just how much trouble Adam and Ellie were in.

Adam tried to calculate the odds of getting both himself and Ellie out of this without getting shot.

They weren't good.

Hands raised, Adam stepped back down to the ring of ground that encircled the sinkhole. Ellie inched right up to the edge of the pit as though trying to put as much distance between herself and Jacobs as she could.

Adam considered joining her there... and immediately felt dizzy. He reminded himself that it was dark. The hole might not even be all that deep.

His guts remained unconvinced.

Ellie's boot scraped against a few pebbles and tipped them over the edge. Three seconds later, Adam heard the soft plonk of a splash.

An idea snapped into place inside his mind.

It was a very, very bad idea.

"Excellent work, Mr. Jacobs," Dawson called out, still huffing with exertion. "Now perhaps we might take a moment... Come to some sort of... agreement..."

"Take a breath," Adam said quietly.

"Why?" Ellie demanded, startling.

"Because I'm about to do something stupid."

"Shoot them," Jacobs ordered.

Adam yanked Ellie into his arms and threw himself backwards—over the edge and into the pit.

They plummeted through a terrifying darkness as gunshots cracked overhead. Then Adam hit cold water with a painful, skin-stinging slap.

He let it take him, still clutching Ellie to his chest. Their momentum broke, gentling to a drift just as his back came up against rubble. Adam shifted, circling one arm around Ellie's waist as he used the other to reorient himself in the water. He pushed his boots against the tumbling, uneven ground and thrust himself up to the surface.

They broke into the air. The darkness around them was nearly complete. Adam could barely make out the shape of Ellie's face as she gasped in a breath and then shoved back from him, water streaking down from the plastered locks of her hair.

He made a hurried study of their surroundings—or what he could see of them in the thickly shadowed gloom. Stone walls rose in a slick, concave curve roughly twenty feet overhead to the gap that had made up the center of the amphitheater. The opening framed a neat circle of roiling, lightning-haunted clouds.

It was a cenote, Adam thought to himself as he recognized the pattern. He had thrown them into a cenote—a natural well created by the long-ago disintegration of some ancient cave.

Lantern light spilled into the opening, illuminating the slick, glistening sides of the well.

Jacobs looked down at them from the edge.

"Finish them off," he ordered.

Pickett appeared, his pale eyes bulging down at them. He was joined by Buller and Price a moment later.

"Get ready," Adam ordered Ellie urgently—and then shoved her into the water.

He dove with her, pushing her down even as she struggled against him. He pulled with his free arm, dragging them deeper as low, muffled drumbeats thrummed against his ears—the impact of gunshots distorted by the water.

Something stung against his bicep. Adam ignored it, continuing to swim until he came up against the smooth expanse of a wall. He held Ellie there as she flailed at his face until his own lungs started to burn.

He pushed up gently against the rocky base of the pool, following the slick shape of the wall as he broke the surface.

It was shallower here at the edges of the well. With his boots planted on the ground, the water lapped at Adam's chest.

He tugged Ellie closer as she hauled in a breath, covered her lips with his hand, and set his mouth to her ear.

"*Quiet*," he breathed.

She nodded. He could feel the way her heart was pounding.

He let his hand fall away but didn't let her go—not yet. Ellie wouldn't like being restrained, but she tolerated it for now—for which Adam was deeply, silently grateful. He wasn't ready to release her... not when the threat still loomed above them.

"Give me the bone." Jacobs' voice echoed down coldly from above.

"One more time," Adam whispered.

Ellie nodded, her face a paler oval against the gloom.

Light flared to life above them. It was far brighter than the lantern had been, like a thousand candles blazing with sudden and impossible intensity.

Ellie's eyes widened with shock, but at Adam's tug, she sank, dropping down to hover just below the surface.

Through the wavering distortion of the water, Adam saw the light grow brighter—and knew that Jacobs was holding the firebird arcanum over the mouth of the cenote.

Even through the water, the glare radiated fiercely. Adam could see the wondering question in Ellie's gaze as she whipped her head around to look at him.

The light dimmed, flickered, and then went out. The cenote dropped back into a darkness that felt absolute by comparison.

Adam drew his head back out of the water, careful to stay silent. Ellie did the same beside him.

As his eyes slowly readjusted to the gloom, Jacobs' voice carried down from above.

"If they are still alive, they will not be able to climb out," he declared flatly. "Let them drown or starve. Either way, they're no trouble to us any longer."

His footsteps crunched against the stones as he moved away.

The others followed. Only one silhouette moved closer—it was Mendez, hesitating at the edge of the well. At a barked order, he hurried after the others, leaving Adam and Ellie alone in the dark.

THIRTY-SIX

$\mathcal{E}$LLIE WAITED FOR her eyes to adjust to the darkness. The hot fury under her skin was a sharp contrast to the cool water in which she stood.

She didn't need to see to know that Jacobs was right. During that moment of bizarre illumination, she had managed to get a brief glimpse of the walls of the hole into which Adam had dragged her. It had been enough to show her that they weren't climbable.

It was entirely reasonable for Jacobs to leave her and Adam there, even if he wasn't sure that they had been shot. He didn't have to be.

They had jumped into a perfect trap.

But that wasn't what pushed a fierce anger up inside of her. Ellie knew that the reason for her quick-burning fury was trivial in the face of their current situation—but she couldn't let it go.

Her eyes had recovered enough to make out Adam's general shape in the darkness, from the line of his shoulders above the water to the hair plastered to his skull.

He started to speak. His tone was uncharacteristically solemn.

"Princess, I—"

"You pushed me under the water," Ellie cut in, her words razor-edged.

"Huh?" Adam returned, obviously thrown. "Wait—you're upset about *that*? What'd you want me to do? Let you backstroke while they were shooting at us?"

"That is *not* what I meant," Ellie snapped in return as she drove a finger into the flat, solid surface of his chest.

The fabric of his shirt clung to him like a jellyfish.

"I told you not to pull that rigidly masculine, protect-the-weaker-sex nonsense—" she began.

"Rigidly...?" Adam cut in awkwardly.

"—with me less than *five minutes* before we fell in here, and what do you do? Shove me down and put your big, self-importantly *male* body—"

"Rigidly masculine," Adam muttered as though confirming it to himself. "Sure. Why not?"

"—between me and the bullets as though somehow *your* person is expendable whereas mine has to be cherished and coddled like a... a prize Pomeranian!"

"You're nothing like a Pomeranian," Adam countered.

"Oh? Then what precious, oh-so-vulnerable creature that is completely incapable of taking care of itself *do* I resemble?" Ellie demanded with a hiss.

"How about a wolverine?" he offered.

"Arrgghhh!" Ellie growled. Her hands clenching into fists as she glared at him. "You are the most arrogant, impossible... just... *dratted* human being I have ever had the misfortune to encounter, and I... I..."

Her anger shuddered, threatening to break—and then collapsed into something far more unsettling.

"*I* am the reason we are both going to die in this godforsaken hole in the ground while those terrible men ravage this city, completely destroying the historical record in the process," she spilled out, "while *you* should still be sitting on your porch at the Rio Nuevo drinking spirits and smoking cigars. Instead, you are going to starve here with me when you might have lived a perfectly happy, contented existence had you never had the misfortune to come blasting into my washroom... Though of course, that was entirely your own decision and not one that I will in any way countenance, implying as it does that any female who happens to emit the slightest... the slightest shriek..."

The words slipped away from her. The panicked rush that had pushed them from her lips spent itself like the ripples of a pond. The echo of her voice sank into the still, careful silence of the cenote until only the soft lapping of the water against the walls remained.

"Done now?" Adam asked carefully.

"I..." Ellie began. She swallowed thickly as her heart worked to return to its natural rhythm. "Yes."

"Good," Adam replied shortly. "Because I need your help with something."

"Of course," she said automatically as numbness settled in where that furious, panic-driven outrage had been a moment before.

"Great," Adam replied and pulled his shirt off.

Ellie's pulse started kicking wildly again. The cenote was still dark, but during her tirade, her eyes had further adjusted to the gloom. There was still a shade of twilight to the sky overhead, and it offered just enough light to keep their prison from falling into total darkness.

She had seen Adam without a shirt before, of course—it was obvious that he would have preferred not to wear one at all if he could've gotten away with it—but never from quite this... *close.*

He was not shaped like any of the men Ellie had known in London—the scholars at her university or the universally insipid suitors Florence kept ruthlessly setting in Ellie's path. There was so much *more* of Adam. All of it was very terribly solid and cut in the most infuriatingly intriguing contours. There were other contours, she knew, on the parts of his torso currently concealed by the water. Ellie had taken note of them against her judgment during those better-lit occasions when he had decided to strip himself down like a wrestler.

"Ah, don't you think you might require..." Ellie began awkwardly. "That is, it *is* rather chilly down here..."

"Hold it out straight," Adam ordered as he pushed the shirt at her.

Ellie yanked the sodden fabric taut between her hands.

Adam stabbed it, neatly slicing his machete through the cotton.

He shoved the knife back into its sheath beneath the water and took the shirt, tearing it the rest of the way with an easy yank.

"Mind wrapping this up?" he asked and turned his left shoulder toward her.

"Wrapping what? Oh blast!" Ellie exclaimed as his movement revealed that a fair amount of blood soaked the upper half of his arm. "You've been shot!"

"It's just a graze," Adam returned stubbornly.

"A bullet has gone through your arm," Ellie retorted, glaring at him. "When exactly were you going to inform me that *someone had shot you?*"

"Once you were done talking," Adam replied. "And it didn't go through me. It just kinda... skimmed along the outside."

He splashed some water up onto the wound, washing away the immediate gore and revealing more of the actual injury. In the admittedly bad light, Ellie thought it looked like a particularly nasty burn.

"That is not cleaning it," she complained. "It needs soap at the very least, and preferably a bit of carbolic."

"Fresh out of carbolic," Adam replied. He poked the wound and tried to crane his neck to get a better look at it.

"Stop that," Ellie said as she slapped his hand away.

"We're in a hole in the ground, Princess," Adam pointed out. "How about you just wrap it up for now?"

Ellie had no good answer to this, even though it was a glum thought. She took the soaked length of Adam's shirt and used it to bind the wound.

The effort required her to move even closer to him. She found herself alarmingly aware of his large, bare body just inches from her hands... her lips...

She snapped herself to alertness. Where on earth had those thoughts come from?

Ellie tied the knot in the fabric a little more tightly than necessary.

"There," she finished awkwardly and took a step back.

Silence settled in as the cool water lapped at Ellie's chest.

"Just how bad off are we?" she finally asked.

"I have a couple of friends in the camp," Adam replied after a brief, telling pause. "If they figure out we're down here, they'll try to come and find us."

"And if they don't figure out we're down here?" Ellie prompted.

Adam didn't answer.

Ellie could puzzle the rest out easily enough. They couldn't shout for help. They would be just as likely to be heard by one of Jacobs' men as they would anybody else. Letting Jacobs know they were alive and anticipating a rescue wouldn't work out well for anyone he came to suspect might aid them. Ellie remembered how Charlie, Lessard, and Flowers had conspired together to get her Adam's knife, and then distract the guards to allow her a chance to escape. It would be desperately unfair to put the three of them in danger.

But where did that leave her?

The thought was more than depressing. It was... *infuriating*. Ellie's temper sparked dangerously as she leaned against the wall beside Adam. She pushed from the stone and whirled to face him with sudden purpose.

"Absolutely not!" she declared.

"Huh?" Adam blinked in return.

"I am not going to die in this well," she asserted. "*You* are not going to die in this well. We are going to find a way to get out of this, together, without endangering your friends. And when we do get out, we are going to make Dawson and Jacobs rue the day they ever *considered* illicitly buying stolen government property to come and loot a priceless piece of Mesoamerican history!"

Adam remained still as he leaned against the wall. He had lowered his head, but he raised it slightly to look at her.

"Sure we are, Princess," he said.

He said it with a smile—but it wasn't his usual reckless, charming grin. It was smaller and ever so slightly sad. A sharp, cold panic flared to life in

Ellie's chest.

"Oh no," she said. "You are *not* allowed to do that. You are not allowed to *give up!*"

"Ellie..." he started.

He sounded tired.

No... it was worse than that. He sounded *hopeless.*

Ellie's mind fought for the logic that would convince him that they could do this. She *needed* to, she realized with a real tremor of fear. This was Adam— the man who had laughed when his boat went over a waterfall. He couldn't have given up hope. If he had... then it might mean that things really were well and truly cooked.

Her logic kept crumbling against the high, slick walls that surrounded them—but Ellie *knew* that there was a way in which she could snap him out of it. She could feel it there inside of her.

She would simply start talking, and surely it would come out.

Ellie took a step closer to Adam to do just that—but as she did, the rubble under her boot shifted, throwing her off balance.

She landed against Adam's chest instead.

Her arms flew up to grasp his shoulders. Warmth flooded through her from every place where she touched him—under her hands, through the fabric of her shirt... her *thigh*, for goodness' sake. She stared up at the grizzled, unshaven line of his jaw and his startlingly blue eyes, which were currently widened with surprise.

All of it felt so desperately right that words deserted her. Something irresistible rose in their place—something that drove Ellie to rise on the toes of her boots and press her lips to Adam's mouth.

Sensation flooded her, sparking her nerves to life—the soft rasp of his stubble, the surprised give of his lips. The solid, male warmth under her hands. Her eyes closed as she let herself fall into the pure, wild feeling of it...

Ellie realized what she was doing.

Her eyes flew open. She pulled back, forcing her hands to release their somewhat desperate grip on his shoulders.

"I..." she began as she flailed about for something—anything—to say. "I... I'm terribly sorry. I shouldn't have... I mean, at the very least, I should have *asked* before I... Oh, drat."

"Did you want to do it?" Adam demanded.

His voice was lower and rougher than it usually was. The way he was looking at her had grown quite intense.

The question was a terribly awkward one. How on earth was she to answer that? Ellie's cheeks flushed with heat despite the coolness of the water around her.

They were facing a slow and terrible death in a pit in the ground. Ellie determined that she might as well be honest.

"Er... well, yes," she admitted weakly. "I suppose I did."

Under the darkness of the water, strong hands slipped around her waist and gave her a firm, powerful tug closer.

Adam's face was inches from her own. The strong lines of it were painted with rich shadows.

His hands felt good. So did the rest of him. Ellie's cheeks flushed further, and something began to move through her—something tingling and warm, like holding a potentially volatile pair of chemical compounds in her hands that she knew would explode the minute she combined them.

"May I kiss you back?" Adam asked as his hands tightened on her.

Ellie's heart pounded in her chest, striking like a quick, compulsive drum at the tight, coiled strength she could feel in his arms.

The words were not a demand. They were most decidedly a question—and Ellie was abruptly certain that when she answered it, everything was going to change.

On one side lay the safe, practical plateau of the rational and sensible choice.

On the other lay a wild, unpredictable abyss that she could not even begin to fathom.

She mustered her logic to face it—but before her logic had a chance to begin, the answer popped to her lips, rising from somewhere else... somewhere much deeper than logic.

"Please," Ellie blurted.

Adam lifted her boots from the ground and devoured her.

It was wild. Relentless. His hands moved over her body—clenching, claiming. His mouth was demanding against her own, the feeling perfectly accented by the exquisite texture of his beard.

He tasted like summer rain and fire. Ellie opened herself instinctively, burning with the knowledge that lips weren't enough—weren't even *close* to enough. She wanted *more*.

Her hands wanted too. She drew her fingers up the relentless planes of his back, and then grasped a handful of his hair, knotting her fingers in the sun-kissed thickness. She pulled herself closer to him—molded and clung.

His teeth grazed her lip and she groaned, the sound emerging from her throat of its own accord.

A hand slipped to her rear. Ellie gasped out an incoherent plea.

It might have been *harder.* Or simply *yes.* It could even have been in Latin. Ellie wasn't entirely sure and did not in the least bit care.

Instinct drove her. She let herself rise in the water, wrapped her legs around his waist, and locked them there. The move brought her higher, giving her new places to explore.

He stole his lips from her mouth. Ellie growled in protest, and he actually *laughed* at her—the absolute rotten bastard—and then set his mouth to her neck instead. He ran his tongue from the curve of her collarbone to a singular little spot just below the lobe of her ear that made her see stars.

Actual stars, exploding behind her eyelids.

She wasn't sure how that was possible.

And as for what was happening below the water... It was... *Dear Lord...*

There was nothing decent about it. There was nothing *scholarly* about it, and Ellie relished every ever-loving bit.

"Bates..." she groaned as he pressed her against the wall of the sinkhole, his hands gliding up her flanks until he pulled her shirt from her trousers.

"Princess," he growled in return and nipped at the line of her jaw.

"I never... I never thought... Well, I mean I *thought*, but I never *realized*..." she began.

"Uh-huh," Adam replied as his hand reached the comfortable, practical lines of her half-corset. It continued up until his thumb slid across the top of her breast.

Those damned stars started popping up across her eyes again.

"You... This... I..."

Ellie had lost the ability to form a coherent sentence. There was nothing left in her but an uncontrollable, animal *need*.

"Oh, fiddlesticks," she declared, and then grabbed his hair, yanked his head back, and kissed him again.

He pressed her harder into the wall. It wasn't hard enough. His hands gripped the collar of her shirt, and then yanked at it. A button sprang free, followed by another.

To hell with buttons. All of them could go. Ellie didn't need them.

She knew exactly what she needed.

She didn't even need words to ask for it. She just clenched her thighs and pulled him even closer.

Adam groaned. He shifted his face ever so slightly to the right and dropped his forehead against the stones over her shoulder. His hands carefully, deliberately lifted from the delicious, inflaming places that they had been exploring on her body. He held them suspended in the air to either side of her.

"Ellie," he said. It seemed to take him a great deal of effort.

"What is it?" Ellie demanded as confusion and a growling frustration rose up inside of her. "What's wrong?"

"I… This…" He swallowed, still very clearly fighting for control of himself, and shook his head. "Not like this."

"Not like this?" Ellie asked as uncertainty crept in.

Adam lifted his face from the wall and looked at her. It was not the look that she had been expecting—or fearing. It was a look that set her nerves tingling again, sparking little fires of the most delicious and terrible anticipation. It was a look that *wanted*.

"If I'm going to take you… every perfect, infuriating inch of you," he elaborated as his eyes moved over her in a way that felt as intense as a touch. "I'm not going to do it like this."

"Every inch?" Ellie echoed roughly.

The words rasped in her throat, which had suddenly gone rather dry. She shifted herself against him involuntarily.

Her legs were still wrapped around Adam's waist. He hissed at her movement and set his forehead to the wall again, this time joining it with his hands.

"Princess. *Please*," he rasped.

"I am really not sure that I agree with you," Ellie countered uncertainly, still clinging to him. "This seems like a perfectly nice place to me."

"We're standing in a damned well."

"Maybe *you* are," Ellie pointed out.

She was not standing on anything at all.

Adam lifted his head again and gave her a look that made her throat even dryer.

"I can't do all the things I intend to do to you," he declared, carefully enunciating each of the words. "Not in here."

Ellie was very intrigued.

"What sort of things?" she demanded.

"I'll tell you about them. *All* about them. Later."

Later.

He almost made it sound like a threat. Ellie found that she liked that. It was a very enticing threat.

"There is only one problem with that," she noted. "Perhaps you forgot in the heat of our recent exertions, but we are still trapped inside this hole in the ground."

"You've got a point there," Adam admitted.

He was still pinning her to the wall. He didn't seem to want to stop. Ellie was entirely amenable to that decision, but now that he was no longer licking her collarbone, a little part of her rational brain began to reassert itself. It itched at the back of her mind as it tried to tell her something.

Perhaps the fact that she was still wrapped around Adam's hips was inhibiting her mental processes.

Reluctantly, Ellie untangled her legs and let them slide back down through the water until her boots brushed against the ground again. She put a hand to Adam's chest. The hand decided it wanted to glide along his hot, gorgeously contoured skin before doing what she had intended it to do—which was very gently push him back.

He moved away from her. He was watching her carefully—and then the carefulness turned to a flash of wicked amusement.

"You're thinking," he pointed out.

"Well, I am *trying* to," Ellie retorted.

"Want me to help?" he offered.

She shot him a glare. "I think you are having the opposite effect at the moment."

Adam laughed at that. It was a very satisfied-sounding laugh.

Ellie stepped a little further away from him and forced herself to focus on their gloomy, damp surroundings instead of the hard, wet, damnably enticing man standing behind her.

She looked up at the mouth of the cenote where the massed clouds of the storm had grown darker.

"No help from above," she admitted and shifted her gaze to the walls. "Too steep and slick to climb. Which leaves what?"

Adam shrugged.

"The water?" he suggested.

Ellie froze as the demanding little itch in her brain grew stronger.

"The water," she agreed thoughtfully as she moved another step farther into it. "The water is... clean," she finished, startled at the word. She turned back to look at Adam in surprise. "It's *clean*. If this was just rainwater, it would be thoroughly fetid by now at the end of the dry season. But it's not. It seems relatively fresh, and..."

She trailed off as the itch turned into a buzz, rising in its nearness and urgency.

"Sinkholes," she said as she turned around slowly. "Cenotes are sinkholes. Sinkholes result from cave systems. Cave *systems*."

She raised her head to Adam with a sudden and shocking hope.

"We need to find out if there's a current!" she declared.

"That'd be easy if we had anything that floats," Adam returned.

Ellie reached into her pockets, feeling through the assorted useful things she had collected. She pulled out the broken pencil.

"Aha!" she declared triumphantly.

She set the pencil down on the surface of the water. It bobbed there. The slightly chewed-upon yellow paint contrasted with the darker surface of the water.

Ellie held her arms out to warn Adam back as she stared down at the little sliver of wood.

"Stay perfectly still, Mr. Bates."

"I've had my tongue in your ear," Adam cheerfully reminded her. "Pretty sure we can drop the 'mister.'"

Ellie shot him a glare.

"Be quiet!" she ordered.

"Me talking doesn't do anything to the water."

"You are distracting me," Ellie grumbled with her eyes on the pencil.

"Not as much as I could be," Adam returned with a wicked grin.

Ellie ignored him. It was more difficult than it should have been, since Adam's threat had done exactly what it was supposed to do, filling her mind with all kinds of delicious notions of exactly how distracting he could be.

And then she saw it.

"Bates!" she whispered excitedly.

"How about Adam?" he countered.

She ignored him, her attention riveted on the pencil.

"It's moving!" she exclaimed.

She pointed at where the slender yellow bit of wood was drifting ever so gently toward the wall as it passed between them.

Adam's eyes narrowed. He zeroed in on the trajectory of the pencil, tracing the line of it back across the water until he locked onto a stretch of dark stone on the opposite side of the cenote.

"Stay here," he ordered, and then dove.

Ellie hissed in protest, startled by his sudden disappearance.

He surfaced on the far side of the well. She could just make him out in the gloom.

"I think I feel something," he announced.

"I'm coming over," Ellie declared.

He held up a hand. "Wait there."

Adam dropped under the water. He popped back up again a moment later.

"There's a tunnel," he announced.

Ellie pushed from the wall and swam across the pool to join him.

"A tunnel?" she echoed as she arrived.

"Three, maybe four feet wide," he confirmed.

"We must try it," she declared firmly.

"Not we," Adam returned as he leaned down to reach under the water, hopping a bit awkwardly as he did so.

He pulled a sodden boot to the surface with a splash and thrust it at her. "Hold that," he ordered.

"Surely the risk would be minimized if the pair of us—"

"Nope," Adam countered, tugging under the water again. "I'll be back in a minute. Well... maybe a little more than a minute."

"Bates..." Ellie protested. He tossed the other boot at her and she caught it awkwardly as he moved away. "*Adam!*"

He paused, and then turned back to catch her by her belt and haul her closer for a sudden, firm kiss.

He smiled at her through the dark.

"That sounds nice," he concluded, and then dropped below the surface.

"Grrraaaah!" Ellie kicked at the water as her frustration peaked. She was still clutching Adam's wet boots. "Incorrigible, arrogant, reprehensible—"

She forced herself to take a breath as she fought for calm... and then hesitated thoughtfully. She shifted her grip on the boots, took a deeper breath, and held it.

And held it.

The breath came out of her in a whoosh as her lungs burned with desperation for air.

The water before her remained still.

It was taking too long.

The realization sparked a quick panic. She could not lose him. Not now. Not like this. Not when she'd only just started to realize... to admit...

She would go in after him. Ellie quickly knotted the laces of his boots together and slung them over her shoulder. She hopped awkwardly, her balance off thanks to her buoyancy in the water, until she had yanked her own boots free.

She would dive in there and pull him back out again. And if he was... If he wasn't... If she had to...

"Stop it," she said aloud to herself, firmly as she tied her own laces together. "Stop it, stop it, stop it. Just go. Just..."

She took a quick, deep breath—and then another, readying herself to

dive. She tried desperately not to think of how it had already been too long.
Too long.

Adam surfaced in front of her with a gasp.

"You absolute rotten bastard!" Ellie exclaimed.

He laughed, his eyes glittering.

"Miss me?" he prompted.

Ellie gritted her teeth as she bit back the string of inappropriate vocabulary that rose to her lips in response.

"There's a chamber," Adam quickly added. "Can't tell how big."

"There was another sinkhole on the other side of the plaza," Ellie noted with rising excitement.

"Then there's a good chance that it's all part of the same system running under the city," Adam replied.

"A system with an exit?"

"Possibly," he cautioned.

"That seems like better odds than what we're facing here," she pointed out.

"Yup," Adam replied. He plucked both sets of boots from her shoulder and swung them around his neck.

Ellie bristled.

"I am perfectly capable of carrying my own—"

"Ready?" he cut in as he patted the boots with a wicked grin. "It's a long way, and we're going against the current. It's a pretty gentle current, but still. Use the walls. Push yourself along. There are a couple of pockets of air along the way, but you'll have to stay with me. And stay calm," he added pointedly.

She fixed him with a glare.

"Have I ever given you any reason to think I am the type to react irrationally?" she demanded.

"You jumped off a balcony with your hands tied," Adam replied.

"I was taking the most direct route away from a pursuer," Ellie retorted.

"You were planning to blow up a boat to get me to listen to you."

"But I didn't!"

"And you tried to set Mendez's pants on fire," Adam finished.

Ellie opened her mouth to reply, and then closed it.

"How did you know about that?" she demanded cannily.

"I saw the burn marks on his trousers," Adam said. "Now—deep breath. Stay close."

THIRTY-SEVEN

𝒜BSOLUTE DARKNESS PRESSED down upon Ellie as she held her breath and followed blindly in Adam's wake.

Her hands caught against the smooth sides of the tunnel. She could feel the pulse of Adam's movements through the water ahead of her. His proximity was the only thing that kept a pure, instinctive panic from closing up her throat.

Ellie kicked against the stone floor as she pulled herself along. The tunnel was just wide enough to swim through. The current was a gentle push against her as she moved.

Fear crept deeper as her lungs began to ache. How much farther did they have to go? What if they had missed the air pocket Adam had described?

They could run out of breath in this dark, cold silence.

Ellie shoved the terror back. She was a scholar. Scholars were rational. She would not succumb to hysteria.

The tunnel could go on forever. She could drown in this dark, forgotten space...

Warm hands caught her and pulled her up. Ellie surfaced with a gasp and dragged in a desperate gulp of air.

Only Adam's hold on her kept Ellie from striking her head against the low ceiling of the little pocket in which they floated.

"That was the longest stretch," he said.

His voice came from close by. The sensation was disorienting, as the world around her was pitch black. Ellie could only feel his hands gripping her arms.

She reached out through the darkness. Her hand found his face and slid to his stubbled cheek. She felt him smile, and the mad pulse of her heart settled a bit.

"You okay?" he asked.

Ellie nodded, and then realized that he wouldn't be able to see it.

"Yes," she replied aloud.

"Deep breath," Adam ordered. "One... two..."

He slipped from her touch as he dropped back into the water. His hand tugged her forward.

Ellie filled her lungs with air and plunged after him.

She pushed herself down the dark, narrow passage, fighting against the water—and then the walls of the tunnel fell away.

Adam's hand grasped her shirt and hauled her up once more. Ellie surfaced with another gasp. The noise echoed hollowly, revealing the space around them to be high and vast.

"We're here?" she asked.

Her voice sounded strange as it floated around her in the total darkness.

"Yup," Adam replied from nearby. "Whatever 'here' is."

His hand still gripped her shirt as though he was afraid she would disappear if he wasn't touching her. He led her forward in the water until her toes brushed up against solid ground.

The slope shallowed until she stood thigh-deep in the pool. She could already tell that it was substantially broader than the cenote had been.

"Do you still have your match tin?" Ellie asked.

"Uh huh," Adam replied through the darkness.

"Perhaps now would be a good time to orient ourselves," she suggested. She was relieved to hear that her voice sounded steady.

Adam released his hold on her. Ellie heard him patting at his body. There was a scratch and a flare of light.

The orange glow danced over his bare skin, his bandaged arm, and the two pairs of boots still slung around his shoulder. The lines of his face were tight with concern as he gazed past her shoulder.

Beyond him, Ellie caught a glimpse of a low, broad cavern dripping with limestone fingers. Water extended around them, flat and still.

The fire reached Adam's fingers. He dropped the match with a curse.

A thicker and more oppressive darkness closed around them. Ellie could sense the pillars of stone that loomed above her.

Something slipped into her fingers. Ellie felt the round shape of the match tin, which was still warm from Adam's touch.

"Light another," he ordered, and then sloshed away from her.

"But where are you—"

"Just light it, Princess!" he called back.

Ellie shook the container. It rattled back at her. The sound was only moderately reassuring. The tin was far from full. If they could only navigate by match light, then they would not be getting very far.

She unscrewed the top and pulled out another match. She fumbled her way to the scratch plate inside the lid, and the lucifer flared to life.

"Well, I'll be damned!" Adam said distantly.

His voice came from somewhere behind her. Ellie whirled toward him. The match snuffed out.

"Drat!" she cursed.

"Hold on a second," Adam called out.

Ellie heard a scratching rustle. The sound struck her as oddly out of place in a cave.

"Say something," he ordered.

"Like what?" Ellie demanded.

"Just make noise, Princess."

Ellie let the first thing that popped into her head fall from her lips.

"Excito," she blurted. "Excitas, excitat."

"Are you... conjugating the Latin verb for *arouse?*" Adam warmly demanded from a short distance away.

"Awake," Ellie cut back shortly. "The Latin verb for *awake.*"

"Pretty sure it also means *arouse.*"

Adam sounded closer, as did the soft splash of his movements, but Ellie couldn't be sure. Sounds echoed strangely through the breadth of the cave.

"Keep doing it," he said.

Ellie cleared her throat, which had gone a bit dry.

"Excitámus. Excitátis. Excitant," she recited.

"How about the imperative?" he suggested.

He was very near to her.

"Excitá," Ellie declared awkwardly.

A hand found her arm. It slipped up to her shoulder, and then rose to caress the side of her neck in a way that sent electricity tingling down to her toes.

"Maybe later," Adam replied.

Ellie could practically hear the wicked grin on his face.

She plucked his hand from her neck and threw it back at him.

"You are an absolute rotter," she informed him.

"Light another match." He sounded not the least bit ashamed of himself.

Ellie fumbled the tin, but managed to catch it. Her pulse thundered at the thought of what might have happened if she had dropped it in the water.

Her hands shook as she took out another match and lit it.

Adam stood right in front of her. He was grinning… and proudly held a dark bundle of sticks in his hand.

"What the devil!" Ellie exclaimed.

"Light it already!" Adam pressed urgently.

Ellie thrust the match forward, setting it to the sticks. In the glimmer of illumination, she could see that they were tied together with rope made of strips of bark.

The tiny flame licked at the wood, and then anchored itself there. Ellie stepped back as it blossomed into a brighter, steadier life.

"That's a torch," she pointed out a bit numbly.

"Yup," Adam agreed. The soft orange glow revealed his form once again.

"But what on earth is it doing here?"

"Dunno," he returned. "I just found it in the basket."

"Basket?" Ellie echoed in surprise.

He pointed, and there it was.

The lake in which they stood ended at a rocky shoreline. More stalagmites sprouted from the stone, interspersed with areas of loose scree. Here and there, Ellie spotted pale, unexpected glints of bone. Most of the fragments looked like the exposed ribs of fish—some of them recent, others crusting over with mineral deposits.

The creatures living in the lake must have been left exposed when the water fell during the dry season, she thought uncomfortably.

The basket was made from reeds woven together with more bark rope. It sat on a slight platform made from a broken stalagmite.

"How is that here?" she demanded.

"Good question," Adam replied meaningfully.

Ellie met his eyes across the glow of the torch.

"Someone else has been here," she said.

"Sure looks like it," Adam agreed.

He pushed the torch into Ellie's hands. She grasped it instinctively and realized that he had another, yet unlit, in his other hand. He tucked it into the back of his belt.

"But how could anyone have carried that basket through the tunnel from the cenote?" Ellie pressed.

"Seems like a stretch, doesn't it?" Adam flashed her a meaningful look and Ellie's heart skipped.

"There must be another way down here," she concluded.

"Yup," he agreed as his eyes glinted warmly. He sloshed through the water with her until they reached the shore. "Let's get our boots back on and see if we can find—ow!"

He jumped back, hopping awkwardly on one foot.

"Ow, ow, ow, ow…" he muttered.

"What is it?" Ellie asked.

"Something bit my toe."

"*Bit* it?" she echoed in surprise.

Adam plucked the torch from her and lowered it to take a better look at the ground. He kept his toes submerged at the edge of the water.

"There!" he announced. "Ugh."

Ellie immediately picked out what he was looking at. It was an insect—a huge one. The bug was nearly the length of her index finger, colored a mottled gray that neatly blended with the stones.

"What is that?" She edged away from it.

"It looks like an oversized assassin bug." Adam pushed the torch back into her hands again. "Feels like it too."

He frowned down at his foot and shook it in the water.

Ellie didn't immediately answer. She raised the torch higher and gazed out across the cavern. The light shifted and flickered across the ground around the stalagmites.

No, she realized with a sick lurch in her stomach. That wasn't quite right.

"Adam?" Ellie said tentatively as she took a step closer to him in the water. "I think the floor is moving."

"Huh?" he replied as he lifted his head—and then his eyes widened.

Adam yanked Ellie back, moving them deeper into the water. He swung his boots off his shoulder and hopped awkwardly in the shallows as he yanked them on.

"Boots," he ordered as he snatched the torch from her.

"Shouldn't you tie them first?"

"Boots, Ellie!" he repeated. His voice snapped with urgency.

Ellie awkwardly tugged on her shoes. The leather stuck against her wet stockings.

"Are those insects dangerous?" she demanded. She wobbled unsteadily on her left foot as she tried to wrangle her laces.

"Maybe? I don't know!" Adam returned. "They're usually the size of a quarter, not four damned inches long."

Ellie managed a knot and let her booted foot splash back down into the ankle-deep water. She took another look at the shoreline—and then wished she hadn't.

The bugs were clustering more thickly now. Glittering gray bodies streamed in from every side of the cave.

Some of them even clung to the stalactites overhead. Their gray antennae waved in the air hungrily.

"Are the normal variety of assassin bugs dangerous?" she pressed.

"They hurt like a bastard," Adam retorted.

The insects swarmed along the edge of the water with their proboscises extending... testing...

Ellie took a step back, wading a little deeper.

"How do they hunt?" she asked as she eyed the swarm uneasily.

"They stick other bugs with some kind of venom," Adam replied. "It paralyzes them and melts their insides."

"Melts their insides?" Ellie repeated with horror.

"Other bugs!" Adam emphasized.

"These are significantly larger, and there are a very great many of them," Ellie protested crossly.

One of the insects entered the water.

It floated on the surface, its thick gray body keeping it buoyant. Antennae waved, legs twitched... and it began to swim.

"Aww hell," Adam cursed.

More of the bugs bobbed into the lake. They weren't exceptionally good swimmers.

Ellie wasn't sure they needed to be. There were a lot of them—and there was nowhere for her and Adam to go.

She sloshed back with him until the water lapped at her knees.

"I think they're following us," she pointed out with remarkable calm.

"Sure looks like it," Adam agreed grimly.

"How are they following us?" Ellie demanded. "These are cave dwelling insects. They shouldn't be able to see."

"How should I know?" He splashed at the water, making a little wave that pushed back the vanguard of the approaching fleet of bugs. "Get!"

Ellie's mind raced through the possibilities.

"Could it be the vibrations?" she mused urgently. "Possibly, but then the insects would have been coming for us from the minute we entered the cavern. Echolocation? No, that's not it. We were speaking as well. It's right here," she said, tapping the side of her head angrily. "I can *feel* it..."

Her gaze locked on the torch in Adam's hand.

"Give me that," she said and snatched it from him.

She waded a few steps away, keeping her eyes on the insects swimming toward them. She focused on their antennae.

Ellie swung the torch out to the right, and then back again... and watched the antennae move.

"Thermoreception!" she burst out.

"What?" Adam shot back, splashing more of the bugs away as he moved deeper.

Ellie hurried over to him through the thigh-deep water.

"Do you see a way out of this cavern?" she demanded.

"I'm not sure," Adam admitted. "It's still too dark at the outskirts of the chamber to make things out."

Ellie looked to the reed basket, which was still stuffed with more pitch-wood bundles where it stood on the shore. Skipping around the nearest wave of insects, she moved as close to it as she dared—and then chucked her flaming torch through the air.

It soared in an elegant arc... and missed.

The torch landed at the base of the broken stalagmite on which the basket stood, burning merrily there.

"What the hell did you just do?" Adam exclaimed.

"I am trying to save us!" Ellie shot back.

"By throwing away our light?"

"They are drawn to the heat!" she retorted.

The nearest insects had turned toward the flames of the fallen torch. They began to skitter closer to it.

Adam's eyes widened.

"Huh," he said with understanding, and then shot her a wry look. "Except your aim was off."

"Only by a foot," Ellie noted.

He sighed and started sloshing forward.

"I'll fix it," he declared.

Ellie grabbed him by the belt and hauled him back.

"Are you mad? You'll be right in the middle of the swarm," she hissed.

"I'll be quick," Adam assured her.

Ellie stared at him.

"Exactly how quick do you think you are?" she pressed.

Over by the torch, the nearest insects reached the flames... and kept going. They climbed into the low, flickering light. Their bodies crackled, crisping and blackening as they added themselves to the fire.

"Pretty damned quick," Adam retorted defensively.

Ellie reached for the dry torch in his belt.

"I'll try again," she said.

Adam shifted his hips away from her.

"Uh-uh! That's our only torch," he protested.

"We can't go anywhere if there's an army of venomous insects in our way!" Ellie snapped.

"You think it's a better idea to navigate through a cave in the dark?"

"That is exactly what we were going to do before you found the torches," she pointed out, seething.

"Yeah, well. Now I found them, which is a lot better than falling into a hole in the ground!"

More of the insects joined the crackling pile by the torch—and more. They crawled over each other to reach the heat of the fire. Their roasting carapaces emitted a low, hissing squeal.

The squeal shifted into a whoosh as the pile of flaming bug corpses extended to the side of the reed basket and the old, dry wood ignited.

Flames swirled up the side of the basket, reached the pitch-soaked torches inside… and burst into an inferno.

A black column of smoke poured toward the ceiling. The cave was blazingly illuminated.

The entire colony of assassin bugs wheeled toward the fire, racing to join it.

"Well, I'll be damned," Adam said.

The light revealed another tunnel mouth on the far side of the dry ground. More stalactites framed the black hollow with teeth-like daggers.

"Come on!" Ellie ordered as she grabbed Adam's arm and tugged him forward.

Adam quickly took the lead. He steered her toward the edge of the cavern, where the stream of insects had already thinned out. As they passed, he kicked a stray few of the bugs out of the way with the toe of his boot.

He seemed to enjoy it a bit more than he strictly should have.

They passed some of the stripped, fleshless bones as they ran—and Ellie realized that she had a fairly good idea how they had gotten there.

Venom that paralyzes them and melts their insides.

She repressed a shudder and hurried after Adam.

Their exit was a wide, dark mouth. The tunnel it framed descended steeply down.

Adam glanced back at the wriggling, insect-fueled bonfire by the burning torch basket.

"We might not want to risk the light until we've got more distance between ourselves and the swarm," he suggested.

"That seems prudent," Ellie agreed.

He offered a hand. Ellie looked at it for a moment in surprise, and then reached over and clasped it.

"Here we go..." he said and led them into the dark.

The light of the bug-fueled inferno flickered softly on the walls of the tunnel for a while as they walked. As it faded, their pace slowed—and then the light was gone, plunging them into an impenetrable night once more.

"Let's take it one step at a time," Adam said. "Feel the ground in front of you before you put your weight down. We could stumble into another crevice or sinkhole at any point down here."

"Indeed," Ellie agreed tightly.

Adam's grip on her hand was a warm anchor. Ellie latched on to it.

They were wandering through an unknown cave system. That was a risky prospect, even under the best circumstances. Doing it in the dark without any of the proper equipment was frankly madness.

Not that they had an alternative.

This was not just any cave system, Ellie reminded herself with a sense of wonder. Someone had left those torches. Even the way the opening of the cenote had been framed by the ball court was clearly intentional.

There had to be some ritual purpose behind it all. The thought touched Ellie with a little chill of excitement. She was walking through the secrets of a lost world.

Hopefully, it wouldn't kill her.

Adam's voice broke the silence that had shrouded them since they'd left the light behind.

"Tunnel's turning," he reported.

"How do you know?" Ellie replied.

"I've got a hand on the wall," he said.

"Should we risk another torch?"

"Would've been nice if we'd had that damned bone," Adam grumbled.

"What bone?" Ellie asked.

"The one Dawson used to light up the temple," he replied. "The firebird bone."

Ellie stopped walking.

"A firebird," she repeated carefully. "As in the mythical glowing creature from Slavic folklore."

"You'd know better than I do," Adam countered easily.

"But in the stories, it's the feathers of the firebird that are supposed to glow." She frowned. "And they are always illuminated unless kept concealed."

"Maybe that's why Dawson had to jiggle it," Adam mused.

"He did *what?*"

"Shook it like a martini," Adam cheerfully returned. "And then the damned thing lit up like a rocket on the Fourth of July. Jacobs used it again in the cenote."

Ellie thought of the wild, impossible light that had glared brilliantly at her through the surface of the water.

"But the firebird is a myth," she protested numbly.

"Yeah." Adam's tone was more serious.

"It's just a story!"

"I know, Princess," he returned quietly.

"And you're quite certain that you... saw that correctly?" she asked, choosing the words carefully.

There was a silence in response. If Ellie had possessed a firebird bone, she was fairly certain that she would have seen Adam cocking a skeptical eyebrow at her.

"Never mind," she sighed. She pressed her fingers to her temple, where the beginning of a headache was coming on. "You saw it."

"I saw it," Adam confirmed.

"Even though it's... impossible," Ellie added.

"Guess not."

She felt him shrug.

"This is..." Ellie let go of Adam's hand. Taking a chance, she reached out and found the wall of the cave. She pressed her back to the stone of the tunnel wall.

She needed to feel something solid. Her whole world was shifting. That was challenging enough, even when one wasn't also swathed in impenetrable darkness.

"This..." she began.

"...makes it look an awful lot like there's probably other stuff like that out there," Adam filled in flatly. "That's what Dawson said."

"Mythological objects," Ellie said awkwardly. "Mythological objects that actually *do* the things they were said to do. But that's..."

She shook her head. Her mind spun as the implication washed over her.

"There are countless stories of powerful objects scattered through the historical and mythological record," she rattled a little wildly. "The Chi Guo Tian Wang—the Eastern King in Chinese Buddhist folklore—possessed a musical instrument that could control the weather. And then there's the Astras of the Mahabharata—weapons of unimaginable power crafted by the gods themselves. The herbs of Asclepius could purportedly raise the dead. The Golden Fleece. The Lance of Longinus… For the love of God, in Iceland there's even a mythical pair of undergarments that produce an endless supply of money. If… If even a *fraction* of those stories are based on some semblance of the truth…"

"It'd sure explain why Dawson and Jacobs are willing to go to such extremes to get their hands on that Smoking Mirror of yours," Adam finished flatly.

Ellie raised her head as a quick, energizing fear snapped through her.

"No," she protested. "They couldn't possibly… That would be…" She shook her head as she tried to clear her spinning thoughts. "The Smoking Mirror is… It's *knowledge*. It's the ability to look into any place or time. The annals say that those who possessed it could see as though through the eyes of the gods."

"Look on the bright side," Adam offered. "It could be worse, like a flying hammer or a flaming sword or something."

Ellie stood up.

"This is so much worse than a flaming sword," she spluttered. "Adam, do you have any idea how terribly dangerous *knowledge* can be? Imagine if you could learn the secrets of every member of Cabinet. If you could see into war rooms. Steal the technology of the future. If there truly are more… more *things* like this out there, you could use the mirror to find them all. It could pave the road for you to achieve absolutely *anything you desired*. Nobody should have that much power—certainly not the sort of people who would hire a man like Jacobs to do their work for them."

Adam didn't answer right away. Silence settled in, thick and tense around them, accentuated by the utter darkness in which they were wrapped.

Ellie was still soaking wet from her drop into the cenote. The cave wasn't terribly cold, but it was cooler than the humid tropical spring of the world above. She shivered.

Adam laughed—a resigned and tired chuckle.

"Aw hell," he said at last. "We really are gonna have to find some way to stop the bastards, aren't we?"

"The two of us. Against a small army," Ellie said numbly as her mind continued to whirl.

"Hey, at least I got my knife back," Adam pointed out wryly.

"And I have a magnifying lens, and a needle and thread in my pocket." Ellie ran her hands over her face, unsure whether she wanted to break out into hysterics or simply lie down on the ground. "We are going to get ourselves killed."

"If it's any comfort, I'm not really sure running away would be any smarter," he said. "It's pretty clear those two don't want to leave any loose ends hanging around. If they do get that mirror, then they could use it to find us no matter where we disappeared to."

It was true, of course. If the mirror could really do all that it was purported to do—which was the risk they were now forced to consider—then Dawson or Jacobs need merely ask it where Adam and Ellie were, and it would show them, as simply as that.

Adam tugged one of Ellie's hands up and pressed something into it. She recognized the feel of the other torch.

There was a scratch and a flare of light. Adam set a match to the pitch-soaked wood and it flickered to life, bringing his face back into view. He looked battered, muddy, and beautiful.

"Thread," he said with a tired grin.

"And a magnifying lens," Ellie confirmed. "I'm afraid I lost the broken pencil—but I do have a flask of some sort of illicit spirits."

"Did you drink any?" Adam asked.

"Goodness, no!" Ellie frowned crossly. "I am sure it is vile."

"Never know until you try it," he pointed out.

She fixed him with an authoritative glare.

"I am saving it for an emergency," she retorted.

"Knife, needle, thread, lens, and booze," Adam listed. He shrugged. "Pretty sure I've made do with worse."

Ellie fought the urge to giggle. "This is madness," she pointed out.

His eyes narrowed wickedly.

"Uh-uh," he countered. "It's *improvisation*. And who knows? Maybe you'll figure out another way to make something explode."

Ellie's mind began to calculate enticingly. "If I do, will you let me do it?"

Adam slipped his arm around her shoulders.

"If there was ever a time to blow something up, Princess, I'm pretty sure this is it," he replied.

The thought was a bubble of excitement inside of her.

Ellie eyed Adam skeptically.

"You aren't going to try to talk me into making a run for it while you attempt to do it all yourself?" she pressed.

"I think at this point, I know you a little too well to bother," he returned with a wry look.

A smile spread irresistibly across her face as she gazed up at him. The warm glow of it pushed away the pervasive chill of the cave.

"I have become inordinately fond of you, you know," Ellie abruptly admitted.

"Well, then, we're gonna have to do our damnedest not to die," Adam replied as he gazed down at her warmly—*very* warmly.

"While we navigate our way through a deadly cave and prevent an army of thugs from looting an immensely powerful magical artifact," Ellie replied.

"Piece of cake," he declared. He made a gentlemanly gesture with his arm. "Shall we?"

"Why not?" Ellie returned, and allowed him to lead her into the unknown.

THIRTY-EIGHT

$\mathscr{T}$HE TUNNEL NARROWED as Ellie and Adam moved on. The ceiling dropped until Adam had to duck to pass under some of the lower curves. Around another turn, the flickering glow of their torch revealed the dark mouth of a perfectly squared opening.

The natural shape of the cave had been carved to form a deliberate doorway. Its three sides were lined with painted rows of Tulan's language.

Ellie took a few steps closer. She reached out but stopped her hand just short of touching the characters. The colors still looked fresh, likely because they hadn't been affected by weather and time like the art above ground.

"I am starting to suspect that this cave has been deliberately modified for ritual purposes," she said carefully as she studied the painted words. "For an initiation, perhaps—some trial for new kings or religious elites. Tulan was also called the City of Seven Caves, but not just any caves. Xibalba—the underworld home of the gods of death. *That's* what is supposed to lie beneath Tulan."

"So you're saying we're in Hell," Adam filled in as he gave her a flat look.

"Er... a ritual approximation of Hell," Ellie corrected him uncomfortably.

"Great," Adam muttered as he took the torch back from her. "Let's go see what Hell looks like."

He ducked through the doorway. Ellie followed in his wake.

A short length of tunnel opened into a chamber full of monsters.

Gruesome, distorted shapes loomed over the moderate space of the cavern. Though they were merely wooden statues, their expressions seemed to grimace with lifelike horror in the flickering light of the torch.

The figures were perhaps twelve feet tall, and were arranged in a rough circle on thrones built of quarried stone that pressed up against the walls of the cave. Any irregular expanses of the cavern's natural shape had been blocked up with mortared rubble. The changes made the space claustrophobic.

The carved shapes were detailed and vividly painted. The gleaming, faceted eyes of an insect and the jaws of a crocodile gaped at Ellie from the dancing shadows.

"Any idea what this is about?" Adam asked carefully. He stepped into the center of the chamber to give the figures a better look.

"I believe they are the Lords of Death," Ellie replied uneasily as she looked up into the bulging eyes of a goddess with a blue face. A noose hung tightly around her neck.

"Sure," Adam muttered unhappily. "Why wouldn't they be?"

He explored the cavern with the torch as Ellie circled the ring of gods.

Bloodstained, canine teeth grimaced at her. Beside them glared the avian eyes of a vulture.

A woman with a skull for a face gazed down from her throne, draped in beautiful finery. Ellie paused in front of her.

"There are twelve figures," she pointed out. "That fits with the accounts from the Popol Vuh."

Adam finished circling the chamber. "I don't see another way out," he concluded.

"There must be!" Ellie replied, startled out of her study. "How else could they have brought all this down here?"

"It's possible there was another branch tunnel we missed when we were moving through the dark."

"If we go back with the torch, we might run into those bugs again. We don't have anything else to lure them away with," Ellie pointed out.

"I don't know what else to tell you, Princess."

Ellie ran her eyes carefully over the walls of the cavern.

"This cave has been heavily modified," she said. "Most of this isn't the natural wall. It's been filled in, particularly around the statues."

"You're saying that the way out must be behind one of the walls," Adam offered.

Ellie stopped in front of the beautiful skull goddess. The statue drew her. It was somehow more comforting than the other gods. The lines of its posture were graceful.

Her eyes drifted to the base of the skull goddess's throne. A lever protruded from a vertical slot in the center of it. It was pointed up.

She looked around. All of the gods had levers. All of the them were up.

"What do you think those are for?" Adam asked.

He stood in front of a giant spider god and tapped the side of the lever with his boot.

The lever thumped down to the base of the slot.

Adam stared down at it.

"Why do I have a feeling that's gonna turn out to be a bad thing?" he said.

Ellie's nerves jarred with alarm.

"It's just a cave," she assured him weakly. "Nobody has maintained any of this for well over two hundred years. What could it really do?"

A low, unmistakable grinding noise roared through the chamber from behind the bricked-up walls. The sound reminded Ellie of opening a giant window. *Counterweights*, she thought.

A stone thudded into place, blocking the tunnel through which they'd come.

Adam immediately raced over to it. He dropped the torch and shouldered at the rock.

Ellie's eyes were elsewhere—on the center of the chamber floor, where she could now see that twelve holes, each a few inches in diameter, had been drilled into the stone.

"It won't budge," Adam announced as he hauled at the base of the slab blocking the tunnel. He gave it a frustrated kick.

The grinding behind the walls stopped. In its place rose a low, sibilant hiss.

"What's that?" Adam demanded.

Ellie gazed down at the holes in the floor with a growing sense of unease.

"I think it's coming from there," she replied.

Adam moved to the openings and reached out to touch them. He yanked his hand back, waving it awkwardly.

"There's steam coming out of them," he declared.

"Steam?" Ellie echoed nervously. "How can there be steam in here?"

"I don't know!" Adam retorted. "Maybe they tapped into a magma incursion or something."

Ellie's interest perked. "What a fascinating suggestion!" she exclaimed.

"Princess..." Adam growled warningly.

A dart of fear tickled at her as the room grew warmer.

"There's nothing to worry about. This is perfectly fine," she asserted. "It must be some kind of test, that's all. If this is an initiation trial, then it makes sense that there are obstacles to overcome. Oh—of course!" she burst out as she remembered. "There were tests in the Popol Vuh when the hero twins went to Xibalba to retrieve the head of their father—"

"Wait—his head?" Adam cut in.

"Never mind that," Ellie hurriedly said. "The Mayan storytellers must have been passing down some version of the initiation rituals of Tulan—and we are walking in the middle of it! Adam, have you any idea of the potential historical implications of that?"

"Not sure I'm too concerned about historical implications at the moment," Adam called over as he made another survey of the cavern walls. "I'm more worried about what happened to your twins if they got it wrong."

"It's different in each of the caverns of Xibalba," Ellie hedged.

"How about this one, Princess?" Adam pressed impatiently.

The heat in the room was rising, as was the humidity. Sweat broke out on her skin as she thought uneasily of the answer to Adam's question.

"They were... ah, roasted alive," Ellie informed him.

"We're looking a bit more like poached here," Adam pointed out soberly. "How do we get out of it?"

Ellie paced the ring of close-packed, looming figures.

"This is the council chamber," she noted. "In the council chamber of the Popol Vuh, the gods of death were trying to trick the twins by putting both real deities and false ones—statues—in the room. If the twins greeted a statue with the same reverence as a god, they would be punished for it."

"In case you hadn't noticed, these are all statues," Adam shot back. He waved a hand up at the grinning crocodile head.

"I can see that," Ellie retorted. Her breath was coming a little more heavily as the heat grew denser. "But there must be something different about them."

"Maybe it's a beauty contest."

"That isn't helping," Ellie pointed out.

"Well, what'd it say in your book?"

"That they were helped by a mosquito," she admitted.

"What?" he exclaimed.

"It pricks each of the gods. The real ones yell about it."

"That's it?" He gaped at her from across the hissing vents in the floor.

"It's a cultural record," Ellie snapped. "It might have been passed down orally dozens of times before it was committed to written form. All sorts of things might have changed since then!"

"Where are we supposed to find a mosquito down here?"

"I don't know!"

The heat was making it hard to think. Ellie felt as though she couldn't draw enough breath.

The chamber wasn't that big. The steam was collecting quickly, and it was *hot.*

At normal atmospheric pressure, steam was precisely 100 degrees Celsius. If Ellie estimated the cubic area of the room, the ambient temperature, and the rate at which the hot vapor was coming in, she could calculate the precise number of minutes they had before they succumbed to heat stroke.

Ellie shook off the thought. She was getting distracted. Her brain was flailing for the wrong sort of answers.

"There is a solution in here somewhere," she stubbornly insisted. "We just have to *think*."

Adam pivoted.

"I'm going to break down the wall," he declared.

Ellie jolted with a quick panic.

"You can't do that!" she protested.

"Why not?"

"This is a priceless piece of Mesoamerican history!"

"It's trying to kill us, Princess!" he shouted back.

"You might smash up whatever controls our way out of here," she retorted as she jabbed her finger at him.

Adam muttered a colorful string of curses and gave the wall a kick.

Ellie stared up at the bulging eyes of the suicide goddess. The figure was depicted with uncomfortable realism, right down to the divots in her flesh where the noose tightened around her neck.

There was something odd about the base of the statue's throat.

She needed to get a closer look at it.

The scholar in her rebelled against the obvious solution. These statues could be thousands of years old. They might be incredibly fragile, with their painted surfaces vulnerable to chipping or marring...

Ellie swayed a bit as the blue face of the goddess doubled. Sweat streamed down her back.

They were going to die down here.

"I'm sorry," Ellie gasped as she grabbed onto the hanged woman's knee. "I'm so dreadfully sorry."

She hauled herself up. Her boots slipped unsteadily on the slick surface of the wood. It had been treated with some sort of oil—likely a natural preservative to prevent insect damage and oxidation, she thought with a distant spark of scholarly interest.

Her toe skidded. Ellie latched onto the statue's enormous arms to keep herself in place.

She pushed herself up, using a wooden arm for leverage, until she was eye-level with the goddess's throat.

The dark spot she had seen from the ground was a hole.

Ellie scrambled her way higher, bracing an arm around the hanged woman's unsettlingly realistic throat, and peered around the statue's head.

A slender wooden tube protruded from the back of its throat.

No, Ellie realized. It wasn't wood. The tube was a carefully shaped piece of hollow bone.

"Oh blast," Ellie blurted as her inspiration crystallized into an idea.

She wondered what sort of bone it was. Probably not human, she thought with uncomfortable relief. Human bones weren't naturally hollow…

…unless someone had hollowed one out.

Below her, Adam kicked at the throne of a giant bug god.

"I don't see a way out of this," he called. His voice was tight with frustration.

Ellie took a breath to steel herself, set her lips to the bone, and blew.

A clear, delicate note floated through the enclosed space of the chamber.

Adam gaped up at her.

"What did you do?" he demanded.

"I… found a flute," Ellie awkwardly replied as she waved at the back of the statue's neck.

Adam met her gaze from across the length of the suicide goddess—then lifted his boot and stomped down on the lever.

Unseen weights moved behind the walls as something ground and cranked into place.

"Was that a good noise?" she asked tentatively.

"Keep blowing and let's find out," Adam retorted. He pivoted over to an enormous anthropomorphic spider and grabbed one of its eight arms to haul himself up.

"Right," Ellie confirmed breathlessly.

She clambered down from the hanged goddess and hurried to the next statue—the bloody-toothed crocodile. She scaled up its body, using its open jaws to pull up to its neck.

She blew through the bone flute that she found protruding from the back. There was no sound.

Across the room, the spider god emitted a haunting, elegant note.

Adam slid down the front of it. He kicked the lever as he went.

Another scrape and clank sounded from behind the walls.

Ellie half-fell down the front of the crocodile. She ran to a god that vividly resembled a rotting corpse, right down to the wooden maggots wriggling in the gaps of its skin.

She eyed it distastefully, but there was no way around it. Ellie climbed up. Her boots slipped on the slick surface. The decaying flesh had been depicted with such realism that she almost expected it to squish under her grip.

Thankfully, there was no squish.

She reached the top, swung herself around to the back of the corpse's neck—and panicked.

"It's not here!" she cried out.

"What do you mean, it's not there?" Adam hopped down from a handsome male god who appeared to have slit his own throat.

"The... the bone! The flute! It's broken off!" Ellie exclaimed.

"Skip it and go to the next one," Adam ordered as he scaled up the torso of a beady-eyed vulture. "If we get through all of them and nothing's happened, then we'll know which way it's supposed to go."

The suggestion was perfectly sensible. Ellie's brain took an inordinately long amount of time to absorb it.

The air was making it hard to breathe—hard to think. She felt dizzy and thick.

"Yes," she said aloud, as though the words could force her body into moving. "Yes, I'll do that."

She climbed down. Her grip on the corpse slipped, sending her into a skid. Ellie caught herself on a handful of maggots.

Adam threw her a worried glance from across the room.

His bare chest glistened with sweat in the light of the torch, which he had jammed into a crack in the stones. His hair was damp as well, mussed and unruly above those piercing blue eyes... eyes that went from dangerous to sparkling with humor in a breath.

And that stubble, which was so scratchy and yet soft at the same time. The way his hands felt when he grabbed hold of her—

"Princess?" Adam cut in. His perfect eyes were lined with concern.

Ellie shook her head to snap herself out of it.

"I'm fine," she assured him unevenly. "Keep going."

He didn't believe her. The fact of it was written clearly on his face—but they were running out of time.

Adam hauled himself up the side of a god with a dog skull instead of a face. Ellie approached the next statue.

This one was some sort of bat. Black wings extended out from either side of it, pointed and leathery. Red eyes caught the torchlight and flickered it back at her.

They looked like glass... or maybe rubies. Were there rubies in British

Honduras?

Ellie's thoughts drifted into possible trade routes.

She shook off the haze and forced herself to climb. Her hands gripped soft fur and leathery skin.

Ellie suppressed a yelp—and realized that it was only wood, lightly textured by some expert, long-dead hand. It had not felt like wood… which meant that she was starting to hallucinate.

Hallucination was one of the more advanced symptoms of heat stroke.

The bat god had fangs. They were long and wickedly pointed.

Yes, Ellie thought distantly. That made sense.

The fangs were not wood. When she touched them, she felt bone.

Perhaps she was hallucinating again.

She reached the back of the bat's neck and found the flute. The note it sounded was a screech nearly too high in pitch for her ears to hear it.

Ellie collapsed back to the ground, too weary and disoriented to climb. The air was so hot—too hot.

She threw herself against the lever. It gave under her weight and clanked down. More noises ground from within the walls.

There was still no way out.

Ellie slumped down on the ground beside the lever.

No—she had to keep going.

She dragged herself to her feet and stumbled to the final statue. The skull-faced woman was framed by a halo of golden feathers and draped in rich, colorful robes.

Ellie had seen her before—painted onto a cheap paper card set in a wooden frame on an altar in Santa Dolores, honored with flowers and candles.

"Santa Muerte," Ellie gasped as her head spun dangerously.

It seemed that the skull-faced woman nodded, as regal as a queen accepting her tribute.

Ellie set her hands on the goddess's knees and pushed herself up. She climbed the figure slowly—a hand to her silk-covered shoulder, a foot on her skeletal hand. She wrapped her arms around the statue's back, clinging to her like an exhausted child as she pulled herself the last bit of distance to her goal.

Her eyes rested on the back of Death's throat.

The bone was broken.

Shadows crept into the sides of her vision. They swarmed there, dancing and shifting. The scope of what she could see narrowed, and Ellie wavered unsteadily.

Her arms gave way. She slid into Santa Muerte's lap, and then fell to the ground as the monsters around her blurred into a kaleidoscope of flower petals and rot.

Adam's face hovered above her. The familiar lines of it were drawn with concern.

"Damn it," he cursed.

Solid arms lifted her as he clutched her to his sweat-slick chest.

"She's..." Ellie groaned.

"She's what, Princess?" Adam demanded.

"Broken," Ellie replied.

She let her head fall against his skin. Her eyes drifted closed.

All of her was drifting. Only the feel of Adam's chest against her cheek and the powerful strength of his arms kept her from floating away.

"That's lovely," Ellie sighed as she drifted deeper.

"Ellie," Adam said. He deliberately jostled her. The shake snapped her slightly more awake.

"Hasss to be one of them," she slurred. "Her or... maggot face... How can we...?"

"You're passing out," Adam declared.

"Ssssallright," Ellie replied.

The world blurred into a swimming dance of color—bones and feathers, jaguar skin and jagged teeth.

"Ah, to hell with it," Adam muttered from somewhere above her.

His body swayed awkwardly as he lifted up one of his feet and stomped down on the lever.

A louder clank sounded from within the walls. Ellie had the vague sense of something benevolent and grotesque moving past her. It reminded her of the shadow of a great wing.

"Thank Christ," Adam coughed. He clung to Ellie as he shoved his back against an enormous, looming object, which moved aside on a well-oiled pivot.

Cool air blasted over her face. Ellie gasped it in as Adam staggered forward. He collapsed awkwardly to a knee, and then to the ground. He leaned back against a wall, letting Ellie fall into his lap.

Her vision slowly cleared. Adam's head had dropped back against the stone. Only the silhouette of his face was visible in the dim torchlight that carried through to them from the other chamber.

She looked past him to see an open doorway cut into the rock. A figure loomed on the far side of it. It was the skull-faced woman, who had swung free of the exit that she had been concealing behind all of her deathly elegance.

Ellie swallowed thickly. Her throat was dry.

"How… How did you know which one it was?" she asked.

"No idea," Adam replied without opening his eyes. "Just guessed."

Horrified alarm made Ellie sit up straighter in his lap.

"You *guessed*?"

"Figured a fifty-fifty shot was better than getting cooked." He cracked a tired eye at her as his mouth pulled into an approximation of his usual roguish smile.

"What if you had guessed wrong?" Ellie pressed, aghast.

"Would've cooked us a little faster." Adam shrugged.

She gaped up at him. "You're unbelievable," she said.

He was definitely smiling at her.

"Thanks." His expression sobered a bit. "Looks like this ritual of yours is meant to kill whoever gets it wrong."

"That would fit with the written accounts," Ellie returned uneasily. "How are we going to get past it?"

"With whatever else is in that big brain of yours," he said. "And luck."

Ellie's stomach dropped.

"That isn't very reassuring."

"Best we've got," Adam concluded.

He shifted her from his lap, climbed to his feet, and extended a hand down. Ellie accepted it and let him pull her upright.

He ducked back into the council chamber to retrieve the torch. It illuminated the way ahead—a low-ceilinged labyrinth of veils, pillars, and stalagmites, which creeped with shadows.

Ellie faced it with grim determination. They would get through this. They *had* to.

Everything depended upon it.

THIRTY-NINE

$\mathcal{I}$N THE DIM TORCHLIGHT, the space around them was shadowy and maze-like. It was not so much a chamber as a throat of stone lined with obstacles. The rock formations were close and awkward. Ellie struggled to see how she and Adam were meant to proceed through it.

"That looks like a path." Adam pointed ahead of them.

The narrow, uneven track twisted through the stones. It was visible for only a short distance ahead of them before turning from view. The cleared ground looked barely wide enough for Ellie to put her feet side-by-side on it.

She took a determined breath and started forward. She had only gone a few steps when Adam let out a sharp hiss of pain behind her.

"What's wrong?" Ellie said as she whirled back to him.

"Damned cave bit me," Adam returned.

He shook out his hand—and a quick, wet splatter darkened the nearby stones. Ellie's pulse jumped uncomfortably at the sound.

Adam noticed it too. He glanced down at his hand and then flashed her a distinctly guilty look.

"Just scratched myself a little," he said.

Ellie grabbed his hand and turned it over. A gash crossed his palm, as clean as the mark of a surgeon's scalpel. Blood welled out of it as she studied it.

"Adam, this isn't a scratch," she protested.

Adam took his hand back.

"It's fine," he insisted stubbornly.

"It absolutely is not. Give it back to me. *Now*," she added when he hesitated.

Adam sighed and gave in.

"There's not much we can do about it in here," he pointed out as she examined him.

"I could sew it," Ellie countered.

"Do you even know how to sew?"

"Of course I do," Ellie replied, and then hedged a bit. "I mean—I despise it and avoid it if at all possible. But I *can* do it. We can disinfect the thread with my illicit liquor."

"I don't think so." Adam tried to take his hand back.

Ellie hung onto it. "You prefer to keep bleeding all over the cave?" she retorted.

"It'll stop," he insisted stubbornly.

"When?" Ellie pushed back.

"Uh—soon."

More blood splatted down onto the stones by her feet.

Ellie pulled her supplies from her pocket and set them out neatly on the ground. She took out a bit of thread and worked to stick it through the eye of the needle.

It took a few tries.

She unscrewed the flask. Tilting it, she brought the fiery-scented liquid inside up to the top. She dipped the needle and thread into it.

"Ready?" she asked impatiently with the flask in one hand and the needle in the other.

"This is a terrible idea," Adam asserted.

"Would you rather do it yourself?" she challenged.

"Maybe?" Adam returned, and then took in the scowl on Ellie's face. "Okay. Fine. You sew me up. Have at it."

He held out his hand. Ellie eyed the cut uncomfortably. Now that he had given her permission to play doctor, she wasn't entirely sure how she felt about it.

She took a deep breath. She could do this. Who knew what could get into that wound while they were scrambling around in the cave? An infection could kill him out here. Stitching it closed was the prudent, rational thing to do.

Ellie steeled herself and sloshed a glug of liquor across his palm.

"Ow—ouch!" Adam complained with a hiss of pain.

"Really?" Ellie raised a skeptical eyebrow.

"It burns," Adam insisted mulishly. "You try pouring cask strength hooch on an open wound and tell me how you like it."

"Well, I doubt you're going to like this much better," Ellie returned as she took hold of his hand and turned it to find the right angle.

There really wasn't a right angle.

This would be just like fixing her socks. The principles were exactly the same... except with human flesh instead of wool.

Ellie stuck her needle into Adam's skin and immediately felt queasy.

He grunted but made no further protest.

"In and out," she breathed deliberately as she looked down at the silver needle protruding from Adam's palm. "Nothing to it."

Ellie wriggled it through to the opposite side of the wound.

Adam's brow creased as he grimaced.

"That's... Mmm." He bit back something else that clearly wanted to come out of his mouth.

"Sorry..." Ellie winced as she tugged the needle out, pulling the thread through with it.

The sight of the string emerging from Adam's bloody hand made her feel a bit dizzy. She forced in another deep breath as she readied for her next stitch—and then froze.

"Do I go back in from the same side or cross over?" she blurted.

"Over," Adam said flatly.

"Are you sure?"

"Very sure."

"How do you know?" she pressed.

"Because I've had stitches before?" he retorted thinly.

"Right, yes," Ellie said carefully, sensing the thinness of his temper. "Very sensible. Crossing over."

She jabbed the needle in again. This time, she managed to get the angle a little better. Pulling the thread through made her slightly less queasy.

She made another jab and started to feel better.

"This really isn't so difficult," she declared as she pushed the needle through his skin again.

"Great," Adam said through his gritted teeth. "Glad you're enjoying it."

"There," Ellie announced a moment later as she made her last pull through the end of the wound. "Do I tie it off now like one of my stockings?"

"Huh?" Adam returned as he raised an alarmed eyebrow at her.

"Same basic principles," Ellie asserted with more confidence than she felt.

She finished the knot. A bit of thread hung from the end of the uneven row of black stitches.

"We need something to cut the—Oh!" she exclaimed as Adam thrust the torch into her hands.

He set the loose end of the thread between his teeth, pulled it taut, and yanked the machete from his belt.

A neat slice severed it right at the knot.

Adam shoved the machete back into place and eyed the wound with a frown.

"Your stitches are all over the damned place," he complained.

Ellie stiffened defensively.

"They are perfectly fine, thank you very much," she countered. "I should like to see you do any better."

"I *have* done better," Adam retorted. "Just wasn't gonna try with my left hand."

At her answering glower, he shuffled a bit.

"But thank you," he replied carefully. "Much appreciated."

"We should bandage it as well." Ellie turned, presenting him with her shoulder. "You may take my sleeve."

"I don't need your sleeve," Adam said as he suppressed a sigh.

"It is still an open wound," she pointed out. "It will take time to scab up properly and we cannot afford to wait around for that. Tear off my sleeve and wrap it up."

Adam narrowed his eyes mischievously.

"So you want me to tear your clothes off you," he clarified.

Ellie's cheeks heated. "The sleeve should be more than sufficient," she returned primly.

"Sure about that?" Adam asked as he loomed a little closer. His newly stitched hand neatly flicked at her topmost button.

Ellie had lost a pair of buttons in the cenote, so the one he touched was already indecently low.

She might lose *all* her buttons down here, she thought thickly as her eyes dropped to the sweat-slicked muscle on Adam's chest. What did she really need them for anyway? Bothersome things, buttons…

"Sleeve," she said through her suddenly dry mouth.

He flashed her a grin.

"Fair enough," he agreed. "Hold still."

"Hold still?" Ellie echoed, and then flinched as the machete flashed up again.

Adam took hold of the shoulder of her shirt and stabbed it. The knife passed close enough to Ellie's cheek that she could feel the soft wind of its passing.

He jerked the blade up, slicing the fabric in two. Taking hold of the cut from both sides, he ripped it apart.

The sleeve severed with a jerk. Adam peeled it down Ellie's arm. The fabric was still a bit damp from her plunge into the cenote and the humid, sweaty warmth of the council chamber.

"We should probably sterilize that with the alcohol as well," Ellie said thoughtfully as she eyed the stained, filthy piece of cloth.

"Sure," Adam replied. "Gimmie the booze."

She took the flask from her pocket and handed it over. Adam flipped it open and tossed the contents down his throat.

"Gahhh," he gasped as he finished. "That really is awful. Who the hell did you steal this from?"

"I took it off Mr. Mendez," Ellie retorted as she snatched the flask back, along with her shirtsleeve.

She splashed the remaining liquor on the fabric.

"No wonder he's in such a bad mood all the time," Adam grumbled.

"There," Ellie declared after firmly binding the wound. "Now we may proceed… though I should very much like to know how you managed to do that to yourself so easily."

"I just touched a rock," Adam complained in response.

"Which one?" Ellie asked, and then realized she didn't need Adam to answer. She could see the splatter of dark blood on the ground where he had been standing. "The torch, please."

Adam handed it to her. Ellie used the light to study the stone column beside them.

She spotted another splash of blood on its surface. Something odd protruded from the center of the stain—a small sliver of black stone.

"Something's stuck here," she said. "It looks like… a tiny little piece of knapped obsidian."

It certainly explained Adam's wound. Obsidian could be chipped into a terribly fine edge. That was why Mesoamerican societies had used the stone to create blades and arrowheads. Though brittle, the facets could be sharper than Adam's machete blade.

Ellie shifted her perspective. From the path, the knife-like sliver would have been nearly invisible.

With a jolt, she realized that there were more of them. A spine of tiny, razor sharp slivers bristled from the column.

"They're all over it!" she declared.

Adam's mouth formed a grimmer line. He plucked the torch from her and directed his sharp blue gaze out over the twisting, maze-like chamber.

Glittering shards of black stone winked at them from almost every surface.

"This place is full of them," Ellie said in slow horror. "We can't touch anything without the risk of being shredded."

"Didn't you say Xibalba had a cave of razors?" Adam asked.

"The House of Knives," Ellie replied uncomfortably.

"Gotta admire their attention to detail," he muttered.

Ellie gazed out at the labyrinth, chilled with fear. The path was a veritable tightrope. They would have to squeeze between stalagmites, duck under veils of stone, and edge around boulders, all of which were lined with blades... and that was just what she could see from where she stood.

Adam's wound was nasty enough, but as long as they could keep it from becoming infected, it wouldn't be life threatening.

A cut to a wrist or thigh could have them bleeding out within minutes on the floor of the cave.

"How are we supposed to get through this?" Ellie burst out nervously.

"Very damned carefully," Adam retorted as he gazed at the death trap before them.

Adam set the pace, and they picked their way forward through the maze. He held the torch overhead as he moved with the slow, careful tread of a stalking panther. Ellie kept her own steps just as painstaking, wary of the glinting daggers of stone that flashed at her in the torchlight from every angle.

Ellie wondered if she and Adam might avoid the obstacle course more readily if they simply left the path. A glance at the black shards shimmering at her from the further reaches of the cave killed that notion dead. The people who had built this place had done their work thoroughly.

Built it, Ellie thought with wonder as she squeezed her way between two close-set rows of knives. All of this had been deliberately constructed by the people of Tulan. The challenges she walked through had likely been pulled from their now-lost myths of heroism and kingship. Those stories had carried such importance that whispers of them had filtered down into the annals of the neighboring cultures across hundreds of years.

"It really is quite fascinating," Ellie said as she lay down on the ground and allowed Adam to drag her under a rippling limestone veil edged with obsidian scalpels.

"I'll appreciate it a bit more when it isn't trying to kill us," Adam replied. He picked up the torch again and turned to see what came next.

The light flickered across another stretch of claustrophobic knife-edged stone formations—but beyond them, a wide black mouth revealed the way to the next chamber.

Adam took a big step over a fallen column.

"Well, that's a relie—" he began.

His words were cut short as the ground beneath his boot gave out a loud, ominous crack.

Adam froze as he looked down. Beneath his foot, the stone of the cavern floor had snapped, revealing itself to be no more than a thin veneer disguised by a few centuries of dust and rubble.

Even as Ellie watched, a few more hairline cracks opened along the edges. The ground Adam stood on jarred another half-inch lower.

He sighed as he looked down.

"What's the betting this opens onto a nice big pit of those razors?" he said.

Ellie swallowed thickly.

"I should say it is probably likely," she replied.

"I'll jump for it," he announced.

"No!" Ellie burst out as she threw up a warning hand. "You'll put more pressure on the fracture."

He met her eyes evenly across the short distance that separated them.

"Then I'm going to step off it. Very carefully," he added.

"I would assume that any change in the dispersion of your weight could be problematic," she snapped back.

There was another soft crack and a shifting of pebbles.

"Leaving my weight where it is sounds pretty problematic as well, Princess," Adam warned.

Ellie made a quick and desperate assessment of the situation. Only one reasonable solution presented itself.

Her gaze shifted to a wide, flat circle of stone that lay just ahead of them. It was a remnant of some long-ago broken stalagmite.

"Set down the torch," Ellie ordered. "*Carefully.*"

"Why?" Adam demanded skeptically, even as he obeyed.

The ground shifted and snapped again beneath him at the slight motion.

"Are there any razors on that limestone shelf to your right?" Ellie prodded. She took a careful step back as she readied herself.

Adam glanced back at the platform. The move elicited another ominous crack from the trap under his boots.

"Nah," he said. "Looks like that bit's pretty—"

"Good," Ellie cut in and launched herself at him.

She had three paces of a running start. She used every inch of it, building up as much momentum as possible. There was just enough time for Adam's face to shift into lines of horrified surprise before Ellie reached the edge of the cracked stone and leaped.

Her shoulder collided with the solid mass of Adam's chest. Her arms flew around his waist. The impact sent him toppling backwards even as Ellie heard the rock giving way beneath his feet.

Adam landed on the shelf with an audible oomph. Ellie was sprawled on top of him.

She lifted her face from a pectoral to assess the damage. He was rubbing the back of his head and wincing.

"Are you intact?" she demanded as she pushed herself awkwardly to a sitting position.

"I… uh…" His expression went a bit blank as he looked down at where she straddled him with her hands braced on the dust-streaked musculature of his chest.

"Are you concussed?" Ellie demanded urgently. She felt a spark of panic.

He slowly let his head drop back down onto the stone and pointed his gaze deliberately at the ceiling.

"Not the time, Bates," he muttered to himself pointedly. "Not. The. Time."

Ellie's cheeks flushed as she realized the impropriety of their position. She scrambled awkwardly free of him and stood up to brush the dirt from her trousers.

Adam levered himself upright. He shook the dust out of his hair with his uninjured hand, and then hopped nimbly back up to his feet on the limited platform of the broken stalagmite.

He looked down at the place where he'd been standing. The floor had crumbled away beneath it, revealing a pit.

"Yup," he concluded. "Chock full of knives." He glanced ruefully at Ellie. "Thanks for that."

He was so very large, filthy, and under-dressed. The room began to feel a bit warmer. Ellie wondered if someone had let steam into it.

"It was no trouble at all," she replied weakly. "Maybe for the rest of this chamber, we should test the ground before we put our weight down on it."

"Sure," Adam agreed and promptly hopped off the platform.

"*Test* the ground, Bates!" Ellie exclaimed with strangled panic.

"What?" he complained. "This part had to be okay or it would've fallen in with the rest." He read the expression on her face and lifted his hands. "Got it. Very carefully."

Ellie gingerly slid her way off the ledge to stand beside him. Together, they turned toward the black, looming hole of the passage.

"What other tests did they have in that book of yours?" he asked carefully.

"There's a House of Bone Chilling Cold," she offered uncomfortably. "Er... a House of Jaguars, and, um..."

"I get the idea," Adam cut in grimly, and stalked—carefully—through the black-mouthed door.

FORTY

$\mathcal{T}$HERE WAS A House of Bone Chilling Cold.

It lay at the bottom of a long, sloping passage, and it was full of running water. The air was frigid enough that Ellie could see the fog of her breath. Only the impact of a recent cave-in saved them from being forced to wade or swim through the freezing depths of the deep, quick-moving stream. Part of the ceiling had given way to collapse into the river. The breakdown formed a natural course of boulders around which the water churned.

The stones were submerged in places. She and Adam waded across them awkwardly. Ellie's boots slid on the slick surface. The water didn't rise higher than her ankles, but her feet still ached from the cold by the time they reached the far side.

Ellie thought of how much worse it might have been if they had been forced to swim.

"Ouch," Adam said. He danced a bit in his boots as they reached the end. "Will you still like me if I'm short a few toes?

The House of Jaguars was less of a danger because all of the jaguars inside of it were dead.

They lay in dusty sprawls of bone on the floor of a vast, open cavern. A latched wooden gate on one side would have kept them contained.

The chamber itself had been deliberately emptied of all but a few columns that the engineers of Tulan had clearly deemed necessary for support. When the cats were alive, the design would have given them free rein to pin down any prey that entered.

Ellie counted the bones of eight animals visible in the flickering light of the torch. Some lay alone. Others had curled up to die together. Nothing had disturbed their remains since they had passed away. The skeletons were still perfectly arranged on the floor of the cave as though the elegant beasts might get up and walk away with a look of feline disdain.

The reason for the cats' fate became clear when Ellie and Adam reached the far side of the vast, echoing space, where another gate blocked the way out.

"They were trapped." Ellie's voice shook with fury. "There are no natural sources of food or water down here. It must all have been brought from the surface. Nobody bothered to set them free."

"Maybe they didn't have time, Princess," Adam said.

"They should have *made* the time."

He set a gentle hand on her shoulder.

"We should keep moving," he said and guided her on.

A smell rose to meet them in the passage beyond the gate. It was faint at first—just a noxious hint to the atmosphere—but it grew stronger and richer as they progressed.

At last, Ellie followed Adam through the mouth of the tunnel into a shadowy, high-ceilinged chamber.

Her feet promptly slid out from underneath her.

Adam had braced himself against one of the stones. He tugged Ellie upright before she could fall, and then grunted with discomfort. She realized that he had used his wounded hand.

Ellie looked down. Their torch was burning lower. She didn't want to think about that too much yet. In the low, orange glow, the floor of the chamber appeared to be covered in thick slime.

The slime was very smelly.

Ellie took a careful step to better balance herself, and the ground crunched lightly under her boot. Glancing down, she saw small animal bones protruding from the sludge.

"What in the name of—" she began, but Adam cut her off by pressing a hand to her mouth.

Ellie started to protest, but he only shook his head. His expression was uncharacteristically serious. He put a finger to his lips, and then pointed up.

Her stomach knotted. The ceiling of the cave was covered in hanging bodies with brown fur and thick, leathery skin.

They were bats—terrifyingly large bats.

Ellie estimated that the animals were roughly four feet in length with wingspans broader than a man's outstretched arms. They clung to the roof of the cave with massive black claws. As she watched, one of them yawned lazily, revealing an array of pale, knife-like fangs.

She could hear the animals around her. The sound was easy to overlook—just the subtle breathing and rustling of a hundred sleeping monsters.

Adam yanked her back into the tunnel. They crouched there together.

"What the hell are those?" he demanded in a whisper.

"I…" Ellie's hands were shaking from the sight of the impossible, living nightmares. "I think they're Camazotz."

Adam ran a hand over his face. He was so filthy that the gesture only smeared the dirt.

"Bat Guy," he muttered unhappily. "Bat Guy is real. Great."

"How could they have survived down here all this time?" Ellie protested.

"They must have a way out to feed," Adam replied.

Feed.

The horror of it swept over her. She thought of the slaughter back on the trail—the wild eyes of the dying man on the ground before her. The holes in his partner's skull. The blood all over the leaves. The ravaged jaguar the day before.

Salió de la noche.

It had come out of the night.

The creatures responsible for that violence were sleeping in legions over her head.

Padre Kuyoc hadn't been lying back in Santa Dolores when he'd warned Adam about monsters. They were here, and they were real enough that Ellie could have reached out and touched them—if the very notion of it didn't make her blood run cold with terror.

She took a breath. Going faint from panic wasn't going to help their situation. She had to *think*.

"How did those twins of yours get past these guys?" Adam demanded.

"I am… not strictly certain that they did," Ellie admitted uncomfortably.

"Fantastic," Adam grumbled. He eyed the entrance to the cavern with obvious reluctance. "How about we try for 'very damned quietly?'"

They crept back out into the sighing, rustling horror of the cavern. Ellie's boots crunched over small bones in the thick slime of guano that covered the floor.

Sometimes the bones were larger.

She winced against every crackle, exquisitely aware of the mass of horrible brown bodies suspended over her head. Adam's low-burning torch seemed painfully bright, but moving in the utter darkness they would face without the torch was even more terrifying.

Ellie let her eyes adjust as the light worked its way into the farther reaches of the room.

The cavern was easily the largest that they had encountered so far. Rock formations dotted the floor and ceiling, though they were closer and less profuse here than they had been in the House of Razors.

To her right, the cavern's expanse was broken by a shelf of stone that rose to within fifteen or so feet of the ceiling. It looked like part of some other cavern that had partially collapsed long ago to merge with this one. The edge of the platform broke off just beneath a ragged hole in the roof that opened to a glimpse of wind-tossed trees and dark sky.

That had to be the way the bats were getting out. The notion made her stomach lurch.

Silently and carefully, Ellie picked her way through the space, following in Adam's track. He muttered a curse as he adjusted his grip on the torch to avoid getting burned. The flame was inching lower. She wondered what they were going to do when it ran out.

There were piles of guano on the floor. Ellie pressed her remaining sleeve to her nose against the smell and glanced up.

"Bates," Ellie whispered. She caught Adam's arm and pointed through the sleeping bodies. "Are those ropes?"

Adam looked up with a frown.

Thick, dark cords wove through the roost. They disappeared behind the remaining columns of stone, slipping out of the torchlight.

"Looks like it," Adam agreed.

"But what on earth are they for?" Ellie pressed.

"Why don't we hope we don't have to find out?" he countered and led them carefully onward.

A ripple of lightning flashed above, sending an eerie purple light through the cavern. Ellie spotted something in the brief flicker of illumination.

She gently tugged Adam toward it, and then bit back a curse as her boots slipped once more against the slick floor.

As they moved closer, the object she sought shifted into the range of the torchlight.

It was a column that rose from the floor of the chamber to the ceiling. It would have been of roughly the same thickness from top to bottom—if a chunk hadn't been neatly cut out of the center of it.

The lower portion was roughly the height of Ellie's waist. It ended in a flat, round platform. Three feet above it, the pillar continued to the ceiling.

The platform was more or less free of guano—one of the only surfaces in the cave that could boast as much. In the center of it sat a knife. The weapon was made of metal that had oxidized to a pale green.

Another flicker of lightning revealed that the pillar had been positioned to aptly catch the light through the opening in the ceiling.

Thunder rumbled distantly through the cavern. The bats above her stirred. Ellie's nerves jangled.

"What do you think it's for?" she said, dropping her voice to the lowest whisper.

"I'd guess it's for fighting them," Adam whispered back as his gaze flashed to the dark shapes that hung overhead.

Ellie considered the blade. Its shape was odd. The artifact was roughly the size of Adam's machete, but the metal jigged and jagged in a way that was oddly familiar to her.

"It looks like a key," she blurted under her breath as the realization clicked into place.

Adam frowned, and then looked past the pillar to the far wall of the cavern. He moved toward it, with Ellie following.

The light bloomed over the stones and revealed the distinct shape of another carved doorway. This one was blocked by a wooden door.

A ring hung from the center. Adam gave it a tug.

"Locked," he announced.

The wall of the cave was angled rather than strictly vertical. It made the door seem more like a cellar hatch.

The ring was bolted into a metal disk embedded in the old, thick boards. There was a narrow slot cut into the center of it.

"Keyhole," Ellie declared.

They glanced back toward the cut pillar together.

"And that's the key?" Adam suggested.

"It seems a reasonable hypothesis," Ellie agreed.

More thunder boomed softly as they returned to the column. The bats shuffled and creaked above them. One of the monsters extended its wings in a stretch. Ellie froze, feeling desperately exposed on the open floor of the cave.

The knife was a dull green shape in the light of the torch as they gazed down at it.

"Why do I feel like there's no way it could be this easy?" Adam muttered lowly.

Ellie grimaced as she looked at the artifact.

"Probably because it's not," she admitted in a whisper. "Perhaps we should..."

"Eh, might as well find out," Adam cut in and picked the relic up.

The top of the pillar jolted up by two inches.

Ellie realized that the surface wasn't stone at all. It was wood, disguised with plaster and dust. The pillar appeared to be hollow. *More counterweights*, she thought with a little burst of excitement.

Her wonder quickly shifted to unease at the creak of something turning under the false platform.

The ropes above her began to move.

Adam whirled with the torch, and the light picked out a row of weights bound with more rope, which were descending the wall of the cavern.

"Ellie..." he began uneasily.

The rest of his words were cut off as a cacophony of oddly resonant, out-of-tune bells shattered through the silence. Swinging clusters of clubs and hammers slammed into the surfaces of the stalactites. The stones rang out in dissonant tones.

With a rustling crash, a barrier dropped into place over the hole in the ceiling, blocking it.

"Drat," Ellie blurted.

The cave exploded into a maelstrom of flying, screeching fangs.

Adam yanked Ellie across the guano-slick floor and tackled her into a nook sheltered by an overhanging rock.

Monsters wheeled through the cave in hungry panic.

"We're supposed to fight our way out of this with *that?*" Ellie shouted over the racket as she waved at the copper knife in Adam's hand.

"Maybe there are more of them than there used to be," he shouted back.

A pair of the enormous beasts swooped closer and crashed against their hiding place. Thick talons swung toward Ellie's face. She lurched back to press herself against the wall.

The bat flopped away, screeching, and Ellie queasily remembered the injuries on the men in the woods.

Of course, she thought with distant horror. Those holes in the man's skull made perfect sense. That was how carnivorous bats immobilized their prey.

Fear flashed up her spine, turning her sweat cold.

Their way out lay across thirty yards of cave swarmed with panicked flying mammals. Even if she and Adam dropped the torch, there was no way they could clear that distance without being attacked. Bats didn't need to see in order to find dinner.

"We need to get a better look at our options," Adam determined grimly.

He started to move out of their nook. Ellie hauled him back.

"Are you crazy?" she burst out.

"This isn't a great hiding place, if you hadn't noticed," he retorted.

He pressed her back as another bat slammed against the stones. It let out an ear-piercing scream.

"If you go out there, you're going to get yourself killed!" Ellie exclaimed.

"That's not *exactly* the plan…" Adam began.

Ellie grabbed him by the arms and gave him a shake—though not much of one. It was like trying to budge a tree.

"I will not lose you to an army of monstrous bats!" she shouted over the racket.

Adam grinned back at her. His face was streaked with filth in the torchlight.

"Careful, Princess," he said happily. "I might start to think you like me."

Ellie let out a growl of frustration.

"Of all the infuriating—" she started.

He cut her off by yanking her in and kissing her.

Fireworks exploded across her nerves. Her hands slipped against the guano on his shoulders as she held onto him.

He broke the embrace and slapped the copper knife into her hand.

"Take this. Back in a minute," he said neatly and slipped out into the darkness.

"Blasted, reckless…" Ellie burst out as she slapped her hand against the stone with frustrated fury.

She was rewarded with a splatter of bat guano against her cheek.

"Yerrrgh!" she cried. She wiped it away with her remaining sleeve—and then jolted back as another bat slammed against her hiding place.

This one fell to the ground before the little crevice where Ellie crouched. It flopped there awkwardly… and then began to crawl.

The monster scrabbled against the stones with the small talons at the peaks of its wings, scratching and squeaking as it skittered toward her.

Ellie pressed herself back against the wall, holding the copper blade out in front of her. She wondered with a vague sense of terror if she would actually have to stab something with it.

A boot swept into the line of her vision as Adam kicked the bat soundly in the chest. The blow sent it rolling across the floor before it winged back up into the air.

"I have an idea," he announced as he slid in beside her. "But it's probably a pretty bad one."

"Is it better than having holes punched in our skulls?" Ellie shouted back.

"Er... probably?" he replied.

"Then fine!"

"I got a better look at the thing that fell over the hole in the ceiling," he said. "It's some kind of woven mat and it's pretty rotted out. I think the only reason the bats aren't busting out of here is because they can't see how weak it is."

"Not see," Ellie corrected him. "Hear. It probably sounds like a solid barrier to them."

"I think we can take it down if we use that ledge to get closer," Adam continued. "But you're going to have to do the work while I keep the bats off of you."

Ellie eyed the shelf of rock that filled the other half of the chamber.

The plan wasn't great—but it was better than hiding in a crack in the wall until something dragged them out of it.

"Let's do it," Ellie agreed.

Adam grasped her hand and tugged her out of their hiding place. They raced across the swarming, squealing chaos of the cavern to the base of the ledge, and then threw themselves against the shelter of a stalagmite.

"I'll give you a lift," Adam said as he extended his hands.

Ellie quickly stepped into them. She scrambled for a grip as Adam pushed her up along the wall of the ledge. Her fingers closed around a crack in the stone, and her boots scrabbled until her toe found a hold. With a grunt of effort, she reached the top and promptly sprawled onto her back.

A vast, black shape swooped over her, close enough for her to feel the wind of it as it passed.

Ellie rolled over and skidded closer to the wall for cover.

Adam's head popped over the side as he scaled his way up. He joined her, tucking in under a natural curve of stone.

They gazed out over their destination—the place where the ledge broke away under the blocked opening to the outside. The air around it was swarming with bats. The animals obviously remembered where their way out was supposed to be and were infuriated to find it blocked.

Ellie blanched.

"How are we supposed to do anything out there other than get ourselves mauled?" she protested.

"I told you. I'll keep them off of you," Adam assured her, pitching his voice to be heard over the whirlwind of outraged monsters.

"And the cover?" she pressed. "What's your plan for that?"

Adam lifted her hand and slapped something into her palm. Ellie stared down at it.

"*A rock*?" she blurted.

"You have a better idea?" he shouted in return.

"I don't even know if I can throw that far!"

"If you can't throw that far," he shot back, "then you're going to have to fight the bats while *I* throw. Which job do you want?"

Ellie swallowed thickly.

"I'll take the rock," she conceded.

"Then let's go!"

With a tug on her arm, Adam propelled her out of their hiding place and bolted onto the ledge. Ellie ran after him, and then skidded to a stop at the end of it.

She froze with shock.

Bats whirled around her, screeching with panic and hunger. Adam had dropped the torch by their feet, which freed his hands to hold both the copper knife and his machete as he stood behind her, facing the maelstrom.

This was fully, completely insane, Ellie determined numbly.

"Bit more throwing would be nice, Princess!" Adam shouted to her as he slammed the butt of his machete into a bat that swooped down at them. The blow sent it screeching off in protest.

Ellie eyed the sagging, half-rotted cover overhead. Steeling herself, she brought back her arm and launched the stone into the air.

It arced out before her... and then fell, missing the cover. Her missile disappeared into the whirling animals.

"I lost the rock!" Ellie shouted.

Adam swung at another bat.

"So find another!" he yelled back wildly.

Ellie dropped to her knees to scrabble through the dirt and guano. Her fingers clasped around the curves of another stone.

She lurched back to her feet and launched it at the cover.

This time, it actually reached the rotting mat... bouncing against it weakly before pinging down to the floor of the cave.

A few more bits of debris rained down around her.

"More rocks!" Adam called out from behind her as he knocked another bat aside.

Ellie scrambled for another stone.

"I found one!" she announced happily. She stood—and then let out a scream of alarm at the bat zooming toward her.

She threw herself to the ground as her hand flailed out for the torch. Grasping it, she swung the flame up.

The bat veered away with a screech of alarm and the smell of scorched fur.

Above her, Adam yelped out a curse, dodging back as another monster swooped at him with its thick, twisted talons extended.

Ellie grabbed the nearest rock and staggered to her feet. She looked down at it where it lay in her palm.

"Make the next one count, Princess!" Adam shouted behind her as he swung his machete again.

Ellie looked up at the dry, sagging timbers of the cover with its trailing tendrils of loose bark and rope.

Her gaze shifted to the torch she held in her other hand.

Ellie dropped the rock. She scrambled forward to grasp a long, thin stick that had fallen with the other debris from the hole.

Bracing the stick between her knees, Ellie jammed the end of the torch onto it. The result was something like a fiery javelin. She gave it a shake to test the construction and was satisfied.

"What are you doing?" Adam called out as he ducked another bat and flailed out with the copper blade.

"I am improvising," Ellie snapped—and launched her makeshift spear into the air.

It arced up beautifully.

The broken stick jammed itself neatly into the tangled mat of the roof… and with a soft whoosh, the whole of it burst into flames.

Ellie let out a whoop of triumph.

Adam grabbed her around the waist and tackled her backwards as the cover collapsed.

The flaming mass rushed past them. It slammed onto the end of the ledge with a shower of sparks before tipping and plummeting to the ground below.

Bats screamed in protest. They wheeled from the flaming, falling debris, and then spilled through the hole into the gusting, storm-tossed night.

The entire colony fled, whirling into the darkness as thunder boomed hollowly through the cavern.

It began to rain.

The downpour was thick and instantaneous. Water gushed down through the opening and splattered against the guano-stained floor.

Ellie watched it all with wonder—and then a lurch of guilt.

"Did we just unleash a horde of hungry monsters on the camp?" she asked weakly.

Adam rubbed his face. "Maybe they're not that hungry," he offered.

He led her back down the ledge to where the remains of the cover smoldered under the perfect circle of the torrent. The embers that had scattered outside the range of the rain were the only source of light in the cave.

The cavern had been a death trap a minute before. Now it was quiet save for the soft rush of the falling rain. The water poured down in a thick, wild curtain, accented by the boom of more thunder overhead.

The last remnants of the debris sizzled as Adam and Ellie picked their way along. They had just managed to reach the door when the flames behind them guttered, dropping them once more into darkness.

Ellie put her hand to the wood and felt across the surface.

A streak of lightning from the storm above them cast a distant, purple flash through the cavern.

She set her hand to the slender gap of the keyhole.

"Give me the knife," she said.

Adam's fingers brushed her arm, and then followed the length of it down.

"Let me," he said, and Ellie pulled away.

She heard the scrape of metal, and then the grate of something turning. She took a quick step back as Adam yanked the hatch up in front of her.

"I've got it," Adam said from the darkness beside her. "Feel your way in. I'll follow."

Ellie's fingers danced out before her to find the edges of the opening. She stepped inside—and immediately began to slip.

"Adam!" she yelped—and plummeted down a smooth, slick tunnel.

She heard his rough curse… and then the thud of the door as he plunged after her.

FORTY-ONE

𝒯HE TUNNEL LAUNCHED Ellie into a jumbled pile of rubble.

She bit out a curse as she landed and felt new bruises spring to life on her skin. The space around her was unimpeachably black.

Ellie struggled to stand, but the loose mess of the ground beneath her shifted. She barely managed to scramble out of the way before Adam crashed into the place where she'd been lying a moment before.

The rubble clattered in protest at his arrival. It sounded oddly hollow.

Ellie crawled toward the spot where she had heard him land.

"Ow," Adam grunted. His hands fumbled for her through the darkness. One of them grasped an arm. The other one latched onto a shin. "Ellie?"

"It's me," she replied as she tried to figure out which end of him was up. Her hand found stubble, and she breathed a sigh of relief.

Awkwardly, she regained her feet, and then caught herself against Adam as the ground continued to clatter and roll under her boots.

"What the hell are we standing on?" Adam demanded.

Echoes told her that this space was smaller than the one they had just left. Water trickled through it somewhere.

Ellie reached down, waving her hand around until it brushed against part of the debris. She grasped the piece of rubble and lifted it blindly before her.

The object in her hand was too light and smooth to be stone. It was the size of a small melon.

Ellie ran her fingers over its contours. They were round as a child's ball... until her fingers dipped into a sudden recess.

That, too, was round, as was a second recess that lay right beside it.

She shifted her fingers lower as an awful suspicion rose in her mind. They

403

brushed across a row of distinctive ridges.

"Adam?" Ellie said carefully as her pulse jumped uncomfortably.

"What now?" he groaned.

"I believe I am holding a human skull."

Adam's hands brushed over hers as he explored the object that she held.

"Yeah," he concluded as he plucked it from her hands. "That's a skull."

She heard the soft clatter as he set it down.

"We're standing in a pile of bones," Ellie said. "Aren't we?"

"Do you really want me to answer that?" Adam returned tentatively.

Ellie's weight shifted a bit. The ground rolled under her boots in protest and she dropped down another inch.

"How many bones *are* there?" she exclaimed.

"Er... sounds like a lot of them, Princess," he said.

"Could they be animal bones?" Ellie pressed hopefully.

"Sure," Adam replied a bit too quickly.

She closed her eyes as she fought a sudden burst of nausea.

"Right," Ellie said thinly.

Closing her eyes didn't make much difference. She couldn't see anything with them when they were open, either.

"I think I'd better chance a match," Adam said uneasily from beside her.

"Certainly," Ellie agreed.

The words came out more steadily than they had any right to, given that something—a tibia, perhaps?—had just cracked under her heel.

Adam rustled in his pocket. A moment later, a tentative spark of light flared to life.

The first thing Ellie saw was his face. He was filthy.

Ellie was filthy as well. She was certain that she was the filthiest she had ever been in her life. It almost made her laugh—but then her eyes adjusted to take in more of their surroundings.

They were not standing in a pool of bones. They were at the edge of a veritable mountain of them.

The mound rose to fill most of the chamber. It peaked on the opposite side, just below a dark opening that Ellie could see in the upper corner.

The mass of the dead was easily three times Adam's height. It spilled out to flood the edges of the floor. From the shape of the pile, Ellie could tell that the bodies to which the bones had once belonged must have been dropped through the hole in the ceiling like so much refuse.

Her gut wrenched with the horror of it.

There were animals in the pile. She picked out the skulls of deer, jaguars, birds, and lizards. There were also people... a very great number of people.

Some of them were small.

Her brain skipped and stuttered as it struggled to think of what that meant.

The match burned out, and Adam muttered a curse.

Ellie grasped for logic.

"This is..." She swallowed thickly. Her throat had gone dry. "This is extremely valuable material for understanding the culture of Tulan, which must provide us with a great deal of insight into how other Mesoamerican societies were shaped. And of course, there are indications that human sacrifice was part of the religious and political practices of the greater region, even if the accounts come primarily from the Spanish conquistadors and must therefore be taken with a healthy grain of skepticism." Her hands were shaking. Ellie clenched them as the words kept spilling out. "Why in the Florentine Codex—"

"Princess..." Adam cut in gently as his hand found her arm.

Ellie pulled in a breath. She felt dizzy.

"There are so many of them," she said weakly.

"Yeah," he replied through the darkness.

"Why are they down here?" she pleaded.

"I don't know," he returned. He squeezed her arm. "I'm gonna light another match, and we're both going to look for a way out of here."

"Very sensible," Ellie agreed.

Her voice was steady even as her insides twisted with something like grief.

The bones were an important part of the archaeological record.

They threw children down here.

The record...

Another match flared to life. The sight of Adam's face was an anchor, reminding her that she wasn't alone.

They would get out of this.

Adam's gaze rose to the top of the charnel pile, where Ellie could see the dark mouth of the tunnel down which the dead must have been thrown.

No, she thought with quick, frantic fear. *Not that way. Please not that way.*

She tore her eyes away from it and dropped them to the ground.

They fell on the shape of a little leather sandal poking out from among the bones by her calf.

Ellie fought the urge to scream.

"Over there." Adam's voice cut through the storm raging inside of her even as the light hissed out once more.

Darkness fell over them again. His hand slipped to her cheek.

"Hey. You all right?" he asked.

Ellie took a breath.

"I am fine," she replied. Her voice was almost entirely steady. "I am a scholar."

"You can be other things, too," Adam quietly replied.

There were lives piled around her boots.

Ellie let herself lean forward. The movement brought her softly up against his chest. It smelled like mud and bats.

She stayed there and drew in a deep, shuddering breath as his hand stroked across her back.

"We should follow the wall," he said. Ellie could feel the vibration of his voice through his skin. "We'll take it slowly."

"Yes," Ellie agreed distantly.

She pushed herself back and straightened.

Adam led them awkwardly across the shifting, treacherous ground until his hand brushed stone. They followed the curve of the cavern through the darkness, shuffling their way carefully through the lesser tumble of the outer edge of the bone pile.

"We're here," he announced.

He lit another match. Ellie gazed up at a long, sloping tunnel, the floor of which had been neatly cut into stairs.

"Looks like we're getting close to something," Adam concluded.

Leaving the mountain of the dead behind her, Ellie tiredly climbed.

Sound began to whisper down at her from the darkness ahead. At first, Ellie took it for the murmur of more water, but after a few steps, it resolved itself into the distant echo of voices.

She gave Adam's arm a warning squeeze.

"I heard it," he murmured back to her.

There was a soft scrape as he took his machete from the sheath.

The voices rose as they continued upward... and then Ellie realized that she could see.

There was just enough light for her to pick out the general line of Adam's shoulders, but the soft glow grew as they moved until more distinct gleams of it painted the walls of their tunnel.

Adam slowed. Glancing back at her, he put a finger to his lips. Ellie gave a silent nod in acknowledgment.

The tones grew more distinct. Words took shape—and Ellie heard a voice that she recognized.

"...size it properly. And don't touch anything!"

It was Dawson.

The sound made her skin crawl. It also banished the lingering tendrils of grief and horror from the pit of bones below, burning them up in a quick wave of outrage.

One thing was certain—whatever lay above them, Dawson wouldn't be there alone.

Adam kept the machete in his hand as they reached the top of the stairs and edged into a dim, narrow room.

The chamber had been deliberately carved from the cave into a regular shape. Its walls were covered in art.

The painted murals depicted images of richness and beauty. A king emerged from the earth, surrounded by well-wishers who anointed his body with oils and painted it with flashes of bright color. A jaguar skin was set over his shoulders, while his long black hair was elaborately braided and dressed.

She and Adam must have stumbled into some sort of antechamber where those who had just undertaken the journey of initiation through the caves were made ready for what came next.

Ellie's eyes halted on an image that showed the king standing in a shallow basin as he was ritually washed by his servants. In the painting, blue water spilled over him from an opening in the wall.

Her gaze shifted up to where a truncated copper tube emerged from the stone just above her head.

Another piece of metal protruded from the base of it, looking remarkably like a handle.

Adam had moved to the farther end of the room, where he pressed himself to the wall as he carefully peered out.

Ellie's hand itched.

She couldn't possibly be considering reaching out and twisting an artifact of a lost culture. It could be incredibly fragile.

It didn't look very fragile.

As she watched, a small bead of water collected at the lip of the tube and then dripped down to the stones under her boots.

Ellie glanced down and saw a small stalagmite growing there.

Her eyes shot to the handle again.

What if she was very, *very* careful?

Glancing over at Adam as if afraid he would catch her, Ellie grasped the handle and gently, gingerly twisted it.

Something grated inside the wall, and a spill of water rushed out, splattering over the top of her head.

Ellie spluttered against it and stepped back as Adam whirled toward her from his post by the exit, frowning with alarm and disapproval.

Elie couldn't bring herself to care. She was far too excited. The water was still coming, splashing across her boots.

"They have plumbing!" she hissed with an excited squeak.

Adam stalked over, grabbed her by the arm, and pulled her to the end of the chamber.

He stopped her at the edge of it, where he turned her to face what lay outside.

"We've got trouble," he muttered at her ear.

FORTY-TWO

*T*HROUGH THE NARROW exit of the antechamber, Ellie peered out at a cavern the size of a cathedral nave.

The ceiling arched forty feet overhead, dripping with elegant stalactites in pale hues. Paraffin lanterns cast a warm glow over spectacular columns and frozen falls of glittering limestone. Some of the formations obstructed her view of exactly what lay ahead of them. Ellie could only make out the vastness of the space—and the sound of voices.

"Careful with that!" Dawson complained. "We don't have a replacement for it."

Ellie drew in a sharp breath. She and Adam had risked their lives to successfully navigate the path of an ancient initiation rite... only to discover that their enemies had made it there first.

"How are they here?" she demanded in a whisper. "They couldn't possibly have traversed through the caves without us noticing them."

Adam turned to peer over her shoulder—and then stopped.

"Er... probably through that door," he replied uneasily.

Ellie looked to where he nodded. In the wall of the cavern across from where they hid, a perfectly rectangular opening had been cut into the rock. Ellie could just make out the start of a flight of steep, twisting stairs in the light of another lantern that had been left there.

"But where does it go?" she burst out.

"The chamber at the top of the temple," Adam replied.

Ellie whirled back to give him a wide-eyed look.

"How on earth do you know that?" she demanded.

He shifted awkwardly and scratched at his stubble.

"Possibly because I maybe opened it for them," he replied.

"You *what?*" Ellie burst out.

Adam tugged her back into the antechamber. "I didn't *know* I was opening any doors," he complained lowly.

"How do you open a door without knowing about it?" Ellie shot back in a whisper.

"All I did was push a button! You know—kind of like how you just turned on the waterworks?" he added defensively as he jabbed a finger toward the water that still trickled from the pipe in the wall.

Ellie pressed her fingers to her temple.

"Perhaps we should both refrain from more button-pushing for now," she concluded tensely. "We need to focus on exactly what our options are."

"We've gotta be directly under the pyramid," Adam concluded.

"How can you be certain of that?" she pressed.

He led her back over to the exit, careful to keep both of their bodies in the shadows. He pointed at the nearer wall of the cavern.

"See that? The stone's a different color at the back of this chamber," he whispered.

Ellie realized that he was right. Though that part of the cave was still fairly shadowy, she could tell that the wall was a much darker gray. What was more, the stone there was free of rock formations even though Ellie could see water actively pouring down its surface.

There was rather a lot of water, she realized.

"The waterfall behind the pyramid!" she exclaimed quietly. "That's why we couldn't see where it went. It's filtering down into the cave system."

A stream flowed from the base of the wall. It was broad, shallow, and perfectly clear. Where it passed near their hiding place, Ellie could pick out each tiny stone under the surface with perfect clarity.

"We must be at the edge of the karst," Ellie mused. "Those mountains would be a harder sedimentary rock, not limestone. The water wouldn't penetrate through them the same way. That means this is where the caves must end."

"We've got bigger problems than geology," Adam muttered. He gently turned her shoulders to direct her attention to the other end of the cavern, where Dawson's voice echoed stridently against the dripping stalagmites.

"Make sure you've measured that correctly!" he ordered petulantly. "We can't risk lifting the artifact and discovering it won't fit."

Boots scraped against stone. A whiff of freshly cut wood drifted toward her as the cave clattered with the sound of hammering.

Adam held up a warning hand, signaling for Ellie to wait as he crept forward. She peered over his shoulder as he risked a better look beyond their hiding place.

The rest of the cavern came into view. It was breathtaking. The space soared overhead, iced with dripping white stalactites. More rock formations covered the ground at the edges of the cavern, but the center of the space had been deliberately cleared and leveled save for the remains of a single enormous stalagmite, which sat in the very center of it all.

The stone had been cut off about two feet from the floor, forming a level platform like the one which had held the copper knife back in the room of monstrous bats. This, too, appeared to serve as an altar for a sacred object.

Ellie could just make out a glimpse of what lay there from where she hovered behind Adam's elbow.

In the gentle hollow carved from the remains of the broken pillar lay a striking glimmer of black stone so flawless that it almost looked like a pool.

It had to be the Smoking Mirror.

The artifact was big. Even though Ellie's angle kept her from seeing it in its entirety, she could deduce that much based on the size of the sturdy crate that Charlie, Lessard, and Pacheco were in the process of constructing on the floor of the cave beside the altar.

The sight of it sparked a wave of fury. Here were Dawson and Jacobs, secure and self-satisfied in their victory as they prepared to pack up their prize and carry it off—and to hell with whatever damage they had done in the process.

It made Ellie want to kick something.

She held back. Besides Charlie and the small company of builders, there were five of Jacobs' armed guards, each of them with their rifles ready. Ellie recognized Buller and Price. Pickett's bulging eyes were fixed on one of the stalactites overhead as though he were puzzling over how it worked.

Staines stood nearer by. Adam's guard looked a bit worse for wear. His cheek was darkened by the rash of an abrasion and the sleeve of his shirt was muddied and torn. He was carrying Adam's Winchester. He handled the weight of it gingerly as though his arm was sore.

Flowers was there as well. His posture was relaxed as he seemingly oversaw the men constructing the crate.

Beyond the mirror, the ceiling on the far side of the cavern lowered to a little more than Adam's height. The shallow stream of water from the falls collected there, deepening from something that would barely cover Ellie's boots to a proper pool. The surface of it swirled with movement. That was a clear sign that there must be some further opening in the cave through which the water was running on to somewhere else.

Ellie filed that bit of information away for later.

"We can't risk prying it up," Dawson complained. "We have no idea how brittle it is or what sort of damage we might do. It will need to be lifted, with men all the way around the circumference."

"There is a better way. Perhaps I could show you."

Ellie startled at the sound of another familiar voice. She risked a farther peek out into the cavern.

Padre Kuyoc stood in the center of it, still wearing his bizarre breastplate of hollowed reeds. He was smiling cheerfully at a sweating, flustered Dawson.

"What the hell is the priest doing down here?" Adam demanded.

"When I saw him in the plaza, he said something about *trying* to get caught," Ellie offered awkwardly.

"So that he could help a bunch of colonizers steal a dangerous magical artifact?" Adam returned skeptically.

Before Ellie could answer, Jacobs stepped from the shadows bordering the clearing.

"How very interesting," he said smoothly as he approached the priest. "And why would you do that for us?"

Kuyoc's eyes glittered. "Because you seem like the sort of men who reward good helpers. And maybe I like rewards," he replied.

From the shadows of her hiding place at the mouth of the antechamber, Ellie frowned.

"The padre didn't strike me as the mercenary sort," she whispered.

"He's not," Adam returned bluntly. "The old man's got another game here. I just hope to hell it's not going to get him shot."

As Ellie watched, Kuyoc reached into the pockets of his trousers. His hands emerged with a neatly rolled cigar and a slender box of matches.

Kuyoc set the cigar to his lips, lighting a match and puffing it to a low, orange light.

He smiled at Jacobs and held the tobacco out to him.

"Share a little k'uutz?" Kuyoc asked.

Jacobs took a step closer. He eyed the cigar thoughtfully without reaching out to take it, and then he raised his gaze to Kuyoc's face once more.

"You wouldn't be here to cause any trouble," he asked, his voice dangerously soft. "Would you?"

Ellie's throat tightened as her pulse quickened with instinctive fear.

No, she thought silently and instinctively. *Don't answer. Don't say anything*

Don't tell him a lie.

"Me?" Kuyoc replied comfortably. His eyes were still sharp. "What sort of trouble could I be?"

Jacobs tilted his head thoughtfully.

"Why don't you tell me?" he calmly demanded.

Kuyoc shrugged.

"None at all, patrón," he returned easily.

Jacobs smiled. The expression was thin as a razor blade. Ellie gripped the stones more tightly.

"Thank you," he replied.

He waved a casual order to Buller.

"Shoot him," Jacobs said.

Adam's arm circled her waist. Ellie hadn't even realized that she had started to charge out of the antechamber.

"Not like that, Princess," he whispered tightly at her ear. "You can't help him if you're dead."

The men by the crate—Charlie, Lessard, Pacheco, and Flowers—had all gone still. The sound of their hammers died as they stared between Jacobs and the priest. Ellie could practically see the wheels churning in Charlie's head. She suspected that Adam's wry ally was frantically calculating his odds of intervening successfully on the priest's behalf.

For his part, Buller was looking uncomfortably from Kuyoc to Jacobs. Shooting a priest must have stretched the limits of his admittedly flexible moral boundaries.

"Hold on!" Dawson protested as he scrambled over to where they stood. "What if he actually knows something about the mirror?"

"Do you?" Jacobs demanded as he turned back to Kuyoc.

Kuyoc's front of cheerfulness had dropped. He looked at Jacobs with all the clarity and discernment Ellie knew him to possess.

"Yes," the priest said flatly.

Jacobs looked thoughtful.

"Tie him to the column, then," he ordered.

Buller and Price moved more readily to obey. The two guards easily hauled the slight, wiry priest to one of the thick stone pillars that punctuated the periphery of the cavern. Staines stumbled over with a length of rope.

"His crazy shirt's in the way," Staines complained. He waved a hand at Kuyoc's homemade breastplate.

"So take it off him," Jacobs snapped in reply.

Kuyoc raised a quick hand as Staines and Price moved to follow Jacobs' command, holding them off. With a few quick tugs on the cords that bound his contraption together, he loosened it, shrugged it over his head, and held it out to the guards.

"Careful with that," Kuyoc cautioned Staines deliberately.

Staines uneasily shoved the garment at Price.

The bigger guard sighed and tossed the bundle of reeds aside. The breast-plate slid across the floor of the cave, coming to rest at the wall right near to where a dark crevice broke the smooth limestone surface.

Could the opening be another way out?

Ellie's brain lurched automatically into a rapid calculation. She considered the position of the antechamber and the angle of the tunnel through which she and Adam had climbed to reach it.

Her stomach sank. The hole must be the other end of the opening that had sat at the top of the mountain of bones. That meant it was the gap through which all those people and animals had been thrown.

Had they been killed right here? She wondered over it queasily as she peered out at the graceful beauty of the cavern.

Price and Staines finished binding the priest to the pillar. The job complete, they ambled away. Staines winced a bit as he bent over to retrieve Adam's Winchester from the floor.

"You said he was trying to get caught," Adam complained in a low grumble. "Was he also trying to get himself tied to a rock?"

"I'm guessing that wasn't part of his plan," Ellie admitted.

Adam gave a tired sigh and rubbed a muddy hand over his features. "Great," he concluded and neatly slipped from the tunnel.

Ellie instinctively dropped to a crouch as she watched him dart across the shallow flow of water and tuck himself behind a rippling stone formation.

No one noticed. All of the men in the room were once again focused on watching the construction of the crate.

With a breath, Ellie followed after Adam.

Her boots splashed down into the cool stream, the sound amplified by her nerves. Ellie hurried through it to the cover of the ragged field of stones that bordered the clearer ground, keeping to the shadows where the glare of the paraffin lights failed to penetrate.

Adam gently caught her arm as she reached him. He pressed a finger to his lips in warning. Silently, he led her through the maze. They darted from stalagmites to thick limestone columns as they circled the cavern, inching their way toward the bound priest.

Finally, Ellie tucked herself behind a fall of debris beside the column where Kuyoc was bound.

Staines and Price had wandered back over to the others. Now that the priest had been confined, nobody paid him much mind.

"Are you all right?" she asked, pitching her voice to a hushed whisper—one that wouldn't be heard over the clamor of the hammering and the constantly rushing water.

The priest sighed and chuckled lowly to himself.

"Why should I be surprised that you are here?" he muttered—then his eyes narrowed as he threw a quick glance toward her hiding place. "How *are* you here?"

"We took the long way," Adam replied from where he hovered in the shadow of a massive stalagmite. He kept a wary eye on Jacobs, Dawson, and their men.

"The Path of Kings?" Kuyoc demanded as his tone sharpened. "The pair of you walked the *Path of Kings*?"

"If by that you mean all the demon god puzzles and skull-eating bats," Adam grumbled. "Then yup. Sure did."

"We're going to get you out of here," Ellie promised with an intent look at the men in the center of the cavern. "But I'm afraid that first, Mr. Bates and I need to make sure those two do not leave this place with that mirror."

Kuyoc startled.

"*That's* why you walked through the caves?" he demanded. "To stop them getting the glass?"

"Sssh!" Ellie urged as Staines threw a frowning look back at where they crouched.

"Well—somebody did throw us in a well," Adam admitted.

Ellie shot him a glare.

"That was you. *You* threw us in a well," she pointed out.

"And what did you plan to do with it?" Kuyoc cut in.

"The well?" Ellie said, confused.

"The glass," Kuyoc repeated with barely concealed impatience. "After you stopped those two from getting it."

"We hadn't really thought that far ahead," Adam said. He scratched his stubble a little ruefully.

"We just knew they couldn't be allowed to leave with it," Ellie offered stoutly—or as stoutly as she could while still whispering. "Because it's…"

Her voice trailed off at the awkwardness of the rest of the explanation.

"An object with the power of a god?" Kuyoc filled in dryly.

"You know!" Ellie gasped.

"What—you think I would be trying to destroy it with a bunch of dynamite if it was just a piece of furniture?" Kuyoc shot back.

"Destroy it!" Ellie squeaked.

"Hold on—*dynamite?*" Adam pressed at the same time.

Ten yards away, Staines turned and frowned.

Ellie dropped. She pressed herself closer against the stones as she heard the guard's steps move closer.

"You talking to yourself, crazy fool?" Staines demanded.

"Praying," Kuyoc corrected him neatly. "For God to protect me from the demons of this place sure to be outraged by your desecration."

The priest flashed Staines a slightly terrifying smile. Staines blanched.

"Shall I ask them to spare your soul from their vengeance?" the priest pressed.

"Yeah," Staines replied. "That would be very nice."

The guard hurried away.

"You can't possibly be serious," Ellie demanded. This time, she carefully kept her voice to a whisper.

"I wanna know more about this dynamite," Adam countered.

"Quiet," the priest ordered as he gazed out over the place where Dawson and Jacobs watched the last nails be driven into the crate. "I'm trying to make a plan."

"I've always been more of an improvisation kind of guy," Adam offered helpfully.

Ellie could practically see the quick, well-tuned wheels of Kuyoc's mind churning. His gaze settled on her with a force she could feel.

"What do you dream of?" he demanded.

"Me?" she protested weakly. "I…"

Possibilities churned through her mind. There were so many things— equality, respect. The feeling of sand under her fingers. The freedom to follow the bright, intriguing instincts of her intellect.

Or was Kuyoc asking her a different question?

The air around her tightened, sparking with the potential of the moment before a storm. Her skin, still damp from her ordeal in the caverns below, shivered with a strange chill—and the answer popped from her lips.

"A woman with a scar on her cheek," Ellie blurted.

Kuyoc's eyes widened with surprise.

"What?" he gasped.

Ellie's eyes flickered to the priest's forehead—to where a similar scar marred his weathered skin.

There were things in the caves below that Ellie now knew were quite capable of inflicting such wounds.

"You were here," she spluttered, barely managing to keep her voice low. "You were here before. You fought those monsters." Her eyes snapped to the pendant he wore beside his cross—the one that looked so remarkably like a great, pointed fang.

"Tell me about the woman," Kuyoc ordered. His eyes blazed with focus.

"I saw her in the desert. In London. And here," Ellie admitted in an awkward, hushed whisper. "In this place. By the plaza. There was... There was ash raining from the sky."

"Did she speak?" Kuyoc pressed urgently.

Ellie swallowed thickly and answered him with the echo of the words from a dream.

"*What do you want?*"

Kuyoc's eyes slid closed. He shook his head and laughed—a dark, tired chuckle.

"Quis enim cognovit sensum Domini?" he muttered.

Ellie's mind automatically translated the Latin scripture.

Who knows the mind of God?

When he opened his eyes again, Kuyoc's look was dangerously intent.

"The mirror was made to grant knowledge," he said fiercely. "But not the knowledge you ask for—not the knowledge you *think* you want. It has no ears. It does not care about your thoughts. It seeks the answer in your heart—in your *desire*. What desire do you hide in your heart?"

The crate by the mirror was nearly completed. In a few minutes, Dawson would order the men to lift the relic from its plinth, set it in the box, and carry it away.

Ellie's chance to stop that from happening was slipping past her.

"How do you know all this?" she demanded. The words burst from her in a frustrated whisper.

Kuyoc's expression softened with sympathy.

"Because I have used it, mija," he replied solemnly. "Because it showed me the way to what I wanted in my heart."

"San Pedro Siris?" Adam quietly guessed.

"Our leader wanted peace," Kuyoc returned flatly. "He thought it would save us from the destruction being wrought by your British, but that isn't how it works. It would only have sentenced us to a slower death."

He pulled his gaze from the men by the mirror, fixing it dangerously on Ellie instead.

"I thought I wanted freedom," he said. "And I did. But the mirror found another dream inside my heart—a deeper dream. *That* was the path it showed me."

Ellie's thoughts snapped to her own dreams—to the splashes of blood on white shirtwaists and the smell of smoke that bled through the air of London as she stood in the midst of a wild, violent ecstasy—and she knew.

"Vengeance," she whispered. The word fell from her lips like a chip of ice.

The fire in Kuyoc's eyes collapsed into grief.

"I walked away from it. It offered me what I dreamed of, and it was a path paved in blood. *Their* blood," he said with a sharp nod toward Dawson and the others. "*Our* blood. I resisted, but it was close. Too close." His gaze snapped to Ellie once more and sharpened with challenge. "Could you do the same?"

Memories flooded in. All the little slights and exclusions, the casual aggressions. How they kept adding up, building inside of Ellie until it felt like they must take on a life of their own and burst out of her skin like a monster.

Fear clenched at her chest.

"I... I don't know," she confessed. Her throat felt tight.

Kuyoc answered with a sigh. For the first time since Ellie had met him, the priest actually looked his age, his shoulders bent by the weight of the burden he carried.

"She would not have come to you if you were not meant to be here," he solemnly declared, and then raised his eyes to the heavens that lay on the far side of the dark stone of the cave. "D'iyoos ka' u-kānān-t-e," he said and shook his head.

"What does that mean?" Ellie pressed uncomfortably.

He didn't answer.

"You passed through the cave below," he said instead. "You saw what was there. If you want to see through the eye of the gods, you must pay for it in blood."

Ellie's thoughts flew to the mountain of bones piled in the cavern beneath them... animals and warriors, birds and children—an avalanche of the slaughtered and cast aside.

All of them were tributes. They were the price the people of Tulan had paid for the whispered secrets of the dark oracle that lay beneath the heart of their city.

"There were so many..." she said helplessly as the horror of it washed over her.

"Then think of how many more there will be if your countrymen take it from here!" Kuyoc countered fiercely. "Ask yourself whether they will hesitate to give the oracle what they must in order to get what they want!"

His eyes were a tangle of emotion—guilt and regret. Hope and fear.

He straightened.

"Cut my ropes, Mr. Bates," Kuyoc ordered. His voice was firm with authority.

Adam glanced out at the men in the center of the cavern, and then darted to where Kuyoc was tied. Crouched behind the pillar, he severed the priest's bonds with a quick twist of his machete.

"Does this mean you've got a plan?" Adam grumbled.

"Sure," Kuyoc replied as he subtly shook himself loose. His eyes remained locked on the place where Jacobs and Dawson were arranging for the men to lift the mirror. "Now give your woman the knife."

Adam startled. His gaze flashed from Ellie to the machete.

"What's she supposed to do with it?" he protested as he handed the blade over with obvious reluctance.

"Use it," Kuyoc replied with a flash of dark humor. "While you and I provide a distraction."

"To do what?" Adam blurted with alarm.

Kuyoc ignored him, looking to Ellie instead. The weight of the machete was awkward in her grip.

"I have given you a weapon," the priest said intently. "Find out what to do with it."

"What—this?" Ellie demanded with a wide-eyed look at the eighteen-inch blade.

The priest gave a huff of exasperation.

"Not the knife. The dynamite!" he replied.

"What?!" Ellie squeaked in protest.

Kuyoc shook his head. "I hope that ghost knows what she is doing," he said.

The priest plucked something from his pocket and tossed it at Ellie, who caught it with fumbling hands as she tried not to drop Adam's enormous knife. She opened her hand and found herself staring down at a book of matches.

The sight sent a ringing note of panic through her, but before she could protest, Kuyoc stepped from the pillar. He raised his hands in the air and began to chant in a stream of mysterious-sounding Yucatec.

"He can't possibly mean for me to use these. Can he?" Ellie demanded, waving the matches wildly at Adam as he slid into place beside her in the cover of the tumbled stones.

"I dunno, Princess," Adam replied as he watched the priest grimly. "If he was talking about that dynamite from the shed, then there's no way that stuff is fresh out of the factory—and I'm guessing you already know what happens to dynamite when it's been sitting around for a while," he finished pointedly.

Ellie did. Dynamite became notoriously unstable the older it was. If Kuyoc had managed to bring some through the bush with him, then he was lucky he hadn't blown himself to pieces with it long before he got here.

But where could it be? The priest had only come to the cave with the clothes on his back... and that crazy breastplate.

Ellie's gaze slid to the bundle of reeds that lay by the dark opening in the cave. A horrified suspicion rose in the back of her mind.

Kuyoc continued to rattle on as he moved slowly towards the center of the cavern.

"What is he saying?" Ellie demanded urgently.

"Er... it sounds like instructions for preserving fish," Adam said.

"Fish?" Ellie burst out in reply, bewildered.

Kuyoc walked past the mirror to where the stream turned and deepened against the far wall of the cavern. Dawson and the rest of the crew stared at him—all of them except for Jacobs.

His eyes pivoted to the pillar where the priest had been tied.

Adam yanked Ellie into a low dash behind the rock formations. They skirted the edge of the clearing and pulled to a stop behind a stone veil. The hiding place was only a few yards away from where Staines shuffled his feet tiredly as he adjusted the weight of Adam's Winchester in his arms.

Jacobs reached the pillar. He picked up the severed ropes clustered at the base of it and studied the obviously cut ends.

His eyes narrowed as he took a more careful, dangerous look around the room.

Ellie forced herself to breathe. The lanterns only offered so much light in the vast, shadowy space, leaving plenty of places for them to conceal themselves.

Jacobs didn't bother to search. Instead, he stalked over to Staines and plucked Adam's Winchester from the guard's limp hands.

Staines startled, almost falling backwards, even as Ellie flinched at Jacobs' abrupt proximity.

Calmly, Jacobs put the rifle to his shoulder and pointed it through a gap in the men to where Kuyoc stood, still keeping up his Yucatec monologue.

"Aww hell," Adam muttered—and vaulted over the stones into Jacobs' back.

Adam's impact sent the pair of them sprawling. The rifle flew from Jacobs' hands, skidding across the floor.

Jacobs twisted like a fish in Adam's grasp and whipped a knife from his sleeve.

Buller and Price whirled. They raised their rifles as Staines scrambled across the floor toward the Winchester. Adam gripped Jacobs' knife-hand as the pair of them rolled across the floor.

Nobody fired, though Ellie watched the rifle barrels track Adam's progress across the ground. He and Jacobs were twisting around too quickly for a safe shot—but that wouldn't last. Either someone would find a clear way to put a bullet into Adam, or one of them would wise up and jump into the brawl to change the odds.

Between the fight and Kuyoc's fish-themed chant by the water—nobody in the chamber was looking at the mirror.

I have given you a weapon. Find out how to use it, the priest had said... and suddenly the meaning of his words snapped into place.

Ellie balked. The priest's plan was insane. Maybe impossible.

But it wasn't as though she had any better ideas.

Ellie sprinted across the floor of the cavern with Adam's machete in her hand. She threw herself against the squat pillar that held the mirror.

Her body slammed up against the truncated stalagmite and she found herself staring down at a flawless, liquidly smooth piece of perfectly black stone.

It was perhaps four feet across. Her guano-streaked, abraded face shone back at her from the surface of it, framed by the reflection of the jagged stalactites overhead. They looked like teeth opening to eat her.

If you want to see through the eye of the gods, you must pay for it in blood.

Ellie felt a quick panic as she recalled Kuyoc's instructions. Whose blood?

A gun went off behind her. The bullet chipped against the stones of the ceiling. Little shards of them rained down.

Her thoughts lurched to her knowledge of Mesoamerican cultures. There was strong evidence for the practice of human sacrifice—never minding the pile of the dead that she had climbed over to get here—but far more frequently in the iconography of the Mayan world, one saw images of priests piercing their own tongues or extremities to make sacred offerings to the gods.

And after all, there was only one source of blood Ellie had on hand.

Wincing in anticipation, Ellie raised the machete and sliced the blade lightly down her arm.

Adam kept his knife sharp. Blood welled up in a rich, red ribbon that unfurled across the pale surface of her skin.

It streamed to her elbow. The first drop of it quivered there, suspended—and then plopped down onto the mirror.

It landed with an impossible hiss. A tiny wisp of smoke curled up from the surface.

Smoke?

It had to be some sort of chemical reaction—but obsidian wasn't a volatile mineral. Nothing in it could react with blood.

Dawson's voice cut through the air.

"Get that woman away from the artifact!"

All the eyes in the room turned toward her.

In a final, desperate moment of inspiration, Ellie slammed her bleeding arm down onto the night-black stone.

The hissing rose as pain burned through her skin. Pale gray smoke spilled up from the point of contact, thick and rich as a smoldering campfire.

Ellie opened her mouth, drawing in a breath to scream.

It tasted of forest, rain, and night—and then the pain was gone as the world around her went dark.

FORTY-THREE

*S*AND STUNG AGAINST her skin. Ellie clutched the trowel and brush in her hands as the storm whipped around her, blurring her view of the brown expanse of the Nile...

Smoke hung over a gray London street. The women around her jostled, screaming, with tears of joy on their faces. Grandmothers and schoolgirls jumped, arm in arm, with the joy of victory. Blood stained the white fabric of their blouses...

Calloused hands traced over her skin as they danced along the length of her thigh. A roughly stubbled jaw brushed against her cheek as she felt the delicious pain of a nibble at her earlobe. She grabbed taut skin and lean muscle. The wildness inside of her rose as the walls crumbled away and everything began to burn...

...and she landed on her back on a floor of cool white tile.

Ellie blinked up at the ceiling of a familiar room.

Over a shelf of fluffy white towels, frosted glass windows filtered the soft afternoon light. A steaming tub frothed with rose-scented bubbles.

She sat up, taking in the clean, comfortable glory of the washroom at the Rio Nuevo Hotel.

"How the devil am I here?" she demanded aloud.

"You aren't."

Ellie whirled, scrambling to her feet, and saw the woman with the scar on her cheek standing on the other side of the tub. This time, she was dressed like Mrs. Linares in a brightly colored skirt and vibrant jewelry.

"How are *you* here?" Ellie spluttered.

The woman circled the tub, running a hand along the smooth porcelain rim of it.

"This was the one desire I could break into," she said distantly as she let her hand fall. "The others were too strong."

"My desire for… a bath?" Ellie tentatively returned.

The woman's mouth pulled into a rueful smile that reminded Ellie of an expression Padre Kuyoc might make.

Ellie glanced down at herself. She was still wearing her stolen trousers and one-sleeved shirt. They were covered in cave dirt and bat droppings. So was the rest of her.

She started to reach for her hair, and then thought better of it. She wasn't sure she wanted to know how bad it was.

The smell wasn't very nice, either.

"Well," Ellie conceded as she dropped tiredly into the chair beside the tub. "I suppose that's fair. But why?" The question blurted out of her. "Why am I seeing you at all?"

The woman sat down on the edge of the tub. She trailed her fingers in the rose-scented bubbles. She was small but strong—beautiful in a way that was easy to overlook.

"The amulet found you," she replied.

Only 'amulet' wasn't quite right. What the woman said was something else—a word that hummed and whispered at the edge of Ellie's consciousness.

All of the woman's words were like that, Ellie realized with a jolt. The ones that came into her mind were only approximations, some of them better than others.

What the woman had spoken was 'amulet,' but also 'fragment,' and 'key.'

Seeker, Ellie thought as another facet of meaning flashed into her awareness and then slipped away again.

"You mean *I* found *it*," Ellie corrected her uncertainly as her hand moved reflexively to the place on her neck where the black disk used to hang.

"No," The woman looked at Ellie from across the room. "That is not what I meant at all."

Ellie absorbed that with a tickling sense of fear. She asked the next question—the one that itched at her uncomfortably from the whitewashed walls and frosted glass.

"Where are we, really?"

The woman drew her hand from the tub and set it regally in her lap.

"We are in the mirror," she replied.

More echoes. More meanings.

Eye. Blood drinker.

God.

A cool fear whispered across Ellie's skin. The washroom around her looked safe and familiar, but something... *unstable* vibrated at her from the lines and the shadows. The tiled floor and the white tub were nothing but a thin veneer over a chaotic darkness that would drive her mad if she actually looked at it.

The more she thought of the veneer, the thinner it became until it seemed as though the contours of the room began to flicker. The shadows grew, and Ellie wondered if she was about to tumble into them—to be chewed up and spat out as something else on the other side.

Suddenly the woman was there. She set a firm brown hand to Ellie's chin. Her grip was gentle but strong as she turned Ellie's face so that it was the woman she looked at and not the room.

Her figure shifted as Ellie watched, from the colorful blouse and skirt to an embroidered huipil like those worn by the women of Santa Dolores. A gorgeous feathered headdress and ornaments of jade. Startling flashes of red body paint and a high-necked English blouse. All of it flickered and twisted around something else that remained steady and unchanging—the dark conviction in the woman's eyes and the scars that marred her cheek.

"Stay with me," the woman ordered.

Other meanings, other senses of her words mingled in Ellie's mind. *Listen. Strength. Hope.*

"Who are you?" Ellie gasped.

The woman smiled. The expression was grim and slightly dangerous.

"Do you really wish to know?" she challenged.

The want bloomed up inside of Ellie, driven by curiosity unsatisfied for far too long. For days now, she had sensed that she was at the verge of discovering something desperately important—something that this woman stood at the center of.

The desire focused, deepened—and the room around her snapped from view, replaced by a flash of vivid, painfully distinct images.

A dark-haired, umber-skinned girl of twelve crawled from a black tunnel to a narrow, painted room. A jagged red wound marred her cheek. Women waited for her there as water splashed from a copper pipe in the wall.

The wound resolved into a scar. The face and body matured, and were decked in jade, gold, feathers, and paint. Her arm wrapped around the throat of a drugged deer. She held an obsidian knife in her hand.

Black glass glittered beneath her as others, older and more elaborately costumed, watched solemnly at her back.

Another word slipped into Ellie's mind as meanings fell over each other in layers.

Initiate. Priestess. Blade.

The woman knelt before an elder who wheezed with weakness. His skin was ravaged by sores as he placed a heavy black stone around her neck.

Bearer. Queen.

A familiar pair of eyes shone with warmth. The delicate hands of the woman who owned her heart roved over her skin, tracking the line of her throat.

An elegant flow of syllables slipped into Ellie's mind—more intimate and more true than what had come before.

Lover. Companion. Ixb'ahjun.

White tile and frosted glass slammed back into place. The silhouette of leaves danced against the window as steam rose slowly from the tub.

"I know," Ellie gasped.

The scarred woman's eyes softened with a gentle sadness.

No—not *the woman*. She had a name.

She was Ixb'ahjun.

She brushed her thumb against Ellie's cheek with a tired affection before she firmed again, straightening her shoulders.

"You want to know who we were," Ixb'ahjun said.

It was not a question. Ixb'ahjun's words were a statement that danced over Ellie's skin. In its wake sparked the familiar, hungry feeling of a burning need to *understand*.

"Of course," Ellie replied.

Even as she spoke it—as she *felt* it—the shadows shifted along the walls. The washroom itched as though a horde of insects crawled behind it. A buzz rose at the back of her mind, whispering of other wants—recognition, respect, freedom.

Ellie did not realize that she had fallen to her knees. Ixb'ahjun stood over her with a calm, unwavering authority.

"Want it," she ordered.

Padre Kuyoc's words danced in the back of Ellie's mind.

The mirror was made to grant knowledge... It seeks the answer in your heart—in your desire.

The woman above Ellie was a ghost—a memory. How was she here?

The grip on Ellie's chin firmed. Another word fell from Ixb'ahjun's lips, harsh and demanding. It felt like a title—a name.

Acolyte. Granddaughter. Warrior.

"Want it," Ixb'ahjun said again.

Yes. She could want it. Ellie had always wanted to know—to learn.

"Show her," Ixb'ahjun commanded. Her voice rang through the ordinary washroom as though it were the great, soaring nave of a cathedral carved from the earth itself, rich and resonant with power.

Knowledge flooded into Ellie.

She reeled against the onslaught of it as the tiled floor beneath her shattered into the sea of thousands of years of history.

Temples rose, curving into the mountains. A city grew and sprawled with elegant architecture and marvels of engineering. Water and stone, paint and music—laughter, joy, ritual.

Progress. Power... and deep beneath the earth—*blood*.

Pierced tongues. Severed earlobes. Birds and lizards. Greater creatures—a screeching tapir, the crimson-flecked pelt of a jaguar.

Captives of war—taut-bodied men with slit throats and opened chests.

Elders and criminals.

The drugged fear of children.

And always the blood.

Bodies piled in the darkness. The glass whispered its truths.

Above, the city thrived. Sparks of wisdom branched out from it to light up the forest with threads of influence that shaped other peoples as they rose, blossomed, fell, and transformed themselves into something else.

Priests wrangled the dark eye like a powerful, dangerous beast, understanding how easily the thirst for more could grow... how quickly terrible it could become.

Then the pale-skinned foreigners arrived, dragging disease in their wake. The desperate push for a solution. So much blood spilled, the most precious and terrible offerings made, only for answers that came in visions of impossible machines, slender points of metal, and fragile tubes of translucent glass.

All of it rippled too far ahead of them—too strange and distant to comprehend and replicate.

Panic. Flight. A civilization crumbling into death and smoke... and then the silence of corpses and the green, relentless life of nature creeping over all that they had built.

Ellie slammed back into the washroom of the Rio Nuevo. She was sprawled on the floor of it. Her head pounded in time with the twisting of her stomach.

How long had she been here? How much time did she have?

Her brain pulsed with knowledge—with dynasties and games, parenting techniques, artistry, engineering, laughter, song, mistakes...

How they built. What they ate. Why they worshiped. How they loved…
It was too vast—too much. Ellie felt as though she would burst from it.
She couldn't. Not yet.

Ixb'ahjun—priestess and blade, queen of Tulan's final hours—stood over
Ellie as she pushed herself to her knees.

"There was never just one of us." Ixb'ahjun's voice rang out through a
space far larger than the washroom. "Not until the end when all the rest were
dead. There were always more, so that if the wrong desire crept into one of
our hearts, the others could see the path to stop it and keep the balance." She
closed her eyes against the pain of remembering. "We all knew of the time
in the earliest days when one blade controlled the stone—a time of burning,
conquest, famine, and death. All that had been here before was devoured by
it, leaving only scattered fragments. The founders of Tulan overcame that at
terrible cost, and it was their wisdom that the stone could only be used safely
with the balance of a council."

Ellie thought of the majestic portrait in the ravine—the assembled figures
that reminded her of the gods of Mayan and other Mesoamerican myths. Not
one but many, all different, each with their own strengths and flaws.

It was… quite brilliant, actually, she thought with a quick burst of
admiration.

Ixb'ahjun knelt, bringing herself to Ellie's level, and fixed her with a serious, challenging gaze.

"Are the men of your world capable of such balance?" she demanded.

Ellie raised an eyebrow at the question. The answer was obvious.

"The men?" she retorted. "Goodness, no."

Ixb'ahjun cocked her head as a flash of humor brightened her eyes.

"The women?" she prompted.

Ellie considered it more seriously. What the mirror could offer to women…

They could find the path to their emancipation. To equal treatment—equal
rights. All of it could be within their grasp…

Padre Kuyoc's voice echoed through the back of her mind.

*It showed me the way to what I wanted in my heart… and it was a path paved with
death.*

The mirror was an arcane force fed with blood—a force that *required*
sacrifice.

Ellie wondered what must be growing—building—inside of something
that had gorged itself on countless hundreds of lives.

Ellie's dreams were big. They were dangerous.

The bigger the dream, the greater the sacrifice.

What would Ellie be willing to sacrifice to pay for her big, dangerous dreams?

The thought of it tore the fantasy away with a sick lurch in her gut—and suddenly she was not in the washroom at the Rio Nuevo anymore.

Ellie knelt beside Ixb'ahjun on a surface of black glass as flawless and dark as a starless night. The cave arched over her head. Stalactites were illuminated by the glare of the paraffin lamps.

Jacobs must have slipped from Adam's grasp. Adam was grappling with Staines now, wrestling him for the Winchester. They were frozen like flies in amber except that their movements slowly, almost imperceptibly, continued to shift.

Padre Kuyoc walked toward the water at the back of the cave. Instead of rushing, the stream undulated, slow and graceful as the shifting of summer clouds. His hands were raised and his eyes rolled toward the ceiling as a dark, self-aware humor twisted his lip.

Dawson's mouth was open in a silent, aggravated protest as his hands waved slowly in the air at everyone around him—at the priest, and at Buller and Price as they swung their rifles into place.

Pacheco held a hammer mid-blow over the nearly completed crate.

Charlie and Lessard were caught in the middle of exchanging a grim, determined glance.

Then there was Jacobs.

He stood two steps from where Ellie herself slumped across the surface of the mirror. Smoke still hissed up in slow, thin curls from where her bleeding arm met the surface. Jacobs' gaze fixed on her with sharp intention. He held a knife ready in one hand as the other reached for her, inch by painstaking inch.

"Why are we back here?" Ellie asked.

The answer crept up from inside Ellie's heart even as Ixb'ahjun answered. "Your desire is changing," she said.

Ixb'ahjun gently took hold of Ellie's hands. The blood from Ellie's wound stained Ixb'ahjun's skin where their fingers intertwined.

"Tell me what you want," Ixb'ahjun ordered.

Ellie fought for the answer through the tumult of conflicted emotion inside of her. "I... I can't let them have it. I need to... I *must*..."

"Feel it," Ixb'ahjun prompted urgently. "Shape it in your heart."

The other Ellie—the one collapsed on the mirror—stirred. The hand of her injured arm clenched reflexively.

Ixb'ahjun flickered. The motion in the cavern lurched dangerously forward for the space of a breath.

The Winchester flew from Staines's hands into a shadowy field of stalagmites as Adam shouted in protest.

Jacobs' hand moved closer to Ellie's neck.

What I want... What I want... What I want...

Ellie's dreams cried out in protest—sand rippling through her fingers, the silence of a rapt and respectful lecture hall.

A cry of victory in the embrace of her sisters-in-arms.

She remembered the bones that lay under her feet—that terrible, forgotten mountain of the dead.

"I have to destroy it," Ellie said as the truth dawned over her, both terrible and undeniable.

Ellie's resolution firmed.

"I *want* to destroy it," she declared.

The ghost across from her smiled, tired and relieved, as she squeezed Ellie's hands.

"Thank you," Ixb'ahjun said—and then vanished, guttering like a candle flame going out.

Knowledge slammed into Ellie's brain.

The blade in Jacobs' hand. Charlie and Lessard hovering a few steps away by the crate.

Dawson reaching into the pocket of his jacket.

A rifle rising to point at Padre Kuyoc as Adam's eyes narrowed with fear and determination.

The breastplate of hollow reeds lying on the ground by a hole into bone-filled darkness, discarded like a piece of trash.

No, Ellie realized with a sharp, clear fear. That wasn't right.

The reeds were not hollow at all.

The mirror told her what she must do—and spilled out the inconceivable chaos that would follow.

Really, it all came down to a simple matter of geology.

"Oh blast," Ellie cursed, her eyes going wide—and then the mirror spat her out.

She slammed back into her slumped, bloodstained body as Jacobs' hand twisted into the back of her shirt.

FORTY-FOUR

$\mathcal{S}$TAINES HAD BEEN BRAVE enough when he had scampered over to give Adam a swift kick to the ribs as he wrestled with Jacobs.

When the chaos that followed left Adam wrestling Staines for the Winchester, the rat-faced bastard must've figured he stood a better chance against Adam's fists than the wrong end of a rifle.

And so he'd chucked it into the stones.

The guard wasn't wrong, though Adam could also do a lot of damage with his fists. Still, that gun would've been very damned handy right about now.

Especially as a wild, familiar light threw the whole of the cavern into stark illumination, and Jacobs grabbed hold of Ellie.

The rest of the cave went out of focus.

Dawson had taken that damned bone out and was waving it over his head. The crazy priest was over by the water, rattling importantly in holy-sounding Yucatec about whatever popped into his head. Jacobs' goons prepared to either shoot or tackle the old man. Charlie and the other guys were conspiring grimly by the crate.

Even Staines, who was gaping up at Adam with well-justified terror as Adam straddled him on the floor—all of it snapped out of Adam's awareness like someone had snuffed out a light.

In its place, there was only Ellie.

Blood dripped slowly down her arm where she'd sliced herself. Her eyes were woozy as Jacobs hauled her off the mirror and the knife in his hand headed for her throat.

Adam was too far away. He wasn't going to get there in time.

The thought filled him with a blind, furious fear—and then a squat, grizzled figure rose from beside the crate.

"Câlice de tabarnak," Martin Lessard cursed resignedly—then drove a practiced fist into Jacobs' kidney.

Jacobs flinched as his teeth snapped together. He twisted instinctively into the injury and let out a grunt—even though he ought to be screaming with pain from the hit.

Adam knew well enough how it felt. Lessard had punched him in the kidney before, and that had just been for fun.

Braxton Pickett, with his eyes bulging more than usual, swung his rifle wildly toward Lessard.

Charlie casually chucked his hammer across the cave. It flew toward the Confederate. Pickett refrained from shooting as he dropped and thereby avoided taking a few pounds of iron to his skull.

It all happened in the space of a breath—but Adam had already shoved to his feet and started sprinting across the space that divided him from Ellie and Jacobs.

Dawson shouted as he waved the glowing bone over his head. Buller and Price whirled to point their rifles at Charlie and Lessard instead of at the priest by the water.

Flowers stood just behind the two guards. The big man neatly reached over and plucked the Enfield from Buller's hands. He tossed it to Charlie.

Adam reached Jacobs and plowed into him.

The blow loosened Jacobs' grip on Ellie. The smaller man twisted into Adam's impact, slippery as an eel. They hit the ground side-by-side, and Adam barely managed to catch Jacobs' knife hand. He stopped it just shy of driving into his guts.

Jacobs was smaller, but he was strong—and damnably quick. It took both of Adam's hands to keep the knife from disemboweling him... which left him with only one other body part at his disposal.

Thankfully, it was a hard one.

Adam slammed his head into Jacobs' face.

Something cracked. The force on the knife hand broke just long enough for Adam to shove the blade away and scramble into a crouch.

Jacobs managed to do the same, even though blood was dripping down from his cheek. Adam's blow had taken him on the bone and split the skin. Jacobs didn't seem bothered by it. His eyes were on Adam with the look of a practiced fighter—one who knew how to watch for an opening.

A few steps away, Ellie crawled unsteadily to her feet, and then flinched as a bullet pinged off the stones beside her.

Jacobs darted in, quick and sharp. He was obviously not a man who won by brute force—which was Adam's usual preferred method—and he still had that damned knife.

Adam was sadly short on knives.

He staggered back to avoid the swipe, batting at the back of Jacobs' hand as he went by—but the guy was moving too fast. Adam hit the other man's arm instead, and Jacobs managed to keep his grip on the blade.

There was probably a clever strategy for dealing with this sort of thing. Adam didn't know it. He just launched himself at Jacobs instead.

Charlie and Lessard had yanked up the crate. They used it as a makeshift shield as they worked toward better cover. Pacheco crouched with them. Charlie peppered off a few rounds at the remaining guards.

Dawson fumbled with his bone as he scrambled for a place to hide. The arcanum slipped from his hands, bounced lightly off the floor of the cavern, and skidded away.

Behind him, Kuyoc had shamelessly darted behind a spill of old breakdown by the stream. The water was rushing faster now than it had been when Adam and Ellie had first entered the cavern, undoubtedly fueled by the rains dumping down on the mountains and the valley outside. The flow of it looked almost like the rapids they'd navigated on the *Mary Lee*.

Ellie made a dash. She bolted across the cave, keeping low as more bullets pinged off the stones.

Still wrestling Jacobs, Adam stumbled up against a low wall of stone—and tripped.

He flailed backwards and slammed onto something flat, hard, and unforgiving.

Jacobs landed on top of him—and immediately sliced the knife in, aiming for a killing blow.

Adam caught his wrists.

Jacobs leaned in, putting his full weight behind the blade as Adam's muscles strained.

The bastard's split cheek was still bleeding. Drops fell from it onto the surface of whatever Adam was lying on.

Where they landed beside Adam's ear, he heard a distinct and surprising hiss.

Smoke coiled into the periphery of his vision in a few tentative wisps.

Adam sucked in a breath, drawing on his reserves to keep his shaking arms up as Jacobs bore down on them. Some of the smoke came with it. It smelled of freshly turned soil and the dew that collected on plantain leaves in the morning.

Time seemed to stretch—and then hold. Shadows gathered in the corners of his vision as Adam was consumed by the dark, skittering sense of something whispering to him from the corners of the world.

What do you want?

"How about... a way... to clock this bastard?" Adam replied through gritted teeth.

Jacobs' eyes narrowed with surprise. For a critical moment, his focus broke... just as a light, impossible burst of knowledge popped into Adam's brain.

It opened itself up to him like a birthday present.

His arms were shaking with the force of holding off Jacobs' blow.

Hell with it, Adam thought numbly. *Why not?*

He shifted his grip to clamp Jacobs' wrists with a single hand, gritting his teeth against the effort of it. He flailed out with the other, slapping it down to the flawlessly flat stone above him.

Something inside of him sang out with the knowledge of exactly how far he needed to reach. As more of that smoke curled up around both him and Jacobs, Adam's fingers brushed against a hard, achingly familiar shape.

He grasped the hilt of his machete and slammed it into Jacobs' temple.

The blow knocked the smaller man aside as he drew in a quick, sharp breath. Adam twisted free and lurched back to his feet—but more than the hit seemed to be slowing Jacobs' reaction.

The dark-haired man wavered, wincing and unsteady.

"No..." Jacobs gasped wildly. "It couldn't possibly be..."

Jacobs shook his head as though trying to knock something out of it. Adam wondered what the hell had thrown the man off—but not for long.

He spun the machete in his grip and faced Jacobs with the blade ready in his hand.

Jacobs' eyes cleared. They locked onto Adam with dangerous focus—and Ellie's voice rang through the chaos of the cave like a bell.

"I am holding a lit match," she called out, lifting a hand where the fragile bloom of a flame flickered against the shadows. "And approximately six pounds of dynamite."

In the other hand, she raised up the sagging form of Kuyoc's homemade breastplate.

"I am about to light it and throw it into the chamber below us," she continued crisply with a nod toward the ragged black opening in the wall of the cave. "If you'd like to escape the collapse of this entire cavern, I strongly suggest that you run."

The blood drained from Adam's face.

"Shoot her!" Dawson screamed.

Ellie touched the match to the cords of Kuyoc's armor and tossed the hissing package of it through the hole.

Across from Adam, Jacobs stared forward with uncharacteristic shock... and then began to laugh.

A deep, earth-shattering boom throbbed through the cavern from below. The shudder of it was tangible through the soles of Adam's boots.

There was a brief, terrible moment of silence... and a crack opened in the ground before him.

"That's not good," Adam concluded, staring down at it numbly.

He whirled away from Jacobs and bolted across the cavern to where Ellie wobbled as the ground shook under her feet.

Stalactites popped like firecrackers overhead, shattering to the ground like bombs.

Jacobs called out an order in ringing, authoritative tones as he waved toward the stairs leading up into the temple.

Staines sprinted for them.

"No!" Dawson screamed as he scrambled out from behind a broken fall of stone. "You can't go! Not without the mirror!"

Adam reached Ellie. He grabbed her arm and tugged her in the direction of the door to the temple.

"No!" she shouted back, hauling him the opposite way.

"What?" Adam exclaimed.

She gripped his arms. Her eyes were clear and intent even as the stones rumbled beneath their feet once more.

Another crack opened near the mirror's pillar and splintered across the ground.

"Trust me," she said.

Adam did.

He let her pull him forward, racing across the cavern as more rocks cracked and plummeted from the ceiling. She yelled to Charlie and the others. With a stream of Quebecois curses, Lessard led the charge to follow.

Kuyoc darted from his hiding place and fell into step behind them with an alacrity that belied his age.

Ellie headed for the water.

At the other end of the cave, Jacobs waved the men into the passage to he pyramid. Dawson lurched back from the mirror as the crack beside it tore wider with an ear-splitting wrench.

The platform on which the stone sat tilted dangerously.

Pickett sprinted past him, and finally Dawson ran.

Something pinged off the toe of Adam's boot and spun across the floor of the cavern ahead of him.

It was a slender little bone, and as Adam watched, it spluttered with flashes of nascent light.

Ellie cast a surprised look back at him—and then snatched it from the ground as she raced past.

She shoved the bone into her pocket as she reached the edge of the deep, churning mass of water at the end of the cavern. She stopped there.

"This is going to sound crazy!" she yelled as Adam joined her.

Adam tugged her into his arms.

"I'm with you," he promised as he gazed down at her.

It was true. The fact of it warmed him up from the inside giddily.

Ellie's face brightened with relief.

"Good," she replied—and then launched herself into the current.

It plucked her up like a leaf and whisked her into a dark, jagged mouth that Adam could now see opened at the far corner of the cavern.

Adam gaped after her.

Kuyoc wheezed with laughter beside him. With a hoot of triumph, he leapt into the water as well and shot after Ellie.

"Are they cracked?" Charlie demanded as he skidded to a stop beside Adam and stared wide-eyed at the water.

A piece of the cave ceiling collapsed. It smashed to the ground a few paces away like the bang of a cannon going off.

Lessard, Flowers, and Pacheco all flinched back from it as they arrived and piled at the edge of the rushing stream.

"Probably," Adam admitted, and then jumped.

The water was cold, fierce, and furious. The current grabbed him like a fist and shot him forward, foaming and churning into the chute that gaped at him like a maw.

Adam was upon it in a moment. The shouts and curses of the other men rang out behind him as they fell or leapt into the water.

He shot into darkness.

The tube of stone was slick. He couldn't have caught himself against it if he had tried. The water raced him forward and shot him around an arcing turn as the tunnel narrowed.

The current quickened, and a shriek from Pacheco echoed off the stones behind him, mingling with the maniacal roar of Lessard's laughter.

The light ahead of him changed. The pitch blackness was moderated by a growing dot of slightly less abysmal gloom—and then Adam burst into the open air of a rain-drenched night, flying out of a dragon-mouthed spout in a frothing cascade of storm-fed water.

He crashed into a deeper pool.

Adam surfaced with a gasp. Pond weeds clung to his shoulder. Ellie grabbed hold of him in the water.

Adam grabbed her back, hauling her to his chest as he made a quick and urgent assessment that all of her limbs were still there.

"It's fine," she gasped over the rushing roar of the water and the pummeling downpour. "I'm fine!"

She was.

So Adam kissed her.

He tugged her close, molding her to his body as he devoured her lips, tasting the warm heat of her through the cave dirt and pond water. Relief washed through him like a tide... until he realized that they were sinking.

He released her, spluttering, and loosened an arm to help keep them afloat as he tried to figure out where the hell they had landed.

It was Ellie's reservoir, the green pond that she'd been so excited about when they had arrived at the city—except it wasn't a pond anymore. It was a rising, frothing whirlpool, fed by the water flying out of the mouth of the feathered serpent. As Adam watched, Lessard shot out of the opening like an ugly, slippery missile. He fell into the water with an epic splash. Charlie followed, with Flowers and Pacheco a breath behind.

Kuyoc was already there. The priest laughed wildly as he splashed at the water and shouted a prayer up to the storm-clouded heavens.

Adam's face split into a grin.

They had made it. It was crazy as hell, but they'd made it.

A thunderous crack resounded through the darkness.

"Was that thunder?" Adam demanded with a burst of alarm.

Ellie blinked at him. Her face paled slightly.

"I don't think so," she admitted.

"Out of the water!" Kuyoc shouted, and then echoed the order in Spanish. "¡Sal, rápido!"

They swam for the wall. The water had already risen enough to bring it into reach. Adam hauled himself onto the ledge and tugged Ellie up after him.

He enjoyed the feeling of holding onto her for a heartbeat before a chorus of shouts rose up from the direction of the plaza, along with a crash of a falling stone—and then more of them, booms like a giant's firecrackers echoing off the mountainside.

"Mada raass!" Charlie cursed as he whirled back in the direction of the sound.

"High ground!" Kuyoc called over the racket. He waved his arm wildly. "*Now!*"

The priest bolted.

Adam raced after him with Ellie at his side. He was vaguely aware of Lessard pulling even. The stocky Quebecois flashed a grin as he managed to outpace them. Charlie stumbled over a rock in the dark and bit out a curse as Kuyoc led them around a skidding turn into an overgrown road between the houses. The old man lost zero ground on them in his sandals.

They skirted the edge of the plaza, where the shouts grew louder. Bones came into sight. The foreman was waving the rest of the expedition on as Velegas shouted out orders from his perch on a boulder.

Aurelio Fajardo slapped a stream of mules into motion. The animals clomped and raced to join them on the road.

Nigel Reneau slid down a short flight of steps. He landed near Adam's side and took off after the priest. Ram and his Bhojpuri companions raced after the cook. Even a pair of Jacobs' remaining guards took about two seconds to decide to desert their posts. They hauled after the remainder of the camp as it raced through the trees and ruined stones.

The road twisted higher as it approached the looming black ridge of the mountains. The trees thinned, and another terrible, rending roar sounded from behind them.

Adam risked a glance back. The pyramid was falling.

The tiers of white stone collapsed inward as the temple sank into a fall of crumbling rubble. Adam spotted a cluster of figures stumbling to the bottom of the staircase. They raced across the plaza even as it fractured under their feet.

Dark shapes swooped overhead and screeched into the night. The monstrous bats from the cave veered from the cacophony of the collapse. Disoriented and chaotic, they fled into the west.

Adam took hold of Ellie's arm and pushed them faster.

The roaring and crumbling noises behind them intensified. The ground trembled beneath Adam's boots as Kuyoc veered them off the ancient road and onto a game track that wended up a sloping ledge of the mountain. He waved them onto it as he shouted, quickly swapping languages.

"Go, go! Kwika! ¡Apúrate!"

The entire camp scrambled up the winding, narrow ledge. The climb was steep. Aurelio's mules, clearly comprehending the urgency of the situation, hopped nimbly over the stones and easily passed Adam and Ellie. Aurelio shouted in the midst of them, grabbed the stragglers by their halters, and hauled them up.

Rain pounded down, making the track slippery and soaking them to the bone as they climbed. The priest picked his way with practiced assurance up the mountainside, taking them higher as more buildings collapsed below them. Trees rustled strangely as they tore from the ground.

At last, the mad caravan spilled out onto a high, broad ledge. Kuyoc stopped as the group collected itself.

Still holding Ellie's hand, Adam made a quick inventory.

Charlie was half collapsed onto one of the stones, where he panted and grumbled more curses. Lessard hocked out a lump of spit and laughed.

Flowers helped pull the last few stragglers up the steep ground to the ledge.

Based on the satisfied look on Aurelio's face, all of the mules had made it out intact.

Pacheco, Lopez, Ram, and the others—everyone else from the camp was there.

And Ellie, of course.

The relief of that made Adam want to fall over a bit—or maybe that was the altitude.

The rain began to slacken. To the east, the underside of the clouds was softly gilded by the rising light of dawn. The tentative glow of it illuminated what was happening below, even as great, rending rumbles continued to resound across the valley.

Adam forced himself to look out over it.

The place where the temple had stood was already gone, along with the ball court where Ellie and Adam fled earlier that night. The reservoir had cracked. The water spilled out in a quick, frothing current.

Farther away, towers crumbled. Sections of trees rustled wildly and then sank from view.

Adam took it in with gaping shock and sudden comprehension.

"The whole cave system is collapsing," he said, voice numb. "This entire place is turning into one giant sinkhole."

"I... Oh dear," Ellie said as she swayed slightly beside him. "I think I might need to..."

Adam caught her and held her upright. She stared past him, eyes wide, as he gently pushed a fall of messy hair from her face.

439

"Hey," he said gently, summoning her attention. "We're okay. Everyone's okay."

Movement caught his eye from beyond her shoulder where the ragged slope of the mountain curved away. In the rising light, Adam picked out a small cluster of figures clinging to the face of the stone above the catastrophic destruction.

It had to be Dawson and Jacobs. Adam supposed it was too much to hope that a temple might've fallen on them.

He had a feeling they weren't the sort to brush off having a prize snatched from under their fingers. There'd be consequences for all of this.

But he could worry about that later.

"Tulan," Ellie said weakly as she looked out over the falling city. "Adam, what have I done? I..."

She was cut off by the sound of a piercing whistle from behind them. Kuyoc had hopped up onto a rock at the far end of the ledge.

"You," he said, pointing at Bones, whose lanky form was mostly collapsed against a boulder. The foreman's clothes were streaked with dirt. "You manage to save any of your supplies?"

Bones let out a short, harsh chuckle. "No."

"Except the mules," Aurelio pointed out defensively. Two of the animals nudged at him with their noses, snuffing for comfort.

"Right," Kuyoc replied with a sigh. "You had all better come with me, then."

He turned and trudged toward another winding path up the mountainside.

"Come on, Princess," Adam said. He took Ellie's hand and tugged her gently from the collapsing remnants of a lost world.

FORTY-FIVE

$\mathcal{K}$UYOC KNEW A shortcut. He led them across the mountains along an obscure sequence of game trails, ridges, and the short tunnel of another cave. They followed the rushing tracks of newly rain-fed streams until the thick, green lushness of the forest opened onto the neatly organized expanses of newly planted milpas.

Shortly afterwards, two girls of perhaps eight and twelve slipped from the trees and legged it up the path, undoubtedly to give Feliciana and the others word of the ragged horde heading for Santa Dolores Xenacoj at the heels of their iconoclastic priest.

The light over the tidy little cluster of houses was golden and warm as Ellie walked up the path to the village. Kuyoc led the way along with a small army of children who had slipped from doors and fences as they approached. They danced around the priest and peppered him with questions.

She could smell roasting meat and the warm aromas of chili and beans.

Feliciana emerged with the other women, who descended on them like a flock of noisy doves. They fussed over Ellie's ruined shirt until Feliciana's granddaughter, Itza, spotted the wound on Ellie's arm and shouted the news of it.

The mass of busy Mayan grandmothers separated her from Adam. A pounded mess of plants was slapped onto her wound, which was then wrapped in a clean bandage.

A wrinkled, fairy-sized woman whom Ellie didn't yet know dabbed the rest of the mud from Ellie's face with a damp cloth. She rattled on in Mopan the entire time, which Héctor helpfully translated.

"She says you need a bath because you smell like rotten plantains," he declared.

At last, Ellie was deposited on one of the stools in front of Feliciana's tidy home, and a plate of food was set in her hands. She tore into it with a sigh of relief and satisfaction, stuffing herself with warmly spiced beans, roasted game, fresh herbs, eggs, and a mass of tortillas.

When she was done, she leaned back against the house and considered all the places where her body ached.

Adam dropped down beside her a moment later. His hand and arm both sported fresh bandages with a greenish tinge, which told Ellie that he had also been poulticed.

He still didn't have a shirt. It clearly wasn't de rigueur to go around Santa Dolores without one, though at least he wasn't breaking any actual indecency laws.

Ellie found that she had a greater respect for indecency laws as her eyes dropped involuntarily to Adam's chest. Even when still slightly filthy and moderately bruised, that torso could cause a riot.

He grinned down at her.

"You look terrible," he said.

Ellie glared at him as he reached over and gave a tangled lock of her hair a little tug.

"Itza offered to comb it, but it would have meant delaying dinner," Ellie retorted. "Which was *not* going to happen. Paolo!" she called, flagging the boy down as he scurried past. His pet chicken followed at his heels.

"¿Quieres más?" Paolo guessed.

"Yes," Ellie replied with relief. "Sí!"

Paolo grinned at her and dashed into the house, where he called out a quick line of Mopan to those inside.

Adam chuckled.

"What did he say?" she demanded.

"Something along the lines of *the foreign lady is hungry as a boar,*" Adam replied.

"I don't care what he calls me as long as he brings me more tortillas," she returned.

"That's my girl."

Ellie startled a bit at Adam's easy, comfortable words. A tumult of unsettling questions sparked to life inside her.

Before she had a chance to ask them, they were joined by Padre Kuyoc The priest had fully washed up and changed into clean clothes.

"Nice sunset," he commented as he plopped down beside them.

He had a cup in his hand. The contents smelled lightly of booze. He raised it.

"To accidentally wiping out every vestige of a lost world," he said.

Ellie's stomach dropped. She had been ruminating uncomfortably over the disaster for their entire walk to the village. She was a scholar, for goodness' sake! She was supposed to learn, document, and preserve—not drop the relics of an entire culture into a giant hole in the ground.

She slowly lowered her face into her hands, overwhelmed by the sheer scale of the disaster that she had created. It felt particularly awful as she sat in the middle of a village full of people who could very likely have claimed Tulan as part of their own heritage... had Ellie not blown it up.

"I'm supposed to honor the past," she said without looking up. "I'm supposed to *protect* it."

Beside her, Kuyoc took another sip of his drink.

"Did you want to destroy Tulan?" he asked easily.

Ellie's head snapped up.

"Of course not," she retorted.

His sharp eyes met her steadily from under a fringe of white hair.

"You followed the path the mirror set for you," he said.

Ellie was painfully conscious of Adam beside her. They hadn't talked about any of that yet.

She had just dropped Kuyoc's potential ancestral legacy into a sinkhole. She could hardly do that and then fail to tell him the truth about it.

"Yes," she confessed.

Kuyoc shrugged. His shoulders relaxed as he took another sip of his drink.

"Well, there you are, then," he concluded.

"That's it?" Ellie demanded with a flash of temper.

"You didn't want to destroy Tulan," the priest replied. "But you wanted something else. What was it? Fame? Wealth? The admiration of your peers—the men who do not think you are capable of doing this work? Did blowing up the cave with my terrible old dynamite bring you any of those things? No." He shot her another careful, penetrating look. "You destroyed the Smoking Mirror. You buried it with the bones of all its dead. If Tulan went with it, perhaps that was the only way to be sure no one would come and try to dig it out again." He chuckled as he looked away again. "You must have wanted that very much."

Ellie absorbed it all with shock. Beside her, Adam was quiet, but she could feel him carefully listening.

She was still a little afraid to find out what he thought of it all.

The things she had seen inside the mirror had blurred in her mind like a dream that she only remembered after she had already staggered from bed for a cup of tea. She recalled the scarred woman's face and a shocking sense of intimacy—of shared purpose. A mind-blasting flood of information that had slammed into her brain, overwhelming her with its sheer volume.

There was no way she could hold it all inside her mind—yet even as she looked around Santa Dolores, small things winked out at her, glowing with a spark of added significance.

The way the stream had been shored up and shaped as it tumbled down to the lake. The layout of the village houses with their tidy front gardens. The flashes of bright jewelry on the arms of the women. How the air mingled with tobacco smoke and the smell of roasting maize.

Ellie was suffused by a sense of the past threading itself through the present, even as so much had very obviously changed.

She should be writing it down, she thought with a jolt of panic. She needed to scribble as much of it as she could on paper before it slipped away from her—but even as she reached for it, the knowledge fled back into the depths of her mind.

Cruzita's voice rang out over the village. A moment later Paolo darted by, clutching his pet hen to his chest. Relieved laughter rang out from where Ram, Pacheco, and several of the other fellows from the expedition sat with a few of the men from the village, rattling off stories in a shifting kaleidoscope of languages.

Charlie leaned against a cashew tree a little further on, quietly smoking a cigarette with a Mayan old timer, as Lessard trimmed his beard with his machete.

Nigel Reneau bent over a soup pot and quizzed one of the older women there about the spice she was adding to the warming chocolate.

Between and around it all ran the children. Aurelio scolded them when they wheeled too close to where the mules grazed in their quickly rigged corral.

It felt right—like everyone was exactly where they were supposed to be. There was a surprising comfort in it.

Adam leaned back against the house with his eyes closed. He was obviously exhausted, but he looked peaceful.

He felt like he belonged there too—dozing beside her with his conspicuous lack of a shirt.

Kuyoc took another sip of his drink as he gazed out over the sunset.

"I think perhaps we are all lucky that you wanted it so badly," he said. He cast his eyes over the warm noise of the village as he set down his cup. "

couldn't do it myself. For me, the mirror was…" He shook his head. and his eyes were tiredly drawn with all the things he couldn't say. "And it would have been too much to ask of the people here. They fought hard for the peace and quiet of this life."

The priest stood up. Adam cracked open his eyes as the older man looked down at them.

"But you two are not looking for a quiet life," Kuyoc noted significantly. "Are you?"

He ambled away from them then, raising a hand to the comfortable greetings of the people of his adopted home.

Adam slipped an arm over Ellie's shoulders, pulling her a bit closer.

"Well, Princess," he said. "You sure know how to conduct an excavation."

Ellie groaned miserably. Her shoulders slumped.

Adam's blue eyes brightened with a laugh, and then sobered a bit as he looked at her.

"What've you got in your pocket?" he asked.

"Magnifying lens," Ellie recited automatically. "A needle. An empty flask."

Adam raised a waiting eyebrow.

"And this," she added awkwardly. She took out Dawson's bone.

It looked like an ordinary humerus from the wing of a largish bird. A few characters had been roughly scraped into the surface. Ellie recognized the language as Glagolitic, an old Slavic script.

She didn't know what they said—yet. She was a little rusty with her Glagolitic.

"How many more things like that do you think are lying around out there?" Adam asked.

"Speaking in terms of pure logic, if we have already encountered two of them, I think we must assume there are a fair quantity of others," Ellie rambled, and then caught herself. "Though of course, there is nothing logical about any of this."

"I've never been that crazy about logic anyway," Adam replied. "I'm more of a winging it kind of guy."

"Dawson… Jacobs…" Ellie burst out. "They couldn't possibly be trusted with anything like the power inside that cave. Nor could anyone who would hire them."

"Can't say I disagree," Adam replied grimly.

"But they'll keep looking for more of them," Ellie filled in. "Won't they?"

"Seems more than likely," Adam agreed. "I mean heck—I'm pretty sure saw their list."

445

Ellie stiffened.

"You saw a *list?*" she echoed urgently.

"It was just some stuff Dawson had scribbled in the back of his note-book," Adam hedged. "I dunno if it was in any order of priority, but the last bit mentioned a dig at Saqqara."

"Egypt," Ellie clarified automatically, and her attention abruptly sharpened as a rising alarm rang through the back of her mind.

"Yeah, Egypt," Adam drawled in reply. "I'm not that bad at geography. I do draw maps for a living."

"But *where* at Saqqara?" she pressed urgently.

Adam seemed to pick up on her change in tone. His expression grew more serious.

"Unas South Cemetery," he replied carefully.

"Unas South Cemetery," Ellie repeated. Her head started to feel tight. "Where Neil is digging?"

"Is… ah… that where he is?" Adam returned tentatively.

"What were they hoping to find there?" Ellie demanded.

Adam took a moment to answer. When he did, his words had an unchar-acteristic weight.

"They mentioned something about the Staff of Moses."

"The Staff of Moses," Ellie echoed queasily. "The one that parted the Red Sea. That unleashed the ten plagues on the Egyptians. Turned water to blood. Brought down a thunderstorm of hail and fire, and then killed the firstborn sons of an entire nation."

"Yeah," Adam answered quietly. "Pretty sure that's the one."

"But they can't possibly…" Ellie spluttered as panic rose in her throat. "For someone like Dawson or Jacobs to possess… For even a *fragment* of that kind of power to fall into the wrong hands…"

She shook her head and fought for some sense of logic.

"If Neil is tangled up in it, he can't possibly understand the real implica-tions," she insisted. "He hasn't the imagination for that. And even if he figures it out, he's not remotely equipped to handle this sort of thing. This is Neil we're talking about. He gets lost in libraries!"

The rest of the truth settled neatly into place. It was as undeniable as it was terribly intimidating. Ellie's heart pounded with it as she raised her head to meet Adam's gaze.

The words fell numbly from her lips.

"We have to stop them," she said.

Adam's expression shifted in a way that made the air around Ellie begin to feel just a little warmer.

"Interesting 'we' you've got there," he noted.

Her heart hammered awkwardly in her chest. For a moment, Ellie considered whether she should try to brush it off—but only for a moment. It took no longer than that for her to know that she could never hide from this and fail to regret it later—no matter what happened in the next few minutes.

"I know there's still… unfinished business between us," she said, picking the words carefully. "I wronged you, and I don't expect you to simply forget about all of that. Because it *matters*. And I…" She swallowed thickly and steeled herself. "I know you think we must get married to protect my family and your friend from being hurt by this mess the pair of us have gotten ourselves into. Of course, I am still staunchly opposed to the entire institution, regardless of situations where a pair of perfectly reasonable adults are being forced to bind themselves together for life for no other reason than—"

"Ellie…" Adam began warningly.

"Wait," she said as she raised her hand. She took another breath to regain control of herself. "What I am trying to say is that I… I don't care. About any of that. I don't give a… a *damn* about it." The curse felt good. Ellie smiled at the way it burst happily from her mouth as she raised her eyes to Adam's once more. "What I do give a damn about is… this."

The word hung awkwardly in the air between them. Ellie pressed on.

"The truth is that I am having a very hard time imagining what it would be like if you decided you didn't want to be around any longer," she admitted. "And I think I am having that difficulty because the notion makes me feel rather desperate—"

"Princess," he cut in firmly, halting the manic flow of her words.

"Yes?" Ellie said weakly.

Adam's arm slid down her back. His hand rested warmly against the curve of her spine as he looked down at her.

"What do you want?" he asked.

The question grew richer and deeper with meaning as it echoed through her mind in the voice of a ghost… in the whispering promise of a god.

What do you want?

There was no need to search for an answer this time. It was right there inside of her, thrumming with certainty regardless of whatever logic might have to say about it.

It simply waited to be spoken.

"You," she replied.

Adam answered her with a grin. It was big and unapologetically happy, and the sight of it warmed Ellie up like someone had lit a cheery little fire inside of her.

The look in his eyes sharpened, speaking to something a bit more dangerous. The little fire simmered further up Ellie's veins, sparking her nerves to quick, delicious life.

"Good," he declared and kissed her.

Someone hooted at them from across the camp. It sounded like Lessard. And maybe that was Flowers who was laughing, and Feliciana telling him to shush.

Ellie didn't really care. Adam's arms were holding her close, and his mouth tasted like rum, waterfalls, and campfires—and thank god nobody had bothered to find the man a shirt, because Ellie was wildly certain that she had never been so happy before in her life.

"Geh wahn room!" Charlie shouted to another raucous burst of laughter—and when they started pouring the chocolate, Ellie didn't even care.

She had everything she could possibly want right there.

NOTE FROM THE AUTHOR

Ellie and Adam's adventures will continue in *Tomb of the Sun King*, Book 2 of the *Raiders of the Arcana* series.

Get a special bonus scene of Adam and Ellie's encounter with the javelinas by joining the mailing list at JacquelynBenson.com/empirebonus.

Make sure you don't miss *The Stolen Apocalypse*, the free *Raiders of the Arcana* prequel novella featuring an afternoon-sized adventure with Ellie and Constance.

Looking for even more? Join my Patreon at Patreon.com/JacquelynBenson to get access to behind-the-scenes updates on the *Raiders of the Arcana* plus early chapters and bonus material.

If you enjoyed *Empire of Shadows*, please consider leaving a rating or review for the book on your favorite online book retailer. It's a great way to give a boost to independent authors like myself.

ACKNOWLEDGMENTS

No book can come to life in a void. This one owes a great deal to many people.

First and foremost, I extend profound thanks to Nicholas & Olivia Atwater. It was Nick who first opened my eyes to the possibility of taking my first novel and truly reinventing it in order to make it the book I always wanted it to be. You wouldn't be holding this volume if it weren't for him.

Olivia unleashed her maniacally detailed eye on my prose, and this book is far more readable as a result. Given that she has hordes of readers clamoring for her to get more of her own books out into the world, I'm extremely grateful for the time she spent with me on *Empire*.

Please also go forth and read both Nick and Olivia's books. If you have any interest in socially-conscious, character-driven fantasy adventures, you will love what they write.

My invaluable beta team—Rosalie Oaks, Chris Mornick, Matthew Doc, Kaitlyn Huwe, Cathie Plante and Nicholas Atwater—further sharpened this manuscript and prompted me to make it even more fun.

The inimitable Lore taught me how to blow up a steamboat and collapse a cave system.

Ruxandra Tarca checked my Latin declensions. (Please check out her books as well.)

Selkkie Designs took a pile of chaotic nonsense and turned it into the gorgeous, on-point cover for this book, while Annalise Jensen gave Ellie and Adam the most perfectly adorable faces.

The writers of the Lamplighter's Guild—Intisar Khanani, Rosalie Oaks, Nicholas & Olivia Atwater, Charlotte English, Tansy Rainer Roberts, and AJ Lancaster—provided industry wisdom and moral support.

And of course, I owe a great deal to Dan for his astonishingly durable faith in my crazy dreams.

Finally, I must extend thanks to all the past readers of *The Smoke Hunter*, who helped me to believe that this story was worth everything that I could possibly give it. I am so happy that now I can finally bring you all the rest of Ellie and Adam's mad adventures.

A brief cultural note:

Both modern and historical Belize are richly diverse cultures in terms of both ethnography and linguistics. As a result, several languages other than English appear regularly in this book.

All of the Kriol phrases were derived from the Kriol-English Dictionary from the Belize Kriol Project. I have used Kriol to refer to the language and Creole to describe the ethnicity of Belizeans descended from the white settlers and Black slaves who were the first non-Indigenous people to live in the region.

The Mopan words and phrases were taken from the Mopan Maya-Spanish-English Talking Dictionary by Charles Andrew Hofling and Narcizo Asij. Blame any grammatical errors on Adam, if you will.

The few bits of Yucatec were gathered from a handful of websites, as I wasn't able to find a more comprehensive resource for that language.

In the 19th century, descendants of Spanish and Indigenous peoples in Belize were most typically referred to as Spaniards. I have chosen to use the alternative term of Mestizo to avoid confusion for modern readers, as it is in more common contemporary use in Belize today.

In researching late 19th century Mayan culture, I consulted a number of contemporary sources written by white American and European scholars. There is unfortunately a dearth of own-voices material on the Maya from that time period. I have tried to read between the lines of the non-Indigenous sources to peel away bias and get at something like the truth, complementing that effort with research into contemporary Mayan identities to create the world of Santa Dolores Xenacoj.

The story of San Pedro Siris is, unfortunately, entirely true, and there is much more to it than I was able to reasonably include in this story. I encourage anyone interested in Mayan resistance to imperialism to read up on the Yucatec Caste Wars—and the ongoing efforts of Indigenous peoples in Mexico and Central America to fight disenfranchisement and oppression.

Tulan, or the City of Seven Caves, is indeed part of the mythologica records of both Mayan and Aztec societies. The city as it appears in this boo is, of course, entirely my own invention, one that draws most of its inspiration from the Mayan archaeological record. I do feel that it is important to note that the question of the extent to which Mesoamerican civilizations may have practiced human sacrifice remains a controversial one. My choice to include it in the culture of Tulan was tied to how I wanted to frame the power of the Smoking Mirror for this particular book. It should not be taken to imply that Mayan city-states routinely engaged in human sacrifice, nor that the Aztec world did so on nearly the scale implied by contemporary Spanish sources (whose narratives were likely shaped by their own agendas, as Ellie points out).

There is some question as to whether the cult of Santa Muerte existed before the 20th century. For the purposes of this story, I have chosen to side with those who theorize that it has roots in pre-Colombian religious practices in Mexico and Central America. Death, of course, has been with us for a very long time, as I find Santa Muerte to be one of its most lovely and compassionate faces, I couldn't resist the temptation to include her in this book.

CONTINUE THE ADVENTURE

THE
RAIDERS OF THE ARCANA

A Raiders of the Arcana Prequel Story
The Stolen Apocalypse
For a determined lady scholar, nothing perks up a
wedding quite like exploding coffins and a priceless
stolen manuscript.

Book One
Empire of Shadows
To race a pair of villains to a legendary city, Ellie
Mallory is forced to team up with maverick surveyor
Adam Bates.

Book Two
Tomb of the Sun King
Respectable lady scholars shouldn't spend their time
in Egypt dodging evildoers, escaping lost tombs, and
chasing down magical artifacts.

More to come.

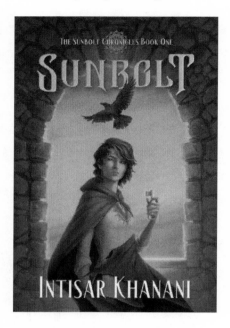

Sunbolt
by Intisar Khanani

The winding streets and narrow alleys of Karolene hide many secrets, and Hitomi is one of them. Orphaned at a young age, Hitomi has learned to hide her magical aptitude and who her parents really were. Most of all, she must conceal her role in the Shadow League, an underground movement working to undermine the powerful and corrupt Arch Mage Wilhelm Blackflame.

When the League gets word that Blackflame intends to detain—and execute—a leading political family, Hitomi volunteers to help the family escape. But there are more secrets at play than Hitomi's, and much worse fates than execution. When Hitomi finds herself captured along with her charges it will take everything she can summon to escape with her life.

Find it everywhere books are sold at Books2Read.com/Sunbolt

The Alchemy of Sorrow

Featuring stories by Sonya M. Black, Angela Boord, Levi Jacobs, Intisar Khanani, Krystle Matar, Virginia McClain, Quenby Olson, Carol A. Park, Madolyn Rogers, Rachel Emma Shaw, Clayton Snyder, K.S. Villoso, and M. L. Wang

Vicious garden gnomes. A grounded phoenix rider. A new mother consumed with vengeance. A dying god. Soul magic. These stories wrestle with the experience of loss—of loved ones, of relationships, of a sense of self, of health—and forge a path to hope as characters fight their way forward.

From bestsellers and SPFBO finalists to rising voices, 13 exceptionally talented authors explore the many facets of grief and healing through the lens of fantasy and sci-fi. In these difficult times, they transform their individual experiences into stories that resonate with audiences who are looking for a touch of magic in their pain.

Find it everywhere books are sold at CrimsonFoxPublishing.com/Book/The-Alchemy-of-Sorrow/

Made in the USA
Columbia, SC
13 November 2024

46467719R00286